HORSES CAN SEE IN THE DARK

a novel
by

MARIETTA BALL

This book is dedicated to Mont,
my partner forever in all my creations.

To Inetta, the friend and colleague who helped to heighten the joys and ease the tribulations of teaching for several years when your career overlapped mine. I am glad you become a forever friend, glad you switched to jr. high when you did, and glad you were given a room down the hall from me. I'm glad you knew me when Mont was still living, glad you know how he completed and fulfilled me. Then the next part of our story starts to sound like fiction. What a difference you brought about in my life after Mont's death. I can't imagine what would have become of me if you

HORSES CAN SEE IN THE DARK

A Novel. POD at CreateSpace.
Available at www.createspace.com/3740117, Amazon.com, and other on-line sources.

A version of the first chapter of this novel was published as a short story titled "Horses Can See in the Dark" in The *Dayton Daily News* and in MOTA 3: *Courage* (Triple Tree Press) after winning top prize in both publications' short story contests.

ISBN-13: 978-1468030228
ISBN-10: 1468030221
LCCN:2012900596

ACKNOWLEDGEMENTS:

I could not have readied this novel for publication without the help of my granddaughter-in-law Tamara, who designed the cover and did the formatting and editing. I am indebted beyond measure to her and to Chris Ewen for helping to make up for my lack of computer mastery, to my entire family for kindly putting up with ten years of talk about "my novel," to Jesse and Mary Lou for proofing, to Ernie and Carole for listening and advising, and to my parents whose respectful curiosity about the flora, the fauna, the topography, and the watersheds of the mountains around us taught me to see things I would not have seen—and to John who insisted I start writing the story and always wanted to hear more.

had not led me to reconnecting with John through that little magazine. I doubt if I would ever have been in touch with John again without that connection, and I doubt I would have started writing this book without his influence. So, to sum it up, you are responsible for this book. It's fiction, but it's the closest I'll come to writing a memoir. I will be honored if you find it readable.

Love,
Marietta
8-4-2012

HORSES CAN SEE IN THE DARK
FORWARD:

Not the Rifle Crack

It was not the crack of the rifle that woke Linc Slaney the day of the killing. R. L. was shaken when Nora Faye asked him about it more than fifteen years later.

"Nothing ever woke your dad," Nora Faye mused aloud, "not even Mrs. Garvens' crowing rooster or Conner chopping kindling right under the bedroom window."

"Yeah, he was a sound sleeper," R. L. agreed. If Nora Faye had known him she would have picked up on the emotion in his voice, but she had met him for the first time just a couple of hours earlier.

"I've thought so often about how he slept through Red Rover games in the rut lane and Ruthie tap dancing on the pump block and even our balls bouncing off the roof," she went on.

She puzzled silently for a moment. "I wonder why the gunshot woke him that morning?"

"It didn't."

She regretted asking the question when she saw R. L.'s now obvious distress, but when she started saying how sorry she was about mentioning it, he motioned that it was okay.

Spreading splayed fingers like blinders on each side of his downcast face, he sucked a long breath through flared nostrils, then reached along the booth seat to take his wife's hand before he managed to speak again.

"I'm truly pleased you brought it up. I'm glad for a chance to talk about it." His voice was husky as he leaned across the table toward Nora Faye and Ted.

Nora Faye couldn't keep from murmuring another apology.

"Don't be sorry," he further assured her. "It threw me for a minute because that very thing was on Dad's mind the last time I got to talk to him. It makes me wish he could have known about you noticing. He said nobody had ever asked him about it, not even my mother. He had kept it to himself until he told me about it right there at the last—the night before he died."

R. L's eyes locked into Nora Faye's. "Dad said he was already up and pulling on his pants when he heard the rifle crack. It was something else that woke him. Something inside his head."

Another struggle with emotion. "That's why he carried such guilt—such unshakable remorse—on top of his grief. He thought he'd been waked to stop what happened and that he had not acted fast enough to carry out what he'd been given the chance to do."

Nora Faye was trembling with despair. "No, no," she protested. "He couldn't have moved any faster. I could see that he was barely awake when he came out the door in his undershirt, with one shoe still in his hand and his belt unbuckled. He hadn't even pushed the hair out of his eyes. Was I the only person who saw that?"

The flood of realization almost swept her off her seat.

"I was. Oh, I was," she whispered. "I could have told him, and I never had the chance."

The four of them sat in anguished silence.

Then R. L. said, "It wouldn't have made any difference."

Nora Faye nodded. "Probably not; I was so little."

"Oh, no. As young as you were, I think it would have given him some comfort to know you realized he acted as fast as possible. But it wouldn't have saved him from feeling like he could have kept it from happening.

"Everybody in my family thought they could have stopped it if they'd just have done something they didn't do or if they'd not done something they did. Nothing could make anybody feel any different. Nothing can save a person from their first reaction to that kind of loss."

The aching wail of "Unchained Melody," playing on the jukebox a few yards from their booth, receded from their gravity until it seemed to be coming from another room, another world. The happy chatter from other booths in the off-campus hangout became muffled to their ears. None of the four looked at another for several moments. Each seemed lost in personal contemplation of R. L.'s concluding pronouncement.

Nora Faye was the first to speak. "Sometimes it seems like that," she said.

CHAPTER 1
CALLIE AND SEELOM

Nora Faye knew there were only four bathrooms in all of Dillard—she'd heard it said many a time—but she didn't know Callie Bennett cleaned three of them until she asked one day, "Why does Callie go to people's houses?"

Her mother said, "She does their housework."

When she asked why Callie didn't come to *their* house, her mother looked at her daddy and said, "Because we don't have a bathroom. Callie works for people that have bathrooms."

Her daddy got the little tender voice he used when he was teasing her mother. He asked, "If we had a bathroom do you reckon it'd give you a reason to do housework or would it mean we'd have to hire Callie?"

Her mother's voice didn't sound tender when she said, "Well, James, maybe you should have married Callie Bennett if you wanted somebody to do your housework." She went on telling him how the people in this hollow who had bathrooms just happened to be the same people that had money to buy cars and pay a hired girl.

Neither of them answered Nora Faye when she asked, "Why don't she go to Mrs. Slaney's house? Mrs. Slaney gots a bathroom."

She felt two ways about it when they ignored her and started talking to each other like this; it made her sad that they usually ended up sounding hateful, but she was glad for the chance it gave her to go check on Callie's horse without interference.

7

From her perch atop the coal shed at the front fence Nora Faye kept track of Callie's daily progress. In the winter Callie came before daylight and left after dark. Everybody said she lived with her old daddy way on up the hollow beyond the tipple, beyond the schoolhouse, all the way at the head of Dillard Creek. She was pretty certain Callie didn't have a bathroom at her own house. She knew there wasn't even a road, so there surely couldn't be a bathroom.

Nora Faye had been past the schoolhouse one time, as far as the place where the road ended. It didn't taper off gradually. There was just suddenly no more road, and the path was almost immediately swallowed by tall weeds. She stared and stared at that spot where the path disappeared.

"How can he see?" she asked her daddy.

"Who?"

"Callie's horse. How can he find the path in the dark?"

"What in the world made you think about Callie's horse right now?" her mother asked.

They were having a picnic. Uncle Eldon had inched his Model A along the gullied road beyond the schoolhouse. He and Aunt Stella were sitting with her mother and daddy on a quilt under the sycamores. Dollie and Bootsie were splashing and squealing in the creek.

Her mother didn't wait for an answer. She never did. "She's just the strangest child," she told Aunt Stella. "Not a bit like your girls. She still talks like a baby, and that horse of Callie Bennett's interests her more than her paper dolls."

Her daddy started unbuckling Nora Faye's shoes. "So you can wade the creek with your cousins," he explained as he peeled off her anklets. "Go play now, Fayzie." He pushed her gently in the direction of the creek.

Then, "Horses can see in the dark," he said. "They never lose their way."

8

She heard Aunt Stella say, "She'll be different after she starts school, Irene. She'll have the other children to play with."

Irene said, "It's not that she doesn't have anybody to play with now; she prefers the horse. She tears all her dresses under the arms hanging on the fence while she talks to that horse. Besides, she can't go to school this year; she won't be five till January. And I don't know if I'd send her even if she was old enough. That old school house is just crawling alive with lice and mites. Even the Slaney children got lice last year, and Berta Slaney is the cleanin'est woman I know."

Her mother was right about the horse; Nora Faye woke up and went to sleep thinking about Callie's horse. She had never talked to Callie, but she talked to her horse almost every day. Not just with words or sounds. She could make the whuffy sound he made when he blew out his cheeks and vibrated his lips, but mostly she didn't make sounds. She talked with looks, with thoughts, with little touches, and with just being there. With smelling him and feeling his breath on her arm, with studying the swirl of his red-brown coat and the tight swell of his sides. Sometimes she brushed the back of her fingers against the warm, soft skin around his nostrils, wondering if anything else in the world felt that way.

The Deetons next door had a bathroom. The Deetons and the Averys next to them, the Slaneys across the road, and then, of course, the Pattersons in the big house on the hill by itself, the mine superintendent's house.

Callie came to that house first thing every morning. She was late today. Nora Faye was already outside. She watched from the coal shed where she was almost hidden by an overhanging branch of the apple tree. Callie's skin was so ruddy some people said she must be an Indian. She tied her horse to the gatepost at the bottom of the

Patterson's long flight of wooden steps. She wore men's overalls and men's lace-up boots and, in the wintertime, a heavy brown coat that looked like a Boy Scout tent.

But today was a hot summer day. Nora Faye saw Callie hang out the Patterson's wash before she came off the hill and crossed the road to the Avery house. She didn't stay long at the Avery's, maybe just long enough to clean a bathroom. She then went back across the road and got on her horse for the mail trip.

She picked up the mail at the post office before noon and took it to the train depot at the mouth of Dillard. After she came back up the hollow with the incoming mail and delivered it to the post office, she went back to the Patterson's house or to the Deeton's next door where Nora Faye sometimes saw her at the ironing board on the back porch.

Nora Faye's mother went to the post office every morning to check for mail and to mail the letter she sometimes wrote at the kitchen table after Daddy went to work. Nora Faye bought a stamp for her War Bond book whenever Daddy left a stack of pennies by her cereal bowl. When Momma got a letter she would stop on the way home, right on the train tracks, to open it and read it before she put it in her handbag. And then she wouldn't talk much all day. She'd sit staring into space looking dreamy and troubled. But today she got no letter.

They waved to Daddy when they passed the store on the way down. He was on the loading dock filling the delivery truck with sacks of feed. He yelled to Momma across the creek, telling her he'd bring home some bologna and crackers for their dinner before he went on his deliveries. But she said she'd make fried bologna and eggs if he'd go home and build a fire right now.

He usually ate Wheaties for breakfast—or leftover cornbread and milk—and he laughed today when Momma called fried bologna and fried eggs a hot dinner. He said,

"Not many a man would let you get away with calling an overdue breakfast a hot dinner."

Momma said, "It's too hot to cook. I wouldn't have let you build a fire if I didn't need hot water to wash my hair." Momma's hair was thick and shiny with a smooth crown. Daddy called it broom-sage blond. She put a few pin-curls at the front to make it full around her face, but she let the back dry natural and bouncy. She didn't push it into waves close to her head and dry it in metal clamps like Aunt Stella.

Daddy built all the fires, and sometimes he cooked their supper, fried potatoes and cornbread or macaroni and tomatoes. Momma said she had warned him that she didn't know how to cook and keep house. Sometimes he didn't say anything, but sometimes he said he didn't know she meant she didn't intend to try to learn how.

She ironed though. This morning she had ironed Nora Faye's blue smocked sundress and her own flowered dimity with cape sleeves. She told Daddy she wanted to go into town for the weekend.

"Send word to Eldon that we want him to come get us on Saturday," she coaxed.

Daddy looked more sad than mad. "You know I get restless there," he almost whispered. "What's wrong with spending some time by ourselves? Why do we have our own place if we're never going to stay home?"

"Well, Eldon's *your* brother. I'd think you'd want to spend time with your own brother."

Nora Faye slipped out to the yard and looked toward the corner fence post that was hidden from the house by the coal shed. This was the time of day when her breath got caught in her chest and wouldn't come out until she got to the spot in the yard where she could see the top of the post. Sometimes Callie tied her horse here after she delivered the mail to the post office, and sometimes she

11

took him back across the road and tied him to the Patterson's gatepost.

Nora Faye always stopped at the forsythia bush beside the front porch. If her heart wasn't beating too loud she could hear the little sounds, the clink of bit and bridle, the scrape of an iron shoe on gravel, a breathy snort. On a warm day like this she could smell him. If the horse wasn't there, she came back to the forsythia bush and crawled under branches that sprawled out and down to make room for a secret playhouse.

But today she heard him, and when she was halfway across the yard she could see the leather reins looped around the top of the corner post. She ran the last few steps. She put her toes on the bottom rail and pulled herself up by the palings as far as she could reach, bringing her face even with his. He jerked his head up and down to say hello.

When she was with him like this she wasn't always sure whether she was touching him with her fingers or just her mind. Her fingertips tingled when she traced her vision over his bony forehead and up his silky ears and down along his jawbone, solid as the wooden mallet Granny Rose used to drive her tomato stakes into the ground.

She had thought a million times how she could get in the saddle if he were tied beside the coal shed. She would be so quick. She would wait until he swung around sideways up close to the shed. She would put one hand on the knob that stuck up in front and one hand on the back of the saddle while she let herself fall against him. Then she would move the back hand to the front and throw her leg up and over the saddle, all in one motion. It was hard for her to think about anything else.

At the supper table Momma started right back in talking about going to town on Saturday. When Daddy wouldn't agree to it she said, "Things can't go on this way, James. I don't intend to be stuck in the head of nowhere day in and day out for the rest of my life."

"You act like you've forgotten that's why we're here, Reenie. We won't be stuck anywhere after we buy us a car in a year or two. We'll be able to go wherever we want."

"I don't see why you thought you had to crawl up a filthy coal-camp holler to a company store to make enough money to buy a car. You could have kept that job in town. Sol Crutcher didn't fire you."

Daddy took off his glasses and breathed first on one lens, then the other, wiping them on his un-ironed but carefully folded pocket handkerchief. His face looked like it did when Nora Faye still couldn't tie her shoelaces after he showed her over and over.

"You know Sol couldn't afford to pay my wages any longer. I've told you how he'd give out so much credit he was going deeper in the hole every day."

Momma said, "Well, all I can tell you is that I'm sick of this place where everybody in the holler knows your business."

Daddy's fork didn't make a sound when he laid it down on the enameled metal tabletop. "No, that's not all you can tell me, Reenie. You can tell me what it is you don't want people to know. They already know about the letter you mail every week. What else is it you've got to hide?"

Momma's forehead was getting red. "And why in the world would anyone be interested in the letter I write my mother every week?" she snapped.

"Maybe because most people's mothers aren't on a troopship in the Pacific." Daddy had forgotten about Nora Faye. He didn't usually talk like this when he knew Nora Faye was listening.

Momma's voice got real quiet. "It's not like you didn't know what you were getting into, James. You can't say I kept anything from you."

13

"But you didn't tell me he sent word about his wife taking up with another man after he enlisted. You didn't tell me you'd started writing him a letter every week."

Daddy was spinning his fork now, not looking at Momma at all, just slowly spinning his fork and watching it like he wanted *it* to tell him something instead of Momma.

"You always think you're so smart." Momma's mouth was getting hard and set now.

"No, I think I'm probably the dumbest man alive to have thought you were being honest when you let me think you wanted to put the past behind you."

"I don't know who's been talking to you, James, but I want you to know that Miss Know-It-All Stella doesn't know half as much as she thinks she knows. I don't know what's got you so upset all of a sudden."

"It's not all of a sudden, Reenie. And, I'll tell you what's got me upset; you call me James, for Christ's sake."

"Have you gone crazy? What else would I call you? James is your name."

Daddy took off his glasses again. His voice was hoarse. "We've been married four years, Reenie, and you've never called me a pet name. You've never called me anything but James."

Sometimes Nora Faye could make her ears shut out their voices, but she couldn't make that happen today. She slipped off her chair and crept out of the house. She didn't know where she was going. She didn't expect Callie's horse. He was usually back at the Patterson's after supper, tied at the bottom of the steps.

But the evening air carried his unmistakable scent and the sound of his jangling bridle. Something good had happened while Momma and Daddy were making each other mad; Callie had tied her horse on this side of the road, and not at the corner near the Deeton's house, but beside the coalhouse. Nora Faye's heart stopped beating for a moment, and then it stoutly carried her through her next endeavors.

She held herself down to a walk across the yard, as though she might scare him away by running—or make him disappear in a puff of smoke like the genies in the bedtime stories her daddy read to her. She put one foot on the coal shed doorsill, as always, and the other on the ledge a good piece up the trunk of the apple tree where a limb had been cut off. The next stretch was to the top fence rail, and the last onto the roof while she grabbed the overhanging tree limb to pull herself forward.

She sat down on the hot tarpaper and wrapped her arms around her pulled-up knees. Every now and then she scooted a little closer to the edge of the roof. She knew immediately she wasn't going to climb on him this time. She felt a calm assurance that there would be another chance for that. This time she studied him.

His back was almost level with the roof. She wouldn't need to pull herself up to get into the saddle, just over. That part should be easier. In her mind she put herself over into the saddle and back several times. When she felt peaceful about it, she let it go and fell into reacquainting herself with the flare of his nostrils and the way his lashes fringed his eyes like feathers. He seemed taller when she looked at him this way, and his rear end looked as wide as the rumble seat in Uncle Eldon's car.

She let her thoughts go into that place where she took complete satisfaction from just being near him. She thought about how deep his eyes looked. She traced her mind around the velvet of his mouth and combed her attention through his forelock.

She was sitting near him but not touching him when she saw Callie coming across the road straight toward her. She had never been this close to Callie; she always ran when she saw her coming. She was surprised to see that her eyes were blue, not black like her tightly knotted hair.

They didn't say a word to each other. Nora Faye didn't move back from the edge of the roof, but she pulled her knees up to her chest again and wrapped her arms around them while she watched Callie fix her saddlebags and gunnysacks, pulling at straps and checking buckles. Then she untied the reins, pushed the horse's rump over with a flat-handed smack, grabbed the front of the saddle, put one foot up into a stirrup, and pulled herself up and over in one smooth effort.

She turned his head with a little lift of her wrist, but just before she swung him away from the coal shed she sort of nodded toward Nora Faye who raised her chin and asked, "Why did you tied him here for?"

Callie didn't say anything, just gave Nora Faye a sideways look out of those clear blue eyes, then touched her heels to her horse's sides and rode off up the hollow.

Momma was packing her travel bag when Nora Faye woke up next morning. She said Gladys Avery was going to take her to town in her car.

"I can't go to town," Nora Faye protested. "Callie's horse is coming. He'll be looking for me."

"Well, I couldn't take you even if you wanted to come with me," Momma said. "I don't know for sure where I'm going."

Hearing that her mother wasn't planning to take her made Nora Faye want to go for a minute until she remembered how she felt last night on the coal shed. Momma told her she was going to take her across the road to stay with Mrs. Slaney until Granny Rose came for her.

Nora Faye said, "Callie's horse wants me to be here when he comes."

"I don't know what time Granny Rose will get here," Momma said, "but she'll come some time today.

"And that horse, Nora Faye, it's a girl horse. I heard Callie call it Sela."

She didn't believe her mother. She didn't make her ears stop hearing; she just didn't believe her.

Granny Rose came on the passenger train and caught a ride up the hollow with the Jewel Tea man. As she led Nora Faye across the road from the Slaneys, she asked her how she'd hurt her lip; then, when she got no answer, she looked again and said she guessed it was just raspberry jam she was seeing.

She said Nora Faye could help her while she got things ready to start fixing supper. While she laid the fire she said she wished she had time to use the soot rake but that she'd have to let that go till another time. "From the looks of things, it's not been done since you moved here," she fretted.

When she got the fire going she started right in cleaning the kitchen cabinet where she said she'd found weevils in the flour bin.

While they were eating supper she said, "I can't stay away more than a night or two, James. My garden's just starting to come in good."

Daddy said, "I know, Ma. I'll work out something."

She said, "I can take Nora Faye home with me."

But Daddy said, "We don't have to make that decision yet."

"What'll you do if she don't come back?"

"She'll come back," Daddy said. His voice sounded more like he was saying he'd never be seeing her again. "She doesn't have anywhere else to go."

"Well, I have to tell you I was a little surprised when she said she was leaving," Rose said. "I'd been thinking lately that maybe she was starting to pick up some of Stella's good ways. Stella's no raving beauty, but she's

17

never given Eldon reason to be anything but proud of her."

Daddy said they didn't need to be talking about that, but Granny Rose went on to say more about how Stella's opinions might be too strong for some people but how she kept a real nice house for Eldon and had never put anything else ahead of her husband and children.

Daddy didn't try to stop Nora Faye when she eased out of the kitchen.

She didn't stop at the forsythia bush; she walked across the yard without one break in her stride and climbed to the coal shed roof. From that point on, time no longer unfolded minute by minute. It was as though everything was over in one second while at the same time it had lasted longer than her whole life. Things happened exactly as they had in her imagination. Until Callie came across the road and lifted her from the saddle she wasn't sure if she was awake or dreaming.

Callie didn't lift her under the arms. She clamped her shoulders between her hands and set her on the coal shed as effortlessly as if she had been a bag of mail or Momma's travel bag. Neither said anything while she checked straps and fixed her sacks. But after she arranged her feet in the stirrups and her hands on the reins, just before she shifted her weight to look like she was part of the horse instead of something sitting on top of it, Callie said, "Ask your daddy if he's all right by it. I don't care none."

As she lifted her elbow and gave her wrist that little twitch she said, "He won't never hurt you."

Then, just as she touched her heels to his sides, "His name's Seelom."

Nora Faye sat on the roof for a long time. She could feel the tarpaper cooling under her bare legs. Ruthie and Billy Ray called to her from their side yard where they were catching lightening bugs. They told her to ask her daddy if she could come over and make fruit-jar lanterns with them, but she said she couldn't come. This was the latest Daddy had ever let her stay on the coal shed. He and Granny Rose were talking on the screened-in porch. She could hear their voices but she couldn't tell what they were saying; the locusts drowned them out. She kept a hold on the tree branch and pulled off the little hard swellings that would become apples. She had tasted them one day. They were bitter, not sour. She dropped them one by one onto the roof where some rolled off and some lodged in seams and wrinkles. She sat by herself until dusk thickened and Daddy called her to come in.

He pulled her up into the porch swing beside him. The locusts were so loud it was hard to hear Granny Rose when she said, "Seems like she don't look as peaked as she did this morning."

Daddy pushed the swing back and forth for a long time after Granny Rose went inside. Each time he pushed, his foot made a little clomping sound and the swing chains jangled like Seelom's stirrups. Finally he said they'd better go inside. He said he would read her the funnies after she got into her nightie. He asked, "Which do you want first, *Alley Oop* or *Red Ryder*?

CHAPTER 2
IRENE

Irene would not return to Dillard. Some details about her immediate destination rattled around loose in her brain while Gladys Avery jounced her out of the hollow in her Plymouth coupe, but there was no indecision about the finality of her departure.

She suspected Gladys was hitting the chug holes on purpose. She knew Gladys had never really liked her, and now she was pouting because Irene wasn't confiding in her, wasn't answering questions about the suitcase or about Nora Faye. Knowing Gladys made the weekly trip to visit with her mother, Irene had not hesitated to ask her for a ride to Wolliver. She gave no explanation, and the sly pleasure of keeping Gladys in the dark helped keep her from acknowledging the little unexpected bubble of panic that tried to form as she walked away from the Slaney's front porch.

As usual, she was oddly comforted to be reminded that Gladys did not like her. It made her feel special, like she was too uncommon to be liked by an ordinary woman such as Gladys. She had come to expect that women would not like her—it had started when she was a girl— and she had learned to take pride in the sense of uniqueness it gave her.

It had seemed, for a short while when they first moved to Dillard, that Gladys might turn out to be something like a friend. She certainly offered more possibility than the other coal camp wives. Irene had heard rumors enough about the high life Gladys once lived to make her think she might not be quick to pass judgment on other people. She and Rollie still liked to liven things up. Irene and James had gone to their house to play poker and have some beers a time or two. Rollie kept a gamecock last summer, and he'd taken James to the fights. James didn't like the cockfights, but he seemed to like Rollie—they worked together at the store—and Irene liked being able to depend on Gladys for rides into town.

But the chummy feelings ended for Irene when Gladys dropped in one day while she was pressing her two Sunday-best winter dresses dug out from the end of the one shallow little closet she shared with James. She liked the straight lines of the simple shifts—or rather she liked the way they accented her spare figure. She had nothing but disdain for all the belts and darts and pleats and shaping on the new styles. (Kenneth had said she was built like a razor strop. He called her a little slab of a girl. She liked that better than anything anyone had ever said about her.)

She'd finished pressing the pale, dusty-green wool-crepe and had put it back on the rack hooked over the top of the open closet door when Gladys took hold of it on each side and pulled it taut. "It could be a pillowcase," she laughed, "or a feed sack."

She waved her hands over her own full breasts and rounded hips. "Can you imagine me trying to stuff all these in there?"

Until that moment Irene had thought Gladys compared her own figure unfavorably to hers. She had even felt a little sorry for her. It had not occurred to her that Gladys could possibly consider herself the more admirably endowed. It was not jealousy closing Irene to all consideration of friendship from that time on; it was more like contempt for someone with such a lack of discrimination.

She'd always been proud of her body. It was perhaps the only place she'd ever felt at home. Except for the last few months before Nora Faye was born, it had always looked much the same. She'd never had awkward growth spurts or baby fat. She'd watched with aversion while one of her sisters went through a big-footed, gawky, long-shanked stage with sharp elbows and protruding knees, and the other one puffed up like a biscuit.

They kept telling her to just wait, that she wouldn't have that same shape in a few years. But her body didn't change like theirs, and she thought they resented that. Ola May, who was plump, bound her chest with long strips of cloth in an effort to squeeze into the middy waist that was as straight as she wanted to be; Addie Lou wore her long-sleeved dress right through the summer heat to hide her bony arms.

The three of them lived with their mother and grandmother, who did not treat Irene the same as her sisters. They used lots of words with Irene while they just grunted and motioned to her sisters. Sometimes it seemed to Irene that the four of them knew a secret code she didn't know, and sometimes it seemed to her that she was the one who knew something they didn't know, something that shielded her from absorbing their signals.

It was the same with the neighbor women. All of the women she knew—the women of Bullhide and the surrounding hollows—whenever they came together in any combination, seemed to share an exclusive history not only setting them apart from men, but making them know, without words, exactly what any other woman needed from them at any moment in time. Irene did not have that perception.

Older women thought she was a schemer, that she was preoccupied with secret plots and dreams. They were wrong. There was an emptiness inside her, but she had never envisioned any plans for filling the void. Young women like her sisters came closer to the truth when they accused her of thinking she was too good for them.

"Good" was the wrong word. "Aware" might be better, aware that this place did not contain what her contentment required. Even at that, she did not have any concept of a place where she might find contentment. She hadn't thought it through far enough to feel resigned. She was careful not to let herself feel much of anything; disappointment lurked vaguely in that direction. It seemed important that she stay numb.

Things changed for Irene when she was sixteen. Old Crance Bradds died, and she went across the hill with her mother to the Bradds' house where the body was laid out. Her mother hadn't been planning on sitting up with the family but, when she heard that Crance's nephew was coming in from Wolliver, she made up her mind to go sit for a while on the chance she might get to see him.

When they got there, the men from the creek were out in the road admiring the nephew's car while he explained how things worked. Irene's mother made a beeline for him. He stood out like a new penny in his shiny shoes and felt brimmed hat, but Irene didn't think he was much to look at except for his get-up, his creased pants and double-breasted overcoat with a velveteen collar.

Her mother asked, "Ain't you Levi and Betsy's youngest boy?"

He said, "That's me, Luther Bradds."

She asked, "Do you 'member who I am?"

He studied her for a moment before recognition dawned. Then he looked almost handsome as a smile spread.

"You're Corrina MacFaron; you're the neighbor girl that made them leave me laying when I broke my leg in the orchard. We called you Corrie Mac."

Her mother beamed. "That uz when we lived in that little house by yorn over back of them big apple trees that'd gone all tall and rangy. You littler young'uns uz always climbing in them trees, and it's a wonder you's the only one ever got hurt. That big holler branch just broke off with you."

"The doctors said I'd have ended up crippled if you hadn't made the others leave me laying till the men come with the corncrib door to carry me home. My brother Oscar was fixin' to try to pack me on his back when you made him stop."

He turned to the men in the road, "Boys, I might not be walking without crutches today if this woman hadn't come along with the good sense to know what to do. She wasn't no more than a girl herself, but she just knew what seemed right.

"The doctors said I might've lost my leg if they'd carried me home like they were fixing to. I've still got a scar something awful." He patted his leg up and down the side to indicate the area.

Her mother said, "I sent that Collins boy up to the barn to bring back a plank or somethin' to carry you on. Your leg was all limp in your britches."

Irene was fascinated for a time—she'd never heard her mother sound proud of herself—but she became restless as they recounted the episode. After they repeated the sequence of events and described the lay of the land several times, Luther went on to tell her mother about his wife Nancy and their three children, their house in Wolliver, and his salesman's job that kept him on the road for weeks at a time. Irene found it so tiresome she was considering lighting out for home without her mother.

Then Luther said his wife didn't like staying by herself while he was away on his job. He said he'd planned on taking his little sister back with him to stay with her.

"That's one reason I came today," he said. "I wanted to pay my respects to Uncle Crance, of course, but I thought it'd be a good time to take Ardell back with me. I hadn't heard she's getting married next week."

Irene said, "I'll go back with you. I can stay with your wife."

She had packed her things in the same travel bag she'd packed this morning in Dillard, the one Luther had brought for his sister to use. It was more space than Irene needed for her things. It would not have been full if her grandmother had not put in the last of the winter-mellowed apples—dug out from the bottom of the barn-loft hay and rolled up in feed sack dish towels with three jars of tomato relish padded with a goose down pillow, along with Irene's two threadbare dresses, one petticoat, and an extra pair of long winter stockings.

Her meager wardrobe proved not to be a problem. Nancy immediately gave her some outfits she culled from her chifferobe, saying she'd been needing to make room for the new things Luther brought her every time he returned from the road.

It wasn't fear that made Nancy want company while Luther was away; she just liked having people around. She liked having someone to talk to, someone to do things with, someone to tell what to do. There were two other girls there full-time when Irene arrived. Irene was sort of a stand-by girl for Nancy to fall back on in case the other two were unavailable. Lavenna Sparks, who lived up Crow Creek, went to high school in town. She'd started staying at Nancy's house during winter months when bad weather made it hard to walk the trace back and forth over Prater Hill, and now she'd become a year-round fixture. Georgine Sayers, from over on Wahoo, had been staying with her ever since she started working at the telephone company. Other girls came and went over the few months Irene was there.

Irene was pleasantly surprised to learn she was not a hired girl. Nancy treated all the girls as her equals. There was no money and little work involved. She was given a place to sleep and plenty to eat just for being there and being ready to do whatever Nancy was in a mood for. They all took care of the children, two boys and a girl of school age, twins Amanda and Otho and a younger boy they all called Dinkum, amazingly untroublesome children who actually took care of each other.

There were dishes to wash up, but Nancy did most of the cooking. Irene realized she felt a twinge of disappointment to discover that, although Nancy liked company while she cooked, she did not want help. Irene had not shared in the cooking at home either. She had done the outside chores like chopping firewood and feeding chickens and hoeing the garden, while her sisters were in the kitchen peeling things and stirring pots and mixing things together with their hands.

Nancy knew everybody in town, and, if they didn't know her, she went right up to them and told them who she was. She liked to put herself out to make people feel special. She did things on impulse, like inviting all the girls in Lavenna's class to make molasses taffy at her house after a school program, or taking Georgine to the movie show on her birthday and getting up in front of the screen before the movie started to lead the audience in singing the birthday song to her. On the twins' birthday she got the idea to sew up little gingham bags with pinked edges for every one of their schoolmates. She sent Irene to the Five and Dime to buy marbles for the boys and jacks for the girls, and she got the bags finished, filled, tied up with twine or ribbon, and delivered to the schoolhouse before their teacher turned out the class for the day.

She acted like she was man-crazy—she talked flirty to all the unattached men in town and even went out with some of them—but, as far as Irene knew, she never did anything Luther didn't know about. She carried on about other men even when Luther was around. It seemed to be a way he liked for her to tease him. He was proud of the fact that men liked Nancy. The two of them acted like it was another honeymoon every time he came home.

One of Luther's business acquaintances, a Mr. Addington, came to see Nancy whenever he came through town. He took her to picture shows and left presents for all of them, discontinued advertising premiums from his sample cases, things like candy dishes or serving trays or a new deck of cards. The nicest thing he ever left was a pair of plaster bookends in the shape of sundials painted to look like burnished bronze. Sometimes he insisted that all the girls join Nancy and him on a drive down the river to the old mill dam or out to the junction pull-off on the other end of town where you could look up to Pine Mountain and spot the fire tower among the trees on the crest.

After one of his visits Nancy said, "It's you Mr. Addington comes to see now, Irene. He's sweet on you. He wants to know if he can come courtin'."

Irene was horrified, though, surprisingly, Lavenna was the one who spoke up. "Why, he's old enough to be her daddy, and he's not good looking enough for her even if he was a young feller. He's ugly as mud." Irene's face showed her agreement.

Georgine scoffed at them. "He's not that bad," she put in, "and, even if that was the truth, you've got to think about how well-fixed he is with that job and a car and all. If you're going to be so particular, you might as well get used to settling for your own company."

When Irene said she'd rather be by herself than be with somebody she didn't like, they asked her what kind of man she liked.

"I ain't never liked a man," she said. "I ain't never thought much about that."

Georgine rolled her eyes and turned to Nancy, "Well, then, you'd better get her started at the Peanut Wagon. You won't want her living out her solitary lifetime here with no spending money of her own."

Most of the girls who stayed at Nancy's house worked, at one time or another, at the Peanut Wagon, in business every day of the week from March through October. It was actually an open-front stand, wedged in between the Crayhill hotel and Sam Hager's dry goods store, but the roasting oven itself sat on a wagon that could be wheeled up to the schoolyard for Independence Day celebrations or football games.

Ward and Maggie Crayhill owned the hotel, the peanut stand, and the ice cream parlor. For several years now, they had left the staffing of the Peanut Wagon up to Nancy. She used a few town girls, but depended mainly on the girls who stayed at her house. She covered it herself if none of the girls were available.

Now she said, "I was already planning to put her to work when we start things up next week. I already told Maggie I'd be breaking in a new girl."

Irene was panic-stricken. She'd stayed in school long enough to learn how to do figures as good as the next one, but she'd never had reason to test her skills. She knew the peanut girl was usually on her own. She couldn't imagine being able to make change and keep records without help.

But her hesitation lasted only until Georgine, speaking as though Irene had no ears, protested, "I was just acting a fool about her starting work. You don't really think she could handle the job, do you?"

Nancy put it to Irene, asking, "What do you say, Missy? Are you ready to join the world of toil, sweat, and simoleons?"

Irene turned away from Georgine's scorn and answered, "I don't see no reason not to."

Though these women were nothing like the women from home, Irene recognized the same sense of kinship among them, a kinship that could move them to talk about her like she was—not a child; they didn't talk past Nancy's children like that—more like she was a decoration. Though Lavenna sometimes lined up with her now, Irene saw her as destined to become one of the excluding circle in the future. Lavenna's occasional differences with the other women seemed to make her more determined to try to be the person she thought they expected her to be. Irene, on the other hand, had felt no obligation to be anybody but herself from the day she'd left Bullhide.

By the time Nancy took her for her first day at the Peanut Wagon, she was more eager than nervous, ready to be part of the commercial bustle she had admired as an observer. The walk to work became a source of pleasure in itself. The moment she stepped out the door into the thin, early-morning air she could hear the Italian stone masons over the way through the trees behind Nancy's house where they were building the bridge that would swing the railroad tracks in yet another direction across the river and through the newly blasted tunnel. She'd felt a little uneasy the first time she heard the men talking to each other in their old tongue, but, after a few days, their voices were like music.

Everything about Wolliver seemed unreal to her, nothing more so than being able to walk all the way from Nancy's house to the Peanut Wagon without getting her shoes dirty, even on rainy days. The streets around the courthouse square looked as glamorous to her as the city streets in the movie shows Nancy had taken her to. Sometimes she pretended there was a movie camera following her as she left Nancy's house at the far edge of the upper bottom to walk on the clean, dry, dirt path that turned into a brick sidewalk before it continued in front of the brick homes of Dr. Betts, with his office through a side entrance, Professor Prior, the school superintendent, and Lenville Stamper, who owned the lumberyard. She liked the hollow sound her heels made on the concrete culvert alongside Frank Roscoe's liquor store, and she felt like a dancer executing intricate steps as she picked her way across the railroad tracks on Main Street. She guessed the wooden walkway in front of the feed store and the movie house would soon be replaced with concrete sidewalks like those in closer to the center of town.

She knew times were supposed to be bad. She'd heard talk about people that didn't have enough to feed their children, about men that couldn't find work. But, compared to the bleak prospects of Bullhide, the signs that signaled hard times to the longtime residents of Wolliver looked to her like a promise of better days. She was newly impressed each morning by all the activity going on no matter how early she got into town: James Houston and Sol Crutcher stacking boxes of apples and potatoes on the sidewalk in front of the Crutcher store, the Hagers arranging a table of fabric bolts and shoe boxes under their dry goods sign, Thaddeus Ward lining up cans of polish in the window of his shoe repair shop, Minna Green sweeping out the ice cream parlor though she'd swept it out last thing before she closed up the day before, Eva Crenshaw fanning out a handful of paper doll books in the 5 & 10 display case, Lawrence Quarls cranking down the awning at the drugstore, a woman with a stack of hymn books bustling into the stone Presbyterian church, and, down on the back streets and up on the hill, tentative sounds of a piano lesson already drifting out of the brick Methodist building, metal locks clanking at the jail, the wide doors of the feed stores and wholesale houses scraping open onto loading docks, pounding sounds echoing from the garage, and trains grinding through town with strings of coal cars. She'd observed all this from the outside, and now she took satisfaction in feeling she was on the verge of becoming part of it.

The hotel lobby was usually deserted when she entered, but she could see through to the long oil-cloth covered table in the dining room where breakfast regulars were eating the gravy and biscuits stirred up by Vessie Blankenship who did the morning cooking for the Crayhills.

Irene let herself into the Peanut Wagon through a side door out of the kitchen. The enclosure was toasty warm even on chilly mornings because Ward lit the peanut oven's bottled gas burner after he stirred up the banked coal grate in the hotel's kitchen range and added a few blocks of coal before daylight. If it was a cold day Irene could leave the front panel closed until the first batch of peanuts was ready, but she seldom waited. After one ritual moment of standing motionless in the cozy dark tranquility, she liked to go ahead and open up to become part of the street. The hinged middle part of the front wall lowered onto brackets to become the counter, and Nancy had showed her how the entire back wall could swing away in hot weather to let a breeze blow through. The peanut stand's rough-planked architecture fascinated Irene as much as the carved oak stairway in the courthouse interested the town historians.

CHAPTER 3
KENNETH

She'd been on the job almost a week before she finally saw Kenneth Mayhall. Nancy kept asking her every day if she'd seen him yet. He delivered the bulk peanuts they bought from Ansel Conley's Wholesale Supply, but his deliveries had always missed Irene's shift. Nancy kept saying he was the best-looking man in town. She said every girl in Wolliver was after him and that she'd be setting her own cap for him if he'd ever give her the slightest reason to hope.

Lavenna looked mortified. "What do you mean? I thought you said he was a married man."

Nancy grinned and sashayed around the room doffing an imaginary top hat and using a Jimmy Durante voice to say, "Well, let me tell you, kid, I'd be willing to forget he's got a wife if he'd be willing to forget I've got a husband."

"Anyway, what kind of wife is it that won't leave her daddy and mommy to come and live with her husband?" Georgine put in unexpectedly. "You can't tell me she's not got herself some kind of friend on the side down there in Perry County where she feels like she's too good to move up here to the sticks. What kind of place is called Glomawr, anyway?"

Nancy laughed as she tap danced around Georgine's chair. "You know an awful lot about him for him to be a married man," she teased Georgine.

Lavenna ignored Nancy's antics. She said she thought Perry County was in the sticks too. She thought it over.

"But, I think Glomawr's near Hazard, and they do say Hazard is a lot bigger place than Wolliver. Looks like he'd a got a job down there. Wonder why he came up here."

"Ansel's his kin, his cousin or something," Nancy told her. "He made some kind of deal with Ansel way back."

After Irene got to know Kenneth, the only thing he told her about his wife was that the marriage had been a mistake and that he was in the process of bringing it to an end.

The first time he made a delivery on her shift, her back had been turned to the counter. She'd just stirred a batch of peanuts and was sliding the tray back into the oven slots.

A man's voice asked, "Are you going to get this latch for me, or do I have to put down my load?"

Irene had not known voices had color. His voice was the color of burnished bronze, liquefied burnished bronze. It flowed down through the center of her bones, displacing the marrow. She was trembling as she straightened and turned.

That's when he said, "Well, aren't you a fine little slab of a girl."

He was balancing a bag of peanuts on each shoulder. She undid the latch and swung the counter aside. He stowed the bags in their special bin at one end of the wagon, then stood back and looked her straight in the face—like he'd taken care of her body with that one comment and was now taking care of her soul.

She finally whispered, "Don't I have to sign that little paper?" and, with eyes never leaving her face, he fished the sales slip and a pencil stub from his shirt pocket.

Irene dropped the pencil when her fingers touched his. They both leaned forward to pick it up and cracked their heads together so hard they staggered back. They recovered, and both started to reach for it again.

Then they started laughing, and laughed so hard Vessie Sparks opened the kitchen door to see what was going on.

"It's okay, Vessie," Kenneth told her. "We're just out here buttin' heads like Billy goats."

That was good enough for Vessie. She was so elated to learn Kenneth knew her name she would have beamed the same way if he'd said they were setting the building on fire.

Kenneth came to the Wagon every day after that, even if he had time to do no more than say hello. Some days he leaned over the counter and talked to Irene while she worked, and some days he came behind the counter and took over her job. Her customers were disappointed when he wasn't there. He kept up a dazzling line of patter, always knowing exactly what each person wanted to hear. He made Preacher Essel's prim wife Polly Ann giggle when he sang "Pretty Polly" to her. He remembered the names of Sally Walper's children, Jasper Potter's bird dogs and Sam Breedlow's cow. He'd juggle filled bags from the warming drawer, or he'd make an elaborate show of filling a bag, peanut by peanut, throwing them up behind his back and catching them in front while he sang, "Yes, We Have No Bananas."

He knew more songs than Irene had ever heard, and sometimes he used them in place of conversation. One day when nobody else was around, he leaned his elbows on the counter and sang, "From this valley they say you are going. I will miss your bright eyes and sweet smile."

She said, "I ain't a goin' nowhere. Are you?"

He grinned wickedly and came behind the counter where he waltzed her around the tiny space singing, "California, here I come."

When it was not her turn to work at the wagon he took her with him on his deliveries. Ansel's business supplied the stock for most of the little country stores in that end of

34

the county, the stores that weren't owned by the coal companies. Kenneth took her up Line Creek and down Smootfork, over Claycroft Mountain, and around Covecamp Ridge. Some of the stores were so out of the way that the roads went right up the creek beds. He showed her off to the storekeepers saying, "I've got somebody here with me today that's prettier'n a spotted pup under a little red wagon." He always winked at Irene when he said this.

In the truck he sang, "I had a dream, dear. You had one too. Mine was the best dream, because it was of you."

He sang to her the day he took her to the fire tower, too. It was the first week in April, far from warm and still as windy as March, but Ansel had given him the use of the truck and he was determined to show her the mountaintop. He'd been talking about it ever since she'd known him. The observation deck wasn't locked. They climbed the narrow stair-steps all the way to the top where the wind gusted through the open sides, almost blowing Kenneth's hat away before he grabbed it in the nick of time. Irene clung to a corner post while he pointed out the wave-like ranges rippling out on all sides. Then, without a word, he unwound her braids and unraveled each strand, throwing her hair onto the winds the way she used to throw corn to the chickens. Her hair ballooned and whipped and yanked at her scalp, and she stood still as a rock until they slid together down into shelter where he pulled the strands around his neck to bind her to him mouth to mouth.

Later, when the wind had died down, he leaned her back between his knees and re-braided her hair while he sang,

"With someone like you,
a pal good and true,
I'd like to leave it all behind
and go and find
a place that's known

35

to God alone,
just a place to call our own."

She felt like she was in that place.

A carnival came to town on May Day, the first one
Irene had seen. The smells and lights and sounds added to
the excitement of being with Kenneth. Odors of hot
cooking grease and hot motor oil mixed together with an
exhilarating sweetness so strong it was deliriously
suffocating. Colored lights seemed to blink in time with
the stirring drone of calliope music. They ate fried pies
and then licked their greasy fingers so they could take a
turn at the string game. Kenneth threw darts to win her a
little celluloid Kewpie Doll dressed in a cowboy outfit
with a tiny ten-gallon felt hat glued on over his curly-cue.
They named him Ragtime Cowboy Joe.

They stood together before a miniature hillside village
built on a truck bed with the gasoline engine chugging and
sputtering to give it life. She was mesmerized by the little
train winding its way through tunnels, over trestles and
among the little houses with lights inside the windows.
She picked the house she wanted to live in; he pointed out
the park where they could loll by the mirror-surface pond
or stroll the leafy paths.

He had to pull her away from the village to take her on
the Ferris wheel where she thought she would die on the
first downward sweep, but where she did what he told her
as they came back to the crest, locked her eyes into his
and lifted her hands from the bar and raised them straight
above her head while she let herself fall into his soul as he
fell into hers.

Next day he brought her the wire-frame Ferris wheel
from Frank Roscoe's liquor store display window. It had
to be turned by hand, but it really went around and had
four tin seats that had held four bottles of whiskey.

Kenneth put flowers in the seats, dandelions and violets. He wouldn't tell her how he got Frank to let him have it. Sometimes she let Nancy's Amanda carefully turn her dolls in it while she kept watch.

When a warm spell hit in mid-month he asked her if she had any britches, any overalls or jodhpurs. She didn't, of course. He came early the next morning with a pair of dungarees and a pair of boots her size he'd borrowed from Ansel's youngest boy, and he told her they'd be gone till late the next day. Ansel drove them halfway up the mountain where he dropped them off in Claude Bender Gap to set out on foot for the trail leading around and up to Highcrest Rock. Carrying two ragged rolled-up-and-tied quilts and sandwiches made of cold side meat on split biscuits, they kept right to the trail so they wouldn't wander into some moonshiner's territory. They slept on the rock that night, and next day wended their way down the far side of the mountain not many miles from the Virginia border, where Ansel and his wife Patsy picked them up at the mouth of Brimstone Branch before dusk.

On the rock that night under the stars Irene talked about something she'd never had reason to talk about, something she never gave a thought to and never thought anybody would want to know. Kenneth told her about his daddy dying last winter and asked if her daddy was still living.

She said, "I don't rightly know who my daddy is."

She told him how she couldn't remember anybody ever living with them but her Granny McFaron. From things she overheard, and especially from things her granny would say, she was pretty sure her sisters' daddy was not her daddy, even though they all went by the name Mosely. She thought her sisters' daddy had died.

"I think that was my mother's only husband. I don't think she was married to anybody when I was born. I'm not sure she was ever married to anybody."

Kenneth said soothing things, and, when she started to protest that it was okay, that it wasn't anything she felt bad about, an unexpected thing happened: her voice suddenly broke and tears stung her eyes. She let Kenneth hold her and stroke her—and she cried—and it was the first time in her life she could remember crying more than a few foreshortened tears at any one time.

As they trekked down Brimstone Branch next day Kenneth told her how he found out about the trail to Highcrest Rock. "James Houston let me come up here with him and some other boys when I first came to Wolliver. James grew up around here; he knows all these hills like the back of his hand. He's the one that warned me about the moonshine stills."

Irene knew James. He was at the Peanut Wagon even more than Kenneth. He worked at Sol Crutcher's grocery store and made numerous daily deliveries to Vessie's kitchen, usually taking a shortcut through the peanut stand. She was aware James and Kenneth knew each other, but she couldn't imagine them hiking up the mountain together.

Kenneth didn't show up at the peanut stand the next day—or the next. On the third day, Nancy told her she heard that a relative came and got him. Irene hunted down Ansel at the warehouse.

He said, "I wish I knew what to tell you, little lady. That uncle of his showed up, and they was gone before I knowed it. That feller's from his mother's side of the family. I don't know nothing about that bunch. The way me and Kenneth is kin is that my mother was his daddy's sister."

Irene was paralyzed. The only thing she could feel was fear, fear that she'd never be happy again, fear that she'd have to go back to Bullhide, fear that Kenneth had found out what she had planned not to tell him until she had to.

Nancy eventually told her Kenneth was gone for good. She'd heard things around town.

Nancy also guessed Irene's condition.

"Is that why he left?" she probed.

Irene shook her head. "He didn't know," she said. "I wasn't sure myself."

"Then you'd better put out some immediate signals to James Houston, little missy. Unless you'd rather throw in your lot with Mr. Addington." Irene's stomach lurched, and not from the reason it had been lurching these past days. Nancy was alarmed. She hurried to assure her. "Don't worry, kid. It's not too late to pull the wool over the eyes of a gullible Little Boy Blue like James Houston."

Nancy's blunt suggestion brought Irene out of her frozen state. She could readily see what Nancy saw, that James Houston might be her lifeline, her chance to stay in Wolliver. She was well aware that she was the reason he routed his hotel deliveries through the Peanut Stand. But the difference between her and Nancy was that Nancy would not be the one living with the effects of the deception, or rather with the effects of the eventual disclosure. Even from the edge of panic Irene was not willing to put herself in a position where she'd end up on the defensive. However, it didn't take her long to figure out a way she could use James Houston without ever having to defend herself. As long as she made sure he knew he was being used she didn't have anything to lose.

So, just short of putting it to him bluntly, she gave him the opportunity to put the idea to her. She cut short his lighthearted chit-chat on his next trip from Vessie's kitchen.

She said, "James, I've been a wanting to ask if you've heard anything about Kenneth Mayhall."

"Just what you've probably heard already, that he won't be coming back."

"Do you know why?" She hadn't plotted out her questions; she was just letting the conversation take its course.

"Nope." He paused a second, "Of course, he *is* a married man. There's a lot of explanations come to mind."

"Well, I don't guess I'll be getting any explanation from him—being that he is a married man."

"Could be that he wanted to come by and talk to you but that his uncle wouldn't let him take the time."

"Could be." She grew bold by his straightforward calmness. "He didn't know I had special reason for needing to talk to him."

James Houston, much to Irene's relief and encouragement, did not bat an eye. He didn't say much more at that moment, but the conversation continued at a pace that seemed right to Irene as he made his continued trips back and forth that day and the next two.

"I guess you'll be wanting to let him know your situation before you take your next step," he said next day.

"I can't be waitin' around and countin' on things that ain't likely to happen. I'll be figuring out how to make do without him."

Next day James said, "So, I guess you might think it'd be better to up and get married to somebody now and let people talk about how fast things moved than to have them counting on their fingers later on."

She'd had enough of this talk. "If you're offering to marry me, James, I need to know why you'd be willing."

James took off his glasses and took his time cleaning them, breathing extra carefully on the lenses and wiping them as usual with his pocket handkerchief.

Finally he said, "Why, you know I've always had my eye on you, Irene Mosely. I might a wished I'd been your first choice but, if you're interested in what I can offer, then I'm happy enough to have things turn out this way."

"What is it you can offer?"

"Not just a piece of paper. I can offer just what I'd be offering if I was your first choice. All I'd need to know is that you really want to pick up where you left off with him and make a life with me."

"How come you'd be willin' to raise another man's child?"

"I'd think of it as your child," he said, "not another man's."

"I do need to move on," she said.

She had Nancy cut off her hair before she married James, had her cut off the braids and then shape what was left into a bob. She carefully coiled the three-foot braids and put them into a claret colored velveteen bag Nancy had saved from a silver teapot she'd long ago given away.

That bag of braids was in a hatbox found some years later on a shelf at Nancy's house after she died; that bag, a little celluloid Kewpie Doll dressed in a cowboy outfit, and the "Red River Valley" lyrics written out in pencil on a brown paper peanut bag. The box had Irene's name on it, and somebody who didn't know any better sent it to Nora Faye.

James was not evasive. He couldn't give Nora Faye answers he didn't have when she asked him if he knew why her mother had kept those things, but he gave her answers to other questions she was asking for the first time.

He said, "I don't know what these things meant to her, but I can tell you that they didn't have anything to do with you or me. They had to do with what she never stopped wanting. The whole time she was with me, it never stopped being the only thing she wanted."

She knew the answer, but asked anyway, "What was it she wanted?"

"To leave," he murmured. "Your mother always wanted to leave. She would never have married me if she hadn't been desperate. She didn't know what else to do. It's just how things were for her, and she never pretended they were any different. She never pretended to be what she wasn't." His voice dropped off out of hearing. "Almost never. "

Nora Faye sucked in a deep breath and asked the other question she already knew the answer to. "You're not my real daddy, then?"

"Not by blood," he answered.

Some men would have felt compelled to pour out a flood of assurances about how she felt like his and all that, but James gave her that same kind of comfort by just saying unflinchingly, "Not by blood."

She had one more question, though. "Why'd you take care of me, then?"

James did not take off his glasses while he contemplated this question. He looked Nora Faye straight in the eye like he was searching for his answer in her dearly familiar face.

"I think maybe that's why all that happened with me and her, Fayzie, so I'd be there to take care of you," he finally offered. "That's the way it seems to me when I look back on it now."

And in an off-kilter, oblique way, that's what Irene thought, too. She so took for granted his devotion to Nora Faye that the times she had almost loved James were not, as it would have seemed, when he was being kind to Nora Faye, but when he was being kind, as usual, to her.

Irene was not as shallow as she struck most people, but her measure of personal rectitude lay in an unhesitating willingness to follow enormously consequential instincts without probing for justification and without looking back.

She was not looking back when she left Dillard. The part of her that had always known she would someday leave James had also known she would leave Nora Faye with him. Except for that one flashing moment when her breath went shallow as she walked away from Mrs. Slaney's steps, her focus had not wavered. Her instinct to take care of details concerning Nora Faye before she left was not a maternal instinct, but one of survival . She felt that her very survival depended on putting this life behind her with one clean slash; she did not want any loose ends requiring her to stick around and give James cause to doubt the finality of her departure.

Though she had not left home with a conscious plan of action, she had sketched a mental outline before Gladys delivered her to Rose's house just a couple of streets over from where she'd lived with Nancy in the Upper Bottom. After she'd told Rose where she'd left Nora Faye, she could walk to Georgine's place.

Nancy and Luther had moved to Lexington a couple of years back, but Irene's dismay at not having the sanctuary of Nancy's house as an option in Wolliver today had been replaced by a plan to make the new home her destination on the first leg of her journey to California. She had enough money to buy a ticket to Lexington. She'd leave Platchet County on the passenger train out of Wolliver this afternoon and be well out of Kentucky by next week. Nancy would lend her enough money to get to San Diego, Kenneth's port of departure.

Since Nancy's move, Georgine had rented the apartment above the barbershop near the train station. She worked the night shift on Wolliver's telephone switchboard. She'd be home this morning and, though she'd not be sympathetic to Irene's plight, Irene knew she would let her stay at her place until train time. Irene had no hesitation about seeking help from women who felt no warmth for her.

She did not divulge her plans to Gladys. For one moment she'd considered having Gladys wait for her and then give her a ride to Georgine's after she talked to Rose, or maybe having her go by Georgine's place first so she could drop off her travel case and not have to carry it across town—the corn on her little toe gave a twinge as she contemplated walking the whole length of the route where she had first started to feel like she was a part of the real world—but she didn't want any delay before letting Rose know what she was doing, and she didn't want Gladys feeling like she was letting her in on things. In spite of her corn, she'd rather go on foot and carry her suitcase as she made one last trip from the far edge of the Upper Bottom into the heart of Wolliver.

CHAPTER 4
JAMES

James returned to the porch swing after he read the funnies to Nora Faye at the kitchen table and then helped her climb quietly into her bed so she wouldn't wake his mother in the big bed. She'd winced while he was washing her face, and he'd found a little discolored place inside her lower lip. At first she couldn't remember how she got it, and then she said she fell off the travel bag. She said, "I didn't poke the screen." He didn't think the cut was going to cause any problem; he'd tried to wiggle her teeth to make sure none were loose.

He knew he couldn't sleep yet, but he'd decided not to risk disturbing her or his mother by turning on the radio to see if he could get more news about the bombings in London. They'd been telling how families were sending their children out of the city, some to live with relatives, some with strangers. He'd seen a newspaper picture of a London mother running alongside the train, stretching to touch her little girl's fingertips through an open window as the train pulled away. He wondered which would be hardest, to let your child go where things were safer—even if it might mean you'd never see it again—or to keep it with you and take the other kind of risk. He thought how fortunate parents were in the U. S., not to be forced to make that kind of decision.

Above the drone of the locusts he could hear a fly throwing itself against the screen. He'd tried earlier to kill it, first with the newspaper and then the swatter, but he'd given up for fear he was going to knock out the screen that was bulged and rusty with little prickly holes here and there. He planned to replace it as soon as he could get enough screen to do the whole porch. Screen wire was hard to come by these days, but he felt he'd be giving in to something low-life if he patched the holes or replaced just the worst panels to end up with a hodge-podge of new and old. Some people were simply removing all the screen, but he thought that looked worse than patches, and he couldn't see how it would help his situation. He'd have to find two more screen doors if the porch had no screen; three doors opened into the house from the porch. Now he wondered if he'd ever do anything about it.

He felt almost relieved that things had come to a head with Irene. He'd lived with dread for so long that he sadly welcomed a new kind of heart-heaviness. It didn't feel so much like a worse ache as a different ache. He knew she would not return. When he'd said she'd be coming back, it was to keep his mother from feeling like she ought to start helping him map out their future. It was usually his way to let things take their own slow course.

His mother was strong-willed but accepting. He had not told her he was getting married, but he'd taken Irene and her suitcase home with him that first day. When Irene went to freshen up, his mother said "Lord a mercy, James, I hope you know what you're doing." But she was kind to Irene, telling her in her matter-of-fact way what a pretty bride she was and telling them both they were welcome to stay there with her as long as they wanted. She even took the train down to Blackey to visit with Clemma for a few days, so as to give James and Irene the house to themselves. She told them she'd been promising Clemma a visit for months.

But there had never been any warmth between his wife and his mother. He'd found a little house to rent cheap in the Lower Bottom where he and Irene set up housekeeping until he got the unexpected chance to come to Dillard.

He'd never talked to his mother about Kenneth Mayhall, but he felt certain she knew the whole story, just as he felt certain he would always be able to depend on her to help him take care of Nora Faye. He'd have to guard against letting her take over the whole job. She would do it if he let her, and he could see how easy it would be to slip into that pattern.

His married life was a pattern he'd slipped into. After he realized Irene would never allow him into her heart, he was determined to focus on the reality of a surface pattern that, in spite of its shortcomings, was more satisfying than his life had been without her. He'd never wanted to marry another woman; it wasn't like he'd made a choice for this life over a possibly more satisfying one.

He had not tortured himself with thoughts of Kenneth Mayhall. He tried to think of Kenneth as the loser; after all, Kenneth was the one doing without Irene and Nora Faye. James was never complacent, but he figured he was living a more satisfied life than most—until the letters started, the letters going back and forth like sticky strands of spider web.

Sol Crutcher, a man not given to speaking his mind, had reacted with a warning instead of congratulations when James told him he needed the day off from work to get married. "Are you sure you want to do this, son?" he asked. "A man can get in enough trouble trying to untangle his own webs without throwing hisself into other people's."

That's when James made the quick decision that life from now on would be simpler if he were never to acknowledge Irene's previous circumstances, even with the most well-meaning people. He pretended to miss Sol's meaning, saying, "I guess it's a real privilege when a man can get tangled in such a pretty creature's web."

Sol recognized his ruse and did not persist. James would not have wavered if Sol had hit him over the head. He convinced himself from the start that it would be enough to spend every day with Irene, to hear her voice, to touch her, to try to please her. And he thought she might have some feeling for him after the baby was born.

The baby had deepened his feelings for Irene at any rate. He thought of Nora Faye simply as their child, as his child. His life proved more than tolerable.

Eldon, of course, knew the circumstances. When Eldon put him on to the letters, he thought he could mark time until they stopped coming. He thought Kenneth Mayhall would find a new distraction if he made it back to the states alive. He did not confront Irene, and he would never have tried to find the letters. He did not want to see words on paper.

Eldon accused him of bringing the whole thing on himself, and James couldn't dispute him. Irene had never given him reason to hope for anything more than what she'd first laid out for him.

Thoughts of Eldon brought the tattered porch screen back to mind. Eldon would have found a way to replace the screen. He had mentioned it to James more than once.

"It's not like it's a big three-sided porch," he'd admonished, "and even that one wall is boxed in at the bottom. It won't take more than a few yards." It was clear that he thought James had not put enough effort into finding replacement screen. Eldon and Stella kept their place neat as a bandbox in spite of Eldon's inclination to buy up great heaps of various goods to resell at the right moment. He had a couple of out-buildings where he stored his clutter.

James's camp house was U-shaped, with three rooms across the back and one at each end in the front. The recessed porch sat between the two front rooms with the front wall boxed in at the bottom few feet and screened at the top.

The fly had stopped banging the screen. Maybe it had dashed itself to death or found a way out. At least he could be sure it wasn't bothering his mother; the locusts had quieted enough for him to hear her soft, regular snoring.

Before he went to bed he would make sure the fly wasn't buzzing Nora Faye. He would tiptoe in like he had every night of her life to make certain she was sleeping peacefully in the wrought-iron baby bed she was still small enough to fit.

He had thought they'd be giving the bed to Tattie's most recent grandchild, but Irene refused to give it up. She didn't want Nora Faye to move to the big bed yet. She said she wanted the spare bed to herself on nights when James's snoring kept her from sleeping. James figured he'd give up the baby bed the next time there was a scrap iron drive. They didn't really need it now. His mother could share the big bed with Nora Faye when she came to help out. Nora Faye usually crawled in with her before the night was over anyhow.

Everybody in Dillard had hunted up every discarded gate hinge and bedspring and rusted-out slop bucket for the recent scrap iron drive. He and Rollie had joined the other men one Sunday to scavenge the abandoned tipple site across the creek behind their houses. Staghorn Collaries had drummed up community participation to show their patriotism. There were rusty bolts and iron plates to pound and pry off the dilapidated coal chute, and iron spikes from the upper tracks along with a broken axle and a bent rail or two to drag down the hill.

James's patriotism went as deep as his neighbors, and he was especially glad for an opportunity to contribute to the war effort since his poor eyesight kept him from enlisting. Though his glasses made it possible for him to function normally, they did not completely correct his problem.

In his heart he was not too sorry his poor vision had rendered him 4-F. Even without the need for thick-lens eyeglasses he could not imagine himself in any kind of combat. When he saw pictures of foxholes or dog-fights or sea battles, they seemed as far-fetched to him as pictures of Biblical clashes or Old West shootouts. He'd heard about some fellas given 4-F status who kept going from one draft board to another until they got themselves accepted. He had not felt a need to do that.

When the war first started, his mother said, "If you'd a just waited it out a little longer, you could have stayed on in town. They'll be jobs again now that it looks like we're going to get into the war."

But he had waited as long as possible. Sol Crutcher would never have fired him, but he was unable to give him a full payday for weeks on end. Even though he and Irene could have gotten by on the provisions Sol insisted he take from their stock, he had no way to pay the rent, and he knew he would lose what peace he had learned to take with Irene if he moved her back in with his mother.

Then he ran into Rollie Avery at the barbershop, and when Rollie asked if he was interested in a job at the company store up Dillard, he'd jumped at the chance. He'd got to know Rollie back on his first wage-earning job, back when he was hauling mail and freight with a mule and wagon from the Bascon train yard to the post office up Sanghill. Rollie had worked up to manager of Staghorn's Sanghill commissary before he'd been relocated to Dillard.

James wasn't surprised when Eldon came next day while they were still at the supper table. He knew he would come as soon as word reached him, and he knew that wouldn't take long. He could imagine the whispered undercurrents that must have followed Irene as she and her suitcase made their way to the train station from his mother's house in the Upper Bottom.

Rose jumped up like she'd been listening for the Ford, but before she could start cleaning off the table, Dollie and Bootsie came running in with presents from the Five and Dime, a new box of colors for Nora Faye and coloring books for all three of them. Stella was close on their heels, saying Eldon needed James to help unload the screen wire he'd brought.

Eldon had swung a deal; he'd traded some lumber for the screen wire. He was good at knowing when a person would be willing to set a low price on something he needed to get rid of quickly: leftover lumber, buckets of paint, loads of coal, one time three dozen pairs of gum boots. Eldon would buy low and keep his ear to the ground until he heard of a need that would push up the value. He worked in the freight office at the Bascon train yard where he often got tips about a possible buy or sale.

When he insisted they start right to work, James protested that there was no need to get into the job this evening. "I know Ma'd like to get back home before dark."

But Eldon said they had plenty of daylight left, more than enough time for this little job. And next thing he knew they were prying off furring strips, tearing off old screen, rolling out the new, measuring, cutting and tacking.

His mother was fixing a pan of dishwater, and Stella was in the bedroom piling things on the bed from Nora Faye's dresser drawer. He knew his mother would set Stella straight; he wouldn't have to get into it with her. The girls were chattering and giggling as they broke in the new colors, but they had taken their coloring books to Nora Faye's bedroom floor, so he was able to hear what

51

the women were saying after Stella went back to the kitchen where she was drying the dishes while Rose washed.

Rose said, "You may as well put her clothes back in her drawer. He's not going to let you take her. Me neither. He says he talked to Mrs. Slaney across the road about her staying over there while he's at work to days."

Stella didn't say much, just that she guessed he'd have to learn the hard way.

CHAPTER 5
THE SLANEYS

While her mother packed her travel bag, Nora Faye had become eager to go to Mrs. Slaney's house. She'd stayed there before. The Slaney children did interesting things, and from their high-up front porch on the corner lot she could see all the places Callie tied Seelom. She wasn't curious about her mother packing a bag. She thought she was probably going to spend a night with one of her Wolliver friends, Georgine or Lavenna. They didn't have children, and nothing about those visits was fun for Nora Faye.

She watched restlessly while Irene changed out of her flowered dimity dress into a plainer one and then rearranged things in the travel bag one more time. She had to take out her box of bath powder before she could close the lid. She told Nora Faye to put the box in her sock drawer. "It's yours now," she said.

Her sock drawer was too shallow; it barely held her anklets and long winter stockings. It wouldn't shut with the powder box. "Well, put it in with your step-ins and petticoats," Irene said. "That drawer's deeper." But it was narrow. Nora Faye had to take out her panties and petticoats and her one-piece winter button-up suits to put the Cara Nome box in the bottom and rearrange her underwear on top.

She could remember when James had given Irene the box of talcum powder for a birthday present. Along with a few words, the cream colored lid was decorated with a little bouquet that looked like a little tree.

"It says 'N' like my name," she said.

"That word is Nome. It's called Cara Nome," Irene said as she unrolled the garters from her everyday stockings.

"What does it means?"

"Cara Nome?" Irene asked. She looked blankly at Nora Faye. "Why, I don't know. I don't reckon it *means* anything. I never wondered about it."

It seemed she took forever getting into her good stockings and her dress-up shoes with sweetheart heels and a strap across the top, the ones that hurt the corn on her little toe. She took off that shoe and stocking and put a special little pad on the corn before she rolled the stocking back up to her knee and once again buttoned the narrow shoe strap. She stood backwards on the vanity stool to check on her seams by looking in the mirror over her shoulder. "Are they straight?" she asked. Nora Faye could never tell for sure.

She went to the porch to look for Seelom before Irene finally came and told her to wait there and not get dirty while she went over to make sure Mrs. Slaney was ready for her. She left the suitcase on the porch, and Nora Faye climbed up on it so she could watch her as she crossed the road and then see her again on the porch steps after she went around the corner to the gate that opened onto the side road.

The suitcase turned over, and, in her efforts to catch herself without punching a hole in the screen, she mashed her lip on the porch ledge. She got a little taste of blood and could feel her lip getting fat. She tried not to let it show when her mother came back for her. She was excited now to think about looking down on Seelom from the Slaney's porch; she didn't want anything to make the plans change.

Mrs. Slaney was waiting for her on the porch steps, wiping her hands on her apron before reaching a hand

54

down to her. "You're just in time to help me make jam," she said. "The children already brought home a gallon of black raspberries this morning and have gone back for more."

She explained further to Irene, "We still pick the berry patches at the Ritter place up the holler here. You know, we were renting that place before we moved down here to the company house. The Hardens that live there now don't bother with the berries, and they say they don't care if we get them.

"But don't let me keep you." She smoothed down her apron and tucked in a strand of hair. "You and Gladys enjoy your day in town. I know it must be nice to have each other's company. Don't worry about Nora Faye; she's never the least bit of trouble."

If she noticed the travel bag she didn't mention it.

Nora Faye said, "I gots to stay on the porch. Callie's horse is coming."

Mrs. Slaney said, "I like to watch him, too. I'll join you out here for a little resting spell when I get this batch of jam into jars. If you want, you can come and try a little taste of skimmed foam before you start looking for your horse. Black raspberries boil up an awful good foam."

Nora Faye followed her into the kitchen where a delicious smell was coming from a big kettle sitting on a dough board on the table. Mrs. Slaney opened the oven and slid out pans of glass jars she said were sterilized now. She set the jars in rows to cool using a special tool to lift and place them so she wouldn't get burned. She explained all this to Nora Faye.

"We've been hoarding our sugar in case they started rationing it this summer. We ate molasses and honey on our oatmeal all through the winter. It takes a lot of sugar to make jam."

She gave Nora Faye a little dish of purple foam she said she'd skimmed off the top of the jam and a little tin cup of cold milk. "It's store-bought," she explained about the milk. "I remember that you drink cow's milk when I give it to you, but most of my children are so partial to the store-bought kind that I told Mr. Williams he didn't need to bring me any more cow's milk unless I let him know."

Sliding open the little door to the warming oven at the top of the stove, Mrs. Slaney said, "There's biscuits in here left from breakfast. Would you like to have one to crumble in your foam?" Nora Faye nodded yes.

Mrs. Slaney stirred the cooling jam and started filling the jars with a short-handled dipper. First she put a wide-mouthed funnel in the jar and then poured the jam into the funnel before she moved it to the next jar. Once, without asking, she poured a little of the warm jam into Nora Faye's bowl. "When the jars are cool, we'll melt the paraffin and pour some on top to seal them." She held up a block of white wax Nora Faye had been wondering about.

"I don't think your mother makes jam, but maybe you've watched your grandmother do it." Nora Faye shook her head. Granny Rose canned things that didn't smell good when they were blanched in boiling water: green beans and red beets and tomatoes.

Just as Mrs. Slaney filled the last jar, the children came home with more berries. Laura Jane put a few in Nora Faye's bowl with a little milk and sugar and showed her how to mash them with the back of her spoon until the milk turned purple. They tasted almost as good as the jam.

The children had purple hands and mouths. They seemed very happy to be covered with berry stains and to be wearing their oldest clothes with rips and holes. They called them their berry-picking duds. They all talked at once while they ate foam and washed up at the kitchen sink and picked burrs off their clothes. They told about seeing a blacksnake and about seeing their old barn cat they'd left behind when they moved. They said the cat stayed with them all morning, stalking them and pouncing from the briers.

Billy Ray said, "Once we thought Donny Stoddard was coming, but it was Mrs. Harden out looking for her heifer and picking a mess of greens."

Mrs. Slaney flashed a questioning look at Lottie, who answered aloud, but softly, "We didn't see a sign of him all morning."

Mrs. Slaney petted Billy Ray a little. He was the youngest, not much older than Nora Faye, and always kind of sickly. She asked him if the others walked too fast for him again, and he said, "Conner packed me."

Nora Faye liked Conner best of all. He was eleven. She kept forgetting the other children's ages. Ruthie drilled her over and over, but, in spite of her efforts, Nora Faye could remember only her own age—and Conner's. Ruthie would act like they were playing school. She was the teacher, and Nora Faye the pupil. She'd put her at the little playhouse table she called a school desk and tell her to sit up straight and not pick her nose. That hurt Nora Faye's feelings, because she had learned long ago not to pick her nose in front of people. She knew it was just pretend, but she wished Ruthie would come up with something different to sound like a teacher. She would hold Nora Faye's hand palm-up and pretend she was going to hit it with a ruler while she forced her to listen to the list. "Billy Ray is six, Ruthie Jo is nine, Conner Eugene is eleven, Laura Jane is twelve, and Lottie Louise is fifteen."

Ruthie would groan when Nora Faye could not recite the list back to her. "What is so hard about a few names and ages?" she'd demand. "I'm not even asking you to learn R. L. and Lissie since they don't live here anymore. Now, what's so hard about learning a few simple facts?"

Mrs. Slaney would tell her to leave Nora Faye alone. "She knows what a four-year-old needs to know. I thought you'd got too old for pretend games and, anyway, I don't see why you want to play something that's no fun for anybody. If you're going to teach her something, why don't you work on the ABCs? What use is it for her to learn your ages? I think you do it just to bedevil her."

But Ruthie would start again as soon as her Mother walked away. Sometimes Nora Faye had to ignore Ruthie, as she eventually had to when she went through a spell of wanting to push her in the doll carriage.

The doll carriage, with its sturdy wicker body big enough for the largest dolls, had sat largely unused for a year or two at the children's end of the long back porch, but when Nora Faye began staying with them, Ruthie became obsessed with pushing her in it or taking it to the side yard where she stuffed her in and let it roll until it stopped. Nora Faye's arms and legs spilled over, and she had to bend her neck at an awkward angle to fit under the sunshade canopy. The path there sloped just enough to keep the carriage rolling after Ruthie gave it a start, and though the ride usually ended in an upset, the thick grass was soft enough to cushion a fall and keep Nora Faye from getting hurt.

But it was no fun when the novelty wore off after the first few rides. She continued to put up with the ordeal only because Ruthie bargained with her for the right to squeeze her in and dump her out. She allowed her to draw with her set of colored pencils one day and gave her a *Mary Jane and Sniffles* funny book another time and even let her dance in her cherished tap shoes.

But Mrs. Slaney did not like to see it, even after Ruthie explained about the bargaining agreement. Nora Faye had had enough, so she was happy when Mrs. Slaney said, "It's not just that Nora Faye might get hurt, but there's no use to destroy the little carriage that way. It's a well-made little buggy that's held up through several of you girls. If you don't want it anymore, then give it to Nora Faye and let her take it home with her to play with her dolls."

Ruthie said, "Nora Faye doesn't play with dolls." Nora Faye mentally disagreed and then realized it was the truth. The dolls she got for Christmases were stored topsy-turvy with the rest of her play-pretties in a wicker laundry basket in a corner of her bedroom. Sometimes she dressed and undressed them, but she didn't play with them like she sometimes played with paper dolls and like she often played with imaginary characters inside her head.

Mrs. Slaney made another batch of jam while Lottie used the last of the berries to put together a cobbler for dinner. Laura Jane and Ruthie went to change clothes, and Billy Ray fell asleep on the back porch cot.

When Mrs. Slaney was washing the jam off her mouth Norah Faye tried not to let her know she was hurting her mashed lip. It seemed somehow that she shouldn't tell Mrs. Slaney about it until after she first told her mother.

When she asked if she could follow Conner to his shop Mrs. Slaney said okay.

Conner did experiments and collected things, put things together and took them apart. He had all sorts of collections in the garden shed at the back corner of the yard. They called the shed his shop. It seemed he was allowed to do about anything he wanted as long as nobody got hurt. His brothers and sisters usually left him to himself except for times like the day they found him cutting glass with scissors. They wanted to try it too. Scrap glass was one of the things he collected—from broken windows and abandoned houses and wherever he stumbled upon it. He held a piece of a windowpane below the surface in a pan of water and used his mother's cast-off sewing scissors with a broken point to cut a valentine heart out of it. It was lopsided and rough-edged, but you could tell it was a heart. He gave them each a scrap of glass and let them try it. It was a nice sensation, even for Nora Faye who could barely cut paper and who had never handled a pair of pointed scissors, much less a piece of broken glass. Conner did most of her cutting while she held her hands on his to see how it felt.

Ruthie caused a commotion and made a mess when she tried to cut her piece of glass without the water. First, nothing happened, and then the whole piece splintered and flew off in all directions.

Conner said he told her so while he picked up the shards and Laura Jane picked little pieces off Ruthie's clothes. When they asked Conner why the glass didn't shatter that way under water, he said he didn't totally understand it, but that the book where he'd read about it said it had to do with molecules and with glass really being a liquid like water. Ruthie snorted at that.

"It's the truth, swear to God," he told her.

Billy Ray said, "We're not allowed to swear."

Conner had read about glass in a science book Mrs. Everhart brought him. He said the molecules in water move real fast, and the ones in glass move so slowly you can't tell they're moving. The water just slows down the reaction of the glass and keeps it from splintering when it's cut.

They all looked baffled except for Ruthie who was still picking tiny glass splinters off her clothes and checking her hands for cuts. She said, "You think we're going to believe that bunch of malarkey?" When he got the book out of the shed and tried to show her the pages, she refused to look.

He laughed and said, "I'll learn all about it some day and explain it so good that even you can understand, Ruthie." She stuck her tongue out at him.

Today he was working with his bee garden. "What happened?" Nora Faye asked in dismay when she saw the glass box in pieces.

"The bees died," he said. "It's my fault. I just wasn't thinking, and what I did was really wrong. I put them in a death chamber instead of a paradise. They need a hive and a queen and drones and workers. They have to be free to gather nectar from living flowers. Most of all, they need a queen."

He was taking apart bricks and glass as he talked. "Anything you do with bees is just play-acting if they don't have a queen. They have complicated societies with certain patterns of behavior. They probably died from heat. The air around them has to be moving. In a hive, there's a certain group of bees assigned to do nothing but fan their wings day and night to keep the hive cool."

He worked silently for a while. Nora Faye waited. She knew he was more likely to continue talking if she did not ask questions.

"I saw Mr. Williams' bees when they swarmed one time. Saw them before he got them back home. Their queen had died or something, and they all flew up in a tree in his orchard and made a great big clump around a limb. I think he put another queen in a hive and hauled the hive out there where they were. The thing I don't know is where he got his queen to put in the new hive. I don't know how he knew she was a queen or where he got her."

Then, after a little silence while he carefully scraped the glass, "I don't know why I didn't ask him about that. Guess I didn't know I was going to be making a bee garden.

"Of course, I'd be ashamed to tell him about the garden now that I see how foolish it was. He'd think I don't know anything. I could make a real beehive someday, I guess, but a beehive is not going to be a simple little make-believe plaything like a bee garden. I'll ask him about the queen next time I get the chance."

Dismantling the bee garden, he soaked the mud mortar in a pan of water if it didn't crumble free right away. He turned the stuck pieces of bricks and glass this way and that before he pulled, scraping with a pointed stick if a piece wouldn't give way, never forcing things that didn't want to move. Every now and then he stretched on tiptoe to reach the top of a rafter with his fingertips. He took down a well-wrapped, single-edged razor blade that he used—handling it with great care—to scrape off mud that didn't come off with water alone. Each time he finished with the razor blade, he rinsed it thoroughly and dried it on his pants leg—gingerly pulling it backwards, so as not to cut the cloth—before he returned it to the exactly creased, white, waxy-looking paper wrapper which slid into a little cardboard sleeve like a stick of chewing gum. He always put the package back on the rafter. He never laid it aside unpackaged even if things looked like he might need it again. He never once mentioned it to Nora Faye, and she did not ask him about it. She did not think the other children knew it was there.

He was a lot like his mother the way he talked to Nora Faye as if she were old enough to understand anything he might say. But with Conner it was more like he was thinking out loud while he allowed Nora Faye to hear. He never expected her to respond to anything he said, but he was kind to her if she did say something.

"Is that a beehive?" she asked, looking at the pieces he'd started laying out.

"A different thing," he said. "This time, ants. I'm trying to figure out how I can tell if I have a queen ant. I think a queen might be just as important to ants as to bees, but I'm thinking the ants will live for a while without one."

He worked silently for a while before he went on. "Ants have complicated ways of living, too, but since they live in the ground I think they might accept food provided in a closed-in place. I'm thinking they might do okay if I can figure out what to feed them…and how to capture enough of them from the same ant hill to start a new colony."

He had the ant structure well under way when a new idea came to him. "Maybe I can leave the bottom open and push it down into the ground right on top of an anthill."

He was sandwiching two panes of glass together with a narrow space between. It looked like a very difficult project to Nora Faye. To hold the space between the panes, he used a thin strip of wood from the bottom of an old window shade she had watched him chop into concise pieces. After sealing three sides with clay mud, he worked hard to tie long strips of stretchy rubber around the construction in both directions. When Nora Faye asked, "What's that?" he told her he had cut the pieces from an old bicycle-tire tube. "It's like giant rubber bands," he explained. "It's what you use to make a slingshot."

As he worked with the rubber bands, some of the mud fell out and he had to redo the caulking job. When it happened a second time, he abandoned the ties and depended on bricks to hold the pieces tight enough to seal. He finished by propping the assembly upright between stacks of bricks, saying that after the clay dried he'd fill the space between the panes with fine soil he'd get from his mother's dahlia bed. "Or maybe I'll dig the dirt out of an ant hill and then put the ant house on top of it."

Nora Faye had seen him use the clay in other projects. It came from one special spot on the creek bank up the side hollow just this side of the Ritter place. He'd brought some back in a jelly jar when they came from picking berries this morning.

"I'm counting on ants not needing special food. I'll give them some sugar, in case they're sugar ants, and a glob of grease, in case they're grease ants, and some leaves—or maybe seeds. Maybe I won't have to put in any food if I can put the ant-hive right on top of an anthill...or maybe that's how I'll get them to come up into the hive, by putting the right kind of food in it." He was musing to himself again, repeating himself, chewing on a corner of his tongue as he worked.

He'd gathered the dead bees found among the wilted flowers on the moss layer at the bottom of the bee garden and, while he waited for the ant structure to dry he began adding the bees to his "dead-board" with stickpins. He seldom killed insects on purpose, but he collected the dead ones he came across—moths, Junebugs, grasshoppers, jar flies, bumble bees, witch doctors, hornets, mud-dobbers, butterflies—and displayed them with penciled labels on a board in the shed. His prized specimen was a gruesome fuzzy brownish blue moth bigger than Nora Faye's hand, the kind that gave her the heebie-jeebs when she saw a live one on the window after dark. He'd been given so many locust shells this summer—it was a year of the seventeen-year locust—that he'd made a separate board for the ones people had collected for him.

Granny Rose came for Nora Faye while Conner was letting her look at a dead bee's stinger under the old scratched camera lens he used as a magnifying glass. Nora Faye didn't think about Seelom until she was back at her own house. She knew Callie had returned him to the Patterson's gatepost when she came back from getting the mail. That's why it was such a surprise to discover him by her coal shed that evening after supper.

After she sat on Seelom that night, she didn't spend much time on the coal shed for the rest of the summer. She thought, for a while, that she'd sit on him again some day—Callie still tied him to the coal shed now and then—but she was always tired when she came home from the Slaney's. Sometimes she fell asleep at the supper table. If she seemed especially sleepy, James would wash her face and put her into her nightie before he fixed them a bite to eat. On mornings when she was hard to wake, he picked her up, quilt and all, and carried her over to the Slaney's where he put her down on the back porch cot.

When she woke on the cot, she always lay still for several minutes, feeling deliciously like she was partly awake and partly still in her dreams. She could hear Mrs. Slaney working in the kitchen if she wasn't already busily setting the back porch table for breakfast. The long porch was screened in, with a big round table at the kitchen end and the cot and some wicker armchairs among the children's playthings at the other.

Waking at her own house was a good feeling, too. Sometimes she woke when her daddy turned on the water—the pipes made knocking noises—and sometimes she woke when he shook down the grate if it was a day he was making a fire in the kitchen stove. Sometimes she didn't wake until he roused her to use the slop jar before he made his morning trip out to the toilet.

After she used the slop jar, he took it out to empty in the toilet while she got herself dressed and climbed up on the bed rungs to pull her covers smooth. He seldom made a morning fire in the summer; they usually ate Wheaties or corn flakes. While he shaved at the kitchen sink he let Nora Faye get the milk bottle from the refrigerator and climb on the kitchen stool to get the cereal box and bowls and spoons from the cabinet.

When Granny Rose stayed with them, Nora Faye slept as late as she wanted and woke to the smell of frying sausage mingling with the pleasingly caustic tingle of hot Fels-Naptha suds chugging in the Maytag.

On the day when Granny Rose finally got around to using the soot rake on the kitchen stove, she told Nora Faye she could play inside or out, but that she couldn't come and go because the doors had to stay shut to keep the soot from blowing.

"It's going to take a while," she warned.

Nora Faye squatted to watch. She found the procedure as fascinating as she'd found Conner's bee garden construction. She'd long been curious about the little long-handled rake in its brackets on the back of the stove, asking her mother about it more than once. But Irene didn't know what it was for. Now, after Granny Rose closed the kitchen doors, shut the windows, and laid newspapers in front of the stove, she loosened the screw in the little oblong plate below the oven door and swung it up out of the way. Then she used the long-handled tool to scrape the soot off the oven wall and rake it into the ash pan while she explained how the caked-on soot kept the oven from baking evenly.

She said, "We'll have to find a place to empty this soot; we'll need to put the ash pan back in its place before we make a fire." She talked like Nora Faye was helping instead of just watching.

Nora Faye said, "Daddy puts his cinders in the road, and Mrs. Slaney putses hers in the rut lane." But Granny Rose said the soot was different from cinders, that they'd have to do something with the soot to keep it from blowing around. She said they'd dig a hole and bury it in the lettuce bed after she got the kitchen put back together. "May as well put *something* in the lettuce bed," she added to herself.

Nora Faye said, "I can read what this word says." She was pointing to the fancy metal lettering above the little soot-rake door. "It says 'Kalamazoo'."

"Elt. That's a big word for a little girl to know." Granny Rose went on to say she reckoned Nora Faye would be reading books before long. She asked if she could name the letters in Kalamazoo, but Nora Faye said N was the only letter she knew. She said, "My name stands for N."

Rose said, "Well, N stands for your name, I guess you could say."

CHAPTER 6
ROSE

Rose didn't exactly mean it when she told James she was surprised about Irene just up and leaving. She just hadn't expected her to do something as mild as running away. She'd always known that Irene would sooner or later do something catastrophic. Leaving was one of the least damaging things to go through her mind—least damaging to Nora Faye and James. If Irene was determined to be with Kenneth Mayhall, then a clean-cut runaway seemed as good to Rose as any way she could have gone about it.

Irene had not told her she was setting out to follow Kenneth. When she appeared on her doorstep that morning carrying the same travel bag she'd had when James brought her home as his bride, she simply said she wouldn't be back and that she needed Rose to go to Dillard and get Nora Faye from Berta Slaney. But Rose knew, and Irene knew she knew.

If truth be told, Rose always felt she understood Irene better than Stella. Her boys knew her well, but she figured they would be surprised to know that about her. She was thankful for Stella. Stella had tightened up the loose edges of Eldon's life. He might have turned out too freewheeling for his own good without his willing surrender to Stella's more practical nature. Stella was an excellent manager.

Rose never had any quarrels with Stella. She was always comfortable around her. The two of them could work together without a hitch to put up a bushel of pole beans or keep a kettle of apple butter simmering all morning without scorching. But Rose could never put herself in Stella's shoes, could not fathom how it would feel to be a person who seemed to have a plan for everything before she did it and who seemed to fit the people she loved into the framework of her plans instead of fitting her plans around the people she loved. Rose had no complaint about Stella's way of doing things, but she could not grasp her core.

Irene, however, Rose understood. She had seen Kenneth Mayhall. Beyond her fierce maternal feelings for James, she could understand the pull of a man like Kenneth. All three of her husbands had been men with that kind of appeal, and Rose knew how fortunate she'd been that circumstances had allowed them to bestow as much honor on her as she had brought to them. She had been in love with all three of her husbands, the kind of love that wipes out side vision as effectively as blinders on a mule. Even so, she could not imagine leaving one of her children to follow a man she loved—the idea staggered her—but then a part of her acknowledged that she had never been put to that test.

She and Irene had never experienced one comfortable moment together. She wondered if that was because Irene could not bear to know she understood her—to know that *anyone* could understand her. Whatever the reason for it, Irene was as slippery as a catfish, her dismissals as sharp as the barbs. Rose had usually been able not to take it personally, and she had hoped James could bring Irene the same kind of comfort Ben had brought to her after she lost Garner and their baby. But the two situations did not compare.

The first time Rose set eyes on her second husband, Ben Calper, she was both elated and mortified by the way he made her feel. Her arousal made her feel she was betraying Garner, but she knew on first sight that Ben was going to make her whole again. Until that moment, she had thought there was nothing that could ever fill the pulsing cavity where Garner and Avanell had been ripped from her.

She was only sixteen when she married Garner Pennington. That was another thing she had in common with Irene. That and the fact she'd left her home as a girl to help out in another home. But the similarity ended there. Rose had expected her exile to be temporary. She'd gone to help out her brother Jimmy's wife, Tattie. Tattie was carrying her fourth child, and the other three were all under five. It was an especially hot summer, and the pregnancy had been a hard one from the start. In the last few weeks before the birth, Rose would often wake in the night to the squeak of the front porch rocker where Tattie rocked and fanned and shifted her weight from one hip to the other. Rose would creep out of bed, careful not to wake the children. She'd tiptoe to the kitchen for a dipper of cool water she'd take to Tattie along with a wet rag for her face. Then she'd sit on the porch floor and massage Tattie's swollen feet and ankles trying to push the blood up to the baby where it could do some good.

She'd meant to go back home after the baby came, but Tattie and the baby were both sickly on until cool weather brought some relief. By that time, Rose was in no hurry to leave Lower Clive Creek; she'd learned how nice it was to live so close to town. They could walk out of the hollow from Jimmy's place and down the main road to Bascon in about the same amount of time it took to walk from the house to the new-ground cornfield at home.

When the baby proved to need so much care, Tattie's sister Clemma came to help out, too. With both of them to take the load off Tattie, she was beginning to gain some strength. She worried about Rose and Clemma working so hard to take care of things, though, and one day in the fall she insisted they go with a neighbor family, the Hayserts, to a molasses stir-off at the Pennington place up toward Sanghill.

Rose had never seen a house as big as the Pennington's except on a picture postcard. With a summer kitchen set apart from the main house, it was two stories tall, four rooms long, and two rooms deep, with porches upstairs and down that ran the entire length of the many rooms. It was painted white and had gingerbread trim along the edges of the porch roofs. There were chimneys on both ends and more along the roof. Some of the married Pennington children lived with their families alongside their parents and their unmarried brothers and sisters in the rooms under that long roof.

And never had Rose seen a group of people so festive as the crowd gathered down past the barn, where a mule tied to a pole went round and round in a circle to turn the mill that squeezed the juice out of the sorghum canes.

Rose was enticed by the rising warm sweetness and mesmerized by the rhythmic motions several older men kept going at the evaporator. They used long-handled stirrers with heads that looked like long, thin, wooden hoes to push the simmering liquid back and forth and through a maze of partitions in the huge metal pan.

The chores seemed relegated to groups of certain age and sex. Men a little younger than the stirrers were cutting firewood to feed the furnace under the molasses pan and were feeding cane stalks into the mill. Still younger men were cutting the cane in the field and hauling it to the women folk who were stripping off the leaves. Little boys were taking turns driving the mule round and round, and little girls were charged with watching the toddlers to keep them out of the skimming hole. In spite of frequent warnings about the skimming hole, one child and at least one young man ended up stepping in the pit where the dark sticky scum was discarded from the first boiling.

Laughing children, chewing on short lengths of cane, ran in and out among the older folks, while courting pairs dipped one cane into the foam kettle and shared two kinds of sweetness at once. As the evening wound down, the women gossiped, babies fell asleep on shoulders, the men took turns feeding the last of the wood into the fire and filling the last of the molasses jugs, young couples wandered into the shadows on the far side of the cane mill, and Rose tried not to stare at one boy who stood out among the crowd like a sunflower in a field of corn stubble.

Coretta Haysert said, "No use looking at him. Ain't no girl on all three forks of Clive Creek don't have her line set out for him. That's the Pennington's youngest boy, Garner."

Rose looked up across the foam kettle into a pair of eyes fixed on hers with such intensity that she dropped her cane into the dirt. Garner came around the kettle and put another length of cane into her hand while he kicked away the piece she'd dropped. He took her wrist and dipped the cane into the sticky brew as tenderly as if she were a baby just learning to feed itself. Out of all the girls on Clive's three forks, Garner Pennington chose Rose as suddenly and completely as she chose him.

He walked to the Wallaces' house with them when they left the stir-off, and he was back next morning on his horse before the Wallaces' cows got milked. He said he was afraid he'd miss her if he dallied. The Hayserts were kin to the Wallaces who had bedded down all the Hayserts as well as Rose and Clemma that night.

Garner told Rose then and there that he'd be coming to Lower Clive and bringing the preacher just as soon as he could locate him. He didn't ask her if she'd marry him; he just asked if she could be ready to come back with him that soon. Rose thought about how Tattie was getting

71

better all the time and told him she'd be ready for him and the preacher.

CHAPTER 7
DECEMBER 1941

Rose woke in surprise to the sounds of Eldon and his family on the porch. She wasn't expecting them until mid-afternoon. She jerked upright in alarm, almost dumping Nora Faye onto the floor. The two of them were bundled under a quilt in the rocker she'd pulled up close to the Warm Morning in the front room. She glanced at the clock to see if she'd napped longer than she thought, but it was just a few minutes after two. Her next thought was about the chicken she'd left simmering on the back of the stove. She threw off the quilt and headed straight for the kitchen range to set the pot off the heat before it boiled dry. Then she went back to get Nora Faye untangled from the quilt.

She'd done something very rare for her; she'd fallen asleep in her chair. She'd been up a good part of the night doctoring Nora Faye who had been plagued with an earache on and off since shortly after midnight. Rose would pour a little sweet oil into a teaspoon and heat it over the light bulb in the bedside lamp. She'd dribble a few drops into Nora Faye's ear, and they'd get a little spell of sleep until the ease wore off. Then Nora Faye would start whimpering in her sleep again and they'd repeat the routine.

The pain had eased after they got up and had breakfast and stirred about a bit, and was almost gone by late morning. After they had a snack to hold them until a dinner planned for later than usual, Rose got the chicken on the stove and the kitchen cleaned up, and they settled down for a rest. Eldon's family would be going to church and back home to change clothes and take care of some other things before they came for a three o'clock meal of chicken and dumplings, so she didn't have to give any thought yet to mixing up the dumplings and cooking down a quart of pole beans and some pickled corn. Eldon dearly loved her pickled corn.

James had planned to work with Rollie last night and into the morning hours, setting up the Christmas toy display at the store. The family's plan was for Eldon to take them all to Dillard after they ate, so the girls could get a look at the Christmas toys today while the store was still closed. That routine had become a family tradition. It sometimes seemed the girls got as much pleasure out of looking at the untouched store display as they got out of their first look at what Santa left them under their trees on Christmas morning.

Rose was in a dither as she tried to deal with several things at once before she got completely awake. She bustled back and forth through the dining room that connected the kitchen and front room. The house had cooled down. She slipped on the coal gloves and started to add a block of coal to the Warm Morning, but Eldon took the bucket and the gloves from her. It didn't strike her until later that he had set the bucket down instead of stoking the fire. Embarrassed at getting caught napping in the daytime, she wasn't thinking straight. She was also concerned that the chicken might turn out tough and dry—it didn't have much fat on it—and perplexed that Eldon and Stella had jumped the gun on dinnertime, even though it was at an odd hour today. Stella was always a stickler about being neither late nor early. Rose was feeling a little frantic as she felt Nora Faye's forehead one more time before she returned to the chicken. She didn't feel hot, and she hadn't during the night. Whatever was causing the earache wasn't making her feverish.

She hurried back to the kitchen to see to the chicken while she explained why they'd been asleep in the rocker. As she poked at the stewpot, flipping each piece of chicken to make sure none were scorched on the bottom, she talked over her shoulder to who she thought was Stella come up behind her in the kitchen.

"She had that earache again, like she had two or three times back last spring when the doctor couldn't say why it was happening. Her mother always said the doctors told her it was nothing to worry about—and it does get better by itself after a day or two—but it's a shame she has to go through nights like this." She took up the teakettle and added water to the almost dry but not scorched chicken pieces.

"If you want to eat earlier than you said, we can go ahead and get dinner together just any time. This little hen I bought at the A&P cooked tender in no time. There's not going to be much broth, but we can make biscuits instead of dumplings and stretch out the little bit of broth to make gravy."

She glanced back over her shoulder when she got no response from Stella, and saw that it was not Stella, but Eldon, standing behind her in his overcoat…standing there looking at her very solemnly and still holding the coal gloves.

She realized, then, that everyone was quiet; the girls weren't chattering and Stella had not started in like she usually did on whatever topic was utmost in her mind. Her heart lurched. She looked through to the front room to make sure both girls had come. Dollie and Bootsie were both there, but they stood beside their mother still wearing their coats. None of them had taken off their coats and none had said a word.

Rose's mouth went dry. She took an involuntary step towards Eldon as she whispered, "James?"

Eldon said, "It's not James, Ma. It's war. We're in the war now. The Japs bombed Pearl Harbor this morning." Rose's fork clattered to the floor.

Eldon bent to pick it up as he said, "Let's bank your fires and go make sure James has heard the news. He and Rollie planned to work right through the night, so he might still be sleeping today. Or he might have got up and gone back to the store to finish things up."

Before she could protest about the chicken, he went on, "We can take the chicken and finish making dinner after we get there." He shook his head when Rose reached to unplug the little Zenith sitting on her kitchen shelf. "We don't need to take a radio; James's is better than mine or yours."

Their tongues and their limbs were suddenly loosed. Stella gave directions to Eldon who was banking the fires while she went to Rose's rag bag to get some old towels to pad a box for the chicken pot and the jars of beans and corn. Rose tried to digest the news while she returned to the front room and reached to take Nora Faye's hand and lead her out of the quilt that kept tangling around her ankles. Dollie and Bootsie followed them into the kitchen where Rose washed Nora Faye's face with a damp washrag. "Just to help her wake up," she said to the other girls.

So, in spite of the world-shaking news, Nora Faye and her cousins got to play with the Christmas toys, as planned, that Sunday, before anybody else saw the display. She could remember first doing that when it was just her and her daddy and momma, and she was so small James had lifted her up to the big table and let her walk about on the red crepe paper table cover among the dolls and wagons and games and books and wind-up toys, like she was in a magic toy land.

Today, she and her cousins were too big to walk on the table, and the excitement among the adults was not the Christmas spirit. Rollie and Gladys had joined them at the store, as though the disquieting news seemed less horrifying if they shared it with other people. The adults went back and forth from the Christmas array to the counter by the cash register where they huddled over the Philco James had set up from the shelf under the counter. The crackle of the broadcast did not keep the girls from becoming engrossed in the display laid out in an alcove usually devoted to men's dry goods: denim p-coats and overalls, coveralls, hats, hunting vests, and work shoes and boots. The first job James and Rollie had tackled had been to stow all those things under counters and in the back room until after Christmas.

They had gone to extra pains to make the alcove look festive, with a big red paper-honeycomb bell hanging over the center of the table and red and green paper-chenille garlands swagged out from it. The decorations for sale were almost as intriguing as the toys. In addition to the ropes and bells, there were strings of colored lights, boxes of fragile colored-glass balls, and packages of angel hair and silver tinsel icicles.

For boys there were wagons, pocket knives, cowboy hats, BB guns and cap pistols, and for girls, china tea sets and dolls and silk parasols. Nora Faye and her cousins were allowed to play with one toy for a short while. They couldn't touch things that might easily get dirty, and they couldn't take most things out of their boxes, but, after they walked round and round the display looking at everything, they each got to choose one toy they were allowed to play with very carefully for a few minutes. Dollie chose a tall doll with blond hair. Eldon took off the see-through box lid and let her straighten the hair and arrange the bows and ruffles. Bootsie chose a set of puzzle blocks she mixed up and then put back together to make a Christmas scene with

77

elves, and Nora Faye was allowed to play with a little clown on a tin tricycle. Her daddy warned her not to wind him too tight, and it didn't take many twists to set him off with his big permanently attached clown shoes furiously pedaling while the attached hands gripped the handlebars. His hands in white gloves, his feet in the big shoes, and his head were tin. His clown suit was real cloth—white with bright dots of every color. A red ruffle around his neck was glued on, as was a white cloth pointed hat topped off with a little red pompom. She could feel through the fabric to tell that he didn't really have a body, just a metal skeleton hidden by the clown suit.

She liked that clown, and she liked a celluloid Santa Clause that hung from an elastic string at the end of a long stick, but she didn't bother to ask Santa to bring her that kind of toys. He brought her things like wooden blocks and rubber balls and a Chinese Checker game. Even her dolls were sturdy rubber Dy-Dee dolls and Raggedy Ann and Andy made of cotton cloth.

When Nora Faye admiringly pointed out the little celluloid Santa, Granny Rose asked what he did. "He just jiggles," she answered. "You give the stick a little jerk and he bounces up and down." Granny Rose said cheap gimcracks like that didn't last any time at all and were just a waste of money. She and Stella turned up their noses at toys made of celluloid and tin and papier-mâché.

Nora Faye never questioned why Santa—no matter what you put on your list—usually brought you things for Christmas that your parents would have brought if they were Santa. Rather than giving away the secret, it seemed part of the magic, that Santa knew how to match toys to families. Although she admired Anna Sue Patterson's dolls, she did not mention a doll like that in the letter to Santa her daddy helped her write. She did ask for a silk parasol though. All three girls had asked, first thing, to play with the parasols in the store display, but they were told they were too fragile. She didn't really expect Santa would bring her a parasol.

Back at the house, the kitchen radio stayed on through the overdue, hurried meal they made of the chicken and gravy and biscuits. While they ate, the girls were kept quiet so the adults could hear the broadcast. After Eldon took his family home, James and Granny Rose lingered at the kitchen table, bending towards the radio they had set down from the shelf. When Nora Faye tried to talk to them about the Christmas toys, they shushed her in a voice they seldom used with her. Her daddy told her to get into her nightie by herself and then come to the kitchen to finish getting ready for bed. Even while he washed her face and helped her brush her teeth, he kept putting a finger to his lips when she tried to talk to him. It hurt her feelings. She went to bed without a bedtime story and almost in tears. Her last thought as she drifted off to sleep was that her ear hadn't hurt any more after she and Granny Rose were awakened in the rocking chair.

Santa brought parasols to all three girls. Nora Faye got a green one, and she liked it so much that it was what she chose later when James said she could take just one new toy to Dollie and Bootsie's house where they went for dinner and where she discovered Dollie got a yellow parasol like hers and Bootsie a pink one.

As much as she liked her green one, Nora Faye would have preferred a yellow one, but she tried not to let it show. However, when Dollie said she had hoped for a green one, they made a swap that left them both even happier.

When Stella saw what they'd done, she grouched a little at Dollie. "I tried to give you the colors I thought you'd like best," she grumbled, "but if you're both better pleased this way, I guess you can do what you want."

Eldon was laughing at her. "Do you realize you just gave away the whole thing?" he asked when the girls were out of earshot.

But she hadn't. The incident did not bring an end to anything. All three girls managed to go on believing in Santa Clause for another few years.

James hoped Nora Faye would always be able to ignore proof like that against whatever she might need to believe in.

CHAPTER 8
R. L.

There was no one particular moment when Nora Faye realized her mother would not be coming home. The first summer without her went fast. The days were spent either with the Slaneys or her cousins or her grandmother—and were so filled from dawn till dusk that her eyes closed as soon as her head hit the pillow. There were no lonely waits for sleep to come, no time to wonder where her mother was and why she had gone away.

Even after the Slaney children started back to school, the days she spent with their mother were filled with one endeavor after another that kept her mind and body occupied. She helped as Mrs. Slaney made grape jelly from the Concord grapes they picked from the arbor up at the Ritter place and made "leather-britches" by stringing fall beans on long thick threads to hang behind the stove to dry. Granny Rose strung beans that way, too, but she called them shucky beans, and Nora Faye had never helped string hers.

Billy Ray was often too sick to go to school. He had severe bouts of tonsillitis that kept him home for days at a time.

Nora Faye was eager to start school herself—she knew there was some speculation about her starting after her birthday and after the worst winter weather was over—but she hoped the other reading books would have stories more interesting than Billy Ray's first grade reader with the binding frayed thin.

The pictures in the dirty yellow reader showed pathways with neat, clean edges like the paths in the Aunt Fritzi comic strips in the funny papers. The neatly snow-cleared walkways or perfectly square grass plots seemed fitting settings for Nancy and Sluggo in the funny papers, but in the school book the artificial neatness took away from the story, what little bit of story there was. The words mainly told the reader to look at the pets and the family members one by one. The book was about a family with two children, Ben and Alice, who had a dog named Blackie and a cat named Whitey. Nothing ever looked dirty or messy and nothing much happened. There were no details in the story and no clutter in the pictures. Nora Faye didn't dwell on them like she dwelled on the pictures in her daddy's *Boy Scoutmaster's Handbook.* After she studied the handbook's diagrams showing how to build a fire, her daddy had let her build a campfire in the back yard while he watched without giving any help. He said she would make a good scout.

Miss Vickers, Billy Ray's teacher, had him read to her from the reader on days she stopped by the house when he was sick. Billy Ray was not a good reader, but Nora Faye listened anyway. She listened when anyone read, but she liked it best of all when Mr. Slaney read to her and Billy Ray from a book called *The Book of Cowboys.* On days when he had time, he read it to them at the table after he finished his noonday meal.

Mr. Slaney worked at night and slept into late mornings. But he didn't need things kept quiet in order to sleep. Mrs. Bledso's husband worked at night, too, and when Nora Faye and Granny Rose talked to Mrs. Bledso at the fence in the morning, they all had to talk very quietly because the Bledso's bedroom was on that end of the house. Mr. Slaney said he could sleep through judgment day just as long as nobody came into the room with him. Mrs. Slaney gave several reminders about the forbidden doorknob before she realized Nora Faye wasn't going to forget.

On days when Mr. Slaney promised to read to them they tried to wait patiently while he savored a cup of boiling hot coffee by pouring it into his saucer bit by bit and blowing on it between careful sips. At last he would push back his chair and fit Billy Ray on one knee and Nora Faye on the other while he propped the book on the table's edge and read them a few pages before he had to stop and take care of home jobs and then get ready to go to work at the tipple where he was foreman on his shift.

Nora Faye studied the pictures long after Mr. Slaney stopped reading. They reminded her of the pictures in the Boy Scout handbook. There were drawings in the margins showing the parts of things or how to put something together. In addition to the diagrams showing how to build a fire, the Boy Scout book showed how to tie knots, how to take care of someone with a broken bone, how to apply a tourniquet, and how to give first aid for a poisonous snakebite. The cowboy book had similar drawings showing the parts of a rattlesnake, the parts of a horse, rifles and their parts, and even the steps to making a saddle. Nora Faye learned that the knob on the front of Seelom's saddle was called the horn. It was hard to wait for the days when Mr. Slaney had time to read to them. Sometimes they begged Laura Jane or Ruthie to read them a bit. It was the story of two city children who went to stay on their uncle's ranch in New Mexico.

When Nora Faye would ask, "What's that?" Laura Jane would stop reading and answer, "The bit," or "The stock," or "The fangs." But Ruthie would ignore her or else say, "I can't read if you keep interrupting." Billy Ray drew pictures of horses and saddles in his school tablet while he listened, but Nora Faye just squeezed in beside the reader and studied the pictures.

All the Slaney children read to Nora Faye. Whatever they were reading, they read aloud to her, even Lottie who didn't have much of anything to do with her otherwise. Lottie read *A Girl of the Limberlost* and *The Trail of the Lonesome Pine*; Laura Jane read Nancy Drew mysteries and the funny-book version of *The Corsican Brothers* and *Swiss Family Robinson*; Ruthie read books about the Bobbsey Twins and the Five Little Peppers; and Conner read Zane Gray books, James Curwood books, *Doc Savage* magazines, and books his teacher, Mrs. Everhart, brought him over the summer: *Tarzan of the Apes, The Last of the Mohicans*, and books about science and geography.

When Conner read aloud he usually forgot Nora Faye was listening, but one day when he was reading *Tarzan of the Apes* she did something that caused him to remember she was there. When he read the part where Tarzan sees a book for the first time and thinks the letters are little bugs crawling on the page, Nora Faye leaned in close to look at the page, and she laughed aloud when, sure enough, it did look like it was covered with bugs. Conner understood why she was laughing, and he laughed too. He read that part again, pretending the letters were crawling up his hands and biting him, making him yelp and drop the book while he frantically brushed them away. He played like he was still trying to read the words while they crawled up his arm. He did it several times while they laughed together.

Except for *The Book of Cowboys* and the ones Conner's teacher brought, the Slaneys got most of their books and magazines and funny-books by swapping with friends and neighbors, sometimes walking miles to make a trade. *The Book of Cowboys* had been a family Christmas present, though, and was not a book for swapping.

Granny Rose read to Nora Faye too, stories from the magazines Stella had brought to Irene after she finished with them. There was a stack of *The Saturday Evening Post* and *Good Housekeeping* and *Colliers* magazines. Granny Rose said magazines were a waste of time, but she got so she offered to read Nora Faye stories more and more often, stories about Babe and Little Joe and, in a different magazine, about Little Brown Koko. Nora Faye's favorite was one where Little Brown Koko and his mother made a gumdrop cake.

Dollie and Bootsie gave Nora Faye *Lassie Come Home* for a Christmas present, and Granny Rose started reading it to her after Mrs. Bledso moved away. At first Granny Rose started to pick up where Mrs. Bledso had stopped, but then she went back to the first and read it all. Mrs. Bledso had read her all of *Heidi. Heidi* was her favorite. She felt like Heidi was a real girl and felt the sadness as her own when Mrs. Bledso read the part about Heidi being so unhappy she walked in her sleep after she was wrenched away from her grandfather on the mountain and forced to live in the city.

James had *The Knoxville News Sentinel* delivered every day so he could keep up with war news. A Gillum boy from the mouth of the hollow made his deliveries on a pony. James always read Nora Faye the funny papers, with Red Ryder and Little Beaver, Nancy and Sluggo, Captain Easy, Boots and her Buddies, Major Hoople, Moon Mullins, Smokey Stover, and Smilin' Jack and his friends: Fatstuff, with such a bulging stomach that a scrawny chicken followed him around to eat the buttons that continuously popped off his shirt, and Downwind Jaxon, whose face was always drawn from the side at that spot just before the nose shows. Before Christmas the newspaper ran a story about Santa and his Elves, with a new chapter each day. James read the daily chapter to her in front of the fire before he banked the grate for the night. By her fifth birthday she could read the titles of the funnies and pick out the letters of her name in the front-page headlines about Japan and Germany.

Every time Billy Ray's teacher, Claudine Vickers, came into the store, she tried to talk James into letting Nora Faye come to school. "She's catching up with Billy Ray," she told him, "and that's just from the little bit she hears me doing with him when I stop by for a few minutes once a week or so. If she came to school every day, she'd catch up with the whole first grade class by Easter time."

James wasn't sure what to do. His mother said, "If you're going to send her to school, you ought to let her come and live with me through the week so she can go to school in town. You know she'd have better teachers and newer books and not have to make that long walk every day. She's too little to walk two miles in the snow and mud. I can walk her up the hill to school in town in no time at all every morning."

James said, "They probably won't let her start in the middle of the school year in Wolliver, but Claudine says she's got room to take her any time I want. She says Fayzie's ready to start school now and that it might be bad for her if she doesn't get to start while she's ready."

The winter had been a hard one, and the two-mile walk and the drafty schoolhouse had been too much for Billy Ray. He couldn't shake off the tonsillitis that had plagued him since the first cold snap. Every time they let him go back to school he came down with a fever again and had to be kept in bed for a while. Miss Vickers sent his lessons home with the other children, and she came by after school every now and then to drill him on his numbers and letters. She told Berta there was no danger of him falling too far behind.

"He'll learn what he needs to learn from his sisters and brother," she assured her. "I know your children read and write even when they're not doing lessons."

On winter evenings the Slaney children did their lessons at the kitchen table while their mother was getting their supper ready. And once a week—every Monday—as soon as they got home from school, they gathered around the big oak table in the dining room where they wrote on sheets of paper so thin they were almost see-through. They called it V-Mail and talked about the war while they wrote. They said they were writing *ar-rail*.

Nora Faye thought *ar-rail* might have something to do with airmail—she knew airmail was letters flown on airplanes to the soldiers and sailors fighting in the war overseas. Or maybe, she thought, *ar-rail* was mail that went to soldiers by the railroad. Or sometimes it seemed that it might be another way to put letters together to make words. She understood the difference between printing and longhand. She knew longhand was the same set of letters drawn a different way and linked together like in the word Kalamazoo on their cook stove. She thought maybe *ar-rail* was still another way to make words, a way that had as much to do with the war and the special paper as the kind of writing. The paper was so thin they had to back it with their tablets to keep from punching through.

One afternoon when Laura Jane was letting Billy Ray print his name at the bottom of the sheet she'd just filled, Ruthie gave Nora Faye her pencil and told her to write something for *ar-rail* at the bottom of her page. Nora Faye printed an almost perfect N, and below it she laboriously strung out all the letters of KALAMAZOO in big, lopsided, sprawling longhand. They all laughed, and Laura Jane hugged her. That was one of the many times when Nora Faye did not understand what she had done to make people laugh and hug her.

But she did understand about *ar-rail* one day soon following that incident when they had folded the thin paper in the special way that turned the writing sheet into its own envelope. As Ruthie carefully wrote on the outside of her envelope, she muttered along with her strokes, "R. L. Slaney," and Nora Faye realized *ar-rail* was a name. When they wrote *ar-rail*, they were writing letters to the sailor whose picture was in a frame on the mantel, their oldest brother, R. L.—Robert Lincoln Slaney was what Laura Jane wrote on her envelope—who they said had lied about his age to join the navy before he was old enough. They sounded proud and sad at the same time when they mentioned that part. Now he was somewhere on a ship at sea.

She had always thought of "Bobby Shafto" whenever she heard anyone say something about someone at sea. Bobby Shafto was a nursery rhyme Bootsie and Dollie read to her from their big book with colored pictures. They didn't actually read Bobby Shafto; they put their heads together and sang it: "Bobby Shafto's gone to sea, silver buckles on his knee. He'll come back and marry me, Pretty Bobby Shafto." But after she made the connection that day, she never thought of the little yellow-haired boy with pink cheeks and fancy buckled pants when she heard the phrase; she thought of the Slaney children's brother, R.L., in his crisp navy hat.

She paid a lot of attention to R. L.'s photograph after that. She took off her shoes and climbed up in a dining chair for a better view of it every chance she got, and she soon had an indelible image of the square-chinned face below the stiff white sailor hat set at a slant on R. L. Slaney's crisp black curls.

There were other pictures on the mantle, two of which were connected to a disturbing tale. The largest picture was one of their sister Lissie standing close to her husband Donald. Donald was holding their baby girl, Donelda. Another picture showed Donald alone in a soldier's uniform, wearing a pie shaped hat with a narrow bill around the front half where the hat peaked.

Nora Faye sometimes had to close her ears when they talked about Donald—they said things that gave her nightmares—but one day when Conner was showing her how to tie her shoes, she let herself think about the things she'd heard. Conner was showing her how she had to pull all the wrinkles out of her tongue before she tightened her shoelaces.

She asked, "Why did they cutted his tongue out for?"

Conner said, "You mean Lissie's husband?"

She nodded yes.

"We don't actually know that they've cut out Donald's tongue. We're just afraid that maybe they have. We know the Japs do things like that; we've heard about them cutting out the tongues of some of their prisoners. We don't even know if Donald is a prisoner of war or if he's dead. They call it missing in action when nobody knows for sure if the soldier was killed or if he was captured. M.I.A. Donald is M.I.A."

"Why do they cutted the tongues?"

Conner said, "It's to make other prisoners tell them what they want to know about our war plans. They show the other captives what they've done, and they tell them that's what will happen to them if they don't talk."

That night Nora Faye dreamed Lissie came home to visit with her baby, Donelda, and when Donelda opened her mouth to cry, she didn't have a tongue.

CHAPTER 9
VIRGINIA

"Ain't nothing like a good cold dope to make a feller feel better." The man on the store porch slid down the wall to a squat like the three other men gathered there. He chugged down almost half of the Dr. Pepper before he took a breath and let the slaking effervescence spread throughout his body. Nora Faye, coming up the steps, reached his eye level just as he lowered the bottle. She came to a standstill. He was talking to no one in particular, but when he opened his eyes and saw Nora Faye intently studying him, he seemed to feel an obligation to connect his pronouncement to her.

He said, "You remember that someday, little girl, when you're old like me and wore ragged and ain't got nobody to love you."

They each studied the other for several heartbeats. When Nora Faye saw the Dr. Pepper bottle, her thoughts had gone to the Dr. Pepper sign on a hillside in good view of the road between Dillard and Wolliver. It was not on a billboard; it was made of whitewashed stones arranged in the grass to form the Dr. Pepper clock circle and the numbers ten, two, and four. When she was with Dollie and Bootsie they made a game of trying to be the first to spot it after they came around the curve. The first to see it yelled, "Ten, two and four!"

When she realized the man was talking to her she said, "You're not old."

For an instant it seemed he might laugh. His eyes flashed a twinkle with crevices showing almost white in the surrounding skin leathered by the daily abrasion of coal dust.

He passed the frosty bottle to the man nearest him before he replied. "No, I ain't old," he said, "and it ain't the truth that they ain't nobody to love me. But I *am* wore ragged." The light went out of his eyes that stared unseeing for a few seconds before he brought his attention back to Nora Faye. "And I sure *feel* old and like they's nobody loves me by the time I come outta that hole ever day."

Another man hunkered a few feet away said, "Nobody but ole John L.. Don't forget how John L. loves you."

"Hmfp. I'll believe John L. Lewis loves me the day he puts the grub in front of my young'uns when they set down at my table with empty bellies."

The other man broke in, "Well, be that as it may about the work down that hole wearing you ragged, that hain't nothing compared to how bad you feel when they hain't got no work for you to go in that hole and do."

Nora Faye was forgotten as the four men hunkering along the wall went on commiserating with one another while they waited for word about work.

James had come out the door. "That's my little girl you're talking to, Clyde," he said to the man with the Dr. Pepper bottle that had returned to him empty after making the rounds. "What kind of ideas you putting in her head?"

"Just telling her how good a cold dope tastes when you're hot and tired, James," the man replied. "I shoulda knowed she was your littlun; she favors you a right lot."

James ignored the remark. "You've not been to work yet; how come you're already hot and thirsty?"

"We had to walk outten the holler. Don't nobody up Steve's Branch got no truck that'll run no more. Randal Fisher stopped by to tell me they's a wanting some extry hands on this shift today, so I rounded up these fellers and we walked down here to see what we could find out. Ain't nobody in the payroll office, though. We thought they'd be waiting to sign us up, but they ain't nobody here and they ain't nothin' on the board out here."

James assured them that Mr. Deeton would be back in the payroll office as soon as he finished his dinner. He fished some pennies from his pocket and wordlessly flipped them to the man in exchange for the empty pop bottle he carried back into the store.

He led Nora Faye through the store and out the back where they went through a routine they followed whenever Nora Faye came to the loading dock. James hopped down off the dock and turned his back like he had forgotten about her. Then he whirled to catch her just as she leapt out into the air like somebody doing a swan dive. He spun around several times while he rolled her like a log up around his shoulders where he carried her to the truck cab and let her slither in like a snake through the open window.

He'd sent word to Mrs. Slaney to let Nora Faye walk over to the store so he could take her with him on a run down to the Vargo store. He gave a wave to Mrs. Slaney where she stood on her front porch watching to make sure Nora Faye got to him okay.

James had proved to have a natural talent for fixing the big milk and meat coolers and the ice cream freezers. In addition to depending on him to keep the units running at the Dillard store, the management had been sending him to Vargo and Sanghill when they had problems with their refrigerated cases.

Charles Wainwright, the Vargo store manager, was an old friend of James' dad, and he and James remembered each other warmly. When James was working on a unit at the Vargo store, Mr. Wainwright would take him home for dinner. He and his wife Virginia had a little girl just a year or so older than Nora Faye, and they kept telling James he should bring his family with him next time and let the women visit and the little girls play together while he worked on the coolers. Virginia worked in the store several days a week, but she said she would take off from work and visit with Irene any time he would bring her.

Virginia was near Irene's age—the Wainwright's marriage was obviously a May-December affair—but James had always made excuses to decline their invitation. He just could not imagine Irene visiting with Virginia Wainwright.

Mr. Wainwright was a Scoutmaster, and he had many tales about how James's dad had helped him explore the hills with his Scouts, showing him overgrown timber roads and electric line right-of-way accesses that led to seldom-trekked places. He had gone with Mr. Wainwright on camping forays and helped him devise ways to let his Scouts test their skills.

"Langdon Houston taught me more than the handbook taught me," he would tell James. "I could never have been a successful Scoutmaster without your dad's help."

James found himself filling his dad's shoes a time or two to help Mr. Wainwright with his present Scout troop, putting Irene on the train to Bascon or Wolliver first, so she could visit with Stella or her friend Nancy while he went on a camping trip.

The train station platform turned out to be an unexpected source of terror for Nora Faye. She had boarded trains without fearsome experiences at Wolliver and Bascon before the move to Dillard, but the trains in town seemed to slow down before they neared the stations, and the station platforms were wide. At Dillard, the first time they waited on the platform as a train neared, they'd all been delivered a shock. It was as though Nora Faye had never before watched a train approach. It came so fast and got bigger and bigger so quickly that it seemed it would not possibly have room to miss the narrow platform. She'd clawed so unexpectedly at James, as she gave a little shriek, that it had momentarily frightened him and Irene as well. The way he told it to her when she was older was that she had screeched and climbed him like a monkey.

She clung to him and burrowed her face in his neck while she held her hands over her ears. He could feel her heart beating. After the engine and the brake noises died down, he said above the hiss of the steam, "You've seen a train before, Fayzie. What's wrong?"

She was still curled into a little ball with her eyes closed when she finally murmured, "It gots too big. They didn't leave room."

So whenever Irene and Nora Faye made a train trip without James, he arranged his time so he could wait with them on the platform and assure Nora Faye the train had room enough. It was some time before she could open her eyes and watch the train coming while she was in his arms. Then gradually, he'd been able to squat beside her and keep his arm around her. And finally, she could stand without flinching, as long as she was holding his hand.

After Irene left him, he had accepted the Wainwrights' invitation and had taken Nora Faye to Vargo with him several times. She seemed to feel right at home with Peggy Wainwright, the way she did with the Slaney children.

"She gots a swing inside her house!" she'd greeted him excitedly when he and Mr. Wainwright went to the house for dinner the first time he'd taken her to play with Peggy while he worked. "And she gots a room that's not for anything but playing." The girls had tumbled out onto the walkway to meet them, and had urged them along to the playroom before Virginia herded them to the kitchen table.

Sure enough, Peggy did have a swing in her playroom, bolted to the ceiling, and the room was for nothing except her play toys. The girls had been allowed to chalk their hopscotch grid right on the dark linoleum beside the chalked floor-plan of a house for their paper dolls.

At first, James was happy to see how openly proud Mr. Wainwright was of his family. He spoke to Virginia with affection and respect, and indulged Peggy in a way that had obviously made her sweet and considerate instead of self-centered. In short, the Wainwright family was everything James had hoped he'd be with Irene and Nora Faye. He found himself becoming more envious with each visit. There was nothing more he could imagine a man needing than a loving wife and family, a job that paid enough to keep them fed and happy, and the time to enjoy his good fortune. After a while the Wainwrights' warm consideration for one another became a thing too painful for him to observe.

Charles told him how he'd met Virginia after he'd been a widower for 14 years. He'd been late to marry the first time, and after just a year of marriage, his first wife had died in childbirth. The baby died too. After he lost them, he had lived by himself so long he'd thought he was a confirmed bachelor. Then Virginia came to Vargo to teach school, and he found he'd been given a second chance at happiness beyond what he could have imagined. He teased Virginia about being stuck with an old codger because all the young men had gone away to the war, but James could see she regarded him so tenderly that she didn't like to hear that kind of joke. He'd sing the jazzy popular song about the men left at home during the war all being too young or too old, until she'd laughingly threaten to leave the room if he didn't stop.

The visits became so bittersweet for James that he stopped taking Nora Faye to Vargo, and he either got his work done before noon or else he would eat a package of peanuts and drink an R.C. at the store, telling Mr. Wainwright he didn't have time to go to the house for dinner.

But, then, one day when Virginia was working at the store she begged him to bring Nora Faye again, even if he had too much work to allow him to join them for a meal.

"You've seen how well the girls play together," she implored. "Peggy doesn't have any playmates in Vargo she's as fond of as Nora Faye."

"It wouldn't even have to be a time you have a job at the store," she went on, brightening as she thought of it. "You could bring her in the evening and have supper with us or you could bring her and leave her to spend the night with Peggy." Her voice fell away as she saw no matching enthusiasm in James's face.

"I wish I could work it out," he said. "Nora Faye always has fun with Peggy, too. I'll see what I can manage, Mrs. Wainwright." He surprised himself with the formality he heard in his voice. Virginia looked hurt.

"I wish you would call us Charles and Virginia," she said. "You make me feel old when you call me Mrs. Wainwright."

"Well, I called your husband mister when I was a boy," he explained, "and I can't break the habit. In fact, Charles and my dad called one another Mr. Houston and Mr. Wainwright, and I still think of him as my dad's friend. I don't mean to make anybody feel old."

Virginia suddenly sounded different.

"James," she beseeched with an earnestness so real it deepened her voice, "please bring Nora Faye when you come to Vargo. You don't need to eat with us, but, bring Nora Faye when you can. It seems a shame for us not to let the girls be together. There's not a lot of people that can make each other happy the way they do, and it seems like it would be the right thing for us to try to work it out."

After that, he took Nora Faye with him now and then, but he didn't join the Wainwrights for a meal again.

CHAPTER 10
MR. WAINWRIGHT

James was restocking laundry soap when they got the news about Mr. Wainwright's death. He had been chuckling to himself as he recalled the smile he got out of dower Mrs. Wooten this morning when she bought a box of Oxydol and he asked, "Do you want me to wrap that, or are you going to eat it here?"

James was content with his job. He liked the exchanges with customers like Mrs. Wooten, and he truly enjoyed making deliveries and keeping the refrigeration equipment in operation. He didn't even mind the housekeeping duties like stocking shelves. If it weren't for his concerns about Nora Faye, he could have considered himself a fairly satisfied man.

A fine sift of soap powder had put him into one sneezing spasm after another, and he had just cleaned his glasses and replaced them and started fitting the last few Oxydol boxes from the old carton on top of the new carton slid in beside the Dreft and Rinso cartons when Mr. Deeton came through from the payroll office to tell them that Mrs. Wainwright had called from Vargo with sad news. Her husband had a heart attack and had died in the night. She knew there was no phone in the store, so she asked Mr. Deeton to let James and Rollie know. She reminded him that James often worked with her husband to repair the coolers and that he helped him with his Boy Scout troop.

Rollie told James he thought it would be a good idea for him to take the truck and go down to Vargo right then and there and take care of the store until the district manager had time to make arrangements. He said James should also find out how they could help Mrs. Wainwright personally. Mr. Deeton said he'd go with him.

By the time James pulled the truck around, Rollie was out on the dock. He said Mr. Deeton had decided not to go until that evening. He handed James the Oxydol box he had packed with a bunch of bananas, several packages of cookies, and a can of coffee. James started to protest—it seemed a useless gesture when Mrs. Wainwright could take the same items off the shelves in the Vargo store— but then he realized it was something Rollie needed to do in order to feel like he was making a difference. But he did unload the box and give it a good upside-down thumping before he put the things back in. He didn't want Mrs. Wainwright to get soap powder tracked all over her floors.

Nora Faye was with his mother in town, so he didn't have to worry about how long he might be tied up in Vargo. His pulse had slowed almost to normal by the time he nosed the truck through the creek and up the gravel incline to the road. It was a relief that Mr. Deeton wasn't going with him. He needed the time alone to collect his thoughts before he saw Virginia Wainwright. There was nothing now to keep him from facing up to something that went to the core of his being, something he had kept himself from acknowledging since the first day he saw Virginia.

He was overcome with conflicting emotions. He felt true sorrow about the death of his dad's old friend, his own friend and mentor. But, he had long realized that the sadness he felt when he observed the Wainwrights together was not just an envy of the kind of union he had hoped to have with Irene. He was jealous, not just because Mr. Wainwright had a happy marriage, but because he had it with Virginia.

It was impossible not to rejoice inwardly now to realize that he and Virginia might have a chance to be together. Though not the slightest word nor signal had ever passed between them, he knew without a doubt that she had feelings for him, too. If they were never to have a chance together, he knew it would be due to other circumstances, not to a lack of feeling on her part.

But those other circumstances might prove to be momentous. His heart had dropped to his shoes when Mr. Deeton delivered the startling news. His first thought was that it might mean Virginia would be leaving the area, that she'd be going back to Cincinnati where she came from. But, when he remembered she'd recently started working full-time in the store, he clung to the hope that Staghorn would be asking her to take over as manager, meaning she'd stay in Vargo.

Though a surprising confidence told him the seeds of a shared future lay between them, a sense of wariness reminded him his own behavior would present him with his greatest challenge. If he said too much too soon, he could destroy what lay there. He'd have to put himself into a state of numbness to get through these next few days—and through the funeral—without saying what his heart wanted to speak. And then, if she stayed in Vargo, he'd have to make a point to see her as seldom as possible and to say as little as possible when he couldn't avoid seeing her.

As he maneuvered the last narrow, rutted stretch of the winding road to Vargo he was glad to have some place to put his concentration before he faced Virginia. The road to Vargo was even more treacherous than the road to Dillard. There was not room enough for two vehicles. If he should meet someone where the road was squeezed between the hillside and the sheer drop-off to the creek, he'd have to do some quick reacting. When the store came into view around the last curve, he was relieved, but he was surprised to see the place looking the same as always, and the people coming and going looking unchanged by the loss of the man who had been such a vital figure in the community.

Virginia was in the house giving directions in a polite but lifeless voice to the Scouts who had volunteered to move the furniture in her front room to make room for the coffin. He could hear her as he crossed from the store to the house on the neat wooden walkway Mr. Wainwright had built.

He would never forget the way her face came to life when she saw him. She thanked him for coming and asked him first thing if she could count on him to be a pallbearer. The loss he suddenly felt was so genuine he was spared the guilt of deceit as he assured her it would be an honor.

She also told him that Andrew Caldwell, the coordinating manager of Staghorn's stores, had asked her to finish out the year as store manager and that he'd told her they were going to ask James to cover it for a week or two so she could take care of funeral business before she returned to work full time.

This time it was not as easy for him to assure her he'd he glad to help without letting her see how terrified and how elated he was all in the same breath. How was it going to be possible, he wondered, not to say more than he should before she was ready? How could he be near her and not speak what was in his heart?

Then he forgot his own dilemma when Peggy came into the room looking lost and aimless. He asked Virginia if she'd like him to take Peggy to stay at his mother's house with Nora Faye until time for the funeral. "I know my mother will want to go to the funeral," he said. "She always says my dad considered Mr. Wainwright one of the best friends of his lifetime."

Marietta Ball

As it turned out, he went for Rose and Nora Faye that evening after he closed the Vargo store, and he took Peggy with him, bringing her to Dillard to stay with them as long as her mother was willing. "I'll bring her home any time you want," he assured her. "I'll be coming to take care of the store every day."

Virginia had been content for Peggy to stay with Nora Faye until the day of the funeral, and James's heart had swelled almost to bursting that he and his mother were able to do something at home as well as in the store to truly help Virginia.

CHAPTER 11
DOLLIE

The school tablet Bootsie and Dollie gave Nora Faye for Christmas had a movie star's picture on the cover. "It's Spencer Tracy," Dollie told her when she opened it.

"Tracy's back and Hepburn's got him," she went on, explaining—when everyone looked dumbfounded—that she had seen that slogan on a poster at the movie theater the time they'd seen a Spencer Tracy movie. She didn't know who Hepburn was, but guessed it was the woman who was in the movie with him.

Bootsie said, "She wasn't pretty. She was skinny and she talked too much, and she had dents in her face. And they didn't sing, either."

Nora Faye didn't find Spencer Tracy to be really good-looking either—not like Bing Crosby. Spencer Tracy's face was sort of lumpy, not smooth and perfect like Bing Crosby's. She liked the way Bing Crosby sang, too. She'd seen him in two movies, "Going My Way" and "The Bells of St. Mary's." They had seen "The Bells of St. Mary's" a few weeks ago, and later, at Dollie and Bootsie's house, she had been telling Granny Rose about the pretty songs Bing Crosby sang and how his wife always wore a long, black coat with a great big hat and scarf.

Dollie laughed and said, "She wasn't his wife. He was a Catholic priest, and priests can't have wives."

"Well, his sweetheart," Nora Faye mumbled, and Dollie laughed even more.

"Priests can't have wives *or* sweethearts," she tittered. Dollie knew about things like this; she listened quietly when her mother was talking to other women, and she remembered everything she heard.

"The woman was a Catholic sister—that's why she dressed that way—and sisters can't get married or have sweethearts either."

Nora Faye protested. "Well, why did she call him father if she was his sister?" And Dollie laughed again, but she hugged her while she laughed, so Nora Faye didn't feel out of sorts.

Dollie explained that "sister" was a word sort of like "doctor" in this case, and that all women who had that job were called sister. She was curious, though. "Why'd you think she called him father if she was his wife?" she probed.

"Well, like your mother calls your daddy," Nora Faye answered. "Your mother calls Uncle Eldon Daddy." And that was true. She did.

They took down the Christmas tree on Christmas day so they could play croquet with the indoor version Santa had brought Dollie and Bootsie. While the girls were at a movie, James and Eldon had set up the game and played a round that ended when Eldon backed into the Christmas tree, getting his bare arm scratched up in the angel hair.

After Stella tried to soothe his inflamed arm with oatmeal paste, she sent him straight to the attic to get the storage box for the Christmas decorations. She and Rose started taking down the tree so the girls wouldn't get into the angel hair when they tried out the game. The girls jumped right in to help when they got home, carefully taking off decorations while they chattered about the movie they had seen that day called "The Sullivans." It was the story of a Catholic family with five brothers serving in the Navy on the same ship. All five were killed when their ship, the USS *Juneau*, was torpedoed by a Japanese submarine.

It seemed, then, that most all the movies Nora Faye had seen—except maybe for the cowboy movies James called shoot-em-ups—were about Catholic people, which was odd, she said out loud, because she didn't know any Catholic people in real life.

But Dollie said, "Yes you do. You know the Berkindoffs, They're Catholic. Haven't you ever noticed how Father Carnaby comes to eat supper with them once a month? He drives that little black two-seater. And he always wears a black suit, like Bing Crosby. Priests dress that way in real life, not just in the movies."

Dollie said the church in Johnston was the only Catholic Church around, and that Catholic people from other towns had to go to Johnston for mass, which was what the Catholics called a church service. Father Carnaby lived by himself in a little two-room house beside the church, and he went around to all the different Catholic families to have his supper. Dollie said he had a schedule, coming to the Plumbos, their neighbors in Bascon, on the last Thursday of the month and to the Berkindoffs in Dillard on the first Monday. "I thought you kept track of things like that from your coalhouse roof," she added, not unkindly.

When Dollie was telling about the end of the movie today, where the five brothers were walking on clouds on their way up to heaven and the youngest brother had to run to catch up with the others—just the way he'd done when they were kids—she laughed and said, "And the thing that makes it funny is that Catholics don't even go to heaven."

"What makes you say that?" Granny Rose asked. She was gingerly folding the angel hair she had stripped from the tree, using just her fingertips, while she muttered about the tradition of putting something dangerous on a tree that didn't even need it in order to look pretty.

Dollie looked for support from her mother, but Stella had left the room. "Well, everybody just knows that Catholics don't go to heaven," she faltered. She glanced toward her dad, but he wasn't paying any attention; he and James had a string of tree lights stretched out where they were replacing the bulbs one by one in an effort to locate the burned-out bulb that was keeping the whole string from lighting up.

Rose said, "I reckon the Catholics have just as much chance as any of us at getting to heaven."

Stella came back just then. She said, "Rose, sometimes, I declare, I don't have any idea what you do believe. Do you think then, that Catholics go to heaven?"

"I don't know if I believe that any of us have a chance of getting to heaven," Rose said, but in such a lighthearted, unserious way that Nora Faye was not concerned.

Eldon had made a trade for a sometimes-operational home-movie projector and a few grainy Gene Autry and Roy Rogers and Hopalong Cassidy movie reels. He showed the movies on a bed sheet they would hang on the wall. Because of the singing, Nora Faye liked Gene Autry and Roy Rogers better than Hopalong Cassidy.

Cowboy movies were sometimes shown at the union hall in Dillard on Saturday afternoons for three cents admission, but James wouldn't let Nora Faye go to anything but Sunday School at the union hall. Any time there was any kind of gathering there, fights were likely to break out—even in broad daylight—among the men and boys who milled around outside. James wasn't willing to risk letting Nora Faye get caught up in something like that. He even went to Sunday School with her if Berta Slaney wasn't going.

And he had to stop letting her go to Sunday School at all after the building shifted on its foundation during a heavily attended union meeting. The upper side of the box-shaped building rested on the ground on the steep hillside, and the side next to the railroad tracks was supported by tall posts anchored only by the large rocks wedged under them. Some folks, who seemed unfazed by the reality of posts that had buckled enough to show it by sight, continued to attend meetings in the building, making jokes about the tilted floor—saying they had leaned to one side on whatever issue was under discussion—but James did not let Nora Faye attend any more activities there.

Volunteers from the Wolliver Methodist and Baptist churches had taken turns conducting the Dillard Sunday School until Fern and Mayo Holder and their grown daughters from the mouth of Dillard took over permanently, using materials donated by the Wolliver churches.

Nora Faye's Sunday School teacher, Evelyn Holder, made the Bible stories interesting by adding details to the short versions from the Sunday School papers. She took great pleasure in teaching the primary girls, and often brought them little gifts and treats. She crocheted them all miniature teacups and saucers she had dipped in sugar water so that they dried stiff and brittle. She happened to bring the teacups on the day she told the story about Baby Moses. When Nora Faye would later think about the baby Moses, she let herself imagine him floating among the river reeds in a stiff little crocheted teacup instead of a basket of woven bulrushes.

In the summer, Brother Crider, the Missionary Baptist preacher from Wolliver, brought volunteers from his church to conduct Bible School for a week at the Dillard schoolhouse. The part Nora Faye remembered best happened during the concluding meeting on Friday evening when the children sang the songs and recited the Bible verses they had learned. They were given certificates for their attendance and for memorizing Bible verses and the names of the books of the Bible. Nora Faye was enrapt when Brother Crider drew a picture with colored chalk while he talked quietly. He told the story of Christ at Gethsemane while he drew the picture and his wife softly played "Have Thine Own Way, Lord" on the little collapsible organ she always brought with her. The room was dark except for a small lamp clamped onto his easel. The picture seemed to take shape magically, and the colors glowed as though a light came from the paper itself. His wife stopped playing just as he made the last stroke on the picture that was given as a prize to the child who had memorized the most verses. Laura Jane won it. That night Nora Faye thought she would try hard to win the picture next year, but she lost interest after she saw it next day. It did not look so special in daylight. It was sort of smudged and messy.

CHAPTER 12
DONNY STODDARD

The only time Nora Faye saw Mrs. Slaney scold Laura Jane was a time she let Billy Ray stay out in the rut lane after Donny Stoddard showed up during a game of Red Rover. Donny stood for a while just watching, out in the open for a change but not taking part in their play. When Billy Ray was called to the other side—just as he broke rank with his side and started across the space—Donny darted forward, bumping into Billy Ray, causing him to fall and skin his knee on the cinders. Donny laughed and went running off up the hollow.

Laura Jane didn't usually get into trouble with anybody—she just naturally did the right things—and she was broken-hearted that her mother was upset with her. She was crying harder than Billy Ray. She said, "I thought Donny was going to play right this time, Mother. You tell us to try to treat him like any other playmate."

Mrs. Slaney was dabbing mercurochrome onto the knee of a whimpering Billy Ray. She said, "I've also told you to bring the little children inside whenever Donny comes around. You can't tell what he's going to do next."

She was quite for a moment, and her voice was gentle but weary when she spoke again. "I guess I was wrong to think you can treat him like other playmates. Bring the little children in from now on, no matter what. You hear me, Laurie?" She gave Laura Jane's arm a little pat.

The older Slaney children could play in the rut lane any time they wanted, but Billy Ray had to ask permission. As unlikely looking a playground as it was, the rut lane served that purpose for all the children who lived in the vicinity where the side stream drained into Dillard Creek.

Back when the row of camp houses was being built high on the hill on that side of the hollow, the rut lane had been the road used by the teams of mules and oxen hauling building supplies on sleds up to the work sites. Then later, a few trucks managed to take that way up the hillside when the company was putting in electricity. The lane shouldered its way between the Slaney's back yard and the Berkindoff's side yard, then swept behind the Garvens' house and around the hillside and up between the row of six small identical houses perched above the new road and three more even smaller houses in a short row above the six. But it had been a long time since anyone had attempted to get a vehicle up on that hill. Every rainstorm deepened the ruts. The Slaneys and Berkindoffs filled the lower ruts with their cinders and with rocks they carried from the branch. If a downpour was not too severe, this filler did manage to capture some of the yellow-gray mud that rushed so readily off the hillside.

If the children were playing games like London Bridge or Green Gravel, Berta Slaney didn't pay much attention; there was seldom an injury during these games. But, even without one of Donny Stoddard's furtive appearances, she kept a close eye on Round Town or Red Rover.

She tried to give her full attention any time Donny Stoddard was around, but it was hard to know when he was lurking in the shadows. He might pop up at any moment. Donny would not take part like the other children. He hovered out of sight and jumped in from nowhere to push and shove and trip. His only purpose was to wreak havoc and ruin the fun of the other children. Sometimes on summer evenings when the children were allowed to play outside after dusk, Donny would hide on the outskirts and lob rocks or dirt clods at them, running off when somebody's dad came out to see what was going on. Most of the adults had given up on trying to be kind to Donny, and they no longer tried to reason with him. Even Berta was at her wit's end. It made her feel real bad to wish a child would just go away, but that's the way she felt about Donny now.

The Stoddards were a different family in several ways. Nobody knew them well. Nobody was sure where they came from originally, though they had lived, for a short while, down near Hotspot before they showed up in Willard two or three years ago. Neither Donny nor his sister Lorraine was in one single school picture. They went back home when they learned it was to be picture day. Nobody thought anything about Donny laying out of school; he headed for the hills more days than not. His sister, however, came to school most days, and she had developed rote answers to use when the teachers asked her about Donny. If he left the house at the same time she did, but disappeared as soon as they were out the door, she told the teacher he got sick and had to go back home. If he didn't leave the house with her, she said he was too sick to get out of bed.

There was a vague rumor about failed health and a behavior change that had come over Donny after a bout with scarlet fever. Nobody believed it. A boy down in Big Dillard really had that happen about the time the Stoddards moved into the hollow, and the neighbors figured that Cad and Lucy Stoddard found the tale a handy way to explain their boy's uncontrollable behavior. Donny did not look sick. He was even a little taller and a little sturdier than other boys his age.

Berta could not find a way to extend her friendship to Lucy Stoddard. Lucy did not answer the door when neighbor women knocked, and she went inside if she saw anyone approaching. Dark window shades were always

111

pulled on all the windows. Lucy usually stayed inside unless she was with her husband, and about the only time the two of them were seen was when they worked out in their garden on evenings Cad was home. Cad was a poker-faced, raspy-voiced man who seldom said anything he didn't have to, even to the men he worked with at the tipple, but he was surprisingly amenable when he absolutely had to deal with people, on the job or on his trips to the commissary. On paydays he did their big trading at the store, and their girl, Lorraine, was sent with a list of whatever was needed between paydays.

One of the only times Cad even let on that he knew about Donny's misbehavior was the winter when the side-branch froze solid and stayed that way for a matter of weeks. Conner had planned ahead. Before the temperature dropped to freezing he'd had the other children help him make a low dam just below a straight stretch in the stream. They cleared out all the big stones they could move and put them in the dam.

Then, after the area froze, the real labor began. Bucket by bucket Conner and the neighbor children carried water from their houses out to the wide place and built it up to form a smooth skating area about nine yards long.

There was only one pair of skates among them: the Wooten boys had a pair of strap-on skates they shared with the others. But after a while, the metal blades lay unused while all of them, including the Wootens, joined in the shoe-sole competition that had evolved. It was a simple but exciting contest that evened out the chances among them, whatever age and size. They launched themselves from the beginning point in whatever fashion they chose—one foot or two, sideways or head on, just so long as they did not change from their starting position— to see who could go the farthest in one slide. Sticks were laid out on the bank to mark the stopping point of each contestant.

Berta was nervous about the endeavor. In addition to the potential for accidents, she worried about the arguments that might arise over different kinds of shoe soles or where someone started or stopped. She was greatly relieved when no quarrels erupted, but she wouldn't let Billy Ray and Nora Faye go out of the yard when the big children from all up and down the creek were there; she made them watch from the back steps. And she was uneasy about letting the girls take part. But when she saw how well-behaved all the young people seemed to be, she relented and let Ruthie compete. Laura Jane and Lottie wanted only to watch. As it turned out, Ruthie was one of the very best racers, knowing naturally how to push off with a momentum that made up for the lack of weight she had to put behind her slide.

Some of the parents began to come to fetch their children near dusk, hanging around to watch and talk for a while. They even built a bonfire at the roadside some nights and let the children continue playing an hour or two after sunset. They teased Linc and Berta about Conner being responsible for all the shoes that were going to have to be re-soled before spring mud time. They told them they should have Conner set up a free shoe-repair shop when the ice melted.

Conner checked the ice first thing every morning and carried a bucket or two of resurfacing water before he went to school. It had turned out to be one of the nicest things that had happened in the hollow in a while. Berta's fears about the bonfires leading to trouble proved to be ungrounded, but she couldn't really rest, fire or no fire, when Linc was away at work. When there were men and older boys around a fire, she watched like a hawk to make certain there was no alcohol being passed furtively from hand to hand.

During the third week, Conner went out one morning to find the ice in shambles. Ashes and cinders from the bonfires had been scattered over the ice surface, and large gouges had been made here and there, probably with the pointed skates that lay bent and ruined amid the mess. The marker sticks were broken and scattered on the ice, and large stones had been smashed onto it.

Later in the morning Cad Stoddard showed up with Donny and a broom and rake and pick. After working for a while, Cad came up the Slaney's back steps and knocked on the porch door. Linc, who was finishing his breakfast, invited Cad to come in and have a cup of coffee with him.

Cad said no, that he'd just come to tell them how sorry he was that there was no way to fix the ice. "I know it was my boy," he said, "I got out of bed when I heard him come in this morning, and he was stinking of wood ashes. Had them all over his clothes.

"I guess you seen that I had him out there trying to make it right, but, come to find out, it's not something that can be fixed.

"If it was anybody but your boy that had made the skating place, I'd know they'd be waylaying my boy and giving him what he's due. The other boys might do it yet, but I've never heard of your boy fighting. I just want you to know I'll not hold it against any of 'em if that's what happens."

Cad stepped back down to the yard and went out the gate and up the hollow following Donny who had gone on ahead of him dragging the ineffective tools.

None of the boys ever gave Donny a beating, and there was very little said about the ruined ice rink. Linc speculated about it to James one day when he came to the store to buy carbide. They were both a little surprised that no fights had followed the destruction.

"I think it's all that killing down in Harlan County, and maybe some people remember those union wars over in

West Virginia back a ways," Linc said. "I think everybody's afraid to quarrel or let their children quarrel for any reason now, afraid it'll get out of hand and turn into that kind of killing here, even if it's not connected with the unions."

James agreed with him. "You're probably right. It would be good to think something good came out of that slaughter. People do shudder in their shoes now when they hear any kind of argument, afraid it could get twisted into union talk. They know how quick a union quarrel can turn into something like a war."

Truth be told, James was a little uneasy saying as much as he'd just said even to Linc Slaney. It surprised him to realize he was thinking that a person never knew for sure who he was talking to when it came to union affairs or how deep another person's feelings might go. Though he'd never given it a thought before this moment, he wondered now if Linc might be feeling him out to see if he could figure out if he was for or against the unions and how strong his feelings might be.

CHAPTER 13
RUTHIE

"Shredded wheat, it ain't neat,
So she makes us eat it in the street.
Shredded wheat, it tastes sweet,
So we don't mind eatin' in the street."

Billy Ray said, "You can't say 'ain't.' You have to say 'aren't'."

Conner—made a little giddy by the unseasonably spring-like weather—got right in Billy Ray's face to go on with his rhyme, stressing the word "ain't" the way brothers and sisters do things like that to each other:

"Shredded wheat, it ain't neat.
She makes us eat it in the street.
Shredded wheat, it's such a treat
We don't mind eatin' in the street."

This time, Billy Ray said, "It's not a street; it's a road. And we're not in the road anyway; we're on the steps."

Conner picked up on that for his next rhyme:

"Shredded wheat, she heard our yelps
And let us eat it on the steps.
We can't eat it in the house
Cause it leaves crumbs for our pet mouse."

Conner put his hand over Billy Ray's mouth to keep him from saying they didn't have a pet mouse. He made up the rhymes while they waited for the confection their mother was making for them on a Saturday morning in February when the slant of the sun finally hinted at spring. They huddled in an ever-moving mass on the back steps like baby birds restively waiting in the nest for parental delivery of their sustenance. All except Nora Faye. She bounced back and forth between the back steps and the kitchen. She'd never seen anybody toast shredded wheat biscuits, and she was curious about the procedure.

"It's messy to eat," Mrs. Slaney was telling her. That's why you have to eat it outside. It gets so crisp that crumbs fly everywhere when you bite into it."

She laid the shredded wheat biscuits on the toast pan and sprinkled them with a mixture of sugar and cinnamon and drizzled them with melted oleo before she put them in the oven.

"The big secret is in catching the oven just right," she explained. "You can't do it in a hot oven. The key is to let them sit at a low temperature for a pretty good spell. It's simple but not easy—and hard to wait for."

After Conner's first time through the rhyme, Ruthie grabbed her tap shoes from the back porch and ran to the pump block. She had them on and laced up in a flash. Then they all chanted the rhymes while she tapped to the rhythm. It wasn't long before she threw off her coat, letting it land on the rut-lane cinders with her cast-off saddle shoes. Conner grabbed a stick and used it to drum on the porch steps while Billy Ray clacked two rocks together. They chanted faster and faster and Ruthie tapped faster and faster.

They got louder as they got faster until Mrs. Slaney finally came to the door with one finger to her lips and the other hand pointing across the road toward the Bledso's house. They knew what she meant. Mr. Bledso slept in the mornings, like their dad, but, unlike Mr. Slaney, Mr. Bledso was not a sound sleeper. They never had to worry about waking their dad. He always said he could sleep through doomsday, just as long as nobody opened his door or came into the room with him, but Mr. Bledso was such a light sleeper Mrs. Bledso tiptoed around their house in her stocking feet while she did her morning housework.

117

Ruthie had been tap dancing ever since she saw her first Shirley Temple movie. Their oldest sister, Lissie, had taken the Slaney children to Wolliver to see, "The Little Colonel" the last time she was home. Ruthie became obsessed. Conner made tap shoes for her from an old pair of Girl Scout oxfords Lissie and then Lottie and Laura Jane had outgrown. They were so worn by the time Ruthie inherited them that she wasn't expected to wear them, but she had kept them on the back porch for times she wanted to go berry picking or play in the rut lane in spite of mud. Conner scraped the corks out of two bottle caps and hammered the metal flat before he used tin snips to cut each cap into two pieces that he fastened to the bottom of the shoes with short upholstery tacks on the heels and toes.

Her mother warned her not to dance in the house or on the porches, but Ruthie had already discovered that the concrete pump block would be the perfect place for best effect. Though only a few feet square, it was big enough to make her feel like she was on a stage, and it magnified the sound of every tap. In addition, the side of the block away from the hill went down in three short steps so that she could do the routine like Shirley Temple did, down and back up with the colored man.

Back when the camp houses were first built, the one communal pump had been installed for the use of this entire section of the community. Later, even the houses with outdoor toilets were given a kitchen sink with water piped indoors, and the pump behind the Slaney's house had been dismantled, leaving nothing but the housing without a handle.

After her mother's shushing, Ruthie had toned her dancing down to a scratchy slide. As she gave her attention to the new footwork, another sound rang out from the side of the pump block. Donny Stoddard had bounced a rock off the concrete target. He had sneaked up near the children, ducking first behind the Berkindoff's toilet and then Mrs. Garvens' chicken house as he landed his rocks with a hollow ring.

Ruthie yelled at him. "I know it's you, Donny. You better stop right now!"

His next rock landed on her coat where it lay on the cinders. He dodged back and forth between the toilet and the chicken house, landing a rock on Ruthie's coat each time he changed position. She was able to ignore it for a while, but then he changed to dirt clods. The clods shattered when they landed, covering her coat with yellow dirt. She jumped to retrieve it just as he lobbed in another rock. It got her on the wrist. She grabbed her coat and saddle shoes and ran to the gate where she stopped and faced in the direction of Donny's onslaught. "I'll be getting even with you, Donny Stoddard. You just wait and see!" she hissed.

She shook the dirt off her coat and put it back on before she took a place on the steps again. She tried not to let on that he'd hurt her; she was afraid their mother would bring them inside and they'd not get to have their shredded wheat. They weren't supposed to argue with neighbor children. If they quarreled, their mother made them come inside.

Conner did what he usually did to keep things from getting out of hand with Donny. He moved away from the other children. He ambled over to the gate like he'd been heading there anyway. He poked at weeds with his stick as he eased out the gate and up the lane past his shop. He squatted to examine something on the ground behind Mrs. Garvens' chicken house, and Donny soon joined him. From a distance they looked like any two carefree boys sharing a moment of idle camaraderie.

Nobody ever knew what he said to Donny at these times. When they asked Conner, he said he didn't remember, that he just said the same things he said with other boys. But, these time-outs with Conner were the only way Donny could be distracted from his campaigns against peace. He didn't usually bedevil a group unless Conner was in it, and then, ironically, it was Conner alone who could sway him from his mischief.

When their mother at last appeared with the shredded wheat, Donny disappeared. But after she had distributed a piece to each of the children, she took the last one—the one she had intended for herself—and placed it carefully on top of the fencepost nearest the gate. As she disappeared back into the kitchen, Donny swooped down like the Saracens and scooped up the shredded wheat biscuit before he dodged behind the Berkindoff's toilet, and once again disappeared.

CHAPTER 14
RUBY CROSS

Ruby Cross looked too perfect to be real. Nora Faye saw her just the one time when Aunt Clemma brought her to Uncle Jimmy's house on Easter Sunday. Aunt Clemma was Ruby Cross's grandmother, and she brought her and two other granddaughters that year. Nora Faye knew the other girls; she'd played with them at Uncle Jimmy's house more than once. But she had never seen Ruby Cross, nor any real girl like her.

She looked like someone from the movies, too somber for Shirley Temple, but maybe Margaret O'Brien. Her coat was a navy blue soft wool crepe with just a little fullness falling from a few gathers at the yoke. It hung in a neat line from her collarbone almost to her knees. A row of mirror-smooth black buttons closed the front all the way to the white file sailor collar with navy blue ribbon trim. Her shoes were black patent leather Mary Janes worn with lace-trimmed white anklets. Her thin, close-fitting, spotless white gloves were eye-catchers, but not as outstanding as the finely woven white straw hat with a shallow rounded crown encircled by a golden yellow grosgrain ribbon that trailed from a bow in back down onto her glossy, thick black hair. The ribbon ends were two different lengths and were notched into vees.

Nora Faye looked around at the other girls in their shabby winter coats that fell open over their new, short, flowered-cotton dresses with puffed sleeves and sashes in the back, or longer, pleated jumpers over short-sleeved white blouses for girls a little older. Most of their new jumpers were made from the same pattern as their winter jumpers, but made in summer-colored, lightweight fabrics. They wore new white sandals or slip-ons. Clemma's other two granddaughters wore new brown and white saddle oxfords, and Nora Faye wore low-top brown buckle shoes that had seemed summery after winter's high-top lace-ups. Now, she felt like she and all the other girls looked dowdy.

Ruby Cross looked like the big dolls Anna Sue Patterson kept under her bed in their closed boxes with clear cellophane windows in the lids. Anna Sue got so many dolls for Christmas—one from Santa, one from each set of grandparents and two from aunts and uncles—that she had never taken two of them out of their boxes, sliding them out to show Nora Faye and the other girls one time when they'd been invited to her house for her birthday party, the only time Nora Faye had ever been in the mining superintendent's big house on the hill.

Today, Nora Faye's daddy had waked her early at home, the way he always did on Easter mornings. Every year he was the one who happened to hear the Easter Bunny just as he was leaving their house and to see just a tip of white tail as he disappeared around the corner of the coalhouse. No matter how quick James was to wake Nora Faye, and no matter how fast she hurried, there were no signs of the bunny by the time she got to the porch. She wished with all her might that she'd be lucky enough to see him. She wanted to see him almost as much as she wanted to see Santa Clause.

"How can he be big?" she asked. And in the same breath, "How can he have hands to carry things?"

James said it was part of the magic.

"Did he wear clothes?" Some of the pictures she'd seen showed him wearing clothes and some didn't. James said he never saw enough of him to tell if he was wearing clothes, that he just saw his big fluffy tail a moment before it disappeared around the coal house or the toilet or the Deeton's house. If he wore pants, then, there must be a hole for his tail, she thought.

She always left her Easter basket on the kitchen table where the bunny could easily find it, empty except for green paper-shred grass. The bunny hid jellybeans in the grass, and wrapped the basket in the gold cellophane paper they left for him along with the bright pink ribbon. He wrapped the basket in the cellophane before hiding it somewhere in the house. Sometimes he put in extra candy, like a few chocolate kisses in their exciting twisted silver foil or a whole box of Campfire marshmallows. Last year he left three lollipops with handles of twisted paper loops instead of sharp wooden sticks.

After a quick run out into the yard in her nightie in an effort to spy the bunny—even one year when it was cold and rainy—Nora Faye came back inside and searched for her basket first thing. After she found it, she threw on her clothes, and they hurried back outside to hunt until they found the five blue eggs hidden in the yard. Those were the eggs they would devil for their Easter breakfast. The eggs she would take to Uncle Jimmy's house later in the day were the ones she and James had colored the day before.

"Why five?" she asked every year, and every year James would tell her to count the spaces in the deviled egg dish. There were ten spaces. "He brings five to fill our deviled egg dish," he would remind her.

"How do we know there aren't more that we didn't finded?"

"Because our dish has only ten spaces. He knows how many eggs it takes to fill our dish."

Sometimes Nora Faye thought she had a vague memory of her mother fixing the deviled eggs for their Easter morning breakfast, but now James did it, letting her help crack and peel the blue eggs and stir in the mustard and mayonnaise before he spooned the mashed-up yellow parts back into the halved whites. He let Nora Faye sprinkle on the paprika.

"Why are his eggs always blue?"

"Maybe he gets them from a robin," James answered.

"Robin eggs are little."

"A magic robin."

It wasn't until they were coloring eggs one Easter time long after she stopped believing in the Easter Bunny that her dad's procedure dawned on her. Their egg-coloring packet would have had a blue dye pill along with the rose and yellow and green and purple they used to dye the non-magic eggs on Saturday afternoons. She had never dyed eggs blue when she was little and never wondered about it, never suspecting that her daddy kept back a pill and stayed up late dying magic blue eggs for her early morning hunt.

She remembered one year when she woke shortly after she had finally fallen asleep the night before Easter. She smelled the warm, vinegary egg-coloring odor, and was up and on her way to the kitchen when her daddy came rushing out of nowhere to put her back in bed. "But, somebody's dying Easter eggs in the kitchen," she protested.

"That vinegar odor stays in the house," James explained. "It's from when we dyed our eggs this afternoon." He went on to distract her with one adventure after another about the Easter Bunny until she fell asleep again.

If Granny Rose wasn't with them already, they picked her up after Easter breakfast and took her with them to Uncle Jimmy's house. You never knew who would be there: always most of Aunt Tattie and Uncle Jimmy's children and grandchildren, usually Eldon and Stella with

Dollie and Bootsie, and often Aunt Clemma and some of her family. Nora Faye knew all of Aunt Tattie's grandchildren and most of Aunt Clemma's, but she had never before seen Ruby Cross who lived near Ashland where her daddy worked at a radio station.

Uncle Eldon's family got there right at the same time she and her daddy got there with Granny Rose today. They had parked among the other cars across the creek and were making their way over the little footbridge when Uncle Jimmy caught sight of them as he returned from the woodhouse. He took his load of wood inside and came back out to wait for them at the gate.

After Nora Faye, Dollie, and Bootsie skirted the honking geese in the lane and got through the gate unflogged, they threw themselves at Uncle Jimmy for a hug, and he went through a routine he always did with them.

"Here's James' and Eldon's boys," he started.

"The girls giggled. "We're not boys, Uncle Jimmy!"

"You're not boys? Well, why in the world did they name you Ralph and Homer and Jasper?"

"Our names are not Ralph and Homer and Jasper!" they shouted.

"They're not?" he asked innocently. "Well, what are your names?"

"We're Bootsie and Dollie and Nora Faye," they tittered.

"Bootsie and Dollie and Nora Faye?" he'd repeat. "Those sure are funny names for boys!"

Then he counted their ribs. He always counted children's ribs to make sure they had the right number. It was very important, he'd explain, that children have the right number of ribs. But he could never get a good count; it tickled so that the children always giggled and squirmed and pulled out of his grasp, and he'd have to start over time and again.

As soon as they greeted Aunt Tattie and the other relatives inside the house, all the children and some of the adults spilled back outside to hide Easter eggs. But the day looked much warmer than it felt, with the sky so blue and the air so clear they belied the chill that sent the grownups back inside. Clumps of grass here and there were so green they looked like they had been colored with Easter Egg dye. The forsythia bushes had just spilled themselves in fence corners and along the lane in piles of blossoms yellow as the sun, and the weigela and japonica buds looked ready to burst open if someone jostled them.

The children had brought their own eggs, and they took turns hiding them for each other to find. In spite of the chill, the first scent of spring-awakened earth rose to waft among them, making them giddy as they ran laughing from one likely hiding spot to another. Only Ruby Cross stood by, looking a little horrified by the tumbling, shrieking children whirling around her. "Come on, Ruby Cross, I saw some over here," Nora Faye called. Then, "Here, Ruby Cross, I'll let you have this one."

The air was suddenly split by a shriek. "Stop calling me that!" the girl screeched, her voice so different from the other children's that they all came to a silent stop.

"Stop calling me Ruby Cross!"

Nora Faye realized the girl was yelling at her.

"I thought that was your name," she murmured. She *knew*, in fact, that it was her name. From the minute she first heard the name Ruby Cross, it had seemed like part of the Easter magic, the magic day. In her mind's eye she had seen a large glittering ruby cut into the shape of a cross. It seemed like this girl had been created for this day.

"What's your name?" the girl demanded of Nora Faye.

When she mumbled that it was Nora Faye, Ruby Cross said, "I mean your whole name. What's your last name?"

"She's Nora Faye Houston," said Dollie, who had stepped up to stand beside Nora Faye.

"Well, how would you like it if somebody called you Nora Faye *Houston,* Nora Faye *Houston* all the time? Why do you always say my last name?" She was screaming and her face was red.

"I thought you were Ruby Cross and something else," Nora Faye whispered, almost unable to get out a sound.

"That's crazy," Ruby Cross yelled. "Who would use Cross for a middle name? We're not like you hillbillies. We don't call everybody by two names!" She stomped off towards the house with her cousins in tow. The other children stood silent for no more than a second before they shook off the hateful intrusion and fell back into their play.

But Nora Faye never forgot the moment, never forgot Ruby Cross, never forgot how Dollie had stepped up beside her when Ruby Cross was yelling at her.

Dollie, in fact, Nora Faye knew, could be counted on to look out for her almost the same as she looked out for Bootsie. It was something she'd always been able to take for granted. That's why it was so hurtful when there was another incident just a few minutes later that took the edge off the good memory she had of Dollie's staunchness.

Roland Warfield was not a cousin. He was a neighbor boy of Uncle Jimmy's who always came from his house on the hill across the creek when he saw that Dollie was there. He was sweet on Dollie. He called her Bascon— even after she moved to Johnston—and always made his presence known by coming up the lane to stand at the gate halfway behind the big snowball bush while he called, "Hey, Bascon!" until she joined him. He was one of the rare people the geese ignored, causing no commotion when he slipped in the gate and up the lane.

Dollie liked him, too. She left the Easter egg hunt to amble over to the gate before he called out for her that day. He asked, "What did your little cousin do to get that prissy city girl so stirred up?" He had made a circling sign around his ear and raised his eyebrows when he mentioned Nora Faye.

Dollie said that it was nothing worth that kind of conniption. Then she asked, "Did you mean that for Nora Faye?" She made the circling motion—and, before he could reply, she added, "There's nothing wrong with Nora Faye."

Roland said, "Well, I mean she's just babyish."

Dollie said, "She *is* a baby."

Then she went on to say something Nora Faye managed to block out of her consciousness for many years. She said, "And even if something was wrong with her, she's not really kin to me. My Uncle James is not her real daddy."

Roland said, "Yeah, I'd heard that." But Nora Faye didn't hear what he said. She no longer heard the other children's voices. It was like the air grew thick to muffle sound, like a cloud went over the sun, and the brilliant grass and forsythia bushes and Easter eggs turned dull. The temperature suddenly dropped to the number on the thermometer, and Nora Faye shivered and hunched up in her scruffy winter coat. It took a long time for the day to regain any of its magic luster for her.

The hurtful thing was the way Dollie backed up in her defense of her and made it sound like something might be wrong with her. She already knew somehow that her daddy was not her real daddy; she'd known that from the time her momma left them. But she didn't know Dollie thought something might be wrong with her. She thought it must have to do with sounding like a baby, like her momma had said. That's what Dollie said, that she was just a baby.

One of the lesser puzzles had to do with the way Ruby Cross said the word hillbilly. Nora Faye had never given any thought to what it meant beyond being what they were called because of where they lived. About the only place she could remember hearing it was in happy teasing talk among adults, and in the song that said "I love mountain music, good old mountain music, played by a real hillbilly band." Everybody seemed happy when they sang that song, and she'd thought they were all hillbillies and that it was something to be glad about. Now, the two-name criteria for hillbillies seemed to rule out Dollie and Bootsie and her daddy and maybe most of the people she knew. And Ruby Cross obviously thought a hillbilly was something to be glad you weren't.

As she got older, it was getting harder to block out things it was best to pretend she didn't hear.

CHAPTER 15
TRUDY MORROW

When Claudine Vickers first stopped by the house to talk to Rose about letting Nora Faye start school, Rose figured the school thing was something to give Claudine a reason to talk to James. She could tell she had her cap set for him, and Mr. Wainwright was still alive, so rumors about James and Virginia Wainwright had not risen to discourage Claudine. But she seemed serious about thinking Nora Faye was ready to start the primer.

When Rose asked about the baby talk, Claudine didn't know what she meant.

"Well, her mother always said her baby talk was going to hold her back in school, the way she says "sitted" and "holded" and things like that.."

To Rose's surprise, Claudine smiled brightly. "Oh, no," she said, "that's not baby talk. Baby talk is if she said, 'Nora Faye sits,' or 'Me sits.'

"That thing she does with verbs is one of the ways she shows she's ready for school. It shows she has an understanding of verb tense. She doesn't always know just how to do it yet, but she knows when a verb should be past tense. There's nothing wrong with how she talks."

Rose didn't know about verbs and tense—Mr. Houston had told her she did fine with grammar without memorizing the rules and parts of speech or trying to change the way she talked—but she was inclined to think Claudine knew what she was talking about. She'd had more schooling than Dillard's other teachers, maybe even graduated from college. The other teachers—in Dillard and most of the coal camps—were girls with one year of college, or even less, who had been given teaching jobs when the men went away to the war. But Rose still had her doubts about it being best to let Nora Faye make that long walk to school.

"I'll tell you what," Claudine said, "I'll say something every time I see James in the store, and I hope you'll urge him at home. It would be a shame to make her wait when she's ready now. It might even make things harder for her later if she doesn't start now. She's done well on the days she's come with the Slaneys, and I have the time to give her extra attention. Our classes are small this year."

"Because of the people that's moved to Dayton and Detroit?" Rose asked.

"And Ypsilanti and Toledo," Claudine added. "The Browns and Linkharts and Manfords all had school-age children."

"Laura Jane and Conner will take care of her," Claudine went on. "You don't have to worry about her getting hurt or anything."

Rose figured she was thinking of Donny Stoddard when she said they wouldn't let her get hurt. She'd heard the tales about how Donny ambushed the children in the quarter mile or so span about halfway between the last of the upper-row camp houses and the tipple. There were no houses along that stretch, not along the new high road nor the old road. The children were supposed to walk on the high road away from the train tracks, but, whether he'd been in school that day or not, Donny would appear, once school was dismissed, to dodge in and out among the trees above the high road, throwing rocks and dirt down at them. If they were on the low road along the tracks, he sneaked along the brim of the high road throwing mud clods down to the low road. Unless one of the teachers walked with them there was seldom a day when someone didn't get books mud-spattered or knocked into a puddle.

Sometimes there were knots and scrapes where a rock landed, but Donny usually managed to keep his onslaught from hurting anyone badly. He knew how to torment them without showy damage that would have brought interference from a parent.

Rose wasn't too worried about Donny. If he got worse, she could walk to the tipple to meet them on the days James let Nora Faye go to school with the Slaneys, but she'd heard them tell how Conner usually took care of it. He would join Donny, wherever he lurked, and walk the rest of the way home with him.

Rose still hoped James would decide on Wolliver for next year, but she had to agree that it seemed to be working out well for Nora Faye on the pretty days now and then that she had gone to school since Christmas.

When she gradually began to go on an everyday basis Rose was glad to see how happy she seemed, going off up the hollow with the Slaneys.

She learned to write her numbers to 100 the very first day she went to school. She could already recite the alphabet, and by the end of the first month, she learned to write the letters without copying. By the end of March she had finished the primer reading book and could make out most of the sentences in the unexciting first-grade reader about Ben and Alice and their dog and cat, Whitey and Blackie.

On her first day, Miss Vickers seated her beside her own desk and wrote out the numbers through 10 and told her to copy them. Nora Faye had done this before when her daddy or one of the Slaney children had given her the list to copy in her tablet, but doing it at a school desk instead of the kitchen table took her into another plane of thought. As she copied the numbers her teacher had written, something clicked for her and, after 10, she continued with 20, 30, 40, 50, 60, 70, 80, and 90, and then

100, 200, 300, 400 all the way to 1000. Miss Vickers pointed out her mistake, but she did not allow her a moment to feel embarrassed. She said that's what she was at school for, to learn. She laughed and hugged her shoulders while she showed her how to go on correctly from 10 to 11, 12, and 13. It was actually the moment Nora Faye realized the patterns numbers have. The way Miss Vickers reacted made it seem of no consequence that she had assumed a wrong pattern at first. It was a simple thing to put the one in front of each number instead of putting a zero after. On her second try she could write the correct pattern up to 20, and in a few weeks time she could not only write the numbers to 100 without copying, but she could add and subtract.

In the reading books she was doing even better. Most of the primer students had moved up, as expected, to the first grade reader well before Christmas. Only Hager Jasper and Ollie Chambers—both from families who lived way at the head of Beegum Hollow and seldom came to school—were still reading in the primer on the rare days when they made it out of the hollow to school, so Claudine put Nora Faye in the first grade reader with the rest, and, in no time, she moved her on up to the second grade reading group.

Nora Faye was pleased with the second grade reader. It had many different stories like one about how bears ended up with a short tail when, in long ago times, one made a hole in the ice and dropped his long tail in the hole to catch a fish. She felt a little sad the first time she read about him going to sleep so that the ice froze around his tail and pulled it off when he stood. But she quickly realized that stories like this were all in fun, where the pain was not real and the point was to get the joke.

Claudine went around feeling almost giddy when James first let Nora Faye come to school. But it wasn't

long until she heard he was interested in Charles
Wainwright's widow down at Vargo, and she couldn't
help but feel she had been used, even though she knew in
her heart of hearts that she, not James, was the one who
had brought up the idea of Nora Faye coming to school.

Claudine had been struck on James for a long time, and
she had privately rejoiced when Irene left him. She was
not a reckless girl; she had subdued her feelings as long as
it was prudent, but when it seemed safe to assume Irene
was gone for good, she just naturally did whatever it took
to put herself in the line of James's attention. It was a
happy coincidence that Nora Faye had often been at the
Slaney's house when she stopped by to help Billy Ray and
that she happened to be ready to pick up on the reading
lessons she was giving Billy Ray. But Claudine knew she
would have found some way to twist it to her advantage
whatever Nora Faye's learning level had been. If she had
shown no inclination to learn, she would have urged
James to let her come to school this winter so she'd get a
better start when she started the primer for real next year.
She tried to make home visits to any of her sick students,
but she realized she had given Billy Ray more attention
than the others. The coincidental connection to James had
been more than she could resist. And now she felt a little
like a fool.

Nora Faye liked almost everything about school,
especially the smells. The pencil shavings and rubber
erasers, chalk dust and felt erasers, wooden floors and
desks worn smooth with age, rubber galoshes, and the
damp-wool smell of their winter clothes with clinging
snow melting by the heat of the coal stove. She loved the
pungent tang of the fresh chunks of coal in the coal bucket
and the smoky smell of the burning coal and ashes and the
hot metal of the stove. The stove was more like a person
than a thing, the way it was warm all the way around with

its friendly welcoming roundness, not just out front like the bedroom fireplaces at home.

Her only disappointment was in not having a permanently assigned seat. Claudine had been moving her around from seat to seat because it seemed to bring out the best in her seatmates. When Nora Faye told her she'd like a seat of her own, she put her at a desk in the back by herself, which wasn't what Nora Faye had meant—most of the others shared the desks in pairs—but she was reluctant to say more.

When Trudy Morrow enrolled, Miss Vickers put her with Nora Faye, and that was okay, too, until the day they were making Easter decorations.

Trudy had something wrong with her from the time she was born. She could not keep up with other children. She was slow to walk and talk, and hard to understand when she finally started talking. Nobody knew just what was wrong with her, but everybody knew she did strange things. She caused her family a lot of heartache, even though people said the Morrows loved her as much as they loved her brothers and sisters and that they always tried to do their best by her.

Her folks had thought there was no question of her ever being allowed to go to school. They had not made the attempt to enroll her when she turned school age last year. Then they heard about Claudine taking James Houston's little girl this year, and they decided to see what she'd say about taking Trudy.

Claudine was not mean spirited, but she felt like she'd been pushed into a corner. Her interest in Nora Faye had been sparked by her interest in James, and after it became clear that she had no chance with James—clear that he had his cap set for Virginia Wainwright—she was feeling hurt and resentful. As for Trudy, Claudine did have more schooling than the other Willard teachers but she'd had no training in how to handle special cases like Trudy. She knew how it would look if she refused to let her attend, though. The Morrows might even go to the county school superintendent and raise a stink. Her involvement with Nora Faye made it too awkward for her to discourage them when they asked her to give Trudy the same chance, and now that James's favor was no longer a factor, Claudine couldn't keep from resenting Nora Faye. She wished she had never started the whole thing.

Her delight in Nora Faye had not been put-on. She thought Nora Faye would have made an impression on her even if James not been in the picture. When she first started tutoring Billy Ray she had a hard time keeping his attention, but after Nora Faye joined them, that was no longer a problem. Nora Faye drank up every word she said, and Billy Ray stayed involved as long as Nora Faye was with him.

It seemed that one day Nora Faye didn't know anything, and the next day she was reading sentences. Claudine took pure pleasure in that, the kind of pleasure that's set apart from any need for recognition. She would have been stunned and would have argued her innocence if someone had pointed out that it seemed she had decided to make James pay by making Norah Faye pay, but there was an undeniable possibility that James's lack of interest played a part in her subtle change of attitude toward Nora Faye.

Having to deal with Trudy was unfair, but she felt a little soothed when she convinced herself that seating Trudy with Nora Faye—who had so recently picked up so much so fast—would somehow be a good way of giving Trudy the same chance. For a while, it went surprisingly well.

Nora Faye sensed that something was not right with Trudy. The teacher told her to help Trudy, but she said it in such a way that Nora Faye felt no burden of responsibility about fixing her. It was a situation calling for tolerance more than anything else on Nora Faye's part. Trudy often tried her patience. She said "huh" to whatever anybody said to her—said it over and over—and then she didn't respond when you repeated yourself. She just stared blankly after all those "huhs." Nora Faye was able to ignore her except in her worst episodes.

Having Trudy for a desk mate had taken the edge off the pure pleasure of being at school, but it never occurred to Nora Faye to lodge a complaint about sharing a desk with her. Not even after the day they were using the colored chalk.

The colored chalk was a dwindling resource carefully hoarded at the back of Miss Vickers' bottom desk drawer. The week before Easter they were working on pictures to decorate the schoolroom windows. The room was abuzz.

Being allowed to have the colored chalk box at your desk was part of the fun when you were working on an art project. The little wooden box with corners Uncle Jimmy called "dove-tailed" was filled with sawdust to keep the chalk from breaking. Most pieces were so small you had to rummage around for them like searching for jellybeans in your Easter basket grass.

But today there were too many people using the chalk at the same time to let the box go to the student desks. It was on the teacher's desk, and the students were making their requests by specific color. Nora Faye raised her hand and made her request for orange to Mattie Bates, a sixth grader who was serving as Miss Vickers' helper. Mattie dug out the piece and handed it to her helper saying, "Take this orange back to the afflicted desk."

Nora Faye pretended not to hear. She didn't know exactly what afflicted meant—she'd only heard it in Sunday School lessons about the lame and afflicted—but she knew it had to do with Trudy being different, and she knew, from the way it had been said, that Mattie lumped her in with Trudy, maybe because she was sitting with Trudy. Next day she asked Miss Vickers to let her sit with Billy Ray. Miss Vickers said first graders couldn't sit with second graders but that she could sit with Molly Eliott if she wanted. Molly proved to be a fine desk mate.

But school was not the same totally carefree delight after that. Nora Faye worried that Granny Rose would hear what the chalk girl had said and that she would be mad at Miss Vickers and would maybe come to school to tell her how she felt. When Miss Vickers took the Easter pictures off the school windows so the children could take them home to give their parents, she stuffed hers into her book bag without looking at it, and, on the way home, she reached into her bag and folded the sheet in half over and over one-handed until it was a little wad. She had been very excited about it before the chalk incident. It was three yellow baby chicks and their jagged-edged empty eggshells beside an un-hatched blue Easter egg on a half sheet of pale pink construction paper. The sky was blue and the chicks' beaks and feet were orange. She had outlined the chicks with orange to make them stand out and had added sprigs of green grass around the eggs and the chicks' feet.

When her daddy went out to fill the coal buckets and use the toilet that night before he banked the fires at bedtime, she reached over the fire screen and threw the wad into the flames although she was never supposed to put anything into the fire without a grownup watching. Ina Morris, a little girl who lived in a top row house, had been badly burned when the sleeve of her chenille bathrobe caught fire as she reached over the screen to throw something into the fire. She'd been in the hospital for months, now, and James and Nora Faye had contributed their boxes of Jello from the kitchen shelf when there was a drive to collect it for her. Jello was the only thing she could eat, and it was scarce in the stores because of the war.

James saw the little clump of ashes from her picture wad, and when he asked about it she told him she had been cleaning out her book bag. That was the first time she lied to him. The lecture he gave her about staying away from the fire seemed mild compared to the lecture she felt she deserved about lying to your daddy.

She lay awake for a long time that night after James finished telling her an Easter Bunny story. At one point she folded back the covers and sat up on the edge of the bed. She wanted to go wake her daddy and ask him what it meant to be afflicted and why Mattie Bates thought she was afflicted. She didn't know why she hadn't told him the truth about the picture. She could imagine how warm his chest and arms would feel as he hugged her to him and explained things. But she ended up lying back down and pulling the covers up to her chin again. What if the explanation wasn't easy? What if he sounded sad, the way he always did whenever she told him about anybody hurting her feelings? What if he should end up comforting her for being afflicted instead of for being mistakenly thought to be afflicted by Mattie Bates?

There was a much more serious incident with Trudy—and inadvertently with Nora Faye—later in the spring, during lunch break one sunny day. The children had finished their lunches and had scattered to various pastimes. The younger children were playing London Bridge in a bare spot close to the schoolhouse, the older girls were sitting in the shade where creek-bank tree trunks curved out over the water to make seats, and the bigger boys were playing a war game that ranged all over the playground. Suddenly some of the boys came to a stop under the back corner of the schoolhouse where it was high enough to allow a person to stand. They were laughing and pointing and acting excited but embarrassed.

Nora Faye went with the crowd when all of them—boys and girls—left their games to see what was going on. When they got to the corner, they could see a shape back in the low space under the schoolhouse. At first it was so dark it was impossible to tell who or what it was. Nora Faye thought for a minute that it might be a monkey like she had seen in a roadside cage at a gas station one time when they made a trip to Hazard to pick up her daddy's cousin Caleb on his way back from the army on a furlough.

Then she saw that it was Trudy. She was squatting over her orange snowball cake—she brought one in her lunchbox every day—with her panties pulled down around her ankles. Bent grotesquely double, she was peeing on the cake while she grinned and giggled. The bow had come off one pigtail and dropped near enough to be splashed by the pee. Her mother always put a bow on each pigtail to match Trudy's dress. She sewed beautiful dresses for her, and Trudy had beautiful hair.

The boys were beginning to whoop and laugh. Laura Jane told them to hush and go away. She stood between them and Trudy and fanned her pleated skirt out on each side to make a screen. She told Miranda Mayfield to go get a teacher fast.

Ruthie started crawling back to Trudy. She was talking to her like you talk to a baby. She said, "Pull up your panties, Trudy. Stop peeing and pull your panties up." Ruthie was trying to spread her skirt out to make a screen, too, the best she could. It wasn't easy, the way she couldn't stand up or even get up on her knees.

Trudy said, "Huh."

When Ruthie repeated her request, Trudy said, "My step-ins match my dress." She couldn't get them pulled up. Ruthie had to turn her on her side—being careful not to get her in the wet dirt—to pull her panties up enough to cover most of her behind, but her skirt was caught in her panties in places where it wasn't up in her face or all the way up over her head. In desperation Ruthie took her by the ankles and started pulling her out to a place where she'd be able to stand her up and straighten her out.

Then a horrific thing happened to Nora Faye. A little giggle erupted from her throat. The confusion and shock of the ridiculous and unbelievable happening right before her eyes, and the demeanor of the other children laughing and giggling—all worked together to take their toll on a rational reaction.

Miss Vickers appeared just as Nora Faye giggled. She said, "You of all people, Nora Faye. I wouldn't think *you'd* have reason to laugh at Trudy."

Mrs. Everhart was suddenly there. She told all the children to come inside with her except for Ruthie and Laura Jane who would stay there to help Miss Vickers. She sent Ruthie up the creek to hunt for Trudy's big sister Janine so they could send Trudy home with her when everything got under control.

Nora Faye had tried not to let her ears hear Miss Vickers' words, but she was not successful. Miss Vickers' comment changed school for her. Never again was there the magic security of utter trust.

Trudy didn't come back to school. Nora Faye tried not to let her eyes turn that way when she passed that side of the schoolhouse on the way to the girls' toilet, but even if she turned her head in the opposite direction, the scene under the schoolhouse, as dark as it was, seemed burned into her vision. Trudy bobbed up and down in the shadows like a monkey on all fours hunching its back up and skittering off to the side.

No sign of the cake was visible—maybe some animal had eaten it—but you could still make out the shape of the hair-bow. How sad, Nora Faye thought, when Trudy's mother had dressed her so beautifully and put those hair-bows on her pigtails every day to match her pretty dresses. She couldn't help but wonder if it would have made a difference for Trudy if she had kept her for a seatmate.

CHAPTER 16
COUSIN NAOMI

Rose planned to turn most of her garden over to her neighbor, Bessie Glassinger, next summer. She could see that James was not going to let her keep Nora Faye in Wolliver more than a night or two at a time. She didn't hold that against him; she was proud of the way he was determined to keep Nora Faye with him. But it meant that Rose spent a lot of her time going back and forth. She knew she didn't need to go to Dillard so often, knew that James and Nora Faye would be fine if she made it no more than once or twice a month to do the washing and the cleaning. Nora Faye was having happy times with the Slaney children, and James was doing a good job of making it seem that Irene's absence was not a tragedy, but Rose discovered that something inside herself was not satisfied if more than a few days went by before she saw Nora Faye.

The passenger train was still making two runs a day, but she learned she could catch a ride with Gladys Avery on the days when Gladys visited her mother in Wolliver once or twice a week. Her mother lived right behind the post office, so Gladys didn't mind looking for Rose as she headed back to Dillard. Rose began to depend on that. She made arrangements with Bessie so that she always kept an eye on her house. That way she could leave town without any preparation. She would make a trip to the post office just about the time she knew Gladys would be headed back home. She'd stop at the alley to look for Glady's car before she checked her mailbox inside the post office.

Then she'd wait on the sidewalk where the brick wall in front of the post office lot made a seat at the corner.

Gladys had told her she was welcome to come on up to her mother's house when she wanted to ride with her, but Rose did not choose to put herself in the position of having to evade the never-ending questions concerning Irene's absence that Gladys' mother always asked.

Today, when she took her mail from the box, she wondered why she was hearing from her cousin Naomi out of the blue. She couldn't recall ever getting a piece of mail from her except for the annual Christmas letter of solicitation for their church mission in Tennessee. Naomi had married a preacher.

She rested her handbag on the high post office writing table and used the pen chained there to start tearing open a corner of the envelope; she guessed it would be better to know right away if it was bad news. Her face reddened and then turned to stone as she read:

Dear Rose,

I am writing to you instead of James because I figure he might not know who I am. I don't reckon I ever saw him except for that one time at your brother Jimmy's house when he was a baby and I was just a girl myself. I want you to let him know right away that we will take the little girl. Everybody knows how long I've prayed for a baby girl of my own. I think the world of my boys, but I've always felt I have so much to offer a precious little daughter.

I had prayed about it especially hard in the Morning Supplications on Tuesday, and when Andrew fetched our mail that day, there was a letter from my sister Francine telling about what happened to your James. I told Andrew that the Lord had just sent me an answer to my prayers by the U.S. Mail.

Now, I want you to know that I've heard the stories about her mother's wayward life and about her real daddy and that, with the Lord's help, I will work past that. It will be a real privilege for me to take such an unfortunate little creature and shape her into a vessel for Our Savior's purpose. I am humble that He has chosen me to entrust with the charge.

My first thought was about how James would have no reason to want to keep the child now, and I want to be sure he understands that we don't fault him about that. No man could be expected to have fatherly feelings for a child brought into the world by such a wife under such shameful circumstances. And I expect that none of you in the family will want to take her into your homes where she would be a sad and constant reminder of the degradation James has brought upon all of you.

The Lord will help me see past that. He works in mysterious ways, and we must have faith enough to accept the tasks He unfolds before us. It is hard to understand why He has not seen clear to let me give birth to a pure, unsullied baby girl of my own, but I do not question His ways if He feels my merciful nature is needed to rescue this poor tainted lamb.

You can work it out with James and then write to tell me when it will be best for us to come and get her.

In His Blessed Name.
Your Loving Cousin,

Naomi

Rose stood perfectly still for a minute, the letter clenched taut between her two hands as she stared unseeing at the accusatory stance of Uncle Sam on the War Bonds poster. Then she ripped the pages down the middle and dropped them into the trash barrel like offal as she headed out of the post office. At the door she stopped, stood a moment in deep thought, and then whirled to return to the tall trash barrel she had to tip sideways before she could retrieve the pieces. She jammed them into her handbag without looking at them.

Several weeks passed before she showed the letter to James, before she even took it out of her handbag. One evening, when she was staying a few days to do some extra cleaning, she found James in the kitchen after he'd read Nora Faye the funny papers and put her to bed. The sight of him shaving by the little mirror above the kitchen sink made her think of the letter for some reason, and she felt suddenly convinced that he should read it. She went for her purse and laid the pieces out on the table.

She said, "I tore this letter up when I first got it from my cousin Naomi, but then I decided I'd better think it over. It seems to me now that it'd be the right thing for you to read it."

James grinned when he saw the torn pieces. "What in blue blazes, Ma? You must have been real mad at somebody. I hope it wasn't me." He ran his spectacles under the faucet and wiped them on a corner of his towel before he came to the table.

"Is Naomi the one that sends the Christmas letter asking for money?"

Rose grunted yes.

It took him a while to line the pieces up close enough to make out the words. He stood leaning over the table when he started, but he sat down as he went along, pushing his chair over to get out of his own shadow cast by the dangling bare light bulb. He held the pages at top and bottom to keep the lines straight. Rose sat across from him and watched his face change from good-natured openness to stoniness.

His eyes were blank when he finally looked up at her. "What made you come around to thinking I should read it?"

"I thought it was the right thing to make sure you know the kind of filth she's going to be hearing. It seemed to me like if I was so mortified to see how a body could think that a way, then maybe it was something you hadn't thought about neither."

James went to the sink and began cleaning up his shaving things, wiping the straight razor and returning it with his mug and brush to the shelf well beyond Nora Faye's reach. He emptied the washbasin, rinsed and wiped it out and turned it upside down beside the dishpan on the shelf under the oilcloth-covered wash table, then hung the towel carefully on its nail beside the razor strop.

"I've thought about it some," he finally said, "but I don't know anything to do about it. It's not like we can stop people from thinking the way they're going to think."

"It's the truth that we can't help how people think," Rose responded, "much less what they say, but I feel like we'll do better by her just knowing there's going to be people doing things like this."

"What'll you do about the letter?"

"Not one thing." Rose sounded resolute. "I'll just let her stew. If she writes again, I'll ignore her again. If she gets on her high horse and comes up here, I'll let her make a fool of herself in front of all the kin."

James grinned again. "That's not very Christian of you."

He let his hand rest on her shoulder for a moment as he walked past her chair. Rose blinked at the sudden sting in her eyes.

CHAPTER 17
GARNER AND AVANELL

The flu hit the Penningtons hardest of any family in that end of Platchet County the winter when Rose's little girl had just turned two. One Pennington baby and three adults died. Garner and Avanell, as well as one of Garner's brothers and his wife had been buried before Rose woke from her three-day fevered delirium.

She knew Garner and Avanell were gone the minute consciousness returned. The agonizing crush of emptiness turned her to stone. She could not climb the hill to see their graves. She was unable to get out of bed, unable to move. Her pain must have been something like the pain people feel in an amputated limb, because her entire body felt amputated from what little mentality returned to her existence. Her waking was like waking under water right beneath the surface and not being able to kick her way on up to air. She was not paralyzed, but she was too weak to move. She could not raise a hand to push the quilt off her face, could not crook a finger to pull a strand of wayward hair from her mouth. The family still lifted her and carried her as they had done when she was beyond knowing anything. They propped her up in the Morris chair before the fireplace and tried to spoon little drizzles of anything liquid down her throat, but she could not swallow. She could not speak. She asked no questions. Pain was the only thing she felt. She had not made up her mind to die, but she was unable to do the things required for living.

Later, she could vaguely recall little snatches of time from those weeks with the Penningtons, but for some reason she had no memory whatsoever of the following weeks spent with Jimmy and Tattie.

When the earliest signs of thaw appeared, Garner's mother, Louisa, said, "We've got to give her a new chance before the roads get too muddy for the wagon.

"I never thought I'd see the day when I didn't know how to keep ever' last member of my own family from dying right under my nose, but she's a goner as sure as Garner and Avanell if something don't change right quick. Why don't you take her down to her brother's house and see what happens?"

Rose was told she'd stayed six weeks at Jimmy's place—showing no signs of recovery—so that he'd borrowed the neighbor's wagon and taken her over to their childhood home up Deep Fold in a desperate effort to jog her into rallying. Again, she had no memory of it. She could move about a bit by then, but her mind was still closed and buried. It was as though her heart did not pump her blood; the valves merely hung loose in their bearings to let the blood slosh sluggishly back and forth. Her mam and pap were too old and frail to tend to her. They sent word to Jimmy that he'd find them all three dead by summer if he didn't come and take her back where she could get the care she needed.

Jimmy didn't know what care to give her that they hadn't tried before, and in his deepest heart he was convinced she was beyond help, but he knew he could not stop trying to take care of a family member as long as there was breath in the body, so he went to see the Stensons about borrowing their wagon again—his meager farm rig would have jolted her mercilessly on such a trip—and was pleased to find Mary Stenson's visiting brother, Ben Calper, willing to fetch her for him since he had to make the trip over that way anyhow to see about getting a job at Mr. Bonner's big Sawmill on Bonners Creek.

CHAPTER 18
BEN

Rose's heart began to pump again as Ben tucked her into the wagon for the trip back over to Clive's Branch. She and Ben recognized and loved and trusted one another as quickly and completely as had she and Garner. He took care of her like he had waited all his life for the opportunity, and after he delivered her to Jimmy and Tattie he came every day to their house and urged her outdoors where he would pad the porch swing with pillows and quilts Tattie provided. He sang to Rose and told her stories while the children sat around their feet like puppies positioned to catch sweet crumbs. He made her wreathes of woven grasses and brought bouquets of violets and dandelions and pieces of sassafras root for tea.

His strong, nimble fingers intrigued her when he taught the children how to weave grasshopper swings from long plantain stems and how to stretch a blade of grass along their thumbs and blow on it to make a sound like a clucking hen or crowing rooster.

She had regained much of her strength by the time Mr. Bonner sent word that a job was waiting for Ben as soon as he could get back to the sawmill.

They stopped at the county courthouse to get married on their way to Bonners Creek where they set up a kind of fairytale housekeeping in the open-air quarters Mr. Bonner provided for them up the branch a little piece from the sawmill camp. Having been the sawmill kitchen before a larger one was built down near the mouth of the branch, their living space was actually a screened-in shelter with only a few of the wooden shutters remaining that could be let down from the ceiling on hinges during a rain storm. It was completely out of sight of the rest of the camp and overgrown with honeysuckle vines that served to give almost as much privacy as walls. Nevertheless, they hung bed sheets on wires they strung around their bed in the center of the one big room. At night, after they blew out the lamp, they pushed the sheets aside and lay together in the soft darkness enveloped by whippoorwill song and stump-dirt musk. Falling asleep surrounded by woodland sounds and smells, Rose marveled that she had not only come back to life, but to a life that was as sweet in its own way as her life had been with Garner and Avanell.

Sometimes when a midnight rain on the tin roof drummed them awake, she lay in Ben's arms and mourned for her loss the way she'd not been able to mourn while her heart was still rock hard.

The words she put together to thank Ben for bringing her back to life and the words he murmured to console her were perhaps sweeter than could have come to their tongues if they had lived in a regular house with solid walls and solid doors. It was as though their feelings were shaped into words that were in harmony with the honeysuckle perfume and bullfrog back-song of their little Eden.

They laughingly called their home Honeysuckle Haven. The unstoppable vine her pap had so hated when it came back year after year to encroach on his cornfield could abound here in all it's perfuming glory without causing a problem for anybody. Ben took a charred piece of wood from their campfire and used it like charcoal to write *Honeysuckle Haven* on a little plank he nailed above the door.

He carried their dinner and supper from the dining room at the sawmill camp. Bed and board were part of Mr. Bonner's agreement with his workers, but there were no other wives in the camp that summer, and Rose preferred not to eat among the men unless Mr. Bonner's wife was with them. When Ben's acceptance of the job had weighed on accommodations for a wife, Mr. Bonner readily offered them the old kitchen for their living quarters through the summer. He said he'd find them something more substantial by fall.

The women of the place, Mr. Bonner's wife and sister and daughters, joined the men for breakfast every morning, so Rose would rise with Ben before sunup and walk down the branch with him to eat breakfast at the table with Mr. Bonner and his lady folk, but Ben carried their dinners and suppers to Honeysuckle Haven in a shallow wooden crate they called their tea tray. Stenciled wording showed that dynamite caps had been shipped in the crate, caps to be used, they guessed, in times when a tree stump had to be blasted out of the ground or a logjam had to be broken up in the river.

At first, Rose could name few plants or creatures in their surroundings beyond the redbuds she recognized by sight and the whippoorwills she recognized by sound, but Ben gave her names for things she had taken for granted all her life, and, in the naming, he gave her a curiosity that distracted her from her sorrow. The more species that became familiar to her, the more unknown ones seemed to appear.

Yellow birds became goldfinches and warblers; blue birds became indigo buntings and nuthatches and jays. She learned to distinguish one bird song from another and to distinguish a squirrel's squawk from a blue jay's complaint, a tree frog's chirr from a jar fly's vibration, and the yellow hammer's punctuated slur from the pileated woodpecker's. On the forest floor he taught her to look for the bloodroot's hidden bloom furled in the sheath of its unopened leaf, and the May apple's solitary bloom concealed beneath its leafy parasol. He even gave her names for ferns and lichens—showing her hickory jacks jutting out from dead tree trunks like shelves and fiddleheads of burgeoning ferns, and promising to fry her a mess of both when they got a kitchen of their own. He said the hickory jacks tasted best in the fall, anyway.

She knew the mitten shapes of sassafras leaves—the Penningtons had a sassafras tree in their yard—but Ben taught her the sycamore and yellow poplar, the dogwood, the "sarviceberry," and the different kinds of "bamma gillies"—the shorter evergreen Balm of Gilead and the tall poplar Balm of Gilead—with their sticky, fragrant little flowerlets. One of the Balm of Gilead poplars stood sentinel by the path near their door.

It was not Rose's first encounter with a Balm of Gilead tree. One also grew near Jimmy and Tattie's front door. Tattie wanted it taken down because it was messy, but Jimmy had left it on purpose when he was clearing the lot for their house. He saw it as sort of an omen of good will. Sitting on the front porch on summer evenings when the fragrance wafted faintly about—and Jimmy was out of earshot—Tattie would admit that the sweet "bamma gilly" scent was worth the bit of messiness. Tattie did not make healing salve from the flowerlets like some of the neighbor women made, but she did carry some of the fragrant little buds in her apron pocket to pinch and hold below her nose when there was a bad odor she wanted to cancel out, like the hog-pen stench on warm evenings when the wind was blowing from that direction.

There had been no foreboding on the day Ben was shot. Rose's last sight of him was as he hurried down the path with a boiled potato in one hand and a piece of cornbread in the other. He had brought their dinner as

153

usual in the tea tray crate, but their first kiss had turned into something serious, and the tea tray sat untouched while they fed a different kind of hunger. It was not the first time they had pulled the curtains closed around their bed at midday, but it was the first time the world had gone away so completely that time had ceased to exist.

"Oh, Lordy," Ben gasped when he realized he was hearing the saw whirring through a fog of bliss. "Mr. Bonner will be up here to pull down our little playhouse and pull me down the path by my galluses."

There had been a delirious little flurry of laughing confusion as she poked spoonfuls of pinto beans into his mouth while he hopped around first on one foot and then the other as he pulled on his overalls and boots.

She watched him out of sight and then turned from the doorway and stretched up on her tiptoes to fix her hair in the little mirror Ben had hung above their washbasin on the tree stump stand. After trying to tuck wayward strands in here and there, she decided she'd have to take out all the pins and start over. That's when she heard the gunshot. She was still standing there with hairpins in her mouth and hands in her loose hair when they carried Ben in and laid him on the rumpled bed, pushing the white sheets aside with his body and leaving great trails of red on everything they touched. The air was tinged with the fleeting Balm of Gilead scent. The men who carried him had picked up the sticky buds on their boot soles and crushed them underfoot as they deposited their burden.

Ben's death turned out to be a mistake so groundless it was unfathomable. A man named George Caulder shot him. Mr. Caulder, a recluse known for his peculiar ways, had married late in life—had married a girl some thirty years younger. From the first day of their marriage he had imagined she was slipping around on him. His latest suspicions centered around the sawmill. He'd told some of the neighbor men his wife was making up reasons to walk past the sawmill and that he knew she was slipping around to have secret meetings with one of the sawmill hands. He said he was spying on her to see who she was meeting…so he could take care of him.

As it happened, Mr. Caulder had crouched in the weeds along the riverbank that day watching the sawmill hands through the late morning hours and into their noontime dinner.

But the sawmill crew looked too unlikely for even a twisted mind to imagine any one of them being involved in romantic shenanigans. He knew some of them; they were the leathery, stolid men who had lived up the nearby creeks and hollers since time out of mind. The ones he didn't know—the ones who came from other parts and slept in the bunkhouse below the mill—looked tired or slow or overworked. They ate with little conversation and returned to their work with no furtive glances toward the meandering paths along the river or up the creeks. Mr. Caulder began to think maybe his wife had not found anyone here worthy of her enticements. It must be somewhere else she was managing to have her secret meetings.

He rose to his feet just as Ben came down the path swallowing the last bite of his cornbread and giving his shirttail one last tuck into his overalls. Ben glowed. His eyes glowed. His skin glowed. He wore his thick, black, glossy head of hair like a king wears a crown. He strode the earth like a man whose every desire is being fulfilled.

Mr. Caulder raised his gun and shot him through the heart.

CHAPTER 19
LAURA JANE

"Millard Farris is going to love that crunchy wing," Conner teased while Laura Jane turned the chicken pieces she was frying in their biggest cast iron skillet on box-supper day. "I can just see him now, gnawing off every bite of meat and then sucking the bone." His pantomime annoyed Laura Jane even more than his words.

"Millard Farris won't be eating this wing or anything else from my box," she responded with more conviction than she felt.

"Well, you know the easiest way to make sure that can't happen. I'm going to go in there and take a peek at your box right now so I can tell Oscar Jones what to look for." Laura Jane made a pretend stab at him with the turning fork as he pretended to head for the closed bedroom door.

She wanted Oscar Jones, not Millard Farris, to buy her box. Oscar had been hinting all week about his plans to do it, but she couldn't be sure he was serious, and, even if he was serious, she couldn't be sure he would have the money. The first problem was how to let Oscar know what her box looked like without embarrassing herself. She couldn't think of a better plan than showing it to Conner, but she was going to wait until the last minute. Part of the day's fun was hiding your box in a pillowslip and carrying it up to the schoolhouse amidst threats of ambush. At the schoolhouse, the boxes would be deposited out of sight on a table behind a strung-up bed sheet. The crowd wouldn't get a glimpse until the auctioneer's helper would bring them out one by one.

The bigger fear was that Millard Farris would buy her box. He'd been sweet on her for a long time, and she knew he always had money; he often bought Vienna sausages and crackers—a treat few could afford—for his school lunch at the Carnahan's little store below the schoolhouse.

He had never been known to come to a box supper, but he'd been telling people all week that he thought he'd come this year. Laura Jane said she'd go home without eating if Millard Farris bought her box.

Even Nora Faye had a decorated shoebox to carry up to the schoolhouse. She didn't really need to keep hers hidden—James would bid a quarter for it with no fanfare—but it was fun to pretend everybody's box was shrouded in mystery, not just those of the older girls with sweethearts. The food in her box and Ruthie's and Mrs. Slaney's was going to taste just as good as that in the boxes of Laura Jane and Lottie, which were steeped in genuine secrecy and suspense.

The box supper was a school moneymaking project. The proceeds were used to buy things like colored chalk and construction paper and a sturdy mug for each child to keep on the shelf by the water bucket so nobody would have reason to drink straight from the dipper. But the tradition would have continued even if it brought in no money. The box supper was a social rite, one of the first chances for a young boy to show his preference for a particular girl, and one of the first chances a young girl had to accept the public attention of a boy.

Mrs. Slaney and the girls had spent the morning killing, dressing, and frying chickens, deviling eggs, baking molasses sweet-bread squares, and cutting pickled beet slices into fancy shapes and wrapping them in old, clean dish towels to blot out the juice so the other food wouldn't get red and soggy. The girls got out the waxed bread-loaf wrappers they'd saved all year long for this occasion. They smoothed the pieces even flatter before they used them to wrap each treat separately.

Ruthie had helped Nora Faye paste a sheet of colored Sunday funnies on her shoebox while she made her own box a little fancier with a small scrap of flowered wallpaper. Nobody had seen the boxes Laura Jane and Lottie decorated behind a closed and guarded bedroom door. Mrs. Slaney packed her own dinner in the box she used every year; a red tin fruitcake box with a winter snow scene painted in an oval on the lid. Billy Ray pointed out each year that the Christmas box was inappropriate for spring, but nobody else paid it any attention.

Everything was carefully planned: James would buy Nora Faye's box, Conner would buy Ruthie's, and Billy Ray would buy his Mother's.

Things were not so cut and dry, though, when it came to either of the older girls. Lottie's dilemma was somewhat similar to Laura Jane's. Her sweetheart, Bill Ernst, was going to stop by the house and walk up to the schoolhouse with her. She'd already told him her box would have wide pink and green ribbons and two big purple crepe paper roses and, just to be certain, she'd show it to him before she took it behind the curtain. But her problem had to do with her former sweetheart, Trace Burnham. Trace had threatened he'd be there to outbid Bill. When Billy Ray asked if she'd come back home without eating if Trace bought her box instead of Bill, she told him that wasn't going to happen. She'd been saving her nickels and dimes to add to Bill's stash so Trace couldn't outbid him.

Mr. Slaney gave a quarter each to Billy Ray and Conner while he was making his breakfast on some overflow portions of the box supper fare. "Don't seem right," he teased, "that the man that has to go to work instead of going to the party has to pay twice for the fixings that everybody else gets to enjoy while he's working."

It's not a party," Billy Ray said, "It's a box supper." And then, "How do you mean you'll pay twice?"

"My money paid for it at the store this morning when you were buying it to cook, and then my money will pay for it again when you buy your boxes at the school house."

Billy Ray said, "Nobody paid at the store. Mother charged it like she always does."

Berta turned her face away while Linc explained to Billy Ray for the hundredth time how every penny they charged at the store came out of his wages on payday. The secret understanding about their store account that Berta shared with James Houston was the closest she had ever come to deceiving Linc in all their married years.

James had wanted to talk about money from the first week Nora Faye stayed with her, but she told him what she knew Linc had told him, that neighbors helped each other without any money passing hands. She knew Linc had repeated the sentiment every time James brought it up with him.

But at Christmas time James told her to give him her list so he could pull her items from the Christmas merchandise and keep them in the back of the store for her. That way, the children wouldn't have a chance to find them at home before Christmas morning, he'd said. Linc left things like that up to her, and she didn't mention it to him when she saw that James had not charged the full amount. She did speak to James about it, though.

He said, "I need your help, Berta. You're the only woman in the hollow I can imagine Nora Faye being satisfied with, and probably the only woman I'd want her to spend that much time with. If you won't keep her I'll have to let my ma take her and keep her in town where I won't get to be with her."

"Well, you know I'll keep her all you need, James. For nothing. And you know how it'd hurt Linc's pride if he knew I'd taken your money."

"He'll never give it a thought, Berta. He's always let you handle the account. And it will hurt more than my pride; I just won't be willing to leave her with you if you won't let me pay you a little something. This is a good way for me to do it without anybody ever knowing anything about it but you and me."

Christmas was not the only time she'd seen the charge slips totaling less than the true amount. When she bought new school tablets and pencils last August—and winter socks and galoshes later in the fall—James had charged her account only a fraction of what they cost. She knew he'd put the rest on his own account.

Linc was saying, "I thought you got your eggs and chickens from Draxie Garvens."

Berta was glad for a change of subject. "Oh, she doesn't have enough at box supper time. The commissary even has to bring in extra eggs. And Mr. Williams brings in eggs and fryers just for the box supper. His boy that lives on Cowan Creek makes a special trip to bring them to him from that egg farm down towards Ice. His boy has a truck."

"Well, I'd never thought about that." Linc combed back his hair with his fingers. "I suppose box supper day does reduce the fryer population quite a number."

The trek to the schoolhouse became an impromptu parade, with more and more families joining the crowd as it moved in festive spirits toward the schoolhouse. The girls guarded their pillowcases like bags of gold, but managed to bring attention back to them if the lack of interest carried too far. There were giggles and little chases, pretend peeps into pillow slips, and even a trip-up and spill (without disastrous results) until the excitement reached fever pitch by the time they got to the schoolhouse.

Mr. Harden, the only man teacher, had been drafted last fall, but Mrs. Everhart served as auctioneer, showing a side of herself that her students hadn't seen as she mimicked the cadence of a real auctioneer.

Lottie's box went up to three dollars before Bill outbid Trace. Nobody else had gone higher than two-ten. The boxes had been arranged roughly by age, and those of the older girls had been auctioned off before Laura Jane's box came out. Nobody scolded Billy Ray when he let slip, "Oh, there's Laurie's!" The boxes' owners were seldom a secret by the time they got out to the auctioneer anyway.

Sure enough, Millard Farris jumped right in with his bid after Oscar opened with a quarter for Laura Jane's box. Millard doubled it. The tension built as the two boys inched up nickel by nickel and then dime by dime until they reached two dollars and seventy five cents. Before Mrs. Everhart could finish her next spiel, an unmistakable voice rang out from the back of the crowd, "I bid five dollars on that box!"

It was Donny Stoddard who had joined the crowd as stealthily as he sneaked around the edges of the children's evening games. Laura Jane grabbed her mother's arm and looked like she was going to cry. Even Mrs. Slaney looked panicked.

Millard Farris did something people in the hollow didn't soon forget: he brought his fist out of his pocket and tapped Oscar Jones on the shoulder. Oscar whirled, looking ready to take a swing at him until he saw that Millard was handing his money over to him. The two boys put their heads together over the fistful of coins, and then Oscar yelled "Five dollars and fifty eight cents!"

Immediately, and as calm as could be, Donny said, "Six dollars." He moved closer to the front, closer to Laura Jane, as he made his second bid.

After rummaging frantically through her purse, Mrs. Slaney looked toward Conner who had grabbed the protesting Billy Ray's quarter to put with his own before he hurriedly took the coins Lottie thrust at him on his way to his mother to see how much she had come up with. He then scurried, fists out, to Oscar who, after a quick consultation, jumped in to raise the bid to six seventy-five.

Donny countered with seven dollars.

Oscar went to seven-twenty five.

You could see James Houston's hand down in his pocket blindly and swiftly counting change. He then reached to take his wallet from his back pocket, but before he got it open, there was a shuffling in the crowd and then a parting, as a man came plowing through with head down and hand out. He grabbed Donny by the wrist when he got even with him and pulled him along as he proceeded to Oscar Jones. It was Cad Stoddard. He went straight to Oscar Jones and thrust a bill into the astonished boy's hand.

He said, "This here boy,"—he held up Oscar's hand like a referee holds up a prizefighter's hand—"this here boy bids ten dollars on his sweetheart's box up there, and this other boy I've got my grip on is on his way home with me where he belongs."

CHAPTER 20
BERTA SLANEY

The sun was out now, but it had rained on and off all morning, leaving the grass and the rut lane too wet for play. The children were entertaining themselves on the front porch. They were singing songs they'd learned from the radio and from the movie they'd seen recently when Lottie and her friend Shelby Jean had been allowed to take them into Wolliver on the bus.

Mrs. Slaney was cleaning the bathroom when Nora Faye went inside to use it. She was down on her knees poking a mop in behind the claw-foot tub.

"The children do a pretty good job with their cleaning except for behind the tub," she grunted as she shoved the mop in and out, explaining her actions to Nora Faye as she always did.

Nora Faye baffled her when she asked, "Why don't Callie Bennett clean your bathroom?"

The question left Berta speechless and motionless for a moment. "Why, I've always done my own housework....with the children's help," she finally stammered.

Though usually good at figuring out where Nora Faye's questions came from, she was stumped this time.

"Why would you think Callie would be cleaning my bathroom?"

"My momma said Callie does housework for people that have bathrooms." Nora Faye was busy getting her clothes back together so she could hurry back to the front porch.

Berta was pleased to hear her mention her mother. She seldom did.

The children crammed Nora Faye into one end of the swing when she got back to the porch. They had her and Billy Ray sitting sideways on the ends with their legs sticking through the arms to leave more room for Laura Jane and Ruthie to squeeze into the seat. Conner darted about here and there, pushing the swing or climbing on the banisters or balancing along the rail as he walked faster and faster and then ran from post to post. They had been singing the songs from all the different branches of military service: "Anchors Away" and "From the Halls of Montezuma" and "Off we go into the wild blue yonder, flying high into the sky." Now they had switched from military songs to "Would You Rather Swing on a Star?"

Mrs. Slaney came to the door every now and then to say, "Don't let my curtains get dirty. Stay up here in this end of the porch, Conner. Don't you knock my stretcher over."

Nora Faye had watched her wash the curtains earlier, swishing them by hand in the bathtub. They were the summer curtains for the front room, made of thin silky material you could almost see through. Mrs. Slaney said they weren't really dirty, that she had put them away clean, but that she liked to freshen them before she hung them for the summer. She left them in a little tub after their last rinse water while she put the stretchers together.

"It always feels good to take down those heavy cretonne things and put up the summer organzas," she said. "Makes it seem like spring's just around the corner."

She warned Nora Faye about the needle-sharp pins that went all around the stretcher rack. She showed her how she had to be careful herself as she unfolded the wooden frame and locked it into position with wing nuts.

Her own children weren't interested in what she was doing, having had their curiosity satisfied the many times they'd seen their mother go through the process, maybe even remembering the inevitable pin pricks when they had taken a turn to help her. Her fingers flew like magic attaching a curtain panel first at the four corners, then at a halfway spot on all four sides, then halfway between all those attachments, over and over and over, until every pin was used and the entire curtain was stretched to fit the frame. Then she'd pull another curtain from the tub and put it right on top of the first, going through the same routine until she had layered the four thin curtains she'd washed in this batch.

Nora Faye had been there one day when Mrs. Slaney took dry curtains off the stretchers in great stiff sheets with a little pattern of swoops and points all around the edges, but she'd never watched her while she put wet ones on the stretchers. Mrs. Slaney let her try it, warning her again about the pricks. Sure enough, she got stuck enough to bring blood right away, which ended her involvement. "I'd sure hate to have to take them off and wash them again if you got blood on them," Mrs. Slaney explained when she sent her back to the swing.

The children told her to suck on her finger to make it stop hurting. "Suck on it till there's no more blood," Ruthie instructed. Nora Faye was surprised at how bad such a little pinprick could hurt and at how much blood welled up from it. She followed Ruthie's instructions.

Ruthie was assigning parts to "Would You Rather Swing on a Star?" She told Nora Faye to listen closely when they got to the part that went, "Or would you rather be a...?" She was to wait until Ruthie pointed at her. Everybody else would stop singing, and she would say "fish" while she made a fish face. They all got the giggles when Ruthie pressed a thumb and finger on either side of Nora Faye's mouth to show her how to make the fish face. But, even after they got over their giggle spell, it was hard for Nora Faye to do what Ruthie wanted. Even when it was something that was usually easy for her, she often got confused and embarrassed when Ruthie put her on the spot with all her instructions.

But she followed directions pretty well this time, since the others had a turn before she did. They laughed and shrieked when others missed their turn or sang the wrong words. Mr. Berkindoff came around the corner on his way to buy his daily egg from Mrs. Garvens. He always teased them. He said, "What's going on here? Don't you children know there's a law against laughing like that on Tuesdays?"

Billy Ray said, "It's not Tuesday. It's Wednesday."

Mr. Berkindoff said, "That makes it even worse then, when you break a Tuesday law on Wednesday." He went on past their yard chuckling to himself as they took up their song again.

Ruthie had assigned parts to "Don't Fence Me In," now, and they had all turned backwards on their knees in the swing. Conner had dropped off the far end of the porch and was watching something in the grass. They were intently listening for their cues when there was a noise behind them, a dog's hurt yelp. They whirled to see Donny Stoddard's dog jumping on their mother's curtains.

Berta knew exactly what had happened when she heard the commotion, and she came running out the screen door looking just about as mad as Nora Faye had ever seen her.

She scolded the children first. They froze as they were, hanging onto the back of the swing, their backs turned to her with their heads twisted around to look at her. "Didn't you see him before he got to my curtains?" There was a muddy paw print on one corner, and a mixture of mud and blood along the edge. The dog had pricked his paw. He went yelping off the porch and down the steps.

Berta was needlessly shooing him off as she yelled at them. Then she called to Donny. "You need to come out right now, Donny Stoddard!"

Donny, to the great surprise of the children, slunk around from the far side of the house instead of disappearing. Berta's wrath even willed him up a step or two as she admonished him, "This is the second time this week I've asked you not to let your dog come in the yard, Donnie. He always makes a mess. He chewed up the girls' doll buggy a few days ago and the porch rug last week. If you're going to have him with you, you need to get a rope and keep him tied. I don't ever want to see him let loose in this yard again."

She was remorseful as she told Linc about it later. " I shouldn't have scolded him like that. He's just a child. But I tell you, it's hard to think of him that way when he seems to set out to cause trouble.

"I guess that's why I hate how I talked to him this time. He really wasn't doing anything on purpose this once. His dog was the culprit...unless he's trained it to cause mischief."

They laughed a strained little laugh, thinking how Donny was the source of most of the discord in the community and how helpless they felt to do anything about it.

"Actually, that dog is seldom with him. It seems to live a life of its own, and I don't reckon he had anything to do with it coming on the porch. But it is his dog and it's his responsibility to keep it out of people's yards, no matter what he has to do to bring that about," she finished weakly.

CHAPTER 21
CONNER

Nora Faye played near Conner's shop while she waited for Mrs. Slaney to come out to hang the wash. Mrs. Slaney surprised her by coming to a stop on the top step and standing there holding the screen door wide open with her elbow. She seemed to forget she was letting in flies and clutching a tub full of heavy wet wash as she put her face up toward the sky with her eyes half closed.

"What is so rare as a day in June?" she asked.

Then she looked at Nora Faye and laughed. "I don't remember which poet wrote that," she said, "but it must have been about a day like this. Just look at that blue sky." She came down the steps and balanced the tub on her hip while she adjusted the prop to make the clothesline a little higher. "Don't want these sheets to drag," she said.

But a moment or two went by before she started hanging her wash. She put her face up into the sunshine again, saying, "Sometimes I wish it could stay June twelve months of the year."

Nora Faye said, "My birthday's in January. I'll be six in January."

"I know you will. And Conner has a birthday this month. He'll be twelve next week." She set the tub down under the clothesline and started hanging towels and pillowslips, shaking out each piece with a crack before she fastened it to the line.

"These ought to dry fast in this little breeze," she said, "whether it blows from east or west."

Nora Faye said, "The Easter bunny hid my basket under the table this year."

Mrs. Slaney paused and studied for a moment and then laughed. "Sometimes it takes me a minute to figure how your mind's going, Nora Faye, but, you're right, I did say 'east or...' "

The Slaney children were scattered this morning. After they helped their mother fill the washing machine and rinse-tubs they'd gone off in several directions. Laura Jane and Ruthie had gone up the holler to swap books with a Baker girl who lived by the schoolhouse. Lottie had gone home with Shelby Jean Harden, Mrs. Slaney had let Billy Ray go down the road with Jack Pollard to play marbles with the Wooten boys, and Conner was on the hill across the branch playing war with Sonny Patterson and Enoch Oldfield in the flat. Nora Faye could hear their voices but she couldn't tell what they were saying except for an occasional shout of "Rat-tat-tat!" or "You're dead, you Nazi!"

She saw Mrs. Garvens next door come out to feed the breakfast scraps to her chickens. Nora Faye hung onto the wire fence for a while watching the chickens peck among the gravel. She tested out how it would feel to be a chicken, tucking her hands into her armpits and leaning forward while she walked on her toes.

Granny Rose said Mrs. Garvens took good care of her chickens but let her children run wild. She let her older girls go up and down the road shouting and quarreling with each other and let her boys smoke cigarettes they rolled and licked closed. Her babies sometimes ran out into the yard without a stitch of clothes on.

Granny Rose never had much to say to Mrs. Garvens, but Mrs. Slaney always talked to her just like she talked to all the neighbors. She called to her now. "Isn't this a beautiful day, Draxie?"

Mrs. Garvens said, "Right purty, I reckon, if a body had time to stand around looking at the sky." She was lacing a length of rusty wire back and forth through the chicken yard fence to mend a hole.

Nora Faye went back to the bare spot in front of Conner's shop. She picked up some smooth stones and began to arrange them into a circle. Then she suddenly thought of something she could make for Conner. She gathered sticks and twigs and started fixing them like the campfire picture in her daddy's Boy Scout Handbook with the twigs for kindling and the bigger sticks for firewood. She knew Conner would recognize what it was. The little teepee of sticks quickly took shape inside the ring of stones.

A sudden loud cracking sound rang out. The chickens squawked and flapped their wings. At first Nora Faye thought Mrs. Slaney had made the noise shaking out her wash, but this sound was different, sharper and clearer but farther away. A movement on the hillside caught her eye. Someone came out of one of the upper houses and ran up toward the flat. Another person popped out of another house and scurried up the hill. One figure ran back toward the houses and a smaller one ran to the Patterson's back yard. The entire hillside took on the look of Uncle Jimmy's mechanical clock with tiny figures that came out the door and jerked around in little circles before popping back inside. For a moment Nora Faye almost laughed. Then a second later she knew something terrible had happened, though she didn't know what. There were shouts and people running now from all directions toward one destination.

Mrs. Slaney's face jerked toward the flat. She made a strange noise and stumbled over her clothespin basket as she lurched forward. Then without taking her eyes off the hillside she came back and picked up Nora Faye. Never looking in her direction she took her straight to the fence and lifted her up to Mrs. Garvens who now stood on the other side saying, "Berta? Berta?"

Nora Faye's foot caught on the fence. Her shoe pulled off and dropped on Mrs. Slaney's side. She didn't think Granny Rose would want her to stay at Mrs. Garvens' house, but that quickly proved not to be a problem. Mrs. Garvens accepted her but, like Mrs. Slaney, she didn't look at her. She set her down and ran to the back gate and out into the rut lane, saying over and over, "Berta? What is it, Berta?"

Nora Faye thought she could reach her shoe through the fence. She got down on her knees and then lay on her stomach to stretch her arm through as far as she could, but it wasn't far enough. She followed Mrs. Garvens out the gate into the rut lane. She thought she'd go in Mrs. Slaney's back gate to get her shoe. A staggered stream of people came hurrying from the commissary now, and strangely silent bystanders appeared on porches and in both the main road and the side road. They all looked dazed. She saw Mrs. Slaney run right through the creek with her shoes on and go straight on up the hill not even looking for the path, grabbing at grass clumps to pull herself upward.

Mr. Slaney burst out of the screen door wearing just one shoe with its tongue bouncing up and down under loose laces. He half hopped down the steps while he pulled the other shoe onto his bare foot. He was in his undershirt. His belt ends slapped around unbuckled and his hair hung in his eyes. Several people ran to him and took his arms while they leaned around into his face to talk to him, but he never stopped, shaking them off and going through the creek and up the hill exactly the same as Mrs. Slaney.

Callie took to the hill from the Patterson's back yard and then disappeared where the flat leveled out. Nora Faye could tell it was Callie because of the overalls. She looked for Seelom and knew he must be across the road when she didn't see him tethered at the Patterson's gate.

Suddenly she saw her daddy in the delivery truck. She forgot about the cinders hurting her foot and started toward him, but he didn't look her way. He drove the truck through the shallow part of the branch where the Slaneys had crossed. Then, in fast, jerky motions, he turned it around with the nose pointing back into the creek. Rollie jumped out before the truck got turned, and then her daddy jumped out and joined Rollie and the others rushing up the hill.

Jack Ballard's mother came running toward Nora Faye. When she met Mrs. Garvens she said, "I'm getting Nora Faye, Draxie. James asked me to get her."

But Mrs. Garvens didn't act like she heard. She just kept staring straight ahead, saying, "What is it? What happened? Did somebody get shot?"

Mrs. Ballard scooped up Nora Faye and said, "Your daddy told me to take you to my house. Somebody got hurt up at the flat, and your daddy's going to drive them to the hospital in Bascon. He told me to take care of you."

Nora Faye said, "My choo got losted," but Mrs. Ballard acted like she hadn't heard. She wasn't looking at her.

Mrs. Ballard's girls met them on the porch, wide-eyed and out of breath. "It was Donny Stoddard, Mommy," Gwinny gasped. "He shot Conner. We were over there with Lorraine when he did it."

Mrs. Ballard clutched Nora Faye so tight it hurt. "Lord-a-mercy!" she gasped. "You mean he told you what he did?"

"No. He said he was shootin' at a target, but Lorraine told him he was going to burn in hell. She said, 'You shot him on purpose and you know good and well you told me you was a gonna do it.'"

Mrs. Ballard set Nora Faye down on the porch. She said, "Gwinny, you take care of Nora Faye. Doris Ann, you go find Jack and bring him home. Bring Billy Ray, too. I've got to go tell somebody what Donny's sister said."

But she suddenly leaned down in front of Nora Faye and looked into her eyes the way nobody had looked at her from the time this all started. She looked like she was about to cry. "What a good little girl you are," she said, stroking Nora Faye's shoulder. "You never cause nobody no trouble. How she could have left you is more than I can understand."

Nora Faye wondered if she meant Mrs. Slaney or Mrs. Garvens. She said, "My choo comed off." But Mrs. Ballard was already rushing away toward the commissary.

It was some weeks later when Granny Rose picked up the odd shoe and said what a shame the other got lost. Nora Faye said, "I know where it falled."

Granny Rose walked over to the Slaney's back gate with her. The house had been sitting empty and silent since shortly after the funeral. They had taken her to see Conner in his casket in the Slaney's front room. It didn't seem like him. He had on a white shirt and white pants. She'd never seen him wear clothes like that. But what she couldn't forget were his feet. He wore no shoes, and his white socks looked silky and almost as thin as women's dress-up stockings.

Granny Rose stood just inside the gate now, and Nora Faye, all by herself, almost tiptoed toward the fence, stumbling a time or two on scattered, darkened clothespins. She saw her shoe right away. It lay on its side exactly where it was lying when she had tried to reach it from Mrs. Garvens' side of the fence.

Something else was just the same: the campfire she'd made for Conner. The stones were still in an unbroken ring, and the sticks had not fallen. She wondered if Conner had liked it.

And then she realized Conner had never seen it.

For the rest of her life, news of any death brought a fleeting vision of a campfire laid out and unseen. From that summer's early June days she carried, in fact, four images that could make her heart plummet: the perfect unlit campfire sitting un-received; Mrs. Slaney's feet taking great long strides through the creek in their lace-up, sturdy-heeled shoes with stockings rolled down on their garters to just above her ankles; her daddy speeding past in the truck without looking her way; and Conner's feet in silky white anklets.

She picked up her shoe and carried it back to Granny Rose, making a wide sweep out into the grass around the packed bare earth in front of Conner's shop.

As it turned out, her feet had grown since the one shoe dropped on the wrong side of the fence. The shoes were too little. She never wore them again.

CHAPTER 22
DEMPSEY GARVENS

Dempsey Garvens suddenly appeared in Nora Faye's back yard one day while she sat on her wooden crate horse. "I've been a wondering what you fellers wuz a doing back here all the time." He nodded in the direction of Mrs. Bledso who was sitting on her back steps peeling apples to fry. Mrs. Bledso didn't acknowledge Dempsey, but she never let him out of the corner of her eye. Nora Faye was thinking that her granny would probably have told Dempsey to go on home, but she'd never really had to do that because he'd never come in the yard when she was there.

"I don't see why you'd sit on this old wooden thing when Callie Bennett said you could sit on her horse." That kind of revelation—almost any time she saw him— showed Nora Faye that Dempsey knew most everything that went on in the holler, though he didn't seem to be around a lot.

"She won't let me get near him. I didn't do nothing to him; she's just done gone and made up her mind that he wouldn't like me." He took hold of the crate with two hands and gave it a good firm jerk as though to test its sturdiness. In spite of the suddenness of his gesture, Nora Faye was not dislodged, and she hung almost limp so she wouldn't be bumped off in case he gave the crate another shake. She wasn't afraid of Dempsey, but she realized you could never know what he was going to do next.

He took a wad of something from the bib pocket of his overalls and pinched off a little piece that he tucked into his cheek with two fingers. "Don't reckon you'd be wanting a piece of this?" he obliquely offered.

She was surprised to see him chewing tobacco. Any time she'd caught sight of him through the summer he was smoking cigarettes he rolled by hand. He would take great pains to extract a single paper from a tiny folder-like packet and arrange it just so along two extended fingers before he took the cloth bag of loose tobacco from his bib pocket with his other grubby hand. The papers reminded Nora Faye of the air-mail stationary the Slaney children used when they wrote to R. L.. Dempsey would tug the bag open with his teeth and carefully sprinkle a line of tobacco along the paper. Then he'd take the little yellow string in his teeth to pull the bag closed before he stuffed it back into his bib pocket and rolled the cigarette, licked it closed, and twisted the ends to keep the tobacco in. Sometimes it took him several tries before he got it lit with one of the kitchen matches he carried loose in his pocket and struck on a rock or the side of a house or anything rough and dry. One time, when he was wearing shoes, she had seen him bend one leg up behind him and try to strike the match on the sole of his shoe, which appeared to be two or three sizes too big. She'd heard it said that the Garvens children never had individual clothes or shoes of their own, that they each grabbed whatever they could lay hands on at the moment, whether it was a fit or not.

Dempsey's cigarette smoking was an example of the kind of thing that made Granny Rose hold Draxie and Arthur Garvens in low esteem. "They'd have to be no-count, sorry people to let a child get away with that kind of shenanigans," she said.

James said Mr. Garvens had a reputation as a capable, dependable worker who was given important responsibilities on the job, but Rose said it took more than being a good tipple foreman to be a respectable family man. "It just don't show good sense to let a child act like a little heathen," she added.

James said at least you couldn't call Mrs. Garvens shiftless, the way she raised chickens and cracked walnuts to bring in extra money for the family, but Rose said that just showed she didn't know how to manage her man's pay. "You know Arthur Garvens draws a bigger salary for working at the tipple than a man gets that goes down in the mines, but she just lets her children squander what he makes on things like candy and soft drinks and tobacco.

"If she knew how to manage, she wouldn't need to sell eggs and such. With her man's good wages, they are living like people that don't know where their next penny is coming from." When Granny got started on the Garvenses, she took a long time to run down.

She went on to say she wondered why Arthur Garvens had married a woman like Draxie anyway. "People say his family were educated people that use to own a big farm down in the foothills that was like the old-time plantations, but that Draxie's people were no more than gypsy stock that traveled around knocking on doors to ask about sharpening people's knives and scissors."

James said, "Oh, well, didn't your sources tell you that Draxie was a great beauty when she was young?"

It was impossible for Nora Faye to imagine that Mrs. Garvens had ever been presentable, much less beautiful. She was sloppy-fat and dirty looking, with gray-streaked, tangled hair she let hang long and loose. Granny Rose said she could make herself look a hundred percent better just by putting her hair up in braids or a knot. She said nothing did more to make a woman look like an old hag than frowsy gray hair hanging loose, whether it was short or long, whether she was old or young.

Nora Faye said young people don't have gray hair, but Rose said some do, when they have a great fright. She said she once knew of a young woman who turned white headed overnight when there was a flash flood that picked her house up and moved it to the other side of the bottom before she could get out of bed and get to her baby's cradle.

Dempsey was Nora Faye's age, but she'd seen very little of him in school. The Garvens children laid out of school as much as Donny Stoddard, but they didn't run with Donny—nobody ran with Donny—nor did they hang around the big bridge at the mouth of the hollow like some of the older boys who played hooky. No one seemed to know exactly what they did to fill their days, but it was generally thought they spent a lot of time with the Caldwell boys, playing poker and shooting craps for money and pitching pennies and playing mumblety-peg and marbles for keeps.

The four Caldwell brothers lived in one of the little camp houses on the very highest row. Their daddy worked in the mines, and there had been no mother with them when they moved to Dillard from Leatherwood. A path through the woods above their house led across the hill to the head of Sams Branch, and people said the Garvenses and the Caldwells went over the hill to Sams Branch almost every day, though why anyone would rather spend their time on the head of Sams Branch instead of on Dillard was hard to figure out. Somebody said the Caldwells had some cousins over on Sams. Nora Faye heard the children at school say the older Garvens and Caldwell boys laid out in a rough log cabin they had built out of saplings near the path that went through the woods.

Dempsey and his brothers had lice last winter and had shaved their heads to get rid of them. Other boys whose heads were shaved for that reason were sometimes so ashamed that they stayed home or wore hats until their hair grew out. But the Garvenses seemed to like theirs that way, and the Caldwell boys shaved theirs, either to be like the Garvenses or because they too had lice. Nora Faye imagined the bunch of them spending a lot of time in their log cabin shaving each others' heads.

As she watched Dempsey twist his jaw around to give his chaw a good start, she said, "I thought you smoked cigarettes."

"Too much trouble," he said. "Too much truck to tote around when you're making quirleys. Hain't hardly no trouble to pinch me off a little piece of this chaw."

"But, let me warn you," he went on, "that you don't never want to take a pinch of t'other kind. This hearn's store-bought, and they mix in a tetch of things that's sweet and juicy. Don't you never take no chaw off a hand-rolled quid—if you was ever offered again and if you was to decide you want to try it—cause that stuff'll make you sicker'n a dog.

"I don't hardly never get sick, but, I'll tell you, when I took a chaw offa one of them things made of rolled-up leaves—they look like a big long cigar that's been looped around and plaited together like a girl's hair—I puked for the whole day. You want to check and make sure it's this kinda squeezed down, square-like, flat-looking kind if you's offered a chaw and if you was to change your mind about taking it."

Nora Faye knew that if Billy Ray were with them, he would have told Dempsey that you're not supposed to say puke, that you're supposed to say you threw up.

Dempsey held out the visual aid, turning it to highlight all sides as he delivered his little lecture, and giving the corners a pinch in an effort to square them up again before he returned it to his bib pocket and fastened it in with the shanked copper colored button.

But he didn't give himself time to work up a good spit before he motioned toward the back of the house. "I done seen you cracking hick'ry nuts there under your house. I wouldn't mind cracking me a few if you've got some of 'em to spare. We cracked so many black walnuts that Mommy says my paws are black for life,"—he held up his stained hands—"but I didn't have no hick'ry nuts this winter."

Nora Faye felt herself sliding from the lathes and drifting with him over to the high place under the back of the house where a peck size basket about a quarter way full of hickory nuts sat beside the chopping-block they used for cracking nuts. He leaned sideways and spat out the chew of tobacco before he grabbed a handful of nuts and one of the cracking stones.

Mrs. Bledso was beside them before he'd dug out the kernels from his first nut with the tip of his pocket knife. She said, "Nora Faye has to stay where I can see her while she plays, Dempsey. If you want to play with her you have to stay where I can see."

Nora Faye said, "You can take some nuts with you. We've got plenty. You can fill your pockets."

And he did. He filled every pocket except the one on his bib, and turned with the manners of a courtly gentleman to say, "I'm right thankful to you. I'd been a hankering fer a taste of hick'ry nut. I don't have nothing against a black walnut—and they do bring us in a pretty penny for our trouble—but they's something that makes you start wanting a hick'ry nut if you hain't had your fill fer a while." He included Mrs. Bledso in these remarks, and she nodded in return and didn't tell him to stop filling his pockets. She said she'd bought a jar of walnuts his family had cracked and had made a cake with them last winter.

Dempsey probably didn't hear her last remarks. He had disappeared as suddenly as he had appeared.

Nora Faye wondered why he'd had no hickory nuts last winter; she and James had found plenty in the fall. Maybe he meant he wasn't allowed to eat them. Maybe he had to put all the hickory nuts he cracked into the jars to sell.

After he left, Mrs. Bledso said they might have been rash. "I guess we should have asked your daddy before we let him take the nuts." But Nora Faye said the nuts were hers and that she was sure her daddy didn't care who she gave them to. Mrs. Bledso used a stick to roll Dempsey's discarded chaw over to the edge of the soft dirt in the crysanthemum bed. She gouged out a hole and buried it.

A week or two passed before Nora Faye saw Dempsey again. He came running through her yard to her back fence to get a better look at a handcar coming up the tracks. Nora Faye had seen the cars before. Her daddy had explained that the men pumping the car were inspecting the rails and ties to see where repairs were needed. Sometimes they stopped the car and made a repair right then and there. One of the workers today was a colored man, and she was thinking about that, but she had not mentioned it to Dempsey. It was as though he read her mind, though.

"Theys teeth ain't really whiter than ourn. It's because Negros' skin is dark that theys teeth look so white." That was exactly what Nora Faye was thinking about.

Dempsey went on. "I bet you think I said something bad when I said *Negro*." He drew out the first syllable and did not sound the last vowel sound like "A," making the word *Nee-grow*.

"I bet you say 'colored' and that your people tell you it ain't right to say *Negro* or *Niggra*. But they's okay to say. It's that other word like that that ain't right.

"My poppy's people call them darkies, but it's probably better to say *Negros* than darkies. But people just keep saying colored, or that bad word if they's bad people. Mommy won't let us say that bad word."

Nora Faye thought she must remember to tell Granny Rose that Mrs. Garvens did have at least one rule. Her granny thought she had none.

But Granny Rose was right about Mrs. Garvens' children doing what they wanted to do without asking permission. When Dempsey saw that the men from the handcar were engaged in a job and might be stopped for a while, he did not go home to ask his mother before he started trying to figure out which way he should go to get a closer look. The handcars had an ephemeral way of disappearing before your eyes, so she could understand why Dempsey was afraid to trust that it would stay put long enough for him to get to it. He said, "I reckon your pap wouldn't want me to be climbing his fence here?"

Nora Faye's expression showed him that he had guessed right. The back fence was a flimsy wire fence that James took great pains to keep looking presentable.

Dempsey thought out loud while he tried to decide which direction would give him a better chance of getting close to the car if it should make a sudden move one way or the other. If he went down to the store bridge to cross the creek he'd have time to catch a glimpse even if they suddenly headed right back the way they came, but if they went on up to the tipple, that would increase the distance he'd have to go to catch up with them—and the workers at the tipple would shoo him off. If they were to head to the tipple he could intercept them at the little trestle if he went up the holler instead of down, but he'd lose them altogether if they went back out of the holler instead of to the tipple.

He decided on the store bridge, and in a twinkling he disappeared from Nora Faye's side and then reappeared at the handcar across the creek, immediately engaging the men in one of his one-sided conversations. He was too far away to hear, but she could guess his words as she saw him unbutton his bib pocket and take out the wad that he offered to the men. One of the men accepted the offer. She could see that Dempsey never stopped talking.

The hickory nuts truly belonged to Nora Faye. She had gathered them herself when her dad took her walking in the woods last fall. James hunted out two burlap bags one gorgeous day, saying he guessed it wasn't too late to find some nuts, and they went down to cross the creek on the store bridge and then double back on the tracks to the ravine beside the old tipple where a faint path went up the point. She knew they would swing around above the overgrown, closed-off drift-mouth and the slate dumps and slag heaps, and into a stand of hardwoods that covered the peaks and dips above the old mines. Then they'd follow the ridge in its natural arc way back of Mr. Williams' farm to come out beside the new tipple and down another ravine there.

Rollie had seen them as they went by his house, and he caught up with them before they left the tracks. By the time they were halfway up the ascent, Jack Ballard and the Wooton boys had hurried to join them, sacks in hand. People liked to walk in the woods with James. It wasn't just that he knew things like which trees were likely to have plenty of nuts in a certain year and how to find trees where squirrels were likely to be cutting, but he knew which areas to avoid to make sure not to stumble onto a moonshine still, and he knew interesting tales about every stand of trees and every fork of a path. His dad had trudged him over many a path in the mid-eastern part of the county, and what he hadn't taken him over, he had told him about. Being in the woods gave James such pleasure that people with him felt happy, too.

He said this day was one that no sane and able person could bear to spend inside a house, and their companions agreed with him. The cloudless sky was as blue as a robin's egg. Goldenrod lined the ditch along the railroad tracks and skipped over the hillside flats, leaping like yellow flames when the sun hit it just right. The sumacs on the hillsides were scarlet, and the maples, where they

183

grew on the summit in a stand, were glowing like great golden walls. The boys raced on ahead, and James and Rollie kept up a steady pace while they talked about the war and baseball teams and such. Nora Faye trailed behind just close enough for James to see her whenever he looked back. He'd told Nora Faye he'd let her gather all the hickory nuts. He said she didn't need to pick up any walnuts, since their hulls left stains on clothes and skin.

He had a system for the walnuts. He kept a big castoff bay door at the loading dock to put under his tires when the creek side was muddy enough that he'd be likely to get stuck. He would take the walnuts over to the store and scatter them out where the ground was hard as asphalt. He'd lay the door on top of the nuts and run the truck over the door a time or two to squeeze the hulls off. He knew how to manage things just right so that it took the hulls off but didn't crack the nuts and didn't embed them in the ground.

The walnuts were messy, but they gave up their kernels with less effort than the hickory nuts. It took a lot of careful work to crack the hickory nuts just right. Maybe the Garvenses didn't fool with them because of that. They were small and hard, and the kernels were difficult to get out in big pieces. But the taste was worth it. She'd hate to think of trying to crack enough to sell. Mrs. Bledso had told her how the Garvens family sat around the fireplace every winter evening cracking nuts, picking them out with hairpins, and putting them in canning jars to sell. Used to be, they had to go door to door or hang out at the polling places on election day to sell their nuts, but Mrs. Bledso said people now came to their door to buy their nuts quicker than they could crack them. Nora Faye thought the people were buying eggs and had wondered why they carried jars.

She was thinking about all these things as she fell farther and farther behind her daddy. They were high on the hillside now on an almost straight stretch where she was still in sight of James in spite of the distance, so he hadn't told her to step it up.

But then he and Rollie rounded a curve so far away she could no longer hear their voices. She felt more alone than she'd ever felt, but she wasn't scared. She wanted to prolong the feeling. She came to a stop and stood there drinking in the smell of drying leaves, rabbit sage, mushrooms and dark, rich earth. Then something told her to look behind her. She turned. A red fox several yards away froze where he was crossing the path. He was just a heartbeat from motion. One dainty front paw was still raised, and his bushy tail was in the middle of a swish. He seemed almost to be levitating. She was reminded of the game they played where they slung one another around and had to freeze like statues when they were released. He looked into her face and she into his. And then he let his tail complete its swish and continued on his way.

She heard her daddy calling and heard his hurried footfalls as he came back to get her. Like a flash she thought of the hubbub she'd cause if she told about the fox. The boys would want to chase it down, and her daddy and Rollie would ask questions about its size and color and the direction it went. And they'd want to know how she knew it was a fox and not a dog. She didn't know how she knew, but she knew it was a fox.

She decided not to say a word. It was the first time, when there was nothing unpleasant involved, that she had ever purposely failed to share a moment of her life with her daddy. If it had been just the two of them she would have told him. But now she knew she'd never tell him, because the feeling would lose something if she told about it later. Her daddy would look hurt because she hadn't told him immediately, or maybe even puzzled and confused, as though not telling right away meant something was wrong with her…or with him. She put all these thoughts behind her and wrapped herself around the quiet, brief joy of the encounter. It was hers and hers alone. She swallowed down the new sensation and stepped up her pace to meet her dad halfway.

CHAPTER 23
STELLA

Stella never dreamed there was any reason not to promise her girls she would let them go to Bible Camp when they were old enough. Camps were held on the River Assembly Campgrounds eight or ten miles down the river from Wolliver where there had been a lumber camp, then a short-lived temporary CCC Camp, and finally a church camp where various churches held week-long revival assemblies in the summer. Stella called the churches that conducted the campground revivals freewill churches, and she dismissed them without much comment.

But then, the three largest churches in Bascon, the Missionary Baptist, the Methodist, and the Presbyterian—churches that generally held Stella's respect—went together and bought the property with plans for shared use of the grounds. The first summer, each denomination took a turn conducting a week-long Bible camp, but low attendance for each camp made it seem advisable to combine the camps into one. Now that her girls were old enough that she might let them go, Stella accepted an invitation to serve on the planning committee.

As the concept of a combined camp was explored in their first meeting, Stella began to look uncomfortable. Reverend Filmore, the Methodist minister who had come up with the plan, explained that the first day of camp would be devoted to an all-around introduction to the format, designed to let the children get an idea of how their neighbors worshiped and how it compared to their way. Then each of the three denominations would have a day to teach about the tenets of their particular church, with Friday a concluding day for bringing the week's lessons together. He drew diagrams on the portable chalkboard where they were gathered in the church basement.

Pastor Richards, of the Presbyterian Church, went on to explain how there would be classes during the morning sessions to introduce the beliefs of the particular church under study, and then in the evening there would be a service like a Sunday morning church service with the children invited to take full part.

Stella straightened on the rickety folding chair and said, "Excuse my interruption, but do I understand you to mean that a child would be allowed to take communion with a church it was not a member of?"

"We had hoped to give the children that opportunity, Mrs. Houston." Pastor Richards responded, and then referred her to Brother Crider, since he knew Stella was a Baptist. "That would come under the plan we discussed, wouldn't it, Brother Crider?"

Brother Crider agreed, saying that the idea was for the children to get a feeling for the entire scope of the denomination under exploration for that day. He stumbled over the chalkboard leg as he positioned himself in front of Reverend Filmore's diagrams and swung an arm vaguely in their direction. "We know this will be something that's not been done before, Sister Stella, but it seemed to us like the children will get a better idea of how their neighbors worship if they actually participate, rather than just hear the procedures described."

Stella's voice sounded like she was barely managing to keep it under control. "You mean the children would be encouraged to pretend-play that they were a member of a church?"

When no one made an answer, she went on. "The sacraments are very serious things that follow a certain order. People first undergo salvation by taking the Lord Jesus Christ into their hearts, then they get baptized to show they have accepted the Lord as their personal savior, and only then do they go on to take part in various sacraments, such as taking communion, as an opportunity for a show of brotherhood with people who believe the same way they do, don't you agree?"

Reverend Filmore responded. "No one would disagree with you, Mrs. Houston, but, the purpose of the camp will be to give an opportunity for the children to get an overall picture of what each church is like. On those three days, the churches will present their unique qualities, and then on the final day, the emphasis will be on the things our three churches have in common, on the ultimate message that makes us all brothers in Christ."

Ennis Butcher, a Baptist who was a clerk at the freight yard, spoke up. "Sister Houston does have a point. It seems we might be teaching the children not to take salvation seriously if we have them taking part in a sacrament before they actually make a profession of faith."

"You surely can't mean they'll be baptized for pretend?" Hilda Strothers sounded distraught, but her question was ignored as someone else chimed in with, "Is that, then, the theme for the week, Brothers in Christ?"

And before anyone could respond to that question, Anna Louise Pierce, who had kept secretarial records for the Methodist church since time out of mind, looked up from the pad where she was taking notes to ask, "Doesn't common sense tell us that little children aren't ready for theological considerations?"

Ennis said, "I think the idea could work if we stick to Sunday School lessons for both the daytime and the evening meetings and leave the Church service procedures out of it altogether, don't you, Sister Houston?" But when they turned to Stella, she was gone.

No one had seen her when she tiptoed quietly out of the meeting. To the surprise of those who knew her, Stella did not say much about it later. In the past, she had been known to take an opportunity like this to make a point of her beliefs. She did not send her girls to camp, and she did say she felt Brother Crider had engaged in blasphemy. For several months she did not go to church nor let Dollie and Bootsie go to Sunday School. But, when they moved to Johnston, she began sending the girls to Sunday School again, and eventually she returned to church.

She went to the Methodist Church in Johnston a time or two before she started in at the Baptist church, and she told Rose she'd just as soon be a Methodist if it weren't that they sprinkled instead of baptizing. "A lot of things the Methodists do are an improvement over our way: the way a new preacher is appointed, for instance," she said. "Their method cuts down on all that politicking and self-important infighting we have when it's time to appoint a committee to chose a new preacher, but I can't see how anyone able to read the Bible can think that baptism means a few sprinkled drops of water."

The baptism topic had not become an issue in their house until one day when Dollie and Nora Faye were playing church-service with their paper dolls, and Dollie was having her dolls get sprinkled instead of baptized. When Stella asked her about it, Dollie said they were Methodists.

Stella said, "Make them Baptists."

Dollie said she didn't have anything to baptize them in, and that, anyway, getting sprinkled was the same thing as getting baptized. She said Betsey Bowers said it was just two ways to do the same thing.

Stella told her that wasn't true, going so far as to get the Bible. She pulled out her sewing machine stool to sit on and started to read the parts of the Bible that had to do with immersion. Dollie didn't look up. She went on moving her paper dolls about as she silently mouthed their conversations. Nora Faye was afraid Dollie was getting herself into real trouble.

But Stella just suddenly closed the Bible, reaching behind her at the same moment to take out one of the long, narrow sewing machine drawers, and, to the astonishment of Dollie and Nora Faye, dumping the bobbins and spools of thread and special foots and pin cushions and scissors and measuring tapes into the top of the paper doll box and thrusting the drawer at Dollie saying, "Here, this will make a good baptismal pool for your dolls."

Dollie asked, "With real water?" Stella just looked at her out of the tops of her eyes with her nostrils flared and her mouth skewed sideways, the way she did when she'd had enough.

Even though the planning committee had ruled out the Lord's Supper and the enactment of baptisms and sprinklings, the general opinion of the community was that the "Brothers in Christ" camp had not been successful that summer. To her credit, Stella did not say I told you so. Neither did she take part in the newly formed planning committee that drew up a brand new format for the third summer's camp. The three churches would work together once again, but this time there would be no mention of the particular tenets of any of the three churches. The emphasis all week long would be on what the three churches held in common, on the shared message of Christian salvation.

Nevertheless, everybody who knew Stella was surprised that she was planning to let Dollie and Bootsie attend the camp. After they moved to Johnston, Stella had become friends with Roslyn Bowers, the wife of Johnston's Methodist minister. People could only guess that her friendship with Roslyn had led her to a new tolerance for other people's beliefs and had helped her to put her trust in the leadership of the church camp. James promised Nora Faye she could go with her cousins.

CHAPTER 24
BOOTSIE

Brother Brightman had lied about his age to join the Navy when he was fourteen. That explained the tattoos he pointed out where they peeked from his collar and shirtsleeves. A gravelly voice, a thick neck, and muscles that bulged under his pale green linen blazer added to the street-kid aura he spun around himself as he talked about the worldliness of his youthful exploits and the simplicity of his late conversion. He was the first speaker on the program for the final night of Bible camp, laying out a few more adventures from the unlikely path that had led him from the rough streets of Baltimore to the salvation of Christ. Nora Faye felt at ease with Brother Brightman. He had been part of the activities throughout the week, teaching them to tie knots and do headstands, and taking them on a long scavenger hunt up the creek one afternoon to find watermelons hidden under a cliff in a cool water hole. The young people had heard enough about his life to feel like he was someone they had known forever, like someone they might have been if they had not been more fortunate.

The Turners were next on the program, a married couple from Philadelphia who looked like twins. They were very blond and fair, with skin that looked transparent. They even dressed identically in lightweight tan and white striped seersucker jackets over plain white open-collared shirts. They didn't so much harmonize as blend into one voice when they sang several duets and spoke very softly to tell about the glories of a life devoted to spreading the story of redemption. This was their first appearance on the campgrounds, and Nora Faye thought they seemed too delicate to have lived there all week. They might possibly have taught crafts in the afternoon, but she couldn't imagine them life-guarding the swimming sessions in the river or running relay races on field day like some of the other counselors had done.

The Madison family then sang a couple of hymns before Brother Posner began his sermon. The Madisons were city people, too—the parents were on the faculty of a Bible college in Chicago—but they had lived on the campgrounds all week, the children taking part just like any other campers and the parents helping to build campfires and cook meals, referee volley ball games and lead sunrise jumping jacks after a prayer at the flagpole before breakfast. Now they moved quietly and quickly—with the Turners and Brother Brightman—from the stage down to the folding chairs on the floor before Brother Posner started to talk.

Brother Posner was the main camp minister who had come from a Louisville seminary to preside over the week's evening sermons and daily advanced Bible classes. He gave the same sermon he had given every night of the week, but it all seemed different tonight. He skimmed lightly over the birth of Jesus and the early years when He was learning in the temple, but when he got to the part where Jesus asked His mother if she did not understand that He was going about the business of His Father, he shifted intensity, lowering his voice and adding minute details that made Jesus seem like a boy who might have attended this very Bible camp. He dwelled on events that made Him seem human: losing His temper with the moneychangers in the temple and telling the crowd that one without sin should throw the first stone. He took Him step by step into the desert and then to Cana and Nazareth, introducing the disciples one by one so that they seemed like schoolyard friends. He related anecdotes to show how Judas might have been Jesus's closest buddy and told stories about Peter to show why Jesus thought He could count on him for anything. Then, he began the part where Jesus is betrayed by these friends who had become His chosen family. He took Him to the garden at Gethsemane, and to Pontius Pilate and Herod. As he walked Him through the heartaches and betrayals and anguish, he was able to make his listeners see things from inside the heart of Jesus, showing how He agonized over the emotional losses and the enormity of the suffering His Heavenly Father had shifted to Him from mere mortals.

He asked his audience to consider how it would have been for Jesus to realize that the father for whom He had tried to be perfect was asking Him to suffer the kind of excruciating physical punishment inflicted on the worst of the lowliest criminals.

And then he went on to depict the ordeal of carrying the cross through the streets, the throb of the crown of thorns on His brow, and the step by step agony of the nails being driven into His hands and the gash being cut in His side, the interminable hours on the cross with His throat becoming dryer and dryer and His pain becoming worse every second. Then—with his voice dropping into an even lower, intimate tone—Brother Posner asked if there was anyone in the audience hardhearted enough to reject the salvation that Jesus had endured for them. He said all this suffering would be in vain if even one unsaved person hearing this message did not open his heart and accept Jesus as savior.

Nora Faye knew what would happen next. The preacher would go on to say that lost sinners just needed to walk down to the front and take his hand to show they had let Jesus into their hearts. Then, a few campers would probably walk forward, and the preacher would have a few quiet words with them and lead them to stand at the side before he joined back in singing "Have Thine Own Way, Lord" the hymn the Madisons had started and the rest of the crowd would be quietly singing now.

She always shut her ears at the last part of sermons like this, the way she had when her mother and daddy had quarreled. She had halfway shut her ears tonight from the time Brother Posner had lowered his voice and begun sounding like he was speaking intimately to certain people. It always seemed like something private was happening that did not have anything to do with her, and she felt like she was intruding if she paid much attention when other people left their seats and went forward. It seemed like some grownup might ask her to leave the room the way they did if they realized she was listening to things she shouldn't be hearing. It was not that she didn't understand what was going on; it was just that she did not feel the situation was one she was expected to deal with. She didn't question what it was that made some people respond to the message, and she never had reason to ponder why it seemed to her like a message for others, not for herself. She had become accustomed to shutting her ears and thinking about other things, maybe the pretty French braids of the girl in front of her or of all the different kinds of shoes the girls along her row were wearing.

She turned her attention to Dollie's white sandals beside her and Bootsie's black ballerina slippers next to Dollie just at the same moment she became aware of something unusual taking place with Bootsie. Bootsie was leaning against Dollie quietly sniveling and snuffling and clutching Dollie's arm like she was drowning. Nora Faye instinctively slid from her seat and onto her knees in front of Dollie to look up into Bootsie's face to see if she could help.

"Did you get sick?" she whispered, thinking of a night this week when one of the girls in their cabin had a stomachache and they all got their flashlights and went down the hill to the toilet with her and stayed while she threw up.

It took Nora Faye a minute to realize Dollie was trying to push her back into her seat. Dollie looked confused but determined. "She'll be all right," she hissed.

Then, Mrs. Spangler, their cabin counselor, tiptoed across the row behind them until she got to Bootsie. She leaned over her, murmuring questions Nora Faye could not hear. Dollie kept repeating in a whisper, "She'll be okay. There's nothing wrong. She'll be okay."

Mrs. Spangler sent Molly Borden to another seat and pushed the chairs apart and came through to sit where Molly had been. She put her arm around Bootsie and kept whispering in her ear while Bootsie kept crying quietly with her back heaving and tears flowing.

Dollie had stopped saying anything. She looked very much like she did the time Bootsie climbed the ladder on the water tank and the time she went out on the lake with David Daws in a leaky little boat. Dollie would just wait when Bootsie did things like this. She knew it would do no good to try to talk her out of it.

She sat very rigid now, staring at her toes, leaving Bootsie's comfort up to Mrs. Spangler. Nora Faye could hear Bootsie saying, "I do believe in him, I do, but it doesn't make any difference in how my heart feels."

Mrs. Spangler had squatted in front of Bootsie's chair now, holding Bootsie to her like a baby. "It's all right, dearie," she cooed. "You've done all you need to do."

It came to Nora Faye, then, that Bootsie was reacting to the preacher's sermon. She was doing what people did when they got saved.

Only it seemed that Bootsie did not feel saved, that she felt more unsaved by the minute. Nora Faye's heart went out to her—and to Dollie sitting helplessly by, not knowing how to comfort her sister. She longed to hug them and tell them it would be okay, but she didn't know how to do it without making a spectacle that she knew her Aunt Stella would not have wanted.

The situation grew more and more serious, with sobs racking Bootsie's body as the preacher went on to speak quietly to the campers who had walked forward. He made brief statements about each of them—three girls and one boy tonight—and two of the girls gave short testimonies. He read through a list of names of all the campers who had been saved earlier in the week. They walked forward in a group, and he urged them all to follow up on their conversion by joining a church when they got home. There was another hymn, "Ring the Bells of Heaven," and then a short farewell-till-next-year prayer by Pastor Richards, made shorter than planned, Nora Faye suspected, by Bootsie's dilemma. Everyone was aware of the situation now, casting worried glances their way. Brother Crider gave a quick run-through of tomorrow morning's schedule, which was just to pack and eat breakfast and go home.

The crowd filed out. All except Bootsie and Dollie and Nora Faye and Mrs. Spangler, along with Brother Crider, Pastor Richards, Reverend Bowers and their wives. A few visiting parents had driven to camp for the final service, and Nora Faye heard their car doors slam and then their engines start up before they drove away. Lights were turned off. Windows were shut. Each time a door was opened, the air felt a little chillier, and Nora Faye could hear tree frogs and night locusts. Sometimes the laughing voices of the campers drifted in as they made their last run of the night to the toilets. Several of the other women counselors came and went. They were mostly mothers from one of the three sponsoring churches. Nora Faye fell asleep for a moment, making a clatter as she almost fell from the hard metal chair. She tiptoed over to the stage and sat on the low step. There was much whispered consultation, with first one and then another counselor exchanging information with another of the adults and then bending over Bootsie and then Dollie. She saw Mrs. Spangler's face turn up to Mrs. Bowers with a question while she kept her eyes on Nora Faye, and she heard Mrs. Bowers answer, while she too looked at Nora Faye, "She's that little girl Stella's brother-in-law is raising."

She lay her head over on the stage where she eventually dozed in and out. Once, before she gave in to her sleepiness, she suddenly stood, feeling compelled to go over to her cousins to see if she could comfort them, but she was afraid she'd be sent to bed in the cabin if she drew attention to herself. She didn't want to be separated from Bootsie and Dollie before she knew they were okay.

Bootsie's crying broke her heart. Nora Faye didn't think she'd ever heard anyone cry for such a long time. She sobbed that she wanted to be saved but that she didn't know how. Mrs. Spangler asked the same question she had been asking over and over, "Do you believe Christ died for your sins?"

Bootsie shook her head yes while she snuffled and blew her nose on one of the handkerchiefs people kept handing her.

"Then, you're saved," Mrs. Spangler soothed. "That's all you have to do."

Bootsie was not soothed. "But I don't feel different," she wailed. 'I don't know how to be sure he hears what I'm saying."

"You don't have to feel different, and you don't have to say words out loud or even in your mind. He knows what's in your heart. All you have to do is believe that He died for your sins. It's that simple, dear."

"It can't be," Bootsie wailed. "There's g-g-got to be m-m-more to make up for all he d-d-id for me." She had to make several attempts to get this said, and then she had another nose-blowing session before she doubled over like she was in physical pain.

She straightened suddenly and thrust out her hands. "They hammered nails in his hands," she moaned, looking down at her upturned palms. She cradled one hand in the other like a wounded bird and hugged them to her chest where she curled around them.

Nora Faye was awake enough to know when Mrs. Spangler left and then came back with their suitcases, Nora Faye's and Bootsie's and Dollie's. Dollie lined them up neatly, close beside her, and kept reaching over to touch them.

In spite of the chill that made Nora Faye curl into a little ball, and the rubber tread with ridges that bit into her cheek, she soon fell into a deep sleep. One time she was aware of a soft, new voice very near her and of someone putting some kind of cover over her. She saw that it seemed to be one of the seersucker jackets that the twin-looking singing couple had worn, and she thought she must be dreaming. "You poor darling," a woman's tender voice was murmuring. "You poor, sweet darling." An angelic face floated above her.

Then, the next thing she knew, the jacket was off and she was being lifted by strong arms. These arms held her against the faint texture of raised stripes as she was carried out into the summer chill. Up close she was surprised to see a few sandy whisker stubbles sprinkled over the chin she had thought was totally smooth.

She was hardly awake when Mr. Turner tucked her into a back corner of the big Packard sedan Reverend Bowers drove. Dollie was beside her and then came Bootsie and Mrs. Bowers. Mrs. Spangler sat up front with Reverend Bowers. Betsey Bowers slept between them, slumped against Mrs. Spangler. Nora Faye was glad neither woman was beside her. She would have hated it if she'd had to be squeezed up close to them, if she'd had to touch them at all.

Mrs. Spangler was turned around explaining to Mrs. Bowers that Mrs. Madison was going to sleep in the cabin in her place that night. "It just seemed best that I be the one to talk to Stella tonight since I'd been in the cabin all week with her girls.

"She agreed that it made more sense for us to bring them home than for her and Eldon to make that drive down here and then turn right around and drive back home," she went on, "but I know this will be a long night for them till we get their girls home."

"Maybe it won't take so long," Mrs. Bowers said. "The Reverend is a fast driver, and there won't be many cars on the road this late."

"Stella kept asking why we didn't call right away, but she'll realize, when she has time to think about it, that there was no way of knowing...of knowing..." She trailed off.

Nora Faye wished they'd hush talking about it in front of Bootsie.

Reverend Bowers said, "I'm confused about the Turners. I thought they had left the campgrounds. Someone said they're scheduled to sing at a service in Hyden tomorrow afternoon...or this afternoon, I guess. Is it midnight yet?"

Mrs. Spangler said, "They did leave. But, they said they got down the road a piece and then turned around and came back because they couldn't stop thinking about that little girl. Said they had to make sure she was all right."

Mrs. Bowers patted Bootsie's leg. "Well I can understand how they felt. She's sure gone through a struggle tonight."

"Not Bootsie," Mrs. Spangler mouthed, jerking her head toward Nora Faye. "It was that one they were so concerned about."

After several seconds dragged by in silence, she added, "You just never know what makes some people tick."

Bootsie sat between Mrs. Bowers and Dollie with her head laid over in Dollie's lap and her eyes closed, but her lids fluttered and her head jerked back in heaving snubs from time to time. She wiggled her fingers a little to show she felt it when Nora Faye squeezed her hand, but she gave no sign that she felt anything else. Dollie sat perfectly still, staring at the back of the front seat with hardly a blink. Nora Faye rubbed Dollie's arm before she sank into another long doze.

Bootsie and Dollie were both baptized a week later on Sunday night. Nora Faye heard Stella talking to Granny Rose about it earlier in the week. She hadn't been paying attention and did not hear what Stella had said to make her granny's voice sound stern. She heard her say, "Just leave Nora Faye out of it. I think it's a shame to let the little ones get all stirred up that a way."

Stella started to speak, but Granny Rose went right on talking, "I know you have your own feelings about it, and that's all right. I wouldn't ever try to make you think different. But James is the one to decide on things like that about Nora Faye. I didn't say anything to try to talk him out of it when he decided to let her go to that camp with the other girls, but I'll sure enough speak my mind to him if you push him to let her be baptized with them. She's too little to know what that's all about."

That's the last Nora Faye heard about it until they went to the Sunday night service at Aunt Stella's church a week later. It was just like any other service Nora Faye had been to in this church, except that the choir was seated down front instead of behind the preacher. She understood why they weren't in their usual place when Brother Crider went into a back room after he stopped preaching, and one of the deacons went up and flipped light switches that illuminated the space where a low velvet curtain extended along an iron bar at the front edge of the choir section's top tier. The deacon pushed the velvet curtain aside. The house lights were dimmed and the choir began singing, "Ring the Bells of Heaven." Stella and two other mothers brought out their girls and led them to brother Crider where he reappeared dressed in a white shirt and pants. Nora Faye realized there must be a pool that had been under a trap door behind the curtain. As she watched Brother Crider lead her cousins and the other two camp girls down the steps one by one she worried about Dollie; Dollie didn't like to put her head under water. But it seemed to go okay. There was no splash or outcry when it was her turn.

When Nora Faye first saw Dollie and Bootsie in their white dresses, she felt envious for a moment, but then as they went down the steps into the baptismal pool she was glad she wasn't with them. She could barely see a corner of the pool, but it seemed to be a dark galvanized metal tank. If she ever got baptized she thought she'd do it in a creek in the sunshine like she saw one time with Aunt Tattie, not in a dismal metal tank.

CHAPTER 25
MRS. BLEDSO

Mrs. Bledso pronounced Heidi's name wrong; she said Hee-EYE-duh. Nora Faye corrected her once but let it go after that. That wasn't her only imperfection as a reader, but she was so engrossed in the story that her flaws were soon easy to ignore. Nora Faye could tell that Mrs. Bledso loved Heidi as much as she did.

Her husband slept in the lower front room, so Mrs. Bledso usually read to Nora Faye in the kitchen, the room farthest away from him. Some mornings they sat on the back steps to read, and sometimes when it was almost time for James to come home, they went to Nora Faye's house and read in her front-porch swing. But usually it was in the kitchen, where Mrs. Bledso would sometimes be cooking a pot of soup beans or mustard greens she'd jump up to stir every now and then.

When it was time for a bag of oleomargarine to be mixed, Mrs. Bledso would sit across the kitchen table from Nora Faye, reading a little louder than usual while Nora Faye kneaded the color into the oleo in its clear tough bag. To her delight, this task had fallen exclusively to her at Mrs. Bledso's house. Mrs. Ethridge insisted on giving her daddy all the butter they needed, so she never got the chance to mix oleo at home. At the Slaney's house, the children took turns. Laura Jane let Nora Faye take her turns, but she hadn't had the experience many times, and it was still a treat to feel carefully until she found the little suspended capsule of liquid color and to pinch it until it burst and then to knead the bag until the color mixed evenly through the white squishy mass. The capsule—no bigger than a shirt button—was a dark reddish brown, but it turned the oleomargarine yellow by the time it mixed all through.

Sometimes she got so caught up in the story she forgot to mix as she listened. But Mrs. Bledso didn't remind her to keep mixing; she was usually just as engrossed as Nora Faye.

After it was mixed, Mrs. Bledso cut a corner off the bag and let Nora Faye squeeze the contents into a fancy round butter mold. It would harden in the refrigerator with the pattern from the mold, and she would turn it out onto a special butter dish that had a fancy cover. This was one of Mrs. Bledso's time-consuming pieces of kitchen paraphernalia—like her potato ricer and apple peeler and strawberry capper—that Granny Rose said just made more work for the cook and dishwasher. The rare times Granny Rose had oleo, she let Nora Faye color it, but then she squeezed it into a square glass refrigerator dish with a flat glass lid that didn't take up much room in her little refrigerator.

Mrs. Bledso said she hadn't bothered to mix in the color before Nora Faye started staying with her. "We just left it white like country butter and threw away the coloring pill," she said as she pressed out the last bit from the corners of the bag. "But it does look cheerful this way." She said they didn't like the taste of oleo at first, but that now they liked it better than real butter. When Nora Faye asked why they ate it when they didn't like it, Mrs. Bledso said the store didn't always have brought-in butter to buy these days, and that Mr. Bledso did not like the taste of country butter. Nora Faye knew that "these days" had to do with the war.

The floor plan of the Bledso's house was a copy of her own, but it seemed very different to Nora Faye because of how different Mrs. Bledso's furniture was and how differently she arranged it. At her own house, the wooden dining table—a white painted drop-leaf style not much larger nor much fancier than the metal kitchen table—was in the middle room along with a trundle-bed sofa, a Morris chair and the refrigerator. There wasn't room enough for the refrigerator in their kitchen because they were leaving that spot empty for the electric stove Daddy was planning to get so her mother could cook dinner without heating up the kitchen on hot summer days and could heat water to wash her hair any time she took the notion. But, they would have to keep the Kalamazoo coal stove for warmth in the winter, so the electric stove would not be taking its place.

Mrs. Bledso had a sitting room where Nora Faye had a dining room, and instead of a dining room like Mrs. Bledso's, they had a junk room, and the door between that room and the kitchen was always kept shut. Mrs. Bledso kept that door open—except for the very coldest winter days—and she was very proud of her heavy, dark mahogany dining table with two extra leaves and eight chairs and a massive mirrored sideboard. She kept a red tablecloth on the table and covered it with a cream-colored hand-crocheted lace cloth. The red showed through the crochet to reflect in the silver tea service always sitting in the center of the table on a silver tray.

In the weeks immediately following Conner's death and the Slaneys' move back to Pennsylvania, James had turned to Mrs. Bledso for help a time or two. At first she said she just didn't see how she could offer him routine help, what with Mr. Bledso being such a light sleeper, but after she realized what a quiet child Nora Faye could be, she agreed to an arrangement with James. His mother came more often and on a regular basis now, but Mrs. Bledso took up the slack on the days when Rose wasn't there.

James was relieved to find that Mrs. Bledso had no qualms about accepting money for the favor. Nora Faye heard him tell Granny Rose the Bledsos were comfortable with the exchange of money because they were merchants at heart. They'd had a little notions store in Wolliver before Mr. Bledso took the mining job, and their son Maynard had a dry-cleaning business in that building now.

Before Mrs. Bledso started reading *Heidi* to her, there were many mornings Nora Faye didn't want to be inside the house. She wanted to stay in her own yard and ride the makeshift horse she had conjured out of a large crate that had housed a new refrigeration unit James had installed at the store. He brought the crate home thinking he might use some of the wood to build the carport he was making for the Plymouth sedan he had bought.

The long lathes of the crate had enough give in them to bounce when Nora Faye straddled two of them and let her legs dangle, and they were tough enough that there was no danger of a break.

James wrestled the crate towards the back corner of his yard where Mrs. Bledso could see it from her windows, and he agreed that, after Nora Faye ate the breakfast Mrs. Bledso insisted on making for her, she could climb the fence back into her own yard and play on the crate unless it was rainy and muddy.

Mrs. Bledso didn't even have to help her climb the fence because there was one easy-to-climb section made of three wide planks going crossways instead of pointed palings going up and down.

Mrs. Ethridge, who picked up their kitchen slop each day, said that section of the fence used to be a farm gate, way back before the tipple and the railroads came and the camp houses were built where the farm once sat. She said when she got married, her husband's family owned the farm, and she and her husband had lived in the big farm house with his family until the mining company came in and bought all the land and tore down the farm buildings. She said Nora Faye's yard and the Deeton's yard had been the apple orchard and that the barn had set on the Bledso's lot. Granny Rose said that must be why Mrs. Bledso's garden always did so well.

Mrs. Ethridge had once showed Nora Faye a squared-off sandstone rock down near the store bridge that she said had marked the corner of the farm lot. It had been pushed to the creek bank when the camp houses were built. Her husband was long dead, and she now lived in a little shack on the Ritter property up the side hollow with her oldest son, Mordechai, who got poisoned with mustard gas when he was in the first war in Europe and appeared to be older than his mother.

Every morning she came by Nora Faye's yard to collect the contents of the slop bucket where they saved their table scraps for her hog, Jack. She carried a big bucket with her and dumped in their scraps and several other neighbors' scraps that she collected on her way to Jack's pen. The bucket at Nora Faye's house hung on a fence post at the back of the yard, and Nora Faye used to walk along with her from the front gate to the back fence while Mrs. Ethridge told her tales of the days before the mines and railroads came in.

She would point to the creek and tell her how clean and sweet it used to be. "All that yellow slime that hangs on the rocks, that used to be moss. And you could catch a fish any time you put your line in the deep hole up where the little trestle is now. Young'uns like you would play in that creek all day long, making dams and making water wheels out of corn stalks.

"But the creek didn't run along here back then. It curved around the hillside there where they filled it in and built the first tipple. Or the second tipple. The first one was down at the mouth of the holler."

She also talked about her daughter, Ida, whose family lived in a little shotgun house up Pryors Run that you could almost see from the little trestle. That's where Jack's hog pen was, in a lot at the mouth of Pryors Run. James had let Nora Faye walk up to the hog pen with Mrs. Ethridge one time and then walk back by herself along the tracks and across the store bridge to come home. He could see her from their yard almost the whole time.

Ida had seven children, and one of them, Henry, had polio. He was in the hospital at Bascon in an iron lung. There had been a newspaper story about him because he was the only polio patient from these parts that didn't have to go away to some city in order to be in an iron lung. The iron lung at Bascon was the only one in the entire area, and Ida's boy needed one just when it was delivered to the Bascon hospital. Every morning, after Mrs. Ethridge stopped to dump Jack's slop in his trough, she went on to Ida's house and stayed there all day with the other children while Ida walked out of the hollow to the mouth of Dillard where she caught the bus to Bascon to spend the day in the hospital with her sick boy. Ida's husband lived in Detroit where he got a job so he could send money for hospital bills. Soon after Mrs. Ethridge passed by, going up the hollow, you'd see Ida coming out of the hollow walking along the tracks, which was the closest way.

At the end of the day—just before dusk—Nora Faye would see Ida walking the tracks back home, and Mrs. Ethridge, then, walking back to her house with her empty slop bucket in one hand and a large egg basket filled with supper for Mordechai in the other hand. When Nora Faye waved to her she could only raise her chin and lift her elbows in a little return salute because of the load in each hand. Mordechai could just barely take care of himself at home and was not strong enough to walk to Ida's and back every day with his mother. He tried to take care of their little garden and their fires at home, while Mrs. Ethridge did the best she could to take care of Ida's garden and her cooking and canning and washing and her milk cow...and her other six children.

On mornings when Granny Rose was there, she made enough breakfast for Ida and all of her children and put it in Mordechai's empty supper basket while Mrs. Ethridge was making the slop transfer at the back fence. Nora Faye saw them in a discussion of it once when she was not near enough to hear what they said. She could tell that Mrs. Ethridge protested only enough to protect her pride, and that Granny Rose made it seem like it was a hard job forcing it on Mrs. Ethridge so she'd not feel bad about taking it. The memory of the transaction left Nora Faye feeling both sad and uplifted.

Seeing Mrs. Ethridge and Ida like gloomy markers to the start and end of each day added to the air of melancholy that hung over everything the first month or two after Conner's death. Nora Faye spent a good part of her mornings on her crate horse, but she hardly bounced on it; it was more of a sway that she kept going as she sang to herself. While Mrs. Bledso worked in the garden on her side of the fence or sat on her back steps breaking beans or shucking corn, Nora Faye sang—almost under her breath—the cowboy songs from Eldon's movies, the doleful ones like "Empty Saddles" and "The Last Roundup."

When Mrs. Bledso asked if she knew the words to "I've Got Spurs That Jingle Jangle Jingle" or "Deep in the Heart of Texas," she shook her head.

Mr. Bledso's light sleeping kept Mrs. Bledso from hooking up her washing machine before he got out of bed, but unless it was wash day, she had everything so well taken care of by the time he left for work that she could sit down with *Heidi* and read until her throat got dry. Mrs. Bledso was the first adult Nora Faye had known who did not act ashamed to cry, who did not give a little laugh and pretend she wasn't really crying. When Heidi was going through her sleep-walking phase, they cried together. Mrs. Bledso turned the book over to hold their place and tiptoed to the spare bedroom to get clean handkerchiefs. After taking out two embroidered, lacy handkerchiefs of her own, she put them back and opened a different drawer, saying, "We'll just take a couple of Mr. Bledso's good-sized ones in case there's another part this sad."

The book didn't make them cry that much again, but there was always a sadness hanging over Mrs. Bledso's life. Nora Faye knew it was partly due to the Gold Star flag hanging in the dining room window. The flag was a white satin rectangle with the narrow sides at top and bottom. A gold colored fringe ran along the bottom edge, and a little wooden bar along the top had knobs and tassels at each end and a thick cord that hung over a nail in the window sash. The white center area was framed by a wide red border of satin with a gold star in the center. That star stood for her son Avery whose picture was in a fancy frame on the dining room sideboard. He had been killed in the army before Nora Faye started staying there. A blue star flag hung in the other front window. It was for her son Maynard who had just got out of the army and opened the dry-cleaning business in Wolliver. Before Avery was killed there was just one flag with two blue stars on it, and Mrs. Bledso said she was a Blue Star Mother. She didn't call herself anything after Avery was killed.

Part of Mrs. Bledso's sadness was because her youngest son, Kelvin, would soon be leaving for his hitch in the service. He had been called up and was due to report for duty at the end of August. He'd actually been drafted a year earlier, but his mother had talked him into asking for a deferment until his older brother got his discharge. They all seemed surprised that his request had been honored, and Kelvin himself acted like the deferment was forcing him to do something he didn't want to do.

"How'd I feel, Mommy, if Claude or Watson had something bad happen to them?" Nora Faye heard him ask his mother in the usual irritable tone he used with her that summer. Claude and Watson were friends of his who had been drafted when Kelvin was drafted.

"Well, it wouldn't make it any less likely that something bad would happen to them just because you'd been doing your turn at the same time."

"It might," he said. "That's the thing. It just might."

Kelvin and his wife Alta lived down past the store in a tiny house between the creek and the railroad tracks, but he stopped by his mother's house every morning on his way home from the hoot-owl shift.

There was no bathhouse at the Dillard mines, but Mrs. Craine, who lived in the old boarding house next door to the Bledsos—the last house in the hollow that had inside running water—had fixed up some rooms in her house with long galvanized tubs where miners could take a bath for fifteen cents and could drop off their clean outfits on their way to their shifts so they'd be there waiting for them when they stopped in to take their baths after work. Mrs. Craine's business was picking up a little, but things were nothing like as busy as they had been before the slump—very few miners now could afford the indulgence of a true bath every day—but there were still lights on in the Craine house at odd hours of the night and a few men coming and going as they went to and from their shifts.

Kelvin took a bath every morning, and he came from Mrs. Craine's to his mother's house to share a pot of coffee and have his breakfast. When he was first married he couldn't eat his breakfast at his mother's house without hurting Alta's feelings, but, after a few months of marriage she didn't mind not having to get up early to cook for him.

Nora Faye could remember back when Kelvin wasn't always in a bad mood. He never seemed to mind whether it was his mother or his wife who cooked his breakfast, but he liked strong, black coffee—strong enough to eat the bowl off the spoon handle, he always said—and Alta did not make strong coffee. He drank a cup of his mother's coffee while she finished making his eggs, and another cup or two while he ate, finishing off the pot with his last bite of biscuit and apple butter. His mother sat down with him as he finished up, nursing her one scant cup for as long as he would sit.

The coffee was a private affair between him and his mother, and was the closest Nora Faye ever heard them come to saying something affectionate to one another. His wife's coffee wasn't actually mentioned by name in their little teasing sessions, but it hung there as the explanation for his stops at his mother's house each day to get a cup of something stronger than the hummingbird tears or pansy petal nectar or fairy wing dew or the other fanciful names he gave to Alta's weak brew. It was part of the teasing he went through with his mother, sometimes as though less to say he enjoyed her coffee than to say he would not be stopping by her house if it were not for the necessity of finding a cup of something stronger than Alta made for him.

The gleaming chrome percolator used for making Kelvin's coffee held the position of honor in Mrs. Bledso's kitchen. As soon as Kelvin left, she unplugged the empty pot, washed it, dried it and returned it to the top of her refrigerator, which had its motor at the bottom instead of on top like the one at Nora Faye's house. It was a point of pride with Mrs. Bledso that she made a pan of clean dishwater to take care of Kelvin's percolator. She couldn't put the pot in the dishpan because of the electric parts, but she sloshed hot soapy water in it and rinsed it with cold water from the faucet and then boiling water from the kettle. The pan of dishwater was for the stem and basket and lid. She never put them into greasy dishwater where she had first washed other dishes.

She did not make her husband's coffee in that pot. He preferred a speckled blue metal stovetop pot. Like the electric pot, it had a glass knob in the lid where you could see the darkening water jump up, but the sound it made was like a slosh, not the crisp cadence of the shiny, chrome pot with its gracefully narrowed top part that expanded into a bulging bottom with a long, curved, tapering spout. In the center of the lid, the little glass knob where the coffee bubbled up was tall and slim, not wide and flat like on the stovetop pot.

Mr. Bledso cooled down his coffee with several splashes of canned Carnation milk. "From contented cows," he always said as he pointed to the words on the can before he poured in just the right amount. He also made a little lesson of it every time he opened a new can of milk, pressing in a triangle of metal on opposite sides of the can. "If you punch just one hole, the air has a hard time getting in to push the milk out, so you get a lot of splashes and gurgles; you have to punch a hole on both sides, so the air can get in on one side to push the milk out the other side." He'd demonstrate the theory step by step as he went along. There was always an opened can of Carnation milk in their refrigerator, the cause of an ongoing argument between him and Mrs. Bledso. She wanted to pour the opened can into a little lidded china pitcher to store it, but Mr. Bledso said it didn't taste the same unless it came straight from the can. Mrs. Bledso compromised by setting the can in a fancy little saucer and she used the dampened corner of a clean dishtowel in her constant efforts to wipe the jagged edges of the opened can. Kelvin always chanted a little rhyme if he was there when Mr. Bledso opened a new can. He censored himself as he went along, "No tail to twitch, no blank to pitch. Just punch a hole in the son of a blank." The blanks were not just because of Nora Faye. She knew he would have said it that way if it were just his mother. Mr. Bledso always looked down to hide his grin, and Mrs. Bledso always scolded both of them, seemingly horrified even by the censored version, although Nora Faye thought she saw a little smile twitching at the corner of her mouth and suspected she was pretending to be horrified because that's what was expected of her. It was one of the few occasions when Kelvin's banter seemed truly light-hearted.

Nora Faye knew Kelvin's anger, always just under the surface, had to do with him putting off the date when he would go into the army, and that the delay had something to do with the blue star and the gold star, but she didn't understand why that made him angry or why there seemed to be something unforgivable between him and his mother. It was as though he felt that her fear had doomed him to a tragic end once he became a part of military life. He said something about that to her one time. "The way you act, Mommy, everybody in this family that goes to fight the war is supposed to end up dead."

Mrs. Bledso was aghast. She said, "There's no sense in you talking that way, Kelvin! What does that say about your brother Maynard?"

Kelvin said, "That's the thing; sometimes it seems like Maynard coming home alive is just as hard for you to take as Avery getting killed."

It was the most forlorn Nora Faye had ever seen Mrs. Bledso. She sat unmoving at the kitchen table for some time after Kelvin left that day. She could not bear to look at Nora Faye who inched closer to her, but reached a hand over her shoulder and blindly patted the hand Nora Faye laid on the back of her chair. It made Nora Faye sad that Mrs. Bledso so dreaded the time when her boy would be leaving for his military hitch, and yet that there was so little joy in the time she had with him while he was still at home.

Stray strands of wiry gray hair had worked loose from the long twisted bun going from the nape of her neck to her crown. Nora Faye wanted to reach out and tuck them back in, but she didn't. She wandered around to the other side of the table and leaned her face in and out towards the unplugged but unwashed chrome percolator sitting close to Kelvin's emptied cup. Her upside-down reflection would get longer and longer until it pinched in at the middle and became two faces. This was the longest she'd ever seen the pot sit unwashed.

Kelvin was put on the day shift for his last two weeks of work, so he'd had his breakfast and gone to work before Nora Faye got to Mrs. Bledso's house one morning soon after that episode. Mrs. Bledso had already washed Kelvin's pot and finished the dishes. They had finished *Heidi,* but she and Nora Faye were sitting on the back steps reading *Lassie Come Home* when they heard people coming through the house. It was three men in miners' clothes. One of the men came out and—without saying a word to Mrs. Bledso—took hold of Nora Faye's shoulder and started talking right to her about the flowers in Mrs. Bledso's garden, while the other men took Mrs. Bledso by the elbows and started guiding her inside as they talked softly to her. Nora Faye felt like she should go with Mrs. Bledso, but it would have been awkward to resist the man who was firmly steering her out into a row of flowers. A few of the little brown butterflies that could always be found on the pink sweet-pea blossoms flew up as the man brushed against the white-washed trellis where the sweet-peas vined. "Do you know the name of these?" he was asking in what seemed to Nora Faye to be a very forced, unnatural way. "I guess they aren't nasturtiums. Nasturtiums are always orange, aren't they?" Then he touched one of the dark red dahlia blooms and said, "I don't know any flowers except for nasturtiums and tiger lilies, and I can see that these aren't either of those. Can you tell me what they are?" And then Nora Faye heard a horrible noise like a trapped animal screaming.

She pulled loose from the man and ran from the flower garden into the house where the men were trying to settle Mrs. Bledso into her wicker armchair. Her knees wouldn't bend. She was sagging in one long piece like a hammock, and her hands flailed above the grip they had on each upper arm.

Then she saw that Mr. Bledso was there, too, other men standing mutely on each side of him where he sat on the wicker hassock like a stone. All of them except Mr. Bledso were in their dirty miners clothes. Mr. Bledso had pulled his pants on over his underwear and had slipped his bare feet into his untied shoes. He just sat and stared at his feet while Mrs. Bledso made the terrible noise Nora Faye had heard from the garden. The men were saying things about a slate fall and a closed coffin and arrangements.

Then there were other neighbors: Mrs. Deeton and Mrs. Berkindoff and Mrs. Ballard, and, finally, her daddy. He took her home. Or maybe Mrs. Ballard had already taken her home before he came. It was hard to keep things straight.

James told her the roof had collapsed in the mine where Kelvin was working, killing Kelvin instantly.

His body was laid out at his parents' house. His own little house was too tiny to hold the mourners. James and Rose planned for Nora Faye to go with them to the funeral in Wolliver the next day, but they were still having discussion about whether it would be wise to let her go over to see Mrs. Bledso at her house today. "Well, you know, the casket will be closed," her granny said, and James nodded and looked at Nora Faye in that way he had of making it seem like he was considering asking her what she wanted to do. The decision was made for them when Mrs. Bledso sent for her—sent Mrs. Ballard to tell James she wanted to see Nora Faye.

When they were still out on her front walk they could hear Mrs. Bledso's voice above the others. Nora Faye did not recognize it at first. She thought maybe a preacher had started delivering a sermon, one of the preachers who used a high, sing-song voice and put in extra sounds between syllables. But then she heard the words and knew it was Mrs. Bledso. She was keening as she talked, wailing that she should have let Kelvin go on to the war when he was drafted, that she should have let the Lord have His way, that she was being punished because she had been arrogant enough to try to tell the Lord when to do things.

Nora Faye had never heard a voice with that sound. Not Mrs. Slaney when Conner was killed. She couldn't actually remember Mrs. Slaney being there when she went to see Conner in his casket. But, that was just it; Mrs. Slaney's grief had shrunk her into something so quiet and still that she seemed to disappear. Nora Faye never really remembered seeing her again after she went through the creek in her shoes and clawed her way up the hill to her boy.

Mrs. Bledso's grief, on the other hand, had exploded her. She seemed to be in several places at once. Alta sat with several others at the kitchen table, Maynard's small family hovered together at one end of the casket, and Mr. Bledso sat beside the dining room door looking much smaller than Nora Faye had thought he was, but Mrs. Bledso scattered herself in sudden bursts from room to room. She clutched one of her lacy handkerchiefs, aimlessly dabbing at the air with it for a moment, and then rubbing it over the casket's gleaming wood and shiny metal hardware. The wicker sofa and chairs had been pushed back against the walls out of the way to make room for the casket in their middle room. "Didn't they pick a pretty coffin?" she'd croon, and then she'd suddenly be at the kitchen table or the dining room door urging the crowd to have a piece of pie or some chicken and dumplings. "They've brought in this big spread," she'd murmur, looking vague and disoriented for a moment. "Somebody needs to eat it."

Then, "Oh, to think he'll never eat another piece of my pie, never set down at my table again, never drink another cup of my coffee!" And she'd wail again, going through a list of self-accusations as she drifted back toward the casket that pulled her like a magnet.

"He'd made his profession of faith." She grasped the proffered arm of Mrs. Ballard who had come to stand beside her. "Some people didn't know about it. He didn't walk down front or anything—he didn't like to draw attention—but the last time Brother Dotson preached a revival, I know he got right with the Lord. A body doesn't have to say something for you to know. I could tell what was in his heart, don't you know?" Her eyes glittered as she stared past Mrs. Ballard for a moment.

Oddly, Nora Faye was not afraid of her in this transformed state. Maybe it had to do with them crying together over Heidi. When the wild gaze finally landed on her, Nora Faye went straight to her without looking to James for permission, and she returned the hug as Mrs. Bledso clung to her while she told her it was her own fault that her boy lay in that closed coffin. "I thought I was a better hand at working out things than the Lord," she moaned. "If I had let the Lord have His way and had let my boy be inducted according to His plan, I wouldn't be standing here beside his coffin now." Out of the corner of her eye, Nora Faye saw her daddy move a step closer before he stopped himself almost like a runner ready at the starting line.

Mrs. Bledso suddenly dropped to sit on the edge of one of the mahogany dining room chairs someone had put beside the coffin. She pulled Nora Faye around in front of her and held a shoulder in each hand while she studied her face like she was trying to find her consolation in it. "You seen how he liked my coffee," she said. "You was always such a good little girl, setting there while we had our coffee and talked. You seen how it was with us." Then she kissed Nora Faye on the forehead and pushed her away, still holding her shoulders and looking steadily into her eyes as she murmured, "For the life of me I'll never know how she could leave you."

Nora Faye assured her, "Oh, she didn't leave me. They're both still here. See them there by the door." She pointed to Rose and James who had not taken their eyes off Nora Faye from the moment she had responded to Mrs. Bledso's outstretched arms

CHAPTER 26
ELDON

Eldon was the one who got the ball rolling on James's divorce. "You're just laying yourself open to trouble if you don't take care of it now," he told James. "It's no telling what opportunities are going to come up now that we're in the war, and you don't want to have that mess hanging over your head if you want to make some changes."

He had never asked James about Virginia, but James figured he saw right through him. He always did. What reason other than interest in another woman would a man in James' situation have for getting a divorce? Eldon went to the courthouse and talked to Robert Yarberry about it. Robert, who had been in school with them, had gone to Louisville to get a law degree before he came back and settled down in Wolliver. Robert took care of it. All James had to do was give him some money when he signed the papers Robert got ready for him.

Looking back on it, James wondered if Eldon had foreseen what was to happen even before Mr. Wainwright died. But, then, that was Eldon's way. He didn't like to leave loose ends dangling, didn't like to settle for something that wasn't neat and tidy and topnotch. It was no big surprise when Eldon got the job as manager of the company warehouse in Johnston and then found a house in time to move his family before winter. In the meantime, he and Stella went on and started Dollie and Bootsie in school in Johnston so they wouldn't have to make a change during the school year. The whole family went to

Johnston with Eldon every morning when he went to work. The girls went to school and Stella went to the house where she worked all day to get it ready for their move.

The company had put the houses up for sale, and Eldon had lucked into a good buy. The people living in a house were given first chance to buy it, but a Blanton family had decided on a move back to Stonega, Virginia after they signed a contract to buy their house in Johnston. Eldon bought it from the Blantons, coming out, as usual, on the good end of the deal. He and Stella worked feverishly to fix it up before the move. They sanded floors and stripped wallpaper and painted, cut doors through the tough wall lathes where there had been no doors, and walled up doors where they existed. Stella worked in the house by herself all day. The girls joined her after school and, when Eldon got off work they all went back to Bascon to have supper and go to bed. It didn't take them long to get things ready to move in.

Knowing how busy he was with his new job and new house, James was surprised when Eldon showed up at the store shortly before closing time one day in late November.

It had been an unusual day for James. Mr. Caldwell, head manager for all the Staghorn stores, stopped by that afternoon and holed up with Mr. Deeton in his office for a half hour or so before they came into the store and got Rollie and took him back with them for another fifteen or twenty minutes. Finally, they all three came back into the store with big smiles on their faces. They came straight to James where he was fitting Mr. Ballard for some new work boots. Rollie took over to give him such a good price on the boots that Mr. Ballard was soon sold and on his way. James started returning shoeboxes to the shelf, but Mr. Caldwell stepped up beside him and slapped him on the back while saying, "I need to talk to you, James. Let your work go for a few minutes and listen to the news I've brought you." Then he offered him the store manager's job at Vargo. He seemed puzzled when James didn't jump at it.

James's heart dropped as it had when he learned of Mr. Wainwright's death, and once again he wondered what this meant about Virginia's plans. He swallowed a time or two before he managed to say, "You've surprised me. I guess I figured the position would be offered to Mrs. Wainwright on a permanent basis."

Mr. Caldwell said, "Well, you figured right, son, but it seems she's been offered a teaching job in Vargo that she decided to take because of having more time at home with her little girl. Their head teacher down there was a man, Joe Turner's boy, and he got drafted. She'll be taking his place."

So, for a second time, James' heart switched from joy to dismay as it swelled to hear that Virginia would not be leaving the area but sank as he wondered how—if he should take the job—it would be possible for him to work in the same community without saying too much to her before she was ready to consider a suitor.

The two weeks he spent running the Vargo store after Mr. Wainwright died had proved to be less difficult than he feared. Virginia was so engrossed in taking care of the things that must be taken care of after a death, and the neighbors had surrounded her with so much attention, that James had not seen much of her. He had thought things might progress smoothly now, and he was waiting until the time would come that he could let her know how he felt.

He surprised all three men by telling them he'd have to think about taking the job. They'd had no doubt but that he'd look upon the offer as a more than welcome opportunity; it would mean a little more money for him and quite a bit more security. Mr. Caldwell said he'd let him think it over for a day or two before he offered it to anyone else.

That was when Eldon showed up, grinning like a monkey and getting in the way trying to help James hurry as he got things ready to close up. James assumed Eldon was grinning about Mr. Caldwell's offer, and he wondered why he was so happy about it. The money wasn't that much more, Vargo was more out of the way than Dillard, the road was in terrible shape, and living in Vargo would further complicate things about taking care of Nora Faye the right way.

He was letting her stay with his mother so she could finish second grade in Wolliver this year. It wasn't what he wanted, but with Kelvin Bledso's death on the heels of Conner's—and with the Bledsos' move so soon after the Slaneys'—he figured it was best for Nora Faye to get out of Dillard where she'd seen so much of death and loss.

He'd been putting out feelers for a job in Wolliver. He felt certain something would turn up. It hadn't crossed his mind that Staghorn might offer him the Vargo job. In fact, he'd thought maybe the timing was going to be just about right for him to approach Virginia soon. He'd thought he would land a job in Wolliver before she would be given the ultimatum of taking the Vargo position permanently or letting it go, right about the time he'd feel free to see if he was right in thinking she had the same kind of interest in him that he had in her. She could quit her job, they could get married, and they could move to Wolliver where he would have found a job.

As he finally got the store closed and started the walk to the house—Eldon had parked at the house—he began to go through the list of drawbacks to the Vargo position before he realized Eldon didn't know what he was talking about. He didn't know about Mr. Caldwell's offer. Once James cleared up the confusion, Eldon beamed and said,

"You can forget about Vargo, my brother. Forget Dillard. Forget Staghorn Collieries. I got you a job in Johnston! I got you the job as bottling plant manager for Pittsburg Coal Collieries Incorporation. They call it the bottling plant, but it's three plants connected. You'll oversee the ice plant, the ice cream plant, and the bottling plant."

James didn't even ask questions. This was ideal. This was the solution to all his problems. He was so delirious he told Eldon about Virginia then and there.

Eldon said he'd better not fool around too long before he made his intentions clear. He agreed that James would have to use a little caution about stepping in before Virginia felt right about it, but he warned him that he'd better not dally while some less wary fellow moved in right under his nose. "Virginia's not a woman men are going to give any peace. Even in wartime. Especially in wartime. Some soldier on leave is going to snap her up before he ships out."

This idea upset James so much he didn't sleep that night. Next day he told Rollie to let Mr. Caldwell know he had decided against the Vargo job and that he needed to talk to him about something else. Then, after work, he drove up to Vargo and knocked on Virginia's door. Peggy was jumping rope in the road with neighbor girls, and when she saw that Nora Faye wasn't with James she just gave him a wave and went on with the game.

Virginia made a pot of coffee while she finished up the supper she was cooking. After James asked her to give him a few minutes before she called Peggy in to eat, she pushed the pans to the side of the stove, poured them each a cup of coffee and sat down at the table with him. He let himself take pleasure from the curve of her long, slender arms. They were bare—she wore a short sleeved housedress—and the multiple creases across the inside of her elbows lengthened and shortened as she raised and lowered her cup and reached without thought to straighten the salt and pepper shakers and the vinegar cruet on a Lazy Susan in the center of the table.

After all the months of worrying and fretting, it was fairly easy for him to tell her what he had to say. He said, "I don't know if it's too early for this, but I can't risk waiting too long and letting some other fellow have his say before I have mine. If it's too soon for me to tell you how I feel about you, just ignore what I say today and let me know when I can say what's in my heart without intruding on your private sorrow."

She smiled with her eyes and said, "I can't think of anything that could give me more comfort than being with a person who is as careful about my sorrow as you are, James. Why don't we just go ahead and see how it feels to talk our true feelings when we're together without worrying about waiting any certain length of time."

That was the end of any uncertainty James had about how to proceed with Virginia. By the time they were married in the spring, he had been on his new job for several months and had moved into the house Eldon helped him find in Johnston. Virginia finished the year of teaching in Vargo, Peggy finished third grade in Vargo, and Nora Faye finished second grade in Wolliver before they joined James in their Johnston house in Coopers Cove where the barrel stave yard had been located in the days when Johnston was being built. It was not surprising that no signs of the cooper's trade remained, for the ravines had been filled in with loads of red dog before winding rows of houses had been built up to where the mountain took on a seriously steep incline.

CHAPTER 27
JOHNSTON

A coal town is as different from a coal camp as a Technicolor movie is from one in black and white, and Johnston was as different from other coal towns as a musical is from movies without song and dance. Wolliver and Bascon—Platchet County's other two largest towns—were not coal towns. They had started slowly, one dirt-floor cabin at a time, long before the railroads came into the mountains to get the coal.

Johnston, however, seemed to have sprung forth full-grown like Minerva, fathered by the Mountain Coal and Steel Company, which sold out to Pittsburg Coal Collieries Incorporation just before James and Eldon moved there. Johnston had not sprouted from native rootstock and grown up gradually like Wolliver and Bascon. The center of Johnston with its brick buildings was a lot like one of the abounding apple tree branches Langston Houston had grafted onto sturdy native stock. It could well have grown from a piece of outland city brick grafted like a hothouse cutting and cultivated to flourish on its mountain host. It took it's sustenance from the veins of coal, the same as all the county now, but, like a grafted branch, it was a marvel of its own features, a self-sustaining community set apart by a cohesiveness that had to do with everything being not only company-owned but company-created. Some of the coal towns in adjoining counties were a mixture of old and new, where a coal company had added on to an already established town, but

Johnston was totally a creation of the Mountain Coal and Steel Company.

On the streets of Bascon and Wolliver, a few red brick buildings appeared side by side with yellow brick, gray or tan cut stone, and wooden buildings painted in various colors. A dwelling house on Wolliver's Main Street, with a facade of smoothly rounded river stones, sat between the yellow brick A & P store and the gray chiseled-stone Presbyterian Church.

But the multi-storied buildings of Johnston were made of identical red bricks that had been manufactured on-site at Brickyard Hollow where—as in Coopers Cove—no signs remained of the industry playing such a crucial role in the creation of the town. Like other company-owned dwelling houses, the houses in Brickyard Hollow were built of lumber, not the red bricks of the schoolhouse, the company store, the warehouse, the recreation building, the office building, the butcher shop, the drugstore, the post office, the train station, the Methodist church, the power plant with its tall smokestack, the mining supply building, the hospital, and the bottling plant that James now managed. Even the tiny jail tucked behind the office building was made of red brick.

The wooden dwellings housing the population would not have been more fascinating in themselves than the Dillard camp houses except for their second stories and the creative ways some of them attained their multi levels. On Mud Flat Row and Slate Dump Row and other rows that faced a road on fairly level land, the second story sat atop the first story in the customary way, but on the inclines, the rear of a house might be jammed into the hillside with the bedrooms downstairs and the front door up the hill on the side of the house, and the kitchen on the back of the top level opening straight out onto a backyard hillside. Or, the lower level might hold the half-embedded kitchen and front room, with the bedrooms upstairs at ground level on the back and two stories above the street in front. When the front of a house faced a sloping road, then the lower-side foundation was skirted to become a tall boarded-up space that most folks just called "under the floor," though some called it a cellar. This space on the lower side of a house—most of which were duplexes with the two sides built in identical mirror-images—might be taller than a story, making the second story of the house tower into the treetops, higher in actuality than a third story.

Along with the image of tree-lined streets and tall, neat, blocky, red-brick buildings, a band was always part of the picture that came to mind when Nora Faye thought of Johnston. She had watched the band perform a year before they moved to Johnston when Stella had an appendectomy in the Johnston hospital. While the adults visited with Stella, Nora Faye had been allowed to sit with Bootsie and Dollie on the top steps of a wooden hillside stairway and watch the high school band practice in the verdant park below.

That stairway was part of a network sustaining the magical MGM musical image. There were wooden walkways and stairways everywhere, flanking both sides of every roadway, whether level or sloped, with platforms in front of each house. If the houses were built around a hillside instead of up, then the walkways went around; if the houses went up the hill, then the walkways went up. Where houses were backed by woods, wooden walkways went up between houses and on past them, right into the woods where paths began. Along the lakeside, where the mine presidents, office managers, engineers and other leading citizens lived in ample, well-appointed, two-story bungalows, a concrete sidewalk flanked the lakeside road, but the wooden walkways extended up to the houses in branches like vines climbing the green hillsides, with one walkway going up so far and then branching out into two tendrils, and maybe a third one on around the hillside.

This walkway system was like a net that held the town together and like a circulatory system that sustained it. The pulse of the town throbbed visibly on its tributaries.

And, of course, the astounding difference between Johnston and a coal camp was that the mines and the tipple were not in sight or hearing of the town. Coal dust did not settle to turn every white dog gray and make every white sheet as dingy when it went on the line as when it came off. Though it was just a few miles up the road, the tipple's grinding rumble did not scrape against every summer dream on hot nights when the economy was thriving and the windows were open.

And so, the town, to Nora Faye, was a place where a band always played a Sousa march in the park, and pleasant people circulated at various levels on the hillsides, clustering on platforms and stringing out along narrow stair steps. Though she knew there had been no dancing and singing the day they watched the band, in her mind's eye she saw people on the walkways dancing and singing in bright costumes while they circulated from one level to another wielding colorful props.

On the Saturday afternoon when they had watched the band, a man was trimming back foliage in woods almost surrounding the hillside hospital, and another man was trimming along walkways and sweeping stairways. At the company store, a man was busy washing the windows with a long-handled squeegee-sponge and a bucket of water. Someone pushed a lawnmower in the grassy strip between the park and the street while another worker trimmed the hedge lines into squared off walls. Children played on the swings and slide and seesaw at one edge of the park. A man with a wheeled popcorn machine set up at the park entrance filled the air with a tantalizing aroma while he popped and bagged and sold the popcorn in jewel-tinted wax paper cones. Children on roller skates and bicycles maneuvered among the people on the well-kept concrete sidewalks and the grassy walkways in the park.

A long, ambling building between the company store and the funeral home housed the complex called the bottling plant, which also included an ice cream plant and ice-making plant. By the time James took over as manager, the facilities were outdated and in need of constant repair. He spent much of his time keeping the machinery running.

Nora Faye and Peggy were allowed to stop by to say hello on their way home from school, and they often found James in the ice plant, down in the huge concrete pit that was surrounded by a chain link fence hung with danger signs. This was the location of the enormous dynamo turning a giant flywheel and fan belt to supply power for the ice-making equipment. James had been hired because of his background with refrigeration, but his experience often fell short of the unique proportions this job presented, and he had to call on his ingenuity and innate intelligence. The fan belt pit was a dangerous, noisy place.

The girls were sent on their way on days when they found him in the pit, but on days when he was not tied to some emergency repair, he took time to explain what he was doing and to let them watch the operation of equipment as fascinating to them as it was labor-demanding for James.

The raised floor of the ice plant was like a giant checkerboard made of thick rectangular wooden lids with narrow walking spaces between. The lids covered narrow, deep metal tanks where water froze into giant ice blocks almost as tall as the girls. When the blocks were ready, the operator used machinery to remove the tanks one by one.

Long chains, which were attached to a hoist-and-pulley rig on high overhead rails, were hooked to a tank. The machinery pulled the tank out of the freezer hole and ran it along the rail to a defrosting hole where it was dipped to loosen the block before it continued to a wooden chute that emptied into the frigid storage room. A smaller chain hooked to the bottom of the tank tipped it up, another swung the lid out of the way, and the block slid down the chute.

Buyers came to an outside dock where whole blocks or pieces of a block were weighed and then loaded into truck beds, car trunks, and wagons and carts of all kinds, including toy wagons. Customers needing ice on a regular basis—those still depending on iceboxes instead of refrigerators—could pay to have the plant deliver their ice supply on a schedule.

The bottling plant—when the conveyor line was running to fill and cap bottles of RC Cola and Nehi soft drinks—was as noisy in its own way as the ice plant. The sturdy glass bottles knocked and rattled with so much racket that it seemed a run would end with piles of broken glass and sticky spilled pop instead of the neatly filled and sealed bottles. Before a run started, Nora Faye and Peggy were sometimes allowed to fill the capping receptacle with the flat metal circles that had a smaller circle of cork glued to the center. The machinery would automatically place a flat circle atop each filled bottle and crimp down to make a seal that looked like a crown. It was a joke between Nora Faye and Peggy that James told them each time they helped how RC Cola got its name from the caps, the RC standing for Royal Crown.

A long narrow stairway ran up one side wall of the bottling room to a small, lofty room in a top corner where vats of highly concentrated flavoring syrups gave off such cloyingly sweet fumes that Nora Faye had to hold her breath to keep from gagging. Peggy never went up; she was too nervous on the steep stairway that had no handrail. Slim lines from each barrel ran down to the mixing apparatus below, where measured amounts of a syrup and carbonated water were automatically added to each bottle on the line before it was capped.

James had three employees to help run the bottling plant and the ice plant, but he mixed and ran and packaged the ice cream by himself to ensure that the mixture did not become contaminated. The three ice cream machines were sleekly streamlined white receptacles on shiny chrome stems bolted to the smooth concrete floor. The walls of the room were covered with ivory colored glassy-looking tiles. All three plants had standards of cleanliness posted on numerous signs, but the ice cream room had twice as many signs stressing how everything had to be super clean. When James was making ice cream, he wore a white smock over his clothes, white cloth shoe coverings, and a white hat like a shower cap. The girls and any other viewers had to watch through a window. No one but James went into the ice cream room while a batch was underway. When a batch was ready—frozen but still soft enough to pour—he filled the paper buckets, lining them up on a shiny stainless steel table where they waited for him to come back with paper lids. Then he stacked them on the shelves of an adjoining walk-in freezer before he returned to the machine and washed and sterilized it according to certain posted procedures.

The ice cream room smelled cleaner than any place Nora Faye had ever been. She had a vague memory of the ice cream parlor in Bascon where Aunt Tattie's daughter, Florrie, and her sweetheart had taken her when she was very, very little. It had that sweetly clean smell also, but that smell was magnified a hundred times in her daddy's ice cream room. She remembered that Florrie let her get the cone with a pointed bottom and three cups in a row— an extra cup on each side of the center cup—for three different scoops of ice cream. They had laughed at her because she wanted vanilla in all three cups.

In addition to the physical labor, the plants required a tremendous amount of paperwork James took care of while sitting on a stool at a high oak desk tucked beneath the syrup-barrel room. When she came upon him perched there lost in his work, Nora Faye was reminded of Bob Cratchit from *A Christmas Carol* illustration in one of her school books.

Sometimes it seemed that he worked as long and hard as Bob Cratchit, too. Though she found the plant procedures to be as fascinating as child's play, she was aware of the enormous amount of work required to keep the machines running and the freezers maintaining safe storage temperatures. James often had to work late, and he usually checked at least one time on Sundays to make sure there had been no temperature drops. But, in spite of the demands of the new job, Nora Faye could see in her daddy's eyes and in the way he walked that he was living in a state of daily contentment like he had not known before Ginny.

CHAPTER 28
BRIMSTONE BRANCH

Something made Nora Faye stir in her sleep. Her muscles began to curl her to a sitting position before she got awake, but when her head was barely off the bed she opened her eyes to look straight into her daddy's face. A look more peaceful than she'd ever seen there caused her to let her head fall back onto the quilt that wrapped her where she lay on the ground in their pine-needle bed near the mouth of Brimstone Branch.

James sat leaning against a tree trunk, his fingers laced together on a drawn up knee. He didn't say a word nor put a finger to his lips. He didn't shake his head even a tiny bit. He just looked at her, and the look told her she need not do one single thing except go back to sleep to show him she recognized the matchless importance of the moment.

Peggy slept on one side of Nora Faye, and Virginia slept beyond Peggy. James's quilt lay undisturbed on the other side of Nora Faye. For a moment she thought the campfire was still burning, but then she realized the light was silver, not golden. Moonbeams piercing the pine branches lit her daddy's face like spotlights on the school stage, and they didn't make a glare on his glasses; she could see his eyes behind the thick lenses.

She was aware, even at her age, that this moment was the apex of her daddy's life. This was the peace and the love and the belonging he had dreamt of and never had before Ginny. She knew he had not been awakened by an animal sound or a creaking tree limb or a shifting log in the ashes of their dead campfire. She knew he had stayed awake on purpose to look upon his happiness with eyes too full of raw emotion for the daylight.

Her lids dropped and lifted a time or two before she drifted back to sleep. Her daddy's face did not change. Nothing changed. Everything was as it should be. She didn't dream about anything at all that night.

This was the second night of an outing that was a honeymoon of sorts—a family honeymoon—and the first get-away of any kind James and Virginia had after they were married.

They started by hiking to Highcrest Rock up the north side of Pine Mountain and then down the mountain to the falls on their first day. Nora Faye and Peggy were worn out when they got to the falls. They sat resting where the widely dispersing spray cooled them after their long trek. James and Virginia frolicked on gigantic boulders in the ruggedly descending hollow below the falls.

At first Nora Faye had been bothered by their playful banter as they disappeared from sight behind one boulder and then reappeared on top of another. The falls made such a roar she could no longer hear what they were saying, but when they were still close enough she was made uncomfortable by the things they were saying and how they were saying them. They were calling each other pet names and saying the same things over and over like they could not say them enough. Virginia squealed a lot as she struggled not to lose her footing on the spray-slick rocks. Nora Faye had never heard her squeal before. She squealed, "Jamie!" and "Jay!" and "Jamesy!"

James, in turn, was saying, "Here, Ginger!" and "Hold on, Gin Gin!" and "Grab my hand, Gingy!"

Nora Faye felt like she was watching people she didn't know. She worried that maybe she herself should be talking differently or feeling different. And then gradually, as the never-ending spray settled on her skin like a moist magic dusting and the smells of pine needles and decaying logs and mossy coverings on rocks filled her nostrils, she fell under the spell dominated by the echoing roar and realized her daddy and Virginia were using words they'd been wanting to use for a long time, that they'd at last found a place that unlocked their tongues to words they'd had but had not had a chance to use. She stopped watching them and watched instead a little bright green fern bobbing in the spray-filled air currents. It jutted straight out from a crack in the wet-slick rock wall and waved and waved and danced and bobbed. She fell asleep, collapsing against Peggy who had already succumbed to the overwhelming peace.

After their campfire supper, they slept that first night at the base of enormous overhanging cliffs in the ravine around beside the falls. The sandy floor made a lump-free bed and the slanted cliffs kept them dry even during a thunderstorm Nora Faye and Peggy slept right through.

Next morning, after more scrambling over the huge boulders below the falls, they sat under a pine tree to rest, and Nora Faye worked with a loose tooth until James was able to pull it for her by taking hold of it with his pocket-handkerchief. The little bit of blood didn't bother her at all because she was thinking about what she had decided to do with the tooth. James took her back down into the ravine and helped her climb to the top of one of the gigantic boulders. He held onto the back of her playsuit while she leaned over and dropped the tooth into the pool on the lower side of the rock away from the turbulence. Then he pulled her close and said right into her ear so she could hear above the roar, "Now a part of you is a part of this place."

When they got away from the roar he said, "I bet the tooth fairy will leave you a dime at home, anyway."

They took their time following the remains of a log flume that followed the stream down to the flat place near the creek-mouth where it went under the bridge to join the Rough Fork of the Cumberland River. Eldon would pick them up at the mouth of the branch tomorrow morning and take them back to their car where they'd left it on the other side of the mountain at Claude Bender Gap. But they had the rest of the day and another night to enjoy their rugged paradise.

A few logs had been left behind for some reason, their enormous girths already padded with green-gray moss. A fallen log across the creek about halfway down from the falls had made an access for James to pick blackberries from long, thick briars hanging out over the creek where they caught the sunshine funneled down between the steep walls of the ravine. He laced cucumber tree leaves together with twigs to make a basket to hold them, and they sat on the end of the log and made their dinner of blackberries, feasting until they could not hold another one.

Before their supper of potatoes and apples roasted in ashes and bacon roasted on a stick, Nora Faye and Peggy played in the creek and explored the woods while James and Virginia cleared fallen limbs to make a place for their beds on the fragrant pine needles. James took them to a spot beside the creek where foul-smelling springs pooled, the brimstone springs giving the branch its name. After he cleaned the surface of one spring, he cupped his hand and took a drink. The girls gagged to watch him and found it hard to believe when he told them people came to fill jugs with the nasty stuff they drank for good health.

He took them to another place where cold air rushed from a small low cave-opening no bigger than a shoebox and almost hidden in a jumble of rocks in the stream bank. The air was as cold as a refrigerator, and James left their bacon there closed tightly in the metal box he'd brought it in for that purpose.

Nothing except Mrs. Slaneys' black raspberry foam had ever tasted as good as the bacon they ate on that camping trip, bacon James roasted over the fire on sticks, to eat on slabs of bread toasted the same way.

CHAPTER 29
MIGGAN NESTOR

People in Johnston who didn't know better sometimes asked if Nora Faye and Peggy—in spite of their different names—were twins. They had similar coloring and similar builds. By the time they started high school they were of similar size. Virginia had saved the Cinderella brand dresses Peggy had outgrown, and when she and James were first married, it had been like another rite of union when she hunted out the dresses and passed them on to Nora Faye. They proved to be Nora Faye's favorite outfits, frilly enough to make her feel special, but sturdy enough to play in without fear of getting them dirty or torn. They were made of flowered cotton prints and had puffed sleeves and gathered skirts, and sashes that tied in the back like most of her school dresses, but they were subtly embellished with a bit of eyelet trim, a spot of embroidery on a collar, a smocked bodice, tucks, detailed buttons, or other touches that made them seem dainty though they were sturdy. With their selvedge edges, French seams, and wide hems, they even won Granny Rose's respect.

She was often the one who ended up letting down the hems as Nora Faye got the last bit of wear out of them. When Virginia added a row of matching rickrack to hide the hem line where it showed faded on one of the dresses she lengthened, Nora Faye did not tell anyone she thought the bright rickrack made the dress look shabby in a way it had not looked with a faded hem line. She found reasons not to wear the dress, though, and that was the first time she felt anything but happy to be wearing Peggy's hand-me-downs. It was still a good feeling to be Peggy's little sister wearing her outgrown clothes, but she was aware, after the rickrack, that other people might not realize it was a happy thing instead of a sad thing. It was the first time other people's possible opinions about her clothing became a part of what determined how she felt about herself.

In spite of this new awareness, she gladly continued to wear Peggy's hand-me-downs until she took a sudden growth spurt in eighth grade and caught up with her in a matter of a few months. They ended up near the same height and frame, and though Peggy's complexion was of a slightly darker hue, no one ever noticed unless they stood side by side. Peggy had not inherited her mother's long thin bones and narrow rib cage and shoulders, and Nora Faye, though of similar bone structure to Irene, had not turned out as boyishly endowed. Their compact but softly rounded figures were more like Rose than either of their mothers. They liked it when someone commented that they were built like their grandmother, catching one another's eyes to smile secretly about their secret that was not really a secret.

It had been difficult for James to let Nora Faye remain with Rose when he moved to Johnston in the spring shortly before he and Virginia were married. With Stella now living in Johnston, there would have been someone to watch Nora Faye until he got home from work each day. But, in the end, he decided it would be harder on Nora Faye to change schools a second time during the one school year than it would be for her to continue to be away from him through the week. He knew she felt almost as much at home with his mother as she did with him.

Much of second grade was a pleasant blur for Nora Faye. The incident that lodged the Wolliver School in her mind—a stage play with brownies dancing around a woodland hut—was something that actually happened before she went to school there.

She had started second grade in Dillard, a depressing two months, the walk to school without the Slaney children starting each day with a forlorn sense of loss in spite of the attention the Ballard girls gave her. Mrs. Ballard had readily agreed to watch Nora Faye after Mrs. Bledso moved away. Gwinny and Doris Ann called her their little sister and made over her like she was a cherished pet, but in spite of their kindness, Nora Faye felt sadder each day, so much so that James began to ask himself if it was wrong not to withdraw her from the Dillard school and let her stay with his mother to go to school in town even if the Wolliver principal should insist that she go back to first grade.

In Dillard it was the expected thing for a child with no school problems to finish the primer and first grade in the same year, but he did not know how they might look upon this in Wolliver since Nora Faye had attended school for less than half a year her first year and had been a year younger than the other first graders. But his mother talked to the Wolliver school principal, Opal Wheeler, who had been an admiring student of his father's, and Opal had okayed second grade enrollment.

For a brief moment James had considered another plan that would have enabled him to send her to second grade in Wolliver while having her continue to live with him. Mrs. Patterson and Mrs. Deeton had always taken turns driving their children back and forth to school in Wolliver on a daily basis, and when Mrs. Bledso moved away, they asked James if he would like to send Nora Faye to school with them in Wolliver each day.

He thanked them for their kindness, and said he'd have to think it over. At first, it seemed the ideal solution. During winter's worst weather, when driving was too dangerous, she could stay with Rose, the way the

Patterson and Deeton children stayed with their relatives in town on those days. And it seemed she'd be happier among strangers in Wolliver than she was among Dillard schoolmates who were sad reminders of the missing Slaney children.

But in spite of their offer, James did not feel totally at ease with the two women whose social position was different from his, and he feared that Nora Faye herself might sense his lack of assurance and feel uneasy with them and their children. Growing up with his parents' respectability fronting him like a family crest, he had never found reason to feel second class to anyone he encountered, but these women were wives of the company bosses, and, from that standpoint, he did not feel on an equal plane. He did not want to put Nora Faye in a situation where she would not feel carefree. In addition, he was afraid she might hear comments about her mother that he did not want her to hear.

Rose understood the situation without any explanation. She was the one to bring it up, and James realized she shared his misgivings about Mrs. Patterson and Mrs. Deeton. That's when they agreed it was time for him to let Nora Faye start living in Wolliver. It was the only way to bring an end to the sad reminders of the Dillard school without putting her in another situation that might hold its own hurtful reminders. James talked to Mrs. Everhart that very day to let her know he would be withdrawing Nora Faye from the Dillard school right away.

If Patricia Deeton and Anna Sue and Sonny Patterson had not been in a school play earlier that fall, Nora Faye might have been apprehensive about the change, but having seen the play in the Wolliver school's auditorium, she was eager to go to school there.

The Patterson and Deeton children were involved for weeks in preparations for the production. Patricia Deeton, a high school student with artistic talents, designed and constructed many of the costumes. She and Anna Sue played the role of villagers, and Sonny was a brownie with a costume made—like the other brownie costumes—of long winter underwear dyed brown and worn with a wide belt cinching in a brown-dyed shirt worn backwards and cut into points along the bottom hem and the ends of the sleeves. Patricia had come to Rose for help with several of the costumes, most notably the brownie shoes. She was having trouble keeping the long, pointed toes from collapsing sideways even after they were stuffed with cotton or wadded-up newspapers. Rose devised a new pattern that solved the problem, and Patricia was so grateful she begged Rose to come to the play and bring Nora Faye.

Nora Faye had been in the Wolliver auditorium for the graduation of more than one relative, but always at night. It was a bleak looking place in the middle of the afternoon, with high windows covered by black shades that did not let in much light on the gloomy fall day of the performance in spite of staggered cracks here and there. The stage curtains were closed. A strange little room in the back-center of the balcony caught Nora Faye's eye as she turned around to watch the school classes file by to take their seats down in front of the parents who were already seated. The little room at back looked sort of like the projection booth at the movie house, and she wondered if there would be a movie.

At that moment the lights went off in the auditorium. The sound of a flute came mysteriously out of the darkness, and a ray of light beamed down from the back of the auditorium to the center of the stage curtains where it created a circle. After several tension filled seconds, the curtains slowly opened as the light turned blue. At first Nora Faye could make out nothing on the stage except for some kind of small three-sided hut with the fourth side open to the audience. Then the beam widened to reveal shadowy figures tiptoeing out of the darkness as they began to dance around the hut that Nora Faye could now see was made of leafy twigs and saplings. The figures were brownies in pointy-toed shoes. The spotlight gradually changed to red and then yellow and white as it crept around the stage highlighting first one area and then another.

The flute was heard again, this time sounding like birdcalls. Something moved in the hut. It was a little girl in a wispy white dress with fluttering sleeves. The spotlight contracted to bathe her in an ethereal, soft, white light. She sat up rubbing her eyes with the back of her fists like she'd been asleep. Her elbows, jutting out to each side, were held high, making her flowing, wispy sleeves look like fairy wings. As the brownies danced around her little house, she joined them, taking a turn first with one and then another before she took center stage to dance alone in the spotlight. Her scarf-like sleeves fluttered constantly as she changed from position to position, first bending her arms with hands near the waist—but never touching her waist—and then with her hands near her eyes again like they'd been when she first awoke. When her hands were near her head, she held them palms forward, drawing opened fingers across her eyes as she tilted first one elbow and then the other up, bending sideways at the waist and extending one leg out straight with a pointed toe touching the floor. The gauzy sleeves never stopped fluttering. Her hands turned palms toward her when she brought them near her waist and bent them at the wrist with delicate fingers feeling at the air. Sometimes it seemed she floated off the stage.

The light beam widened to reveal a forest with leafy trees and dangling vines. For the next hour Nora Faye was so completely lost in the magic world before her eyes that she would not have known her own name if she'd been suddenly asked. She totally forgot that Sonny's brownie suit was really long winter underwear. She forgot, in fact, that Sonny was one of the brownies. He looked as unearthly in the colored lights as everything else on the stage.

From that day on, Nora Faye was eager to start school in Wolliver and, in her second week of school there, she realized that the girl who had danced with the brownies was the girl sitting beside her in reading class. The girl's name was as otherworldly as her stage role. She was Miggan Nestor. Nora Faye was almost speechless in her presence.

Second grade in Wolliver seemed like a continuation of the stage presentation she'd witnessed, taking on the qualities of a fairytale occurrence happening to someone else. She walked through it in a kind of trance. She could do her lessons well enough to require no special attention. Her teacher, Mrs. Crawford, seemed surprised that she could read so well. She had a talk with Mrs. Sherman, the third grade teacher and, starting in Nora Faye's second week, she was sent to the third grade room when it was time for reading lessons. It was Miggan Nestor who was assigned to walk her back to her second grade room just to make sure she didn't get lost the first time.

For the first few days Nora Faye was shy without friends or cousins to do the talking for her, but her new classmates immediately began to look out for her. Shirley Bastin, who lived down the street from Granny Rose, took her under her wing right away.

On Sundays she got to be with Peggy—sometimes they were all at Johnston and sometimes James and Nora Faye went to Vargo—and by the time she and Peggy started living together that spring, they could hardly remember not being together.

CHAPTER 30
PEGGY'S VOICE

Nora Faye enjoyed the security that came with being Peggy's little sister. She knew Peggy's reputation was the reason some people were nice to her. Everybody liked Peggy. In addition to her pleasing personality, she had a beautiful singing voice that opened doors for her and won the admiration of the entire community.

When Peggy became a solo act, a tangled emotion of part pride and part envy gnawed at Nora Faye. At first, the four of them had sung together: Nora Faye, Peggy, Bootsie and Dollie, but their act was built on the novelty of the songs, not on anybody's singing talent. After Peggy started singing by herself, it wasn't just that Nora Faye felt envious of how good she was, but she resented sharing her with everybody. People acted like they had a personal claim on her, like she belonged to them. A part of Nora Faye understood the reaction. Peggy sang as well as Judy Garland or Shirley Temple, and she inspired that same kind of adoration.

When she was not performing, people treated her the same as any likable child, and this was what was really hard for Nora Faye to face up to: she knew she was more envious of Peggy's natural likeability than she was of her uncommon singing talent. Even though most adults had treated Nora Faye well all her life, she felt it was because she did not stand out in any way rather than that she had any outstanding qualities. She could not imagine how it would feel to have a talent like Peggy's, and she was in awe of the way Peggy stayed the same, even after people started treating her like she was special. She thought she could not have stayed the same if people admired her the way they admired Peggy, who was so unassuming that people could almost forget about her dazzling performances when she was not on stage. Nora Faye sometimes wished Peggy would mess up on stage or have a temper tantrum somewhere…anywhere.

By fifth grade, Peggy was the expected main act of every show in town. Her fourth grade teacher, Mrs. Spangler, was the wife of the high school chorus teacher, and the two of them were co-sponsors of the school's three big talent shows a year. Mrs. Spangler took her under her wing that year and helped her work up a wide selection of songs.

Her all-community debut came during her first spring in Johnston when the Kiwanis Club asked her to sing "Short'nin' Bread" for their annual minstrel show. The Kiwanis Club show was a very important event with a program that seemed to be trying to showcase all the talent in town. A small group from the high school band opened with Dixieland jazz, followed by a large group of high school girls in evening gowns and boys in their best clothes—ties and jackets if they had them—singing Stephen Foster songs. A group of seventh and eighth grade boys sang Hoagy Carmichael's "Lazy Bones" and "Ole Buttermilk Sky," and girls the same age sang "Skylark" and "Star Dust." A set of high school twin sisters sang "It's Only a Paper Moon" and "Elmer's Tune," and a fifth-grade brother and sister act sang "Mr. Five by Five." A young history teacher in a beard and top-hat recited Lincoln's Gettysburg Address . A high school boy played a trumpet solo and a high school girl named Helen Royce did two dance numbers reminding Nora Faye of Miggan Nestor. Two fifth grade boys recited poems by James Whitcomb Riley, and an eighth grade boy gave a humorous declamation he'd written himself.

Two men in blackface—two of the Kiwanis Club members—sitting on stools in front of the curtain at either end of the stage, made comments and told jokes between acts. One of them, who introduced the acts, was the leader. The others called him Mr. Interlocutor. Sometimes a group of men in blackface came out between acts to do a skit in front of the closed curtains, and the final act was the stage full of what seemed to be the entire membership of the Kiwanis Club in blackface, taking center stage one by one to make one joke after another and do little dance steps between. The Interlocutor, Mr. Kellerman, was the one who had asked James about letting Peggy sing in the show.

Peggy got her first glimpse of blackface makeup when a young Kiwanis Club member, new to the tradition, rehearsed his skit in makeup early on to get a feel for it. She knew she did not want to do that. She hunted out Mr. Kellerman and told him she was sorry to back out of the show, but that she hadn't realized she'd have to wear that kind of makeup.

He laughed kindly and told her she would not be wearing blackface. He thought it was the mess she didn't want to deal with. He said, "No wonder such a pretty little girl doesn't want to put that stuff on her rosy cheeks." He said nobody wore blackface except the Kiwanis members, that it was a long and honored tradition that meant a lot to them.

So she stayed in the show, but when she was given a wig of pickaninny curls, she just quietly refused to wear it. She did wear a dirty-looking torn shirt and raggedy little cut-off pants with a knotted rope belt and uneven galluses, and no one seemed to notice the missing wig.

She told James and her mother she did not want to be in another minstrel show. She told them the rehearsals took up too much time, waiting through all the many acts before her turn came, but she told Nora Faye she wasn't

249

sure why she had such bad feelings about it. Even without that venue, she was Johnston's most often seen performer.

For a short while it was mistakenly assumed that all four girls had pretty singing voices. Stella launched their act in a small Woman's Club production she helped organize her first winter in Johnston. She put the act together after she heard the girls singing in the porch swing one rainy late-summer day while she was thinking about working up a number for Dollie and Bootsie to sing in the show.

The four girls were entertaining themselves by teaching songs to each other. One thing Nora Faye missed about the Dillard school was the Friday afternoon entertainments when the teachers forgot about the routine lessons for the rest of the day and had the biggest boys push back the folding doors between the two rooms. After a spelling bee and a math competition—and sometimes a states and capitals bee—the teachers led the children in songs together, songs like "Listen to the Mockingbird" and "My Old Kentucky Home." Then the students entertained by performing whatever songs they wanted.

She especially liked the way the Sexton sisters sang. They lived way up on Dillard and hardly ever came to school for a full week, but they almost always came on Fridays for the singing. They sang old-timey sounding war songs: "There'll Be Smoke On the Water, the Land and the Sea;" "I'm Writing This Down in a Trench, Mom;" and "When the Roses Bloom up Yonder, I'll Be There." Nora Faye became friendly with Helen Sexton who spent recess and the entire lunch hour one Friday going over and over the words to "I'm Writing This Down in a Trench, Mom" until Nora Faye learned it in that one day. Helen was an olive skinned wisp of a girl with a long neck and long straight, dark hair framing her heart-shaped face. She was the prettiest girl Nora Faye had ever seen, and the maroon colored scar on one side of her face, swooping from her ear almost to the corner of her mouth made her seem even more beautiful. It was a clean line that pulled no features out of shape. Nora Faye realized the scar most likely came from an agonizing calamity, and she was ashamed of her envy, but she could not help wishing she could know how it would feel to have something so dramatic marking her face. She had never heard anyone mention it, when Helen was around or when she wasn't.

The songs the Sextons sang weren't the songs the girls were singing the day Stella was listening. Nora Faye and Peggy were teaching Dollie and Bootsie the boy-girl songs they'd learned in their schools, the ones like, "Reuben, Reuben" and "Paper of Pins." They often sang those for their own entertainment.

Stella didn't have the musical ear to distinguish one voice from another, and she didn't pinpoint Peggy's talent as being any greater than the others, but she did recognize that they had exactly the substance she'd been trying to create for Dollie and Bootsie's act. So, instead of one pair, there were now two pairs of friends to sing "Once There Lived Side By Side Two Little Maids." Virginia made costumes for them, blue checked gingham pinafores—like the song said—over white puffed sleeve blouses with white Dutch bonnets. Dollie and Nora Faye had natural pigtails; Bootsie and Peggy had artificial ones made from yarn and attached to their hats. Mrs. Bowers, the Methodist minister's wife—and Dollie's piano teacher— played piano for them, as well as for most of the other acts in the show. She was the one who first pointed out to Stella that it was Peggy who had the voice.

Stella had the four of them do their number again for the school's next talent show and had Peggy and Nora Faye, without Bootsie and Dollie, sing "Reuben, Reuben." Both acts were crowd pleasers and the girls were invited to present them for several civic groups before they outgrew their costumes.

Peggy and Nora Faye continued to get invitations to do the boy-girl songs and some other numbers like "Rubber Dolly" and "Don't Sit under the Apple Tree" that they sang in regular clothes. It was evident to some who knew music that Peggy's voice carried them, but the novelty of the pairing kept Nora Faye in the act until there was an incident making her think she'd better bow out before she brought embarrassment upon herself.

When they came offstage one night, Mrs. Spangler's visiting sister who was helping backstage, enthusiastically praised them for their cleverness, saying, "That's so skillful the way one of you sings just off key for the entire song. Which one of you manages to do that?" Peggy looked stricken for a moment before she forced a giggle. "That's part of the act, making everybody guess," she tossed off. Nora Faye realized then that Peggy had always known what had come as a shock to her at that moment. She didn't perform again.

Sometimes she would suddenly be overwhelmed with shame to think of all the times she had exposed herself to ridicule by singing without knowing she was singing off key. Sometimes she even felt angry at the people, especially Peggy, who had let it happen. But Peggy said nobody ever noticed whether they were singing well or not, that their audiences just enjoyed the kind of songs they sang. When Nora Faye asked how long Peggy would have let her go on singing if Mrs. Spangler's sister hadn't said something, Peggy said she had always figured something would happen to bring things to a natural end.

Without a partner, Peggy sang a different kind of song, moving rapidly from the novelty numbers to perky pop hits to sentimental pop hits to love songs. Her mainstays for a while were "Buttons and Bows," "I'm Looking over a Four Leaf Clover," and "If I Knew you Were Coming I'd A baked A Cake." Then "The Old Lamplighter," "Far Away Places," "A Tree in the Meadow," and "Now is the

Hour," right on into "My Happiness," "On a Slow Boat to China," and "I Beg Your Pardon." Granny Rose was bothered by "On a Slow Boat to China." The girls could not figure why that number, out of the long list, was the one that hit her as inappropriate for a young girl to sing.

Until she started high school Peggy's stage clothes were no problem. If she needed something other than one of her best dresses, her mother or Rose made it for her. But as she got older, a formal gown often seemed called for. Rose and Virginia could have made them, simple prom-style formals with full gathered skirts and fitted waists and tops—but the fabrics were expensive and often unavailable. Before it became an issue, the problem was solved by Betsy Fryman, a hometown girl who lived across the street on Coopers Cove. She always called herself that—a hometown girl—meaning she had lived all her life in Johnston. She was actually a young wife and mother who had married straight out of high school and started her family right away. She had three young children, but she had sentimental memories of her high school days, when she had been the one to sing in the local shows. So when Peggy began singing more adult songs, Betsy insisted on giving her the two evening gowns she had saved. "They're just hanging there taking up precious closet space, and they'll be out of date by the time my girls grow into them, anyway," she said. After Betsy contributed hers, there were other young mothers who wanted to see their old gowns appear in public even if those days were in the past for them. Before she knew what had happened, Peggy found herself trying to find a place to hang her several evening gowns, and the talents of Virginia and Rose were called upon for making alterations instead of making entire dresses.

CHAPTER 31
THE BEGINNING OR THE END

The day when half of the student body—grades six to twelve—was marched to the Johnston Cinema to see a movie called *The Beginning or the End* was unlike any school day so far. Nora Faye's teacher, Mrs. Amberson, somberly prepared her class for the outing, telling them this was one of the most solemn occasions of all their schooldays. They were seeing the movie, not to be entertained, she said, but to learn the stories behind the atomic bomb, to learn the history and the implications. There had been some disagreement in a faculty meeting about whether sixth graders were old enough to understand the movie, she told them, but she was one of the teachers who argued for their right to see it. She said they might not understand all of it but that the older students would not understand all of it either.

They were part of a very special generation, she went on, the first generation to grow up in the atomic age. The world could never go back to the way it was before Hiroshima. She told them they must learn all they could about atomic energy because, though they had nothing to do with developing it, they were the ones who must figure out how to manage this awe-inspiring but frightening power source which could be used for accomplishment or for destruction, a source that came with a scope of possibilities and responsibilities beyond anything the human race had yet to face. If it proved to be true that this new source of energy could replace other sources—including coal—then they were the generation who would have to figure out how they could make it happen without destroying themselves with it. They would be the first generation with means to move away from consumable energy sources and supposedly turn the earth into a non-depleting, self-perpetuating planet, or they could be the first to destroy the planet in the wink of an eye. The bomb would hang over their heads for the rest of their lives, she said, no matter what they did or didn't do.

One by one, smiles dropped off the faces of Nora Faye's classmates, and, throat by throat, big swallows silenced happy whispers. When her class joined the others in the hallway, it was obvious that all the teachers had given similar preparation; the groups were all subdued. When Nora Faye saw Peggy and Dollie outside in the alley and then on the sidewalk at the theatre, she didn't give them even a tiny smile. A slight bend of her wrist near her hemline was the closest she allowed herself to come to a wave. She struggled to keep her fingers from wiggling. She noticed how pretty Peggy's feet and ankles looked today in the brown penny-loafers she wore without socks. Most of the girls in her class wore bobby socks with fat rolled-down cuffs, but Peggy didn't like that look for herself. Nora Faye's feet were still a size smaller, but she was eager to get rid of her Girl Scout oxfords and try out Peggy's loafers. She studied her own feet for a moment wondering how her lace-up oxfords would look without anklets.

She didn't know how she was supposed to be feeling about the movie, but the others seemed to be a little unsure also: a little afraid and yet a little excited. The entire mass of students was like a hive of bees just barely humming but possibly on the verge of erupting into some kind of chaos. She remembered Conner telling her about the swarm of Mr. Williams' bees he'd seen collect on a tree branch in a great tangled clump. She would not have been surprised to see the entire student body suddenly take off in one big clump for a spot somewhere way up on the mountainside.

There was extra effort to keep lines straight and the pace steady, but the teachers wielded these efforts with looks more sadly serious than stern or hateful. The procession wasn't quite as somber as a funeral procession, but that's what came to Nora Faye's mind. She almost giggled to think it was kind of like they were going to their own funeral.

But her main concern was Buddy Holbrook who was seated in front of her alphabetically in the schoolroom and had therefore ended up in front of her in line. She was in danger of getting into big trouble because of Buddy. Mrs. Amberson had already thrown several looks their way when Buddy kept insisting—with elaborate mimed motions—that she get in front of him. She finally took his offer in desperation, thinking it was the only way to stop his antics, but Mrs. Amberson immediately motioned that she should return to her spot behind him. She cringed to think of the other ways Buddy might bring Mrs. Amberson's wrath down on her before the movie was over. The other girls told her Buddy was saying she was his girlfriend. He had been making her life miserable in the classroom by constantly making a show of his interest. He hurried to the board when their row was called up in arithmetic class so he could pick out the longest piece of chalk and present it to her like a trophy, and he always picked her first whenever he was the one to choose sides for anything.

She did not want to be Buddy's girlfriend and did not want people to think she was. She had not liked or disliked him before he started his romantic campaign, but even if she had liked him, she would have recognized his interest as something bound to get her into trouble with Mrs. Amberson.

Dilemmas like this did not come up with Peggy, who had a way of discouraging boys she didn't like without making them feel bad. She told Nora Faye some things she could say to discourage Buddy without making an enemy of him, but Nora Faye knew Peggy's words would not work for her. They wouldn't come out of her mouth if she should try. She figured things like that had to come naturally. It would sound right only if it came to your own mind.

Peggy knew how to talk to people. She always had a boyfriend and many other admirers. She talked sweetly to all of them, but not in a false-hearted, double-timing way. She was naturally kind and understanding, and she just knew what to say to make people feel good. When Randall Mayfield brought her a big box of candy on Valentines Day, Peggy somehow managed to refuse it, while, at the same time, making Randall feel good about himself for bringing it to her. At her subtle suggestion, he ended up sharing it with the whole class, and they all ended up thinking Randall was a great fellow.

Nora Faye didn't remember what Peggy told her she had said to Randall, but she'd seen her manage other awkward situations with that kind of results. Peggy might not have told her about it at all if she had not wanted to give Nora Faye an example of how she might handle Buddy Holbrook, and she only told her about Randall bringing her the candy; she didn't tell her how it turned out that he gave it to the class instead of her. Nora Faye wouldn't have known about that part if their neighbor, Mrs. Shannon, had not told Virginia. Mrs. Shannon had witnessed the event when she took cookies to her daughter's classroom, and she gave an account to Virginia in Nora Faye's hearing. She said, "I sure wish my Betty Jo had that knack, but she's so awkward about it that I don't see how she'll ever have a boyfriend."

It was not that Nora Faye did not want to have a boyfriend, but she never seemed to like the boys who liked her—like Buddy Holbrook—while the ones she did like were not interested in her. She had no desire to compromise.

She had thought it would be nice to be Jackie Glenville's girlfriend, until he got mad at her when he thought she had betrayed him by supplying snowballs to Doug Sam Boyd one winter recess when the boys were having snowball battles from behind snow forts. The girls were making snowballs for the boys, and Nora Faye was delighted when Jackie asked her to make his. She had liked Jackie for some time and she hadn't been able to figure out if he liked her.

But an unfortunate mix-up ensued after Doug Sam destroyed Jackie's fort. He asked Jackie to pair up with him behind his fort. This seemed to be according to rules, as far as Nora Faye could tell, so she joined in with her friend, Susanna, who was making Doug Sam's snowballs. Nora Faye thought the snowballs were going into one communal pile between the two boys, and she was adding an armful to the pile when Jackie jumped up and asked her why she was helping Doug Sam instead of him. Doug Sam turned to see what the distraction was, and two well-placed snowballs landed smack in the faces of Jackie and Doug Sam as their fort was attacked and destroyed by Foster Boggs.

Doug Sam laughed and started building another fort, asking Nora Faye if she would like to make his snowballs this time. Nora Faye declined, but Susanna was mad at her because Doug Sam asked her, and Jackie was mad at her because he thought she'd been helping Doug Sam. She hurried to catch up with Jackie who was headed toward the schoolhouse door. She tried to explain, but he wouldn't hear what she was saying. He stopped and turned suddenly, saying, "I should have known you wanted to help him. When we were arguing about who could have first chance at asking you, he said I could go ahead because you would turn me down anyway and wait for him to ask you. What I don't understand is why you agreed to help me when you really wanted to help him."

Nora Faye's head was whirling. It was more than she could take in to think of two boys fighting over her and of the passion her supposed slight had brought to one of them. It was the first time it had ever occurred to her that a boy might have this kind of interest in her, much less that two boys might have equal interest. That realization made her feel good for a moment. It seemed flattering that they wanted to claim rights to her in front of everybody. But, on second thought, there was a part of her that very much didn't like that they had argued over her before asking her what she wanted, and that what they were fighting over was the use of her snowball-making skills the way they might fight over a good slingshot or BB gun.

Before she could say anything, Jackie whirled and continued toward the schoolhouse. She felt mad enough that she scooped up a two-handed wad of snow and pressed it into a ball that she flung at his head just as he reached the door. He dodged as the door opened and Mr. Stamper, an eighth grade teacher, came out. Her snowball hit Mr. Stamper in the chest. Nora Faye's breath sucked in and she felt like she might faint. She thought this would be her first bad-conduct trip to the principal's office. But Mr. Stamper just frowned and looked surprised. He gave his head a little disapproving shake when he saw who had hit him, brushing off the snow with one nonchalant swipe as he said, "You children need to look where you're throwing."

Her situation certainly did not end like Peggy's valentine experience. Nothing good came out of it for anyone. Susanna made such a fuss about Doug Sam's rejection that Doug Sam didn't want anything more to do with either of them, and Jackie's stubborn refusal to hear her explanation left her feeling angry and frustrated. She wrote him a note that afternoon saying, "I thought they were supposed to go into one pile after you and Doug Sam started fighting in the same fort." She wrote small and tore off the little note and folded it a couple of times before she dropped it on his desk. He wadded it even smaller without looking at it and put it into his mouth where he made a great spectacle of chewing and swallowing it.

So, with this kind of past experience with boys who supposedly liked her, Nora Faye had no interest in responding to Buddy Holbrook, but she didn't know how to discourage him without making a scene. She dreaded sitting beside him during the movie. It occurred to her that he might even try to hold her hand. Susanna had told her the way a boy let you know he wanted to kiss you was by holding your hand and secretly wiggling one of his fingers in your palm. She knew how mad Mrs. Amberson would be if she caused any kind of stir on such a solemn and carefully planned occasion.

She was saved when Buddy was the last one to fill a row and she was directed to go all the way over to the end of the next row before she took a seat. She was too far removed from Buddy to be in danger of an incident. And watching *The Beginning or the End* might have had a sobering effect on Buddy in general, because that was the last time he offered Nora Faye a place in line or showed any interest in her, and she never again heard that he was calling her his girlfriend.

The walk back to school was still far from routine, but the other students seemed to have lost their apprehension. They appeared to be feeling like the worst was over as they tried to hold out just a little longer before they risked a total return to normal behavior. Nora Faye, however, was filled with dread, not about the atom bomb, but about the possible classroom follow-up to the movie. She was afraid she'd be asked what it meant, and she knew she couldn't say. Her classmates didn't seem to be worrying about being put on the spot. They didn't seem to be thinking about the movie at all.

It was not what she had expected. It was not just a war movie. She had a hard time following the stories. There were romance stories along with the story of getting the bombs ready and making the decision to drop them. She felt a little less awed when she realized it was a movie with actors playing parts, not the actual scientists. She recognized the handsome young newlywed scientist; she'd seen him in other movies. But, in another way, she wished it had been the real people. Having actors play the roles made it all seem a little phony after the big buildup.

She could understand that this bomb was much worse than other bombs, but she wasn't sure how a bomb could be a source of energy, or if the words nuclear and atomic meant the same thing. And she couldn't see why it was going to hang over everything that happened to them from now on, the way Mrs. Amberson had warned.

When she realized on the walk back to school that Buddy wasn't going to be bothering her any more, it was a relief to have one less reason to worry about getting into trouble with Mrs. Amberson. She got off to a bad start with her early in the year, and she had been struggling to make up for it ever since.

One of the first classroom projects Mrs. Amberson launched with them was a unit on how to debate. She said debating skills would serve them well throughout their school years and for the rest of their lives.

She caught Nora Faye's full attention when she said debating would teach them how to disagree without losing their tempers. Angry arguments made Nora Faye's stomach hurt, but she liked the idea of disagreeing in a friendly way. She had deplored it when her daddy and mother argued hatefully, but she found it comforting when he and Ginny disagreed about things without getting mad.

James and Ginny had fallen into a routine of pushing their chairs back after supper and nursing a cup of coffee while they continued with discussions they'd started while they were eating, discussions about the Marshall Plan and the Truman Doctrine, whether Ginny should take a teaching job, or whether they should have a garden at the back of the yard next year. They didn't always talk about things from the news and they didn't always agree, but the nice thing was that their voices sounded the same whether they were agreeing or disagreeing.

Sometimes Ginny would jump up and empty a kettle into a storage bowl or grab the broom and push it back under a cabinet where her eye had landed on some crumbs, but her sudden spurts of domestic application did not interfere with the flow of the conversation.

Nora Faye and Peggy washed the dishes and cleaned up the kitchen around them, sometimes listening to James and Virginia and sometimes so caught up in their own conversation that they paid no attention to their parents' discussions which set the mood like background music. Sometimes James and Ginny drifted from side to side as they discussed an issue. Sometimes, when they had strong differences—as they did about the garden—they reached no common ground, but Nora Faye could tell it made no difference in how they felt about each other.

That's how she wanted to be able to talk. She, herself, found it impossible to argue without getting emotional, so she usually tried to go along with people even if she disagreed with them. Learning how to disagree without crying or feeling defeated sounded like the perfect way to attack the much-despised weakness.

After Mrs. Amberson spent a day teaching them the basic rules of debate, she let them suggest topics for future discussion. She wrote the topics on the board as she called on the students one by one. Nora Faye raised her hand immediately. She knew exactly what she wanted to hear debated: why the two schools should be united, the regular school and the colored school.

One of the few disappointments about living in Johnston had been the discovery that there was a separate school for colored children. She'd always been curious about the colored children she glimpsed when she visited in Johnston, and she had looked forward to going to school with them.

She was surprised and sad when it first sank in that the big white frame building across the railroad tracks from her school was a separate colored school. Nobody talked about it. It wasn't so much like it was a touchy subject; it was just something that was settled. Even her daddy had no insight for her. It seemed to be something he'd never wondered about. "I reckon they'd rather have their own school," he'd said after some deliberation. "They have their own churches and pool hall and barber shop. The men even have their own lodge building. I guess they feel comfortable in their own places," he finished up. "They'd not feel any more at home in ours than we would in theirs."

She knew Mrs. Amberson was going to be pleased with her topic, because she kept saying, "Don't repeat the same ideas. See how original you can be." The board was almost covered when she finally got her chance to contribute, and she felt light-hearted and assured—almost smug—as she said, "There should be just one school for the colored children and us so that we'd all be together." She had even remembered to make it a statement instead of a question.

Everything went silent. The few hands yet waving in the air dropped or froze in place. All eyes locked on Mrs. Amberson's face.

Mrs. Amberson first smiled a fleeting little indulgent, squinty-eyed smile, then her lips pursed, her eyelids dropped halfway, and her nostrils flared. "Nora Faye," she said with an air of great patience. "Take a look at the topics on the board. If you'd been paying attention to the list, you would realize how inappropriate your suggestion is. We'd be wasting our time to debate things we can't influence. Notice how all the items on the board deal with things that are part of your real world. See if you can think of a more suitable topic and I'll come back to you."

Her classmates exhaled, and Mrs. Amberson returned to calling on them as she added to the list of topics like: cats make better pets than dogs; girls should be allowed to play football; boys should be cheerleaders. (Those two got lots of laughs.) Bugs Bunny is funnier than Woody Woodpecker; school vacation should be in the winter instead of summer; (That one came from Joe Bradson who liked to be different.) Lincoln was a greater president than Washington; Bing Crosby sings better than Frank Sinatra; football is harder to play than basketball; the wolf would be a better symbol for America than the eagle.

Nora Faye guessed Mrs. Amberson didn't really mean it when she urged them to think up original topics—the one about the wolf was the only one with any originality—and she didn't think her classmates had any more influence on the listed topics than they had on her topic.

She did not try to think of another one.

After they saw *The Beginning or the End*, she wondered if Mrs. Amberson would have let them debate whether or not President Truman did the right thing when he ordered the bomb dropped. On the one hand, she told them the bomb would always hang over their heads, but, on the other hand, how could the atomic bomb be part of their real world if the colored children were not?

CHAPTER 32
THE ROCK

Susanna didn't stay mad after the snow-fort incident. She forgot about Doug Sam and had a new boyfriend the very next day. Nora Faye was glad things had not changed between them. It was from Susanna she learned the ins and outs of the town and the routines of the children. Susanna's older sister, Rayelle, was Peggy's friend, and there were four other girls near their ages who lived on their stretch of Coopers Cove. James and Virginia let them do almost anything they asked as long as some of these neighborhood girls were involved.

It didn't take Nora Faye long to learn how friendships were built partly on silly, meaningless, repetitive things that made you feel like you were part of the group, things sort of like singing with the Slaneys in their swing or chanting Conner's rhymes on the back steps.

But the things among her Johnston friends were somehow less personal and more of the outside world. It wasn't just that the Johnston things came from movies and radio shows—so did some of the songs she sang with the Slaney's—but she never thought about "Would you Rather Swing on a Star" without remembering how Ruthie had squeezed the sides of her mouth to make her look like a fish.

It seemed to her that her Johnston friends were doing what everybody else did, rather than making up their own things like Conner's rhymes. The Bugs Bunny exchange, for instance, a favorite with her and Susanna, would get the same response with anyone you started it with, whether or not they knew what you were doing. One person would start by saying something like, "You've got *updoc* in your hair" or "Oops. I spilled my *updoc*." The other would ask, "What's *updoc*?" and the first would say something like, "I didn't know your name was Bugs Bunny." That's all there was to it, the supposed purpose being to spring it on someone who had not heard it. But those in the know seemed to enjoy bantering it back and forth as much as they enjoyed pulling it on the unaware, the challenge being to come up with fresh ways to set it up.

Nora Faye didn't know the origin of another routine Susanna had taught her, but somebody said it came from a Bob Hope movie. She and Susanna repeated it several times a day. It started whenever one of them complained about something. The other would say, "Well, that's life."

"What's life?"

"A magazine."

"Where do you get it?"

"Drugstore."

"What's it cost?"

"A nickel."

"I don't have a nickel."

"Well, that's life…"

It could on and on until something happened to turn their attention to some other delicious silliness.

Even harder to resist was a little song everyone joined whenever one person started it, the point being to claim the most attention by being as melodramatic as possible:

Blood on the saddle.
Drip, drip.
Blood on the trail.
Splash, splash.
Cowboys a dying.
Ooooooooh.
Horses a neighing.
Naaaaaaaay.

This is the end of my tale.
Swish, swosh.

Susanna lived five houses down from Nora Faye, on the same side of the road. It was from her yard Nora Faye often gazed up at Ransom Rock, the Rock hanging above Cooper's Cove. Her own house sat too close in to the base of the mountain to give a view of the rock when she looked up from her yard.

She loved her house. Several things made it special. It was the last house built on her side of the street, so there was nothing but woods on the upper side as well as the back. And it stood alone, without being attached to another house. Her yard went all the way around her house, and she was able to look out windows in all four directions. The houses up to Nora Faye's house in Cooper's Cove were identical, two-story, double-sided, mirror-image houses with three rooms in a row downstairs and three upstairs on each side.

But where the mountain became suddenly steep, the lot was big enough for only one unit in Nora Faye's house, which was tucked into its own little cove. It also had it's own layout to fit the curve of the hill. Downstairs, the living room and dining room faced the street, with the kitchen on the back.

Something else making Nora Faye very happy was the bathroom that was upstairs with the three bedrooms. This was not the first time she had lived with the luxury of an inside bathroom—Granny Rose's house had a bathroom, one her granny told her Grandpa Houston had built at the end of what had once been a long back porch—but she felt especially lucky to think how close they came to having no bathroom in Cooper's Cove. Theirs was the last house on the street with a bathroom. A tank truck called the honey wagon came at scheduled intervals to clean out the toilets behind the houses built higher on the hill.

She could see a totally different world from each upstairs window. The back bedroom she and Peggy shared had views in three directions, the window at the highest elevation of the house giving a vista out over the roofs of the lower houses and threading west through spaces between several intermeshing spurs to reveal a glimpse of the road up the mountain to the lower gap where the ditch on one side of the road drained into the head of the Kentucky River and the ditch on the other side into the Big Sandy River via Buckhorn Creek.

The road doubled back up the mountain to go south through the out-of-sight pass to Virginia. It seemed odd to Nora Faye that you would go straight up the mountain to go south; south had always seemed downhill to her. Around the mountain from the pass was the enormous out-jutting Ransom Rock standing sentry directly above her house.

The opposite bedroom window was just a few yards from the steeply inclined forest floor that sloped straight down from the rock, and the back window looked onto the hillside spur rounding out their cove across the little salamander-inhabited stream trickling down behind the house. James and Virginia's bedroom window at the front of the house looked out over houses to the east and to the place where a trail led through the woods to the schoolhouse.

Across the street, houses continued on up and into the highest reaches of the cove. If you went past the yard of the highest house and on into the woods, you could curve around to come down in Brickyard Hollow where Bootsie and Dollie lived. The double houses on the higher lots of Coopers Cove had only four rooms on each side. Then there were little one-story, three-room houses nudging right into the trees. The road forked in three directions several houses above Nora Faye's house, one fork going to the edge of the woods and two forks looping around and back down into the lower road.

On their first Christmas Eve in the new house, snow began to fall just at dusk. The house was full of voices and excitement and Christmas smells. Granny Rose was there, and Eldon's family. The sharp tang of the Christmas tree blended with Granny Rose's traditional Christmas Eve supper smells: cornbread, salmon patties, a mix of mashed vegetables including turnips, parsnips, carrots, and sometimes—when she had them—little knotty clumps she called Jerusalem artichokes that were the roots of a few tall, gangly-stemmed plants with yellow flowers that grew at the back of her garden, wedges of lettuce with mayonnaise, and for dessert, gingerbread cake with cinnamon applesauce. The other girls were still rearranging things on the tree in the living room, James and Eldon were working on the tree lights—as they always seemed to do throughout every Christmas season—and Stella and Virginia were pouring milk and water and putting the last touches on the table while Granny Rose mashed the vegetables.

Nora Faye had been sent upstairs to get an extra chair, but she stayed on where she could go from room to room, from window to window, to see the snow coming down on the different worlds around her house. It looked like a different snowfall from the different windows. When she looked out the highest window she could see great drapes of snow whipping like sheets on Virginia's clotheslines up one hollow and then another. At the back window she could watch the ground slowly turn white where the cove gave protection from the wind, and from the upper window she looked right onto the steep forest floor and saw individual flakes settling softly on packed, brown leaves and collecting one by one on mossy tree trunks. At the front window in James and Virginia's room she could look up and into the wind to see the flakes coming at her like a magic crumbling of the sky.

This was not her first snowfall, of course, but it was the first time she had watched from an upstairs window and had felt like she was among the flakes as they came down. She breathed on the windowpane and quickly drew a six-pointed snowflake in the condensation before it dripped and ran down the glass to make a puddle on the shiny ivory painted windowsill.

When the family began to call her she didn't answer right away and did not go down until she took another tour from window to window, trying to give each of her senses a chance to experience all of it one more time as she wondered what it would feel like to be standing on the edge of Ransom Rock in the middle of this snowfall right now.

There were several tales about how Ransom Rock got its name. One of the most often-repeated had to do with Indians holding white captives in a cave under the mountain until a ransom of horses, hides and moonshine was delivered to the rock. Their teachers said it was probably untrue. No caves had been discovered under the rock, and moonshine production on a large scale was not so common until a later time. Another story had to do with an Indian called Chief Ransom who would sit on his white pony at the very edge of the rock while his braves made raids on the few scattered settlers in their cabins below. Nobody seemed to seriously believe either tale, but after she heard the story of Chief Ransom, Nora Faye could not stand on the rock without thinking about how scary it would be if you were sitting on a pony that might lurch suddenly closer to the edge.

James took them straight up the mountain to the rock the very first Sunday the entire family lived in Johnston. It was the shortest approach, but an extremely steep climb.

They were puffing for breath by the time they got to the base of the rock where a rusting but sturdy steel cable was strung at an angle up the receding stretch of the rock's lower end. They used the cable to pull themselves up, hand over hand, shortening the climb by saving the many steps around and up that would have been required without it.

James guessed the cable had been installed back in the days when hikes to the rock were a routine Sunday diversion for the people of Johnston. He said back in the boom time of the early years, the coal company made trails for its employees to follow on their hikes up to the rock. The climb had been the recreation of the office workers and store clerks and teachers and nurses and whoever lived in the big lakeside boarding house called the clubhouse. There had been trails of varying lengths and steepness, but they had all become overgrown as people took up less strenuous ways of entertaining themselves. Except for the cable, James found no definite trace of the old trails.

Later, Nora Faye saw photographs from those outings. The walls of the offices where they paid their bills for electricity and water and coal deliveries were decorated with huge blow-ups of old photographs from those early days. The women wore long-sleeved, dark colored, high-necked dresses that hung almost to their ankles, and you could tell they wore several petticoats under their skirts. Nora Faye wondered how they kept from fainting from heatstroke while climbing those steep trails in their hot outfits. She had steamed in her sleeveless blouse and shorts.

CHAPTER 33
FRANKIE PORTER

It is not the mountains' elevation that brings on the closed-in feeling some people experience when they live down in the midst of a mountain range; it is the sameness of the peaks. If the mountains are all near the same height, with none offering the prospect of a lofty vista, they can begin to give the feeling that they are folding in on a person. Nora Faye thought people were not as likely to get that smothered feeling if there was one peak taller than the others. Looking up to that peak would remind you there was a place to go when you needed to be higher than anything else.

The Dillard mountains, though not towering, were all near the same height, and they smothered Mrs. Garvens. Nora Faye didn't think Mrs. Garvens ever went to gather nuts with her family. She had never heard of her climbing any of the mountains for any reason—but even if she had gone to the top of one of the mountains she would have seen nothing to help her catch her breath. The maple trees were beautiful on the path where Nora Faye had seen the fox, but there was no overview from the top of that hill or any of the others.

When Nora Faye was playing in the Slaney's side yard, she often heard Mrs. Garvens huffing and puffing as she worked with her chickens and grumbled to herself about being trapped under these never-ending mountains like dominoes stood on their ends and ready to fall on a body. "Oh, for a breath of fresh air from a spot where you can see for miles down the road," she would moan while she fed and watered and gathered eggs and set hens and tended to the never-ending job of mending the chicken-wire fence.

Miss Sheedy, one of a pair of missionary ladies who came to the Dillard school to give Bible lessons, was from Illinois. Her partner, Miss Hollowron, had teased one day about how she sometimes had to take Miss Sheedy up to the fire tower on top of Pine Mountain to let her get her breath. They used the smothering story to make a lesson about how the feeling of being unable to draw in a good breath—as though she were covered, head and all, by a heavy rumpled blanket, Miss Sheedy said—is the way people feel when they are covered with sin. Going up to the lofty overlook was the way it felt to go up to Jesus with your smothered feeling, they said.

Nora Faye was not sure if Miss Sheedy really felt smothered or if she made up the story to teach the lesson, but Miss Sheedy and Mrs. Garvens both came to her mind when she would play alone on her front porch after Conner died and the Slaneys moved away. She guessed the heavy feeling hanging in her chest must be something like what they said they felt. The song about the bear going over the mountain roiled in her head. She did not sing it aloud—it seemed she did not have breath enough for singing it aloud—but she barely hummed it over and over to herself as she swang back and forth. "The bear went over the mountain, the bear went over the mountain, the bear went over the mountain, and what do you think he saw? He saw another mountain, he saw another mountain, he saw another mountain, and what do you think he did? He climbed the other mountain, he climbed the other mountain..." She felt sadder and sadder as she pictured the bear going mindlessly over mountain after mountain after identical mountain.

But the mountains around Johnston did not make her feel that way. Living below Ransom Rock, she was reminded of Heidi being so happy on the mountain with her grandfather. She felt like she lived *on* the mountain, not *in* the mountains. Though her mountain was not tall as an Alp, and her house did not stand alone way up on the side of the mountain like Grandfather's, living in her Coopers Cove house made Nora Faye feel a little like she thought Heidi must have felt.

She had hiked up to Ransom Rock only a few times, but she always knew it was there with it's sweeping vista, and she could recapture the feeling she got on the rock even as she lived day by day so close to its base that she could not see it when she looked straight up. She had learned to send her mind to the rock when she needed to put it on something pleasant.

She knew the rock was not the pinnacle of the mountain, though it gave that impression when you looked at it from below. When you took the highway up the mountain and through the pass to Virginia, you could see how the mountain went on up beyond the rock.

James did not know the mountains in this edge of the county the way he knew the ones where he'd grown up near Wolliver, and he did not have the time to explore them like he would have when he was younger. But he was greatly impressed with the majesty of the rock and with the drama of the three watersheds where they headed up within yards of one another in the pass. One of the first things he'd done after he decided to move to Johnston was to take Nora Faye up to the state line where he parked and got her out of the car to walk her from the ditch on the Kentucky River side of the road across to the Big Sandy ditch on the other side of the road, and then the few yards over the state line to the place on the Virginia side where the first few headwater trickles would eventually follow gravity's pull to the Stockard River that also fed into the Big Sandy through the Breaks.

Of all the waterways, the one that engrossed Nora Faye during her first weeks in Johnston was the trickle at the back of her yard coming straight off the mountain without passing through any stretch of civilization. It reminded her of what Mrs. Ethridge had told her about how children used to play in the Dillard creek before the coal companies came into the hollow. James tried to follow their Coopers Cove branch up the mountain on one of their first treks to Ransom Rock, but it was impossible. The tiny trickles feeding it branched from all directions and changed pathways from rainstorm to rainstorm. It was not fed by a spring, and it varied with the weather, drying up in some stretches for months at a time. Behind their house it sometimes came close to drying up, but even in the driest times the salamanders and crawdads survived in mud under the rocks. The salamanders repulsed Nora Faye as much as they fascinated her, but they did not keep her from enjoying the branch. She often gravitated toward it when she was in the back yard, and often found herself turning rocks in search of the slimy salamanders that made her want to run away once she found one.

On a spring morning during her earliest days in Johnston, she was in the branch trying to coax a crawdad out of the mud when she heard children's voices nearby. At first she thought it was happy chatter. She picked up on a sing-song, teasing tone and was reminded of Conner and how he would make up a rhyme to fit the occasion. But when she came up out of the branch and saw a group of children in the yard two houses down, she knew immediately that their chant was not good natured. They were obviously teasing a little boy who stood by himself near a chopping block with the axe raised to his shoulder. She could tell he was almost in tears although he was making threats to his tormentors.

They chanted, "Frankie, Spankie, lost his hankie. Poor, poor little Frankie." He gave the axe a shake as he replied with something unintelligible.

Nora Faye walked down to the yard and straight over to the boy. He looked neither afraid nor hostile as she approached. He somehow knew she was friendly, just as she knew he was harmless. "Why are they teasing you?" she asked.

"I don't know," he said. "I never know."

The children simply disappeared, and before she knew what was happening, she and Frankie Porter were sitting on the chopping block telling one another the stories of their lives. His mother was very sick. With what, he didn't know. She wasn't bedridden and she didn't take medicines, but doctors had done something to her brain back in the winter that made her stop being herself. She just did not seem to be a complete person anymore. She could do some things up to a certain point, and then it was like she forgot what she was doing. She could no longer cook meals or do the washing and ironing or any housekeeping chores. She wasn't able to take care of him. He lived with his aunt and uncle in a place called Betsy Lane where he had just finished first grade. He was visiting at home for a few days, now that school was out, to see if his mother would be well enough to take care of him for the summer. He didn't think it was going to work out. Nora Faye noticed, then, how there was dried milk around his mouth and how his hair did not look combed.

She told him about living last year with her Granny Rose to go to school in Wolliver and how her mother had left when she was just a little girl and how her daddy had married Virginia whose girl Peggy was now her sister.

She asked him to come up to their house, but he said he was not allowed to leave his yard. He said even though his mother did not seem to know he was around, his dad said he had to stay in the yard anyway. He told him if he ever found out he'd left the yard that he would no longer be allowed to live with them. When he told his dad that his mother never looked at him or said a word to him, he said it didn't matter. He said it might upset her if she looked for him and didn't see him.

Nora Faye went to his yard every morning for more than a week. She tried to get there before the other children were out and about. Frankie was usually waiting for her no matter how early she arrived, but she waited on the chopping block if he wasn't out yet. They sat on his back steps and talked, or played at the back of his yard where someone had long ago built rabbit pens. They wove a little fantasy world where the rabbit pens were new and were full of rabbits, which they named and described to one another. They played with the imaginary rabbits the way Nora Faye and Peggy sometimes still played in their secret world before they fell asleep at night. In bed, they whispered and didn't move except to do something like arrange a pillow so that it became a log that, as fawns, they nudged up against, lying absolutely still while their mother went to feed in the meadow. Nora Faye and Frankie created the same kind of magic world where they let the rabbits scamper on the grass and eat little piles of clover they pulled for them before they had them burrow under the bushes to sleep in a heap. When they had to leave them, they put them back in the cages, but they never shut the doors. The rabbits were free to come and go as they pleased.

One day while they played at the rabbit pens, they noticed little silent explosions in the dead leaves under the big oaks on the hillside across the branch. The leaves would fly up in one spot and then another, and, just when everything seemed quiet for good, they would fly up suddenly in another place. Finally they could see it was birds scratching under the leaves and making them fly into the air. A small flock worked an area of the forest floor like they had rehearsed their routine so that they stayed a foot or two from one another. Their markings were unusual, black heads and backs and tails with reddish-brown sides. The tail had a touch of white, and the breast was pure white from the vee-shaped line where the dark throat ended and the curved lines where the rusty sides ended. It was hard to get a good look, the way they disappeared under the leaves from time to time.

They were so engrossed in watching the birds they couldn't believe it was time for Frankie's father when he rapped on the windowpane. He came home at noon every day. He would pull the kitchen curtain aside just far enough to peck on the glass and motion for Frankie to come inside. After he gave Frankie and his mother some lunch, he took Frankie for the afternoon to his mother's cousin's house near the place where he worked in a mine office. The cousin was an old woman who could not walk without her canes. A hired girl stayed with Frankie's mother. His mother never came to the door. Nora Faye never caught even one glimpse of her.

The next morning Nora Faye sat on the chopping block for a long time, but Frankie didn't come out. She didn't see him ever again and did not hear a thing about him until the week after Christmas when his dad knocked on their door one evening. He said he'd been visiting with Frankie in Betsy Layne and that he'd brought Nora Faye a Christmas gift Frankie had sent her. He did not come in, saying he had to get home to Maureen.

Wrapped in white tissue paper with a narrow red ribbon, it was a little box he'd made for her out of wooden popsicle sticks. He'd written her name on the bottom with red and green crayons, but he spelled it wrong. He spelled it "Norah Fay." On the inside of the lid, in penciled lettering so faint it was barely discernable, he had written, "I luve you mor than ennyboddy. Frankie."

Virginia looked distressed when she read the message on the upturned lid. She said, "Oh, Jay, look what he's sent her. That poor little boy."

The box filled Nora Faye with sadness. She hunted out her mother's Cara Nome powder box and put the two boxes together in one of James's sturdy cardboard ice cream tubs, padding them with the crumpled tissue gift wrapping. She labeled the tub with her name and pushed it to the back corner of the little closet she shared with Peggy.

It did not come to her to wonder about the identity of the teasing children until after she left home to go to college. The children in her new neighborhood were still only vaguely familiar or were strangers to her on the day she first saw Frankie, and she had not even looked their way. She was glad it had not entered her mind to wonder who they were. They were just a gray mass. She wondered if she would have been a part of the mass if she hadn't been new to the cove. She had a flashing memory of how she had giggled when Trudy Morrow was scampering like a monkey under the schoolhouse and how Laura Jane and Ruthie didn't laugh at all and just seemed to know how to do the right things.

CHAPTER 34
SUSANNA AND RAYELLE

Susanna soon told Nora Faye she'd found out it was not just a kiss a boy wanted when he wiggled his finger in a girl's palm, but she was vague about what he did want. Nora Faye had picked up on the great mystery from several sources, but there were still big gaps in her knowledge. When Margaret Docket's mother grew fat one summer, it was Rayelle, Susanna's older sister, who said she was pregnant.

Then she looked at Nora Faye and told Susanna to take Nora Faye and get out of the bedroom before she barricaded the door. Peggy said, "Let them stay. Nora Faye's no baby. She knows everything I know." And Susanna said it was her room, too, that she could stay if she wanted to. So Rayelle was outvoted, and the younger sisters were allowed to witness the rite of passage taking place in the bedroom.

Rayelle and Peggy were getting ready to shave their legs, Peggy—at Rayelle's urging—for the first time. Rayelle had carried in a pan of warm water and a new bar of Camay soap before she shut the door. After she wedged a desk chair under the doorknob, she climbed up on the vanity stool to dig out the safety razor she'd hidden at the back of the closet shelf in a box of Kotex. Everything was hush-hush and secret because she wasn't supposed to be shaving her legs. She said her mother belonged to a holy roller church where they believed it was a sin for a woman to shave her legs or cut her hair or wear jewelery. But her mother hadn't noticed Rayelle's smooth legs so far.

Nora Faye wasn't sure what Virginia would think. The topic hadn't come up at home. She guessed Peggy had decided to go on and do it and find out later how her mother viewed it. She knew Virginia shaved her own legs—or used hair removal cream from a tube—so it seemed she wouldn't be too upset.

The girls worked up a lather with the soap bar and slathered it onto their legs before they took turns making long downward strokes with the razor, twisting this way and that to get to the backs.

Rayelle was swishing the razor in the pan of water when she suddenly looked right at Nora Faye and said, "I bet you don't even know what 'pregnant' means."

Nora Faye was reminded of Ruthie and the way she used to put her on the spot. She stammered, "It means a good smell."

The other three girls erupted into laughter they immediately tried to shush. When they got quiet, Peggy whispered, "You're thinking of fragrant," but she didn't tell her what pregnant meant. The subject was dropped as suddenly as it was brought up.

Instead, Rayelle began giving instructions on shaving. "You must never shave dry," she lectured. "And never stroke in the wrong direction. The hairs will grow back stiff and dark if you don't shave in the direction they're growing."

Nora Faye asked, "Why do girls do it, then?"

"What? Shave?" Rayelle asked.

Nora Faye nodded.

"Well, you wouldn't even ask that question if you were old enough to understand the answer." Rayelle had a way of laughing sort of fondly as she talked to somebody, so that she could say something seemingly offensive without hurting a person's feelings. "That's why you had no business staying here today, girlie. When you start wanting a boyfriend, you'll not be needing to ask such a question."

Nora Faye did want a boyfriend, as a matter of fact, but she did not feel compelled to shave her legs. After today, she thought she might try to avoid the process forever.

"Ouch!" Peggy hissed as she cut herself again. The little cuts didn't seem to hurt much, but they turned the lather pink and then ran in tiny red rivulets even when the nicks were so small you couldn't see them. The Jergens lotion they applied when they finished the job did hurt, though. They sucked in their breath and said it burned like alcohol.

They didn't make any nicks under their arms, being extra careful as they raised their arms straight overhead and tucked their heads under their arms like cats taking a bath while they worked carefully. Peggy had brought her special deodorant to share with Rayelle, an unselfish gesture, considering how much the small bottle cost. She would never have had such an expensive brand if not for the formal gowns she wore when she sang. She had to make the tiny bit go a long way. There was a special applicator in the frosty blue bottle the color of Evening in Paris perfume bottles. The thick deoderant looked blue in the bottle, but it dried clear, and it really did keep you from sweating so much. Stella bought a bottle for Peggy when she bought one for Dollie after Dollie had a beautiful claret colored wool dress with ruching on the bodice that was ruined in one time's wear where perspiration made big discolored circles under the arms and made the fabric mat together.

Peggy told the story as they finished shaving under their arms, and Rayelle said, "She should have worn dress shields," but Peggy said she *was* wearing shields. "They wadded up when they got soaked," she said. "You must not sweat much or you'd know how useless dress shields really are for girls who truly need them, like Dollie." She went on to say that, thank goodness, she didn't sweat like Dollie, but that she liked the security of using the special deodorant when she sang. "I'd hate it if I ruined one of the dresses after people have been nice enough to give them to me."

You couldn't find the deodorant in stores, but Stella knew a beautician who ordered it for her. She gave a bottle to Peggy for a Christmas present and said she hoped the other girls were not going to perspire as heavily as Dollie. "Some women do and some don't," she said.

Virginia gave Stella the money to get it for Peggy after the first bottle, and she said she was glad Peggy needed to use it only when she was dressing for a performance. Peggy would probably have been okay without it, but Virginia said there was no use to take the chance.

Peggy hadn't stopped to think how, even without nicks, the deodorant might burn after shaving under their arms, so when she made the first dab under Rayelle's arm, she was as unprepared as any of them for the violent reaction. Rayelle shrieked and almost knocked the precious bottle out of Peggy's grasp. She dropped facedown on the bed where she pulled her knees up under her and rocked back and forth with one hand squeezed tightly in the stinging armpit while she bit a corner of a pillow to keep from screaming.

Her mother didn't come to investigate the shriek, but as soon as Rayelle got her breath back, she began hurrying to return the razor to its hiding place and to sneak to the bathroom to empty the pan of water and get rid of all signs of her transgression.

Virginia didn't seem very concerned when Peggy showed off her shaved legs that evening. "It's just that once you start, you can't stop," she said. "I was hoping you'd both put it off as long as you could. Fourteen is young to start."

When Nora Faye asked why you couldn't stop, Virginia said, "Oh, it just looks bad once you've shaved. The hair grows back coarse and thick."

She didn't say anything at all about the shaving being connected to wanting a boyfriend. Nora Faye wondered if she was somehow unaware of that or if she wasn't saying anything about it because she thought they were too young to be thinking about it.

She had told them together about having periods. Both of them pretended not to know a thing, but they actually knew about it from Aunt Tattie's granddaughter, Willa Dean, who had given them and several other girl cousins the facts in the far toilet at Aunt Tattie's one day as she gave a demonstration of how to attach a fresh pad to a sanitary belt. "That's why girls start carrying purses," she said. "So you have a place to carry extra pads, and to carry used ones if you change in a place where you can't throw it away. Mommy won't let us put ours down the toilet hole at home. She makes us burn them ."

"You have to make a fire in the toilet every time?" Nora Faye asked forlornly, and the other girls laughed in the affectionate way they had with her. Willa Dean explained that they had a spare slop jar in the toilet to collect them until a burning day when a fire was built in the trash pit down by the creek. "That toilet's just for us girls. The boys have to go to the one over by the barn."

Nora Faye was thinking that having periods caused girls a lot of inconveniences beyond the main one of having your body out of your control for several days a month. It made her feel good that Virginia included her when she gave Peggy the talk, but she wasn't eager to face the inevitable. She didn't especially dread it, but she felt no big yearning to become a woman. Virginia said some girls started having periods younger than others, and that Nora Faye could possibly start before Peggy.

She didn't start first, but she wasn't far behind. In the meantime Elizabeth Barstowe had added to her knowledge when she gave a demonstration in the school restroom of how to use a tampon. She didn't actually make use of the tampon; she just displayed it while she gave directions, saying her mother claimed only bad girls were able to use them before they were married, but that her older sister told her that was just old-woman talk, that she and her friends had secretively used them since they were in high school. Elizabeth hadn't had the nerve to use one yet, but she carried it in her purse in case she should feel daring some day. She gave details about having babies as well as having periods, but she said nothing about a girl shaving her legs and nothing about what happened between the time a girl started having periods and the time she had a baby.

By eighth grade, when the girls and boys were sent to separate rooms to see a film about bodily changes they were soon to expect, most of the girls had already started having periods, and Nora Faye had figured out that shaving your legs was something you probably did to look like you thought you should, not necessarily something your hormones actually prompted you to do.

She had also figured out that makeup was in that kind of gray area, too. Girls invariably wanted to use makeup when they reached a certain age, making her think maybe hormones did have something to do with that impulse.

She'd noticed a strange thing about makeup; the girls who used it were mostly those who did not need to—who were pretty without it. Unattractive girls using makeup just called attention to their ugliness, and most of them stopped after their first experiments with it. These unwritten laws of makeup usage had first come to her attention way back when she was just a little girl in Dillard.

The girls who settled down in Dillard, getting married and having children right after they finished school or dropped out, never experimented with makeup and would have been ridiculed if they had.

However, if a girl went away in her teens—either to go to school or to take a job somewhere—she often came back home for her first visit with makeup on her face. If she was pretty, it was accepted—even if she did not do it well—but if she was ugly, she was mocked like those people who came back home with an accent.

The oldest Garvens girl came back for a visit flaunting a phony sounding northern accent after she went away to work in Detroit. For months after she went back to Detroit, people mocked her with a cruel little rhyme. They said before she went away, she would say, "I saw a *cayfe* go down the *payth* to take a *bayth* in a minute and a *haylf*." The A sounds in this first part were long and drawled. "But when she came back," they went on, "she was saying, 'I saw a *coff* go down the *pawth* to take a *bawth* in a minute and a *hoff*." Nora Faye heard the same rhyme applied to many different people—always girls, come to think of it. Maybe boys were no more prone to taking up accents than they were to wearing makeup.

There was no rhyme for the makeup situation, but when a girl did not follow the rules, she was teased just as mercilessly. The rules dictated that a pretty girl would be tolerated while she learned to use makeup so sparingly— or so skillfully—that it could be ignored, and that an unattractive girl would be ridiculed until she left it off altogether.

Until she was in college it had not occurred to Nora Faye that makeup could be used to conceal the flaws of ugly girls and to highlight their best feature so as to take attention off less attractive ones. It had not occurred to her that even ugly girls probably had at least one good feature. She'd thought of makeup as something used to draw attention to the beautiful, not to conceal the ugly. She felt self-conscious when she wore makeup, but when she got to college she learned that some girls were self-conscious without it. She watched her roommate, Shirley—no matter how early she had to get up for a class—stumble to the mirror and apply pancake makeup and eyeliner and mascara before she left the room.

One evening, when they decided suddenly to go to The Cellar, Shirley stopped at the mirror to freshen her face and said she didn't see how Nora Faye had the courage to go out into the world without putting on makeup. Nora Faye had been thinking the same thing about Shirley, that she didn't see how she had the nerve to go out into the world with her face made up that way.

Nora Faye didn't think of herself as ugly, but neither did she think of herself as beautiful. Lipstick was the only thing she and Peggy ever used. Peggy didn't use pancake makeup even on stage. She had inherited enough of her dad's olive complexion to keep her from washing out in the spotlights, and she'd managed to stave off the attempts of enthusiastic stage makeup people to further enhance it for dramatic effect.

Nora Faye learned about makeup being used as an enhancer in a girls-only assembly in her first year at college, but it was too late; she did not think of herself as a makeup user, and it was too late to change. She did what her mother had done; she put on lipstick and then touched the tip of a finger to her lips before she blotted, stroking that finger along her cheekbone to leave the very slightest smudge of a blush. Her mother had finished with a dusting of face powder over everything, which Nora Faye did not do. Her mother also used rouge sometimes instead of lipstick on her fingertip. The rouge came in a tiny flat container barely bigger around than a quarter with its own tiny flat puff, but her mother didn't use the puff; she picked up the color by touching her finger to the little rouge cake the way she touched it to her lips. Nora Faye always meant to see if she could find a little container of rouge next time she was in a drugstore, but she never remembered to do it.

A few months before high school graduation, a young woman representing a group of personal-care and cosmetics companies came to school to talk to the senior girls about personal care regimens. Their senior sponsor, Mrs. Rutledge, meeting with the senior class in the library right after lunch that day, sent the boys to their regular classes after explaining that the speaker was not what she thought she had scheduled. The school secretary had made a mistake, thinking this was the personal motivation speaker they'd had last year. But the mistake was not realized until the representative showed up in the principal's office with boxes of complimentary toiletries packets and cosmetic samples for girls. The principal decided to let her give her talk since she was already there and already paid for.

Mrs. Rutledge said the representative would be up to talk to them just as soon as she finished signing some papers in the principal's office, and that they could just relax and enjoy their afternoon off. She pointed to a stack of boxes. "Those are the samples she'll be giving you. The office had some boys go ahead and carry them up here, but you mustn't get into them until she gets here." When she got to the doorway, she turned back for a parting word. "I don't think you'll find her to be boring," she said. "She doesn't look any older than you girls."

Even with that warning, her youthful appearance was so confusing that when she showed up they wondered if she might be a student helper the speaker had brought with her or maybe a new student who was lost. She wore a navy blue suit and plain black medium heel pumps, but she still looked too young to be any kind of sales representative. The girls looked around for a teacher or principal to tell them what to do, but Mrs. Rutledge had left right after she'd explained about the mix-up, and the librarian, Miss Buckwalter, had gone into her workroom and shut the door.

The girl in the navy blue suit, however, eased their minds when she started right in by saying, "I know, I know. I look like a little girl playing grownup, but I'm actually twenty-three, and I've been doing this job for two years. I was lucky enough to get it the week I graduated from college."

She said her name was Lexie, and she launched right into her presentation, which covered everything from how to file your nails to how to tweeze your eyebrows to how to get the most shaves out of a razor blade. She told them how to use makeup techniques to enhance their good features and downplay their bad ones, how to brush their teeth so that it also kept their gums healthy, how to spot-clean their suede jackets, and—in case they were going to college—how to live on cafeteria or sorority-house food without gaining weight. She said pamphlets about eating a healthy diet came with the sample packages of Ayds diet candies they would receive, along with Ipana toothpaste, Gillette razor blades and countless other samples.

Time sped. Nora Faye could not believe such trivial subject matter had held her attention. When Lexie asked if there were any questions, almost every hand in the room went up. They asked about everything from how to talk to a boy, to how to talk their parents into letting them get a strapless dress for the prom.

The first question was about talking to boys. Lexie sounded stern when she said she was not supposed to answer that kind of question. "I'm supposed to talk about things that tie in with the products I brought. I'm not a counselor of any kind."

But the girls ignored her protest. As though she had said nothing to discourage them, they continued to restate their questions. And with no mention of her surrender, Lexie just suddenly began to talk about what they wanted to hear.

Nora Faye never forgot the things she told them. She said the way to talk to a boy was the way you would talk to anyone you wanted to spend time with. First of all, you would actually listen, not just pretend you're listening. You would be thinking about the person you're talking to, not about yourself. She said, "You don't need to know anything about what the boy is talking about. It can go even better when you don't know, because what you want to do is listen and ask questions or make comments to move his topic forward."

She gave examples. "Suppose a boy is talking about his ham radio hobby. If a girl says, 'Oh, our neighbor had a ham radio and I always meant to go over and find out about it, but I was volunteering as a candy striper at the hospital that year, and I was so busy with that and with school work and taking life-guard classes at the swimming pool that I never had a chance to talk to him about it before he had to stop doing it because his antenna was messing up people's radio reception,' she's showing no interest in him and giving him no help in going on with what he was trying to talk about." Lexie gasped for breath while the girls laughed at her impression of the fictional girl.

"But if she asks, 'How did you get started with it?' or makes a comment like, 'That sounds like it could take up a lot of time,' then she's hitting the ball back to him, just like in a game of ping-pong. If she responds by talking about herself, it's like she's let the ball go by her while she polishes her paddle, and a boy, or anybody else, can't play if you don't do your part by returning the ball."

And she didn't stop there. "Of course, if he never wants to talk about anything but himself, then, after you've known him for a while, you'll want to ask yourself if you really want to spend a lot of time with a boy who never puts the ball in your court. But you'll want to make sure you gave him a good example by returning his balls. (The girls were so absorbed they did not snicker.) When they have a good example to follow, people can learn how to converse successfully without knowing it's happening."

In addition to that off-the-agenda advice, Nora Faye also never forgot what Lexie told them about filing nails and tweezing eyebrows. It crossed her mind, after she went away to college, that she did not remember anything the speakers had said at her baccalaureate service or graduation ceremony, but she always remembered that the girl named Lexie said it does not matter if you file from the middle to the sides or from the sides to the middle, but that the important thing is not to move the file back and forth over the nail, to always go in one direction. And, as for eyebrows, she said to never pluck above your brow, to always pluck below, so as not to destroy the natural line. When someone asked about hairs growing back stiff and dark once you start shaving your legs, she said it was a myth. She laughed. "But I know I'll not change your minds about it. If you think it's true, that's the way you'll see it."

The scene from that bleak February afternoon came back to Nora Faye through the years. She was intrigued by the way her classmates implored a twenty three year old girl who was there to advertise toiletries to solve their most personal problems. Lexie was there only because of someone's scheduling mistake. Her purpose was to advertise the products of her sponsoring companies, and she told them outright that she was only a few years older than they were and that she was not trained to give personal counseling. But the questions they asked her touched on the most sensitive areas of their lives.

In later years, Nora Faye came to realize that Lexie had spoken with quite a bit of wisdom, but she suspected her classmates would have asked their questions no matter how she had answered. It was as though they were ready to be led by anyone they might possibly cast in the role of a leader.

Someone asked Lexie what she'd majored in to prepare for her job, and she laughed and said her major had nothing to do with her position. She'd majored in Political Science and minored in Philosophy, and had applied for this job thinking they wouldn't even give her an interview. "Maybe there's a lesson there for high school seniors," she added. "Don't hesitate to go for a job you want even if it seems you're not prepared for it."

After Lexie answered a question about using mascara, Janice Akers suddenly stood and said she needed advice about her family situation. She sank back into her chair as she went on to say she wanted to go to college, but that she didn't know how she could leave her mother to take care of her brother without help. Her younger brother had been born with a condition that kept him from developing beyond the infancy stage mentally and developmentally although he kept growing physically. She said her mother had used up all her strength taking care of him, that he had to be lifted and carried and fed and cleaned up just like a baby. Janice said she did not see how her mother could go on doing what she'd been doing, and that she was afraid she'd be expected to step in and take her mother's place now that she was graduating, because she was the only girl in the family. She had an older brother and a younger brother. Her history teacher had told her she would be winning the history scholarship at graduation time, and she wanted to go to college and become a college history teacher. She wanted to know how she could make a life for herself without making it seem like she was an uncaring monster who was turning her back on her family.

The room had gone totally quiet. Nora Faye knew vaguely that Janice had a retarded brother, but she had no idea he was so profoundly afflicted. She'd never considered how Janice carried the constant burden. While they laughed and chattered in homeroom, she'd never thought to wonder how Janice got herself to school each day and kept her attention on her schoolwork. In a class enrollment of less than sixty people, she was stunned to realize she knew almost nothing about Janice. Her question had taken the air from the room.

But Lexie did not flinch. She said Janice absolutely must find an adult she could talk to: a teacher, a minister, a neighbor, anybody who could let her talk about her situation. "Maybe the teacher who told you about the history scholarship." The girls could not hold back little titters at this suggestion. They told her the teacher was Coach Brawley, who had as much personality as a fencepost.

But Lexie said she should not rule out anyone. "You might be surprised about who will listen to you. If the coach will listen, start with him. No matter what his personality is like, he'll have a certain respect for you because of the scholarship." She looked right at Janice. "I don't mean to avoid your question," she said, "but it is too big for me to deal with. I don't know how you've accomplished what you've done so far. I should be asking you for advice." Her eyes were filled with urgency as she looked over the twenty-five girls. "I hope you'll each do what you can to help Janice find an advocate. Who knows? One of your parents—or you—might be the one who can help her move toward a solution."

The girls began to applaud. Nora Faye joined them. It seemed appropriate, although she wasn't sure if they were applauding Lexie or Janice. Maybe both, she thought.

When the dismissal bell rang at the end of the day, the girls were still asking questions. Lexie was sitting on a desktop and they had pushed their chairs into a circle around her. When Miss Buckwalter came out of the workroom she was aghast to see them still there in her library. She said, "You bus-girls are missing your busses! You need to go now!" She sent Susanna to tell the bus drivers to wait. Then she told the other girls to put the chairs up on the tables so the janitor could sweep.

"You can't just come in the library and put the chairs in a mess and leave them that way." It was not until then that she realized Lexie was not one of the students. A little put off balance, she said, "And I'm sure this young lady needs to get on with her day."

Lexie asked if she could leave the samples there in the library for the girls to pick up tomorrow, "The girls kept me so occupied I didn't get around to passing out the sample kits," she explained with a little laugh.

Miss Buckwalter looked stymied. She didn't answer. Some of the girls hurried over. "It's okay, Miss Buckwalter," Donna Ellis said. She turned to Lexie. "We'll take the boxes to the principal's office and pick them up tomorrow morning and take them to the senior homeroom. We'll take care of it."

Nora Faye had seldom heard Donna speak out about anything, and when she did speak she usually sounded sullen and hateful. "I'll help," she told Donna. Other girls picked up the remaining boxes.

Years later she wondered what Donna Ellis remembered most from that day. What transfiguring spot had Lexie touched in her that nobody else ever touched? Was it something about Lexie that opened them up to new considerations, or was it just the right time in their lives for considering things that had not been important in the past?

CHAPTER 35
JAMIE

Nora Faye or Peggy sometimes asked James and Virginia about emptying the laundry room so one of them could move into it. That was usually when something had happened to make them feel more cramped than usual in their small room with the one big bed, or when they'd had a quarrel about one of them taking up more than her share of the space. But they knew they would miss each other's company, and they always let it drop before any action was taken. From a practical standpoint, nobody in the family could imagine how they could get by without the extra storage space provided by the laundry room. Even if the girls had separate bedrooms with their own closets, they would not have as much room as they had on the storage racks in the laundry room. The laundry room had a freestanding rack for hanging their clothes and one for Virginia and James.

They called the third bedroom the laundry room because that's where Virginia hung the wash on rainy days. Clotheslines were crisscrossed from windowsills to doorsills, and a big electric fan was stored there to blow the clothes dry.

In addition to laundry lines and clothes racks, there were shelves and chests and boxes for storage of winter clothes in summer and summer clothes in winter and for any closet overflow, which increased as the girls got older. The room also served for storing Christmas decorations, winter quilts and blankets, galoshes and snow pants, picnic baskets, a folding Boy Scout cot, outgrown toys, overflow pots and pans from the kitchen, a punch bowl, a folding table and chairs, an extra mattress, and all the other household detritus a family collects over the years. Nora Faye and Peggy gave Granny Rose their bed when she came to stay, and they slept on the extra mattress on the laundry room floor.

The girls didn't usually mind sharing a room. They got along better than most sisters, each remembering the earliest days of their parents' marriage when it felt too good to be true to have a sister to whisper with until you fell asleep.

So, it was a shock when they came home from school one day when Peggy was a junior and Nora Faye a sophomore to find their clothing rack crammed into their room, and the other clothes racks and laundry room shelves and boxes crammed into corners of every other room in the house. They found Virginia in the laundry room where she had just hung new wallpaper.

"You're just in time," she burbled from her perch atop a ladder. "I can't do the border without help." She seemed to be trying to hold back laughter, her eyes twinkling with some kind of private joy.

"After we get the border up, you can help me clear out the last few things so I can give this floor a good cleaning and waxing tomorrow," she babbled on, as though she were oblivious to their puzzled stares.

Nora Faye was surprised that Virginia was going to the trouble of waxing the floor and replacing wallpaper that was in good shape in a room nobody but family ever saw. Then she was stunned and puzzled when she realized Peggy had tears in her eyes.

"Oh, Mother," Peggy gasped. "Oh, Mother!"

Nora Faye did not know what was happening. She felt so left out that it was a physical ache. It must be that Peggy had figured out why this room had become so special to Virginia, and it must be some private understanding only mothers and daughters could have between them.

Peggy and her mother were looking at one another with faces so radiant and full of emotion that Nora Faye averted her eyes, letting her gaze fall to the floor where she studied the pattern on a roll of border Virginia had unfurled for several feet. Her eyes gradually took in the pattern of the border—teddy bears and toy horses and baby blocks—and slowly her brain made the unmistakable but never before considered connection.

"There's going to be a baby?" she yelped, and ran to join Peggy and Virginia, who held out their arms to take her in.

"See how it's going to work?" Virginia was excitedly darting from one corner of the room to another, pressing out invisible bubbles from the faintly swirl-patterned wallpaper and sweeping her hands over it in great big hugs. "See how the wallpaper is neutral enough to be okay for a baby and also for an older child, and how it and the border fit either a boy or a girl. As it gets older I can change just the border to make it suitable, and the walls will be fitting on through the years, whether it's a boy or a girl."

She picked up a length of border and started rolling it out on the table she'd made from saw horses and plywood sheets James had stored under the floor after their earlier refurbishing. "I've already got my border cut into pieces," she said. She moved the ladder closer to the wall and began stepping off the distance from the ladder to a place where she positioned the kitchen stool.

"Fayzie, you'll be on the ladder," she said. "I'll hand the pasted piece up to you, and you'll put that end in place and hold it snugly while I stretch up to take it from you and pass it on to Peggs. As soon as you take it, Peggs, I'll grab the other stool and climb up to hold it here in the middle. By stretching, we can reach along the entire length and get all the bubbles out before we do that with the next strip."

It was amazing how making room for the baby did not feel like an impossible imposition. After discarding what they could, they somehow managed to squeeze all the clothes and storage shelf contents into various other rooms or into the closet James built in a corner of the dining room and in a storage bunker he built under the house on the highest end. He put up new laundry lines in the dining room, fancy ones that rolled up out of sight when not in use.

But Nora Faye was astounded—after Jamie was born—by the enormous amount of work a baby generates. The roll-up feature on the new clotheslines proved to be unnecessary; the lines were always in use. The clotheslines—sometimes both outside and inside—stayed full of diapers, and the ironing board was never put away. Virginia washed diapers almost every day, and, as she ironed them, she folded them in complex ways that changed to fit Jamie as he grew. Little pans of water sat on the kitchen drainboard with Jamie's stained clothes presoaking before Virginia hand washed them. The big pot of boiling bottles seemed to have a permanent spot on a stove burner, and rows of sterilized Evenflo bottles and nipples and rings were always laid out on clean dishtowels on the kitchen tabletop awaiting formula. Virginia had changed to bottles when Jamie had not gained the amount of weight the baby books recommended after the first few months.

When he started eating solid foods that summer, Nora Faye volunteered for the task of walking up to the last house in the cove every morning, where Mrs. MacGlothen raised chickens like Mrs. Garvens. Nora Faye took a nickel with her to buy one freshly-laid brown egg for Jamie's mid-morning meal. They bought their other eggs at the store; Mrs. MacGlothen, like Mrs. Garvens, did not have enough chickens to sell eggs in large quantities.

Virginia hadn't meant to travel with Jamie until he was older, but when she got word that her dad was terminally

ill with leukemia, she decided she wanted her children to
see him before he died. He hadn't seen Peggy since she
was a baby and he had never seen Jamie. Virginia's
feelings for her father were not warm. He was an educated
man, a county clerk, who was respected by his colleagues
and his community. But he had mistreated his wife,
talking to her like she was his servant instead of his wife.
The sad circumstances had not pulled Virginia close to her
sister. Neither of them had been able to forgive their dad
for treating their mother cruelly, and being with her sister
made Virginia feel they should have been able to do
something to change his malicious behavior. She blamed
him for her mother's early death from heart problems. But
it suddenly seemed important to her that her children see
him before he died. And James. James had never met her
father.

As they made their plans for the trip to Covington,
Tattie got word that her granddaughter, Rowena, who
lived in Cynthiana, was having a difficult pregnancy. She
wrote to her grandmother saying she wished she could
come and spend some time with her and bring Aunt Rose,
since Rose always had such a good way with women who
were having a hard time carrying their babies.

James and Virginia quickly made plans to take Rose
and Tattie with them as well as Stephen's daughter Druci
who would stay with her cousin until the baby came. They
would route their trip through Cynthiana and drop them
off on their way to Covington. Nora Faye was
disappointed when James told her there would not be
room enough for her to go, that she would stay with Dollie
and Bootsie. She tried not to act like a baby, but she felt
left out. She knew there was no reason for her to see
Peggy's grandfather, and she certainly understood that the
car would be too crowded if she went, but she had looked
forward to making the trip.

She could tell how much her daddy hated leaving her
behind. He gave her another five from his wallet just
before he got into the car. He'd given her a five earlier in

the morning, but she knew he was giving her money because he didn't know any other way to show her how he regretted going without her. She tried to cheer him up. "I'll have a good time here," she said. "It's going to be like one long party. We're going to the movies tonight and to the skating rink in the morning. Aunt Stella says we can sleep on the back porch tonight. There will be Susanna and Betty Jo and some of Dollie and Bootsie's friends." He still looked like he felt he was betraying her.

The pajama party did help to keep her mind off the trip she was missing, and the movie had totally engrossed all of them. Spreading their quilts and blankets on the screened-in porch Eldon had built right to the edge of the woods, they smoked cigarettes from the pack Betty Jo had sneaked from her daddy's carton of Lucky Strikes and entertained themselves singing and dancing the Debbie Reynolds' numbers from the movie they'd seen, *Two Weeks with Love*. Nora Faye thought Ricardo Montalban was the handsomest man she'd ever seen.

Her throat started feeling scratchy as they were going through "Aba Daba Honeymoon" for the tenth time, and she stopped trying to sing. By the time they started falling asleep one by one, her ears were hurting worse than they had in years, and her throat hurt more by the minute. She thought it was the cigarettes and the night-air dampness from the woods, until she suddenly felt like her mouth was filling with hot water. She barely made it to the bathroom before she threw up.

Her second run to the bathroom woke Dollie, who went to get her mother. Nora Faye was so sick she hardly felt embarrassed when she raised her face to see Stella, in her housecoat with her hair in pin curls, and the girls in their pastel hued baby dolls all gathered round to watch as she retched helplessly over the commode.

As she weakly recited her symptoms to Stella, she reminded her that she never got real sick when her ears hurt. Stella said this was different. She said she could tell just by feeling her forehead that she was burning up.

Stella made the quick decision to take Nora Faye to Coopers Cove to care for her there, in case this was something contagious. "I'm sorry to roust you out, Daddy," she explained when she woke Eldon so he could drive them, "but I don't want to be responsible for letting any of these other girls get sick." She changed out of her nightclothes but grabbed one of Dollie's coats for Nora Faye to throw on over her baby doll P.J.s.. To her own surprise, Nora Faye was barely able to sit up when Eldon helped her ease onto the back seat of their Pontiac Chieftain. Stella sat back there, too, with a bucket ready, just in case. When they got to the house, they had to halfway carry her up the stairs.

The next couple of days were like a dream. She had a vision of Stella shaking down a thermometer and putting it under her tongue, and then sitting on the edge of the bed to hold it in the right place.

When she shivered until her teeth chattered, Stella put on more quilts and blankets, and when that didn't touch the chill at the center of her bones she fixed a hot water bottle to put next to her skin. Then, before she knew it, Nora Faye woke, kicking off covers and feeling so hot she thought she'd surely go up in a cloud of steam.

Once when she woke, Stella was embroidering, sitting in the rocker somebody had brought in from Jamie's room. The shiny little embroidery hoop glinted like a halo as she turned it this way and that, and Nora Faye saw the reflections before she got fully awake. She had a brief memory of her mother embroidering something on a little wooden hoop, and she wondered what it was she had made. She couldn't think of ever seeing anything around the house decorated with embroidery, no pillowcases or dresser scarves except the few Granny Rose had made. But Granny Rose didn't do much embroidery. She said her fingers were usually too busy doing necessary work to have time left for gewgaws and frippery.

One time she woke for a few moments to see Stella ironing a baby blanket, with the ironing board set up in the hallway just outside the bedroom door. When she came awake later to the soothing comfort of something warm being tucked into her throbbing ears she understood then that Stella had been warming the blanket for her by ironing it.

Another time Stella was asleep in the rocker, her head fallen sideways onto one shoulder

When Nora Faye woke, her throat would feel dry as sawdust. She was so thirsty she felt she must somehow get out of bed and drag herself to the bathroom where she envisioned putting her mouth under the faucet and drinking until she could hold no more, but she would fall asleep before she could act on her compulsion. She had a dream where she was at her school desk drinking from a quart size canning jar full of delicious cool water. The teacher told her to put it away, but she raised her desktop and hid behind it where the teacher couldn't see her while she gulped down the pure, sweet water.

Another dream was more disquieting. A fever had broken, leaving her to shiver in her clammy pajamas. She was awake enough to know she was freezing, but not enough to pull up more covers or to make a sound to wake Stella. She couldn't see Stella, but could sense her in the chair. She was aware it was a dream when she saw herself standing outside her body, and she was not surprised to see that she was wearing white clothes like Conner wore in his casket. Nor was she surprised to see Conner, himself, standing on the other side of the bed. The thing that fascinated both of them was the fabric of their clothes. It was like fish-food flakes. Then, rather than being something they wore, their garments were part of them, sort of like fish scales, but light and dry like the fish food flakes Bootsie fed her goldfish, white and slightly iridescent. She and Conner didn't move anything but their eyes. They didn't hold their hands up in front of their eyes or turn their bodies this way and that, but their eyes studied the other's splendor in breathless awe.

Then Stella was shaking her and hugging her close, yelling her name over and over, and then shaking her again. When she was finally able to open her eyes, Stella dropped onto the edge of the bed, alternately holding her close and pushing her away to look into her face. She said, "You had me scared, little girl! I couldn't get you awake."

After that, whenever Nora Faye made a sound, Stella would rush even more quickly to the bedside while she said soothing things. But she couldn't let her have water. She would remind her that it made her throw up. She motioned toward the pan on the floor. "You've been so sick you don't even remember." She wiped her face with a cold washrag, letting her first touch it with the tip of her tongue.

Another time when she moaned for water, Stella spooned a tiny ice chip onto her tongue, and then Nora Faye realized what had made the pounding sound she'd thought was part of her earache. Stella had wrapped ice cubes in a dishtowel and pounded them with a hammer to crush them. Her ears had been pounding with such pain she'd thought the hammering was the pain she could hear.

She wasn't sure at first if it was real or a dream when she heard a whispered conversation between Stella and Eldon at the top of the stairs. Stella was giving him instructions to pass on to the girls about how to take care of things at home, and giving him a list of things to bring to her. She told him to have Bootsie and Dollie call each of the girls to find out if they got sick, and she told him not to come any closer to Nora Faye's room. As he turned to go back down the stairs Nora Faye got a whiff of the cigar odor that always hung in his clothes, and she gagged. Stella came running in time to get the pan to her.

Once, when Stella was helping her ease onto the commode during a feverish spell, the contrast in temperature when the back of her hot legs first touched the cool seat was as painful as being burned, and the shock went all through her body, drawing her up almost into a fetal position.

She went right to sleep when she got back to bed, and woke this time to hear Stella again whispering to Eldon at the top of the stairs. She was saying, "She never asks for her daddy or anybody. Remember how Dollie kept asking for me that time she had a fever, even when it was me doing something for her? Nora Faye doesn't question anything. She accepts whatever I do. She never complains. I've never seen a sick child take it all so stoically. It's almost scary."

By the time the doctor came, she knew it was the doctor and not a dream, but she could not stay awake long enough to talk to him after he put the stethoscope on her chest and back and felt up and down her throat and under her chin with a finger and thumb. Stella told him first about the deep sleep she'd had trouble waking her from, and she explained about the vomiting and earaches and sore throat and fever. He left a bottle of liquid medicine that Stella spooned down her throat every few hours. It came back the first several times, but after a while, it began to stay with her.

Stella read to her one day from the "B" volume of the Britannica Encyclopedia she'd found lying on the vanity stool, and when Eldon tiptoed up the stairs a little later, he found them both sleeping peacefully, Stella with the encyclopedia draped across her chest opened to the entry about bats.

It was the first time she'd heard Nora Faye breathing regularly, Stella told Eldon after he woke her. When Nora Faye woke later that day, her ears had stopped hurting, and when she drank some tea and ate a few bites of dry toast she held it down. That night the two of them listened to the Jack Benny show. It was the first time it had occurred to either of them to turn on the little bedside Emerson Nora Faye and Peggy often listened to as they fell asleep at night.

The doctor didn't know what was wrong with her, but Stella did not get sick. Neither did Eldon nor any of the other girls. Several weeks passed before she began to feel like herself. Her hair felt thin and brittle, and she fell asleep in the daytime. She began to keep a jar of water in the refrigerator, and when she woke from those naps she would go for it and drink almost the whole quart in one gulp.

James and Virginia and Peggy all felt responsible for her illness, as though she would have stayed well if they'd been there, but Stella said thank goodness she hadn't gone with them and got sick away from home, maybe even in the car.

Things were different between Nora Faye and Stella, but not in a way that anyone but Nora Faye would notice. She had never really given much thought to Stella as a person. She was just Dollie and Bootsie's mother who had strong opinions and definite notions that her daddy and Granny Rose protected her from at times. She and Stella had never before dealt with one another on an individual basis, and she thought maybe Stella was as pleased with what she'd learned as was Nora Faye with what she'd learned.

When Stella was talking, Nora Faye now listened to what she was saying, trying to sift out something to help explain what had caused her to care for her so tenderly. The practical side of her thinking left her with no illusions about the main reason she had nursed her rigorously and without relief; it was so that her own family would be spared the illness, not necessarily because she felt any personal devotion to her. And yet, she had gone far beyond basic care. There had been something extremely kind in the way she met every need and in the way she managed to make sure Nora Faye was spared the embarrassment that could have accompanied accounts of such intimate, unpleasant tasks. Even if she'd been a little child, Nora Faye could have felt debased, knowing what unpleasantness a person had endured to take care of her,

305

but Stella's matter-of-fact accounts did not go into details and were always slanted so as not to leave her with any sense of shame about being an almost full-grown girl requiring the kind of sometimes-disgusting care you have to give a baby.

The situation was the opposite from what Nora Faye was aware could be expected from some adults you thought you knew. Once, for instance, years ago, when Aunt Tattie's Florrie had taken care of her for a day, she made it sound like they'd had a warm and wonderful time together as she recounted the day for Rose and Tattie, when, in fact, she had given Nora Faye scarcely any attention and had been gruff whenever she asked for anything.

Stella, on the other hand, had given her total attention to Nora Faye, taking care of the most repulsive tasks with matter of fact efficiency and going out of her way to try to ease her pain—like with the baby blanket she warmed for her ears and the ice she crushed for her thirst. But she didn't mention these efforts when she was asked about the ordeal. She said, "Oh, we didn't want anybody else to get sick, and Nora Faye was such a good patient that I used the time to get a little rest, myself."

It was not that Stella pulled her to her side for warm hugs or anything like that now, but she did make Nora Faye feel good when she would flash her a special little smile, for instance, and say something about the two of them knowing all about bats, before she went on to tell the story about reading from the B volume of the encyclopedia, like it was something that set them apart from others. Nobody else would notice the subtle change, but sometimes when their eyes happened to meet, a secret look passed between them that made Nora Faye feel, not that she was beholden to her aunt, but, surprisingly, like they were somehow equals now.

CHAPTER 36
AFRAID

Because James did not work in the mines, the threat of mining accidents—the prevailing fear in both Dillard and Wolliver, of course—had not really touched Nora Faye. But she was aware of that threat and of other ever-present communal fears connected to the coalmines and trains and train tracks. On Dillard she'd been warned never to go near the copper colored body of water gathered in the concave top of a slate dump near the deserted tipple site behind their house. James took her up the hill to show it to her one time and impress on her what a dangerous place it was. The sides sloped steeply into the deep and desolate pool. It looked like something on the moon. There was scarcely any vegetation and no large rocks around the pool, meaning there was nothing to grab onto if your feet slid out from under you on the slippery slate debris. If you slid into the water—even if you could swim—there was nothing to grab onto to get out. The bank just kept crumbling off and rattling down into the water. James went back into the trees and gathered some fallen limbs to demonstrate how there was nothing to catch anything that started sliding down the incline.

There was a tale about a girl who slid into the pool and drowned. Boys knew to be careful, because they had grown up secretly exploring the out-of-bounds place and dealing with its dangers, but the girl had never been there, and she thought she was being careful.

There was also a tale about a boy who was smothered in the sandbox, which was an open-topped wooden structure the shape of a coal gondola built adjacent to the tracks near the little trestle a couple of houses up the hollow from Nora Faye's house. Sand was stored there to put on the rails in icy winter conditions when the wheels needed traction. Again, the problem was that there was nothing to grab hold of to save yourself when the sand started sucking you down in an avalanche. James had gone over to shoo children out of the box more than once. It looked like the perfect place to play, the temptation underscored by a ladder up the backside of the box. He tried to explain to the children why it was dangerous, but they usually ran when they saw an adult approaching, and he seldom got close enough to give them an explanation. He and the neighbor men living closer to it just yelled at children to drive them out when they saw or heard them. James had tried to talk to Mr. Patterson about putting some kind of locked cover on the box for safety reasons, but nothing ever came of his efforts.

Another danger had to do with putting nails or pennies on the track in front of an approaching train. The flattened, misshapen items would become a novelty for the boys to carry in their pockets if all went well. But, if a train wheel hit at the wrong angle it could shoot the piece of metal instead of flattening it, turning it into a sharp projectile traveling at a fast rate of speed, something like a bullet. There were sad accounts of children being blinded or gravely injured.

There were also tales about lost limbs and deaths when someone got caught between coal cars as they were shuttled back and forth to be loaded at the tipple. The general rule was to stay away from the tipple and the gondolas that were sitting there, but of course the situation became a challenge to the more adventurous boys. Some of them knew where a lever could be pulled to cause a hissing sound like escaping air, and they made a game of trying to locate an unwatched car so they could do this.

In addition to these concrete fears, there was an overhanging fear of random violence, like the fear of what could happen if a union meeting should go out of control and spill its fights over into the community, or fear of card games getting out of hand and leading to knifings or gunshots.

One time on election day three young men riding horses had come thundering up the hollow and into the schoolyard when the children were outside at noontime. They circled the yard a few times, shouting and waving fists and open pocketknives in the air before they took off back down the hollow without incident. A few parents followed them to the schoolhouse, and even though they met the horsemen in their gallop out of the hollow, some of the parents continued their trek, needing to know their children were okay. James came to the schoolhouse in the company truck. He left Nora Faye at school. Come to find out, the riders were from down at the mouth of the hollow, just boys not used to the moonshine someone had given them that day. They had headed up to the schoolhouse simply because that was one of the few ways they might go without getting out on the main road. But Nora Faye felt uneasy for a few days, and some of the children had become hysterical and had not come back to school for a while. She was astounded to be told it was only three horses. At the time it seemed like at least a dozen—and she could have sworn it was rifles and sabers they waved above their heads.

The fears in Johnston were of a different sort, but there were lots of things to be afraid of. The undercurrent in the lake was one of the first things they were warned about. The cold mountain water feeding the lake at the end farthest from the dam supposedly rushed to the dam at the bottom of the lake, staying on the bottom because of its temperature. Then, when it hit the dam, it recoiled—now warmed a little by the upper layers—rushing back at an even faster speed just above the current that was running the other way, setting up crosscurrent warps that pulled a person down and tossed him about beyond rescue. The most often repeated story concerned a young bridegroom who had been thrown into the lake on his wedding night as part of his shivaree. He drowned when he was pulled down by the crosscurrents and so did one of his friends who tried to rescue him.

Another cautionary tale concerned a boy who was struck and killed by a car when he rode his bicycle down the hill from his house and out onto the road in a blind curve, and yet another was about a boy who was killed when lightening struck the fire tower in the forest on the opposite side of the highway from Ransom Rock. Other fears involved deadly cottonmouth moccasins and blasting caps. The snakes supposedly abounded in the swampy places up Crandall Hollow where the dairy farm was located. A man who took care of the dairy cattle had almost died from a moccasin bite years ago, and anybody who had to go up the hollow took great care to stay alert and stay on the paths even now.

Nora Faye had never seen a blasting cap, so she felt that the blasting cap danger did not concern her. But the men who came to school to give safety talks said it was that very thing that made them dangerous. Children picked them up because they didn't know what they were. There were tales of lost fingers and lost eyesight. Every now and then safety officers from the mining company came to school to give warning talks, leaving the teachers with posters showing what the caps looked like and why it was important to report it to an adult and not to pick it up if you found one

James and Virginia gave the girls warnings about the lake and about bicycle safety and—in their last years of high school—a new fear, the fear of shootings between truck miners and whoever it was who opposed them. They did not let the girls spend time in the homes of friends whose dads were involved in truck mining.

Nora Faye and Peggy were no longer allowed to go to Shirley Bastin's house when they were in Wolliver with

Granny Rose. Shirley's dad now made his living from the truck mines he owned, and he drove one of his own coal trucks home every night. A group of unidentified men who waylaid him when he came home late one night shot up his truck as he parked it beside his house, grazing his shoulder with a bullet and frightening his family and the neighbors. Granny Rose kept the girls close to home whenever they came to stay with her until Mr. Bastin moved his family out to the country. She was relieved when they moved, remarking that Mrs. Bastin was a good neighbor but that—even without the shooting—her husband's big trucks were breaking up the street and leaving trails of coal dust and debris through the Bottom. "There should be some kind of law to keep people from bringing big coal trucks into neighborhoods like this," she concluded.

Nora Faye was confused about the identity of the aggressors. The common assumption seemed to be that it was union men. "I though it was union men who got shot at by company thugs," she said to James, and he explained how that had been the situation in past violence, but how things had changed as coalmining methods had changed. "Truck miners are now in competition with the big mining companies the union men work for. There's going to be a still newer set of circumstances if strip mining becomes the main method of mining in the future. Then I don't know who'll be fighting who. I guess it might be the railroads that'll be feeling the pinch."

These communal fears did not cause Nora Faye any unease. It would have seemed that she had every reason to feel serene and satisfied. Mrs. Amberson was the only teacher to be anything but kind to her, and she had always been warmly included by her classmates. She and Peggy had their separate groups of close friends, but they got along with each other's friends. Though she never seemed to like the boys who liked her and to like the ones who didn't, boys, to her surprise, courted her favor even though she did not have Peggy's natural way of saying the right thing in every situation. But she was never totally content. She felt she was somehow not like normal girls, which made her impatient with herself in light of all this benevolence.

She surprised herself at how brave she felt when it came to answering questions in class and even standing up in front of the room to recite a poem or read a report or explain a math problem. What made her feel she was not normal was something that happened in casual times with groups of friends or classmates. Between fifth grade and high school most of these occasions involved no boys— boys formed their own groups during those years—but there were girlfriends in profusion. In addition to the times when there were gangs of friends at their house, there were things like study periods with teachers who let you talk all period, or groups gathered on the stairs to wait for the entry bell in the morning, or her Home Ec. class in ninth grade where the girls chattered as they worked at the sewing machines or stoves.

Her uneasiness was not a fear of being left out or of saying the wrong thing or of any of the more usual fears suffered by girls her age. She was afraid of the feeling of isolation that descended upon her when she was surrounded by friends but was feeling that she was not like the other girls. No matter how warmly she was included, no matter how much she was enjoying herself, she often felt like an imposter, like she was of a different breed that looked the same on the outside but had different internal mechanisms—sort of like the wind-up clown from the Christmas display whose clown suit hid a skeleton of bare metal rods instead of flesh covered bones. Things that made the others extremely happy or extremely sad were not things warranting that kind of emotion in her heart.

Things that seemed important to them seemed trivial to her. Sometimes even Peggy seemed like one of the aliens. She could understand why Peggy liked to look pretty when she was performing, but she could not understand why the exact shade of lipstick or nail polish was so important. One time when she had an evening performance coming up, Peggy spent the entire day trying one color of nail polish after another, going through the malodorous mess of removing the previous color and starting all over, time after time. The various shades just looked pink to Nora Faye, but Peggy said some had an orangey tinge and some had a bluish hue and some were too rosy. After she'd apply a color and wave it dry, she would hold her dress up under her chin and walk past mirrors, trying to catch a glimpse of her nails unaware, as though trying to see them through the eyes of another person. Nora Faye could not understand such an obsession.

When their bedroom was crowded with a whole bunch of girls caught up in this kind of fixation, Nora Faye ended up observing instead of participating, her inner being retreating to a secret place behind her face. The others seemed to thrive on getting absorbed in details. Once, it was the length of Rayelle's prom dress. She had the other girls pin and re-pin it, making minuscule changes after climbing onto the vanity stool and slowly turning for inspection. She took out the stitches and started over even after all the girls agreed she'd found the perfect length and she had hemmed the entire front half of the full gathered skirt. For some reason she felt compelled to try it on one more time before she finished the job, and somehow it did not look the same done up with stitches instead of pins. She started all over again, pinning all those pins just a fraction of an inch shorter. As the girls argued over the hem length, Nora Faye felt like she was of a different species. How could a fraction of an inch make that much difference?

She had enjoyed shopping for her first prom dress with Ginny, but as for the length, she felt satisfied with any of them that hit roughly midway between knee and ankle, ballerina length. She had planned to wear one of Peggy's formals to her first prom, but Ginny suddenly felt Nora Faye needed to have her own dress and had taken her to

Bascon at the last minute to look for one. They had pastel shades in mind when they started shopping, with cap sleeves or shoulder straps, but they stumbled upon a rich brown satin strapless dress that took their breath away when they saw how it made Nora Faye's light brown hair look blond and fiery. It was more than Ginny had meant to spend, but she said they didn't have to feel like it was a splurge, considering that Peggy would be able to use it later for her performances. She didn't say one word about it being strapless, though she had been ignoring other strapless dresses as they shopped.

Nora Faye didn't always feel alienated, and it wasn't just with girls. Sometimes she felt that way with boys. She could understand doing things you wouldn't ordinarily do in order to be with a boy you wanted to be with, but she lost interest even with boys she liked a lot if there was no common ground. It seemed if she liked a boy as a friend, she had no physical interest, while if he made her go giddy there was no meeting of the minds.

Fletcher Howell in freshman algebra class had been a friend. They were allowed to work with other people when Mr. Minton gave class-time for doing homework assignments, and she and Fletcher—who sat beside her— discovered they made a perfect team. She was good at figuring out what the reading problems were asking, and he was good at working with figures. As sophomores, they had a study hall in the library where they did their Latin homework together, and when they were juniors they were in the same homeroom and sometimes waited together on the stairs for the entry bell to ring where they fell into deep discussions about the books they were reading or movies they'd seen.

But when he asked her to go to the prom their junior year, she felt smothered and trapped. She didn't know how to say no, but she knew instinctively she would be sorry she'd said yes. She'd always known that, for her, physical appeal would have to precede friendship with a boyfriend, though all the articles in *Seventeen* magazine said it should be the opposite.

She figured Fletcher had asked her not just because they'd studied so well together in past years, but because they had enjoyed being together in a Saturday morning folk dancing class Miss Ellis and Mr. Trollinger held in the school gym that winter. But she knew the prom would not be like the folk dancing class. At the prom they would be dressed up, sitting at a table with other couples who, unlike them, would be all agog over having the opportunity to touch and hold each other close. She'd never had any physical interest in Fletcher, and if that kind of interest in her was what had prompted his invitation, it surely dissipated in the awkwardness engulfing them at the prom. She felt more and more like she was in the wrong place with the wrong person. It wasn't a nauseating kind of distaste that coursed through her body when they took the dancing position—his right hand on her back, his left hand holding her right—but rather a muscle ache stemming from the strain of trying to make sure her body did not send any misleading signals. She mourned the waste of the wonderful brown dress, but that is exactly why she had felt one of Peggy's would do; she had not thought her date was special enough to warrant a special dress.

That prom date ended the warm comfort she and Fletcher had between them, and the few times she'd been thrown with him afterwards, things felt painfully stilted. She gave the dress to Peggy.

It was Brad Carnahan who made her heart beat fast. That's why she had signed up for the folk dancing class. Coach Brawley had urged his basketball boys to take the class to improve their gracefulness on the court, and she'd seen Brad's name on the list.

But Franny Harmon pounced on him—arriving breathless for the first dancing class in her cheerleader outfit with its pleated skirt—drawing the attention of the whole group as she explained she hadn't had time to change after a picture-taking session. She monopolized Brad's time during that class and all the rest.

Nora Faye didn't get a chance to talk to Brad during the dance classes, nor anywhere else until toward the end of that summer when they were both at the swimming pool one afternoon. When she saw him coming her way from the other side of the pool she made a dash for her towel so she could tie it around her waist to hide her legs. She was self-conscious about the way her knees didn't touch unless she bent one leg. She thought it made her look bowlegged. Peggy said it looked better than being knocked-kneed, and Susanna said nobody else would notice, and that it was better than the way her thighs rubbed together. But Nora Faye felt deformed.

Brad waylaid her before she got to her towel, backing her into a little corner beside the concession stand to ask her what she'd been doing all summer. She pressed against the hot chain link fence, trying to avoid the prickly weeds poking through, while she artfully bent one knee in front of the other, until Brad's forthright interest made her forget about her legs. Come to find out, he had been as interested in her as she was in him, and he told her how disappointed he'd been when she seemed to be too wrapped up in Fletcher during the folk dancing sessions to give him any attention. He walked her home from the pool that day, and they made a date for a movie later in the week.

It was a beautiful, clear night. After the movie she took him around the long way home. He sang "Walkin' my Baby Back Home" to her, and she felt like the kind of girl Jane Powell and June Allyson played in movies, with the boy she liked also liking her, and everything turning out so right.

But the one thing not perfect was that Brad didn't have anything to say about the movie they'd seen. She wanted to do what she always did after a movie; she wanted to examine it from every angle. She wouldn't have expected him to have much to say if it had been Elizabeth Taylor in

"Cynthia" that she saw last week, or Jeanne Crain in "People Will Talk" the week before that. But they'd seen "The Day the Earth Stood Still," which she thought was more a boy's movie. He said, "It was a good story. That's all I ask of a movie." And that was that. When she kept talking about it, he said he'd never before heard anybody go on so about a little ole movie. "What's the matter with you, girl?" he growled deliciously as he pulled her to him for a kiss.

She liked the kiss so much she made another date with him, and then another, on into their senior year. But by the time they were on their way home from a winter date—a Christmas party at the house of their senior sponsor—she realized his kisses weren't enough to make up for the lack of common interests. It was pretty easy to break up with him since he had lines of girls waiting their turn. He'd gone back to the party that night and had walked Margaret Bannister home and was still going with her at prom time.

She ended up asking Betty Jo Shannon's cousin, Roger, to her senior prom after he asked her to his. He lived down the road toward Pikeville and went to school at Virgie. He'd spent weeks at a time at Betty Jo's house as they were growing up, and Nora Faye had liked him well enough but had never thought of him as boyfriend material. She borrowed back her brown dress for his prom and borrowed a pale green one for her prom, and she had a good time at both proms and on a few movie dates that followed. She was starting to think maybe her theory was wrong; maybe the physical part could come later, after things started with a friendship. She was beginning to feel she might possibly get serious about him, when he sent her a note by Betty Jo saying he had started going with a girl who lived closer. His note said, "I'm sure you always felt the way I did, that we were just having some kicks together until we met the right person, and I guess you'll be happy to hear that I think I may have met mine."

She didn't answer his note. What could she have said? Thanks for letting me know what a faint impression I made on you?

It seemed to her she was doomed to a future without a boyfriend. If a boy appealed to her physically she didn't have anything in common with him mentally, and vice-versa. And she'd rather be by herself than with a boy who didn't really appeal to her.

CHAPTER 37
TED

She saw Ted Hunt her first day on campus. She had only a fleeting glimpse of him that day, but she remembered him when she saw him the second day at the freshman post-registration mixer hosted by the sophomores in the student union party room. She was on her own. Shirley, who was her roommate, was saying goodbye to her parents who would be going home after their late lunch, and Peggy was busy with her responsibilities as one of the party hostesses.

It had come as a shock yesterday when she suddenly felt overwhelmed by the size of the university. She'd visited Peggy on campus so often she'd thought she was familiar and prepared. But after she registered yesterday, she'd suddenly realized that knowing where buildings were located was not the same thing as being able to get from one building to another on time.

Peggy's feelings had been hurt back when she realized Nora Faye was even considering colleges other than the university. "I thought we'd always planned to go to the same school," she said, "even if we can't room together till you're a sophomore." Freshmen were required to live in a freshman dorm, but Peggy had plans for them to share a dorm room next year, or maybe to rent a house or apartment with other girls off campus.

Nora Faye's choice of colleges had not been a snap decision. She'd considered smaller schools—she knew the university might feel too big—but she thought being with Peggy would balance out the size.

"You'll get used to things in no time," Peggy soothed, "and you'll never get homesick like I did last year, because you'll have me."

Nora Faye wasn't homesick, and she had not thought she needed any kind of assurance until reality set in yesterday. Though she and Shirley Bastin had never been bosom buddies, their paths had crossed so often over the years—in spite of the caution James and Granny Rose took after Mr. Bastin's coal truck was ambushed—that she knew her well enough to know they'd get along okay. So she said yes when Shirley called one day back in the summer to ask if she'd like to room with her. James had no objection; he did not see how Mr. Bastin's truck mine involvement could put Nora Faye in any danger at school. He asked her not to accept a ride home with Shirley's family, but that was the only restriction he asked for.

Peggy's first year had been such a happy one that, for her, coming back to campus had been like coming back home. But even with Peggy's reassurance, Nora Faye felt increasingly unsure. If she was this nervous today, how was she going to manage with classes tomorrow? She wished she'd gone to a smaller school: to Morehead with Susanna or Lincoln Memorial with Dollie and Bootsie.

This welcoming party seemed a frivolous waste of time. She was thinking she should be making practice runs or doing something to help prepare for getting around campus tomorrow. She became more fretful by the moment and was seriously considering leaving the party if she could locate Peggy to let her know what she was doing.

As she scanned the crowd for Peggy, she saw Ted Hunt for the second time, and her heart lurched. Her eyes were drawn to his hands with long graceful fingers that looked to be moving like those of a guitar player or a piano player. Everybody else seemed to be struggling not to have an accident with the refreshments. Even the girls looked awkward as they juggled sandwiches, cookies and punch, and the few boys who had managed to avoid mishap while picking up the flimsy paper plates and cups now stood unmoving with everything frozen in ham-fisted grasps. But Ted held cup and plate with ease in one hand while he fed himself with the other and even managed to gesture as he talked. His angular grace didn't just take her mind off her growing misgivings; it made her absolutely dizzy.

She managed to get swept nearer to him where a few upperclassmen from the newspaper staff were explaining to a group of freshmen that they did not need to be journalism majors or English majors to work on the newspaper. They were inviting them to a staff meeting.

When Ted asked if the paper still came out every Thursday, one of the newspaper fellows sounded very pleased as he looked up in search of the questioner. "Is that you, Hunt? Glad to see you back. I never could get you interested in the paper before. You planning on checking us out this year?"

Ted said, "Maybe." Nora Faye liked the way his voice sounded earnest and playful at the same time.

She was confused about him having been on campus in the past and yet not seeming to be one of the hosts today. The newspaper staffer was having the same thoughts. He asked, "Why are you at this freshman thing? Are you one of the hosts?"

Ted said, "Not a host. Just thought I might see some familiar faces if I crashed this party."

Another boy said, "I think I saw her face back by the ping-pong table." The group laughed, and Nora Faye's heart went heavy.

When she was jostled again, she maneuvered so that she ended up beside him, turning to him to ask, before she lost her nerve, "Do you play the piano?" He looked confused, then disappointed. He studied her face, looked toward the refreshment table, then returned his gaze to her.

"You're looking for Ted Nettleby," he said. "I'm Ted Hunt. Nettleby's over there by the punch bowl—or he was a few minutes ago. He'll be at the piano when the entertainment starts."

She laughed, surprised at how comfortable she felt with this boy who made her feel so giddy. "No, I'm not looking for a piano player named Ted." But she suddenly felt not comfortable enough to confess she had been admiring his hands. "I thought somebody said you played," she fabricated.

He asked if she played, but she was jostled away before she could answer. The crowd had parted in two big waves to make way for a boy in a football jersey who hopped onto a small, low stage and spoke into a mike, announcing that Peggy Wainwright was going to sing something for them. The room erupted into applause and shouts and whistles, and then a hum of excited comment. The boy on stage was grinning like he'd told a joke. He playfully motioned for them to get quiet, and made a show of trying to start talking again while the chatter got louder every time he tried to speak. "I have no idea what song she'll be singing..." The crowd went insane with noise and laughter, and he was shouting now, "But some of you may have heard her sing a certain number last year." The clapping and hooting and whistling didn't let up until the other Ted sat down at the piano and Peggy stepped up from the crowd. She smiled and gave a little wave before she went to the piano bench where she leaned over Ted Nettleby and touched the sheet music as they exchanged a whispered word. Then, after a short piano riff, she raised the mike and began to sing "Blue Moon" so perfectly that Nora Faye felt like this was unreal. She'd been hearing Peggy sing for a great part of her life—and she was always perfect—but today she was in another realm. She sounded as smooth and professional as Rosie Clooney or Doris Day. The crowd was transfixed. The minute she started to sing, everyone froze in place. It seemed that the entire room took a deep breath, and then, when Peggy got to the lines that began, "And then there suddenly appeared before me…" just like in a movie musical, the entire crowd joined in as one, making the walls vibrate.

This was a tradition. She remembered now. Peggy had told her about it. But she'd had no concept of the magnitude. She'd pictured a few people in a small room. Peggy had told her how her class had spontaneously chosen "Blue Moon" as their theme song and had chosen Peggy to lead them in singing it at every possible occasion.

And now, as though unable not to, she joined them as the song continued, "…the only one my arms will ever hold. I heard somebody whisper 'please adore me,' and when I looked the moon had turned to gold."

A little of her apprehension subsided. She looked around for Ted Hunt. She wished she could tell him, "That's my sister!"

But being so proud of Peggy made her nervous in a way. She was afraid she would be expected to be as talented and sweet and smart as Peggy. For the first time ever, she was glad she and Peggy did not have the same last name. These thoughts brought her back to her worries about the size of the university. She still felt like she was out of her league, but seeing Ted Hunt had moved her to consider that maybe she would be able to adjust, after all.

She saw him again on the first day of classes when he was suddenly in a group that had gathered casually on the front steps of the science building before heading to the cafeteria for lunch. But, as much as she regretted losing a chance to be with him, she'd decided she'd have to stop by her dorm and pick up the books she'd need for afternoon classes before she ate lunch. Then, once in her room, she looked at her notebooks and realized she needed to organize the notes she'd taken in her morning classes. She skipped lunch altogether.

Just as she started out the door on the way to her one o'clock, Shirley and some other girls burst in giggling and out of breath. It took her a few minutes to figure out what they were saying. They were teasing her, saying how surprised they were to learn she was such a schemer, a girl who knew how to arouse a boy's interest so quickly. Then, she was in happy disbelief when they finally got themselves calmed down enough to tell her Ted had asked about her after she slipped out of the group. They said he asked, "What happened to that disinterested girl? I thought she was going with us."

She looked up "disinterested" in the dictionary. That's the first box she unpacked—the one with the dictionary— when Peggy came to her room that evening to help her finish unpacking.

In spite of no disasters on her first day of classes, Psych 101 was yet to be faced, and it loomed with some dread. Peggy and her crowd had warned her that Dr. Mesker probably wouldn't have a slot left for a freshman—his classes filled early—and they'd said she should wait until next term to take the course if she couldn't get Dr. Mesker now.

So they were happy for her when she got into his class on registration day, but she was dubious about the class participation they kept telling her about. They said after the first few class sessions Dr. Mesker would talk very little himself. He had the class divide into pairs, and after giving brief directions at the beginning of a class period and allowing time for the pairs to discuss assigned topics, he would use the rest of the time to question them about their discussions of the topics.

It wasn't just that she didn't like the idea of talking in class, but the thought of listening to all that hot air from other students seemed like it would be an ordeal. "I know how that goes," she protested. "There are always a few bores who love the sound of their own voices. I'm supposed to be here to gain from the wisdom of my trained professors," she struck a statue-of-liberty pose, "not to hear a bunch of wind bags making noise. I've been in classes like that, and one person always ends up going on and on."

Peggy assured her Dr. Mesker knew how to keep that from happening. "He really is something special," she tried to soothe. "I promise you'll agree with me. You were so lucky to get him."

Peggy was right. In the very first class meeting it became apparent that Dr. Mesker was such a good teacher he made it look easy the way he conducted discussion with a tight but invisible rein. Tall and gaunt, and rumored to have been in a POW camp during the war, Dr. Mesker, with a scraggly beard and deep-set eyes, looked more eccentric that he behaved. Without ever appearing heavy handed, he never allowed one person to monopolize a discussion.

However, she began to feel uneasy toward the end of the first class period as he gave directions for the structure that would carry through until the end of the term. They were to pair off today and, from that time forward, they would discuss all assigned topics with their partner, after which, students he called on would give a summary of the partner's viewpoints, not his own. Nora Faye had not understood, from Peggy's description, that she'd be with the same partner all semester. It sounded like it could be an interesting experience with the right partner but like carrying an albatross if she ended up with a bad one.

When Dr. Mesker instructed them to pair off with someone they didn't know very well, somebody piped up to ask how he'd know if they paired up with a friend. He gave the expected answer about supposing college students were mature enough to want to profit from a course they were buying, rather than to play tricks on the teacher.

Nora Faye saw no one she recognized, so anyone in the class could have served as her partner. Rather than milling about the room with those in search of a partner, she decided she might as well ask the girl in front of her if she wanted to pair up. She leaned forward, but before she could tap the girl's shoulder, Ted Hunt dropped into the chair beside her, saying, "You don't know me—you think I'm Ted Nettleby—and I don't know you at all. So we meet the criteria, don't we?" And Nora Faye became partners with Ted Hunt.

When Ted went on to say he thought such a disinterested girl would make a good partner, Nora Faye's heart beat fast, and she asked what he meant by disinterested. Before he could answer, she continued, "I heard about you calling me disinterested yesterday. I looked up the word."

He grinned. "I hoped you'd hear I asked about you." He threw the question back at her. "What do you think I mean by disinterested?"

She said she hoped she hadn't appeared indifferent, and he said she hadn't. He was arranging his long legs under the desk. "I just finished reading *The Razor's Edge,* he went on. "Maybe you know how Maugham's narrator describes the main character as disinterested. I'd been waiting to meet somebody who doesn't seem to be self-centered so I could use the word that way."

Nora Faye had read *The Razor's Edge* just the month before, the first of many coincidences to unfold between her and Ted Hunt day by day. "Larry?" she asked, and then went on after Ted nodded, his eyes wide in disbelief, "I read *The Razor's Edge* this summer, too. I don't remember where the word disinterested was used, but I thought of Larry as just the opposite. I thought he was extremely self-centered, the way he gave up a real life to wallow in his self-absorbed search for answers. Disinterested surely isn't the word for him."

As they talked, two or three classmates came by to see if Ted already had a partner. Other students milled about them seeking and settling into their new partnerships as Nora Faye and Ted fell into the kind of discussion that was to bundle them into one package from there on out.

"Well, maybe his disinterestedness (she loved the way he could roll out such an uncommon word in such a common manner) lay in the sense that he wasn't always promoting himself the way self-serving people do: that he was searching for the meaning of life rather than searching for a way to force his idea of the right kind of life on other people. He was looking for answers instead of trying to tell other people how to think."

"But, in a way he was telling Isabel how she should think; he wanted her to think it would be the right thing for her to give up material things and join his spiritual search. And wasn't it selfish the way he abandoned her for his search?"

"Oh, but wasn't she the one who abandoned him, in that she refused his invitation to join him in his search?"

"Some choice!" she started to say, but Ted shushed her with a finger. "Okay, maybe 'open-minded' would be a better word to describe Larry…and you. I'm willing to let go of Larry, to let go of Maugham altogether if I have to, and call you open-minded or not self-centered instead of disinterested."

"Based on what?" she teased. "How could you know if I'm not self-centered?"

He said he'd heard her in a conversation at the president's welcoming party. She well remembered her first glimpse of him at that party, of course, but she didn't know he'd been near enough to hear any conversation she was in. "What were we talking about?" she asked.

He grinned—the grin that was soon to become as dear to her as the air she breathed. "*Lady Chatterley's Lover*, as a matter of fact," he said, and Nora Faye did remember the conversation. She blushed, although the conversation had been nothing to feel embarrassed about, and she did not remember that she had said anything.

A girl in the group had been telling them about her parents' adventures smuggling in an uncensored copy of the book on their return trip from Europe. The conversation was about the drama of the smuggling, rather than the content of the novel. Nora Faye was pretty sure Ted hadn't been close until the group was breaking up, but he teased that he'd heard a lot more than she realized.

"I noticed you because the question you asked that girl moved her along in her tale about her parents instead of centering things on yourself. Other people were commenting about their opinions of the book or about their experiences with custom inspectors or about their trips to Europe. You didn't talk about yourself."

She said, "You seem to read a lot of fiction for a science major," and he told her he started out majoring in English Lit, saying, "Can't break the habit."

Then, "How'd you know I'm a science major?" he asked.

"One hears things," she teased.

He scooted his chair closer to hers. "Yeah, one does. I've heard, for instance, that you realize you're destined to marry me." He pointed to her name where she'd written it on her notebook cover. "I've heard you've already got my initial on your luggage." Nora Faye smiled to herself to think of the N. F. H. on her graduation-gift Samsonite.

So they became partners, and their partnership continued beyond the class, into second semester, through the summer, and—except for one sad period of separation—right on through her sophomore year. Both of them, as well as Peggy, had taken summer jobs in Lexington.

For Dr. Mesker's purposes, she and Ted had probed one another about all the items on the syllabus: personal things like early influences and present outlooks, as well as assigned case histories, textbook chapters, society's expectations, lists of terms, periodical articles, and current headlines. Being forced to sum up another person's viewpoint was a good way to force a person to truly listen and to lose the habit of looking at things from just one side. And knowing that your opinions were going to be summed up by someone else was a good way to force you to try to express yourself clearly. Having a partner whose outlook so closely paralleled your own made the job harder instead of easier. She had to stay alert to not miss the small ways their opinions sometimes differed.

She was happy to concede to Peggy that the class was truly interesting and that Dr. Mesker was a brilliant teacher. Peggy said, "Well, you'd be sitting pretty no matter what kind of teacher Dr. Mesker turned out to be. Who wouldn't thrive with Ted Hunt for a class partner? I've never been so jealous in all my life!"

"*You*, jealous?" Nora Faye squeaked. "Well, it's about time I give you reason to be jealous. I've been jealous of you all our lives. You, with your voice and your looks and your grades, your talents and your personality. And now, with your...your sex appeal. All I hear about, everywhere I turn, is how every football player on the squad is trying to date you." Nora Faye was only halfway teasing. The part about Peggy's attributes was all true—and about football players wanting to take her out—but she was exaggerating the jealousy. She usually felt more proud than envious of Peggy, and when she felt jealous, it was a unique mixture of feelings that put her in the position of feeling grateful for the very situation that made her jealous. She was almost as solicitous of Peggy's happiness as her own.

Peggy was persevering about Ted. "Well, I'm just saying," she went on, "that there's not a girl on campus who doesn't envy you for capturing Ted Hunt's heart. The quintessential Renaissance Man. I heard more about him last year after he went home than I heard about the boys still on campus."

They were inseparable, Nora Faye and Ted. They laid out their entire lives before one another. She could not remember which conversations they'd had in classrooms and which on park benches or in juke-joint booths. It all ran together. He knew more about her than anyone else, or, at least, she'd told him more about what she felt and thought than she'd ever told anyone else, even Peggy.

Nothing about herself seemed insignificant when she told it to him, and nothing he told her about himself seemed insignificant.

His mother died when he was fourteen. Breast cancer. He lived with his father in Middlesboro above the family hardware store where his family had always lived. He worked in the store from the time he was a little kid. He had a genius brother thirteen years older who was a physics professor at Cornell. Ted had ignored his brother's urgings to come to Cornell two years ago and had instead enrolled at the university to be near a girlfriend who was enrolled at Transylvania. That romance had ended before classes began, and he'd had several other girlfriends since then, but nothing serious. He started school with plans to major in English Literature but had switched to Library Science and then Geology. He'd finished his first year and had just started the second when he had an emergency appendectomy and then a severe bloodstream infection he developed in the hospital. If it had happened a few years earlier—before penicillin—he would have died. He had to withdraw from school and go home for a long recuperation before he started over again this year. Like Nora Faye, he was keenly aware of how his father had put his well-being before his own. He felt extremely grateful for the way his dad had taken care of him when he was sick and the way he'd tried to keep their home the same for Ted after his mother died and his brother moved away.

Nora Faye and Ted walked every sidewalk on campus and on all the streets surrounding school, and she spent hours with him while he worked on his car in his friends' garage. They sat on park benches, in stairwells, on library steps, in the student union building, in the campus grill, in borrowed cars a few times early on and in Ted's car after he got it running, on long hallway floors with their backs against the wall, and in little hole-in-the wall sandwich shops near campus… talking incessantly.

"Why?" she asked him about one of her memories after another. "Why did I just stand by instead of participating in my life?" She hadn't known she needed these answers until he was there to anchor her while she asked the questions.

"I seemed to curl up like a possum when people showed interest in me." She wondered why she hadn't accepted Callie Bennett's offer to sit on Seelom again—why she stayed in the backyard that fateful summer where she couldn't even see Seelom anymore—and why she didn't take the opportunity to get to know Callie. "I know she would have taken me up the holler to see her old daddy if I'd acted like I wanted to go. She somehow knew what I needed at such a crucial time in my life, and yet I never did try to find out how she knew or why she cared. And not just Callie Bennett. Others, too. The Turner couple who sang, for instance; I could have located them. I could have thanked them for their kindness to me and could have tried to find out what compelled them to drive back to camp to check on me that night after they were on their way to Hyden."

She wondered why she hadn't asked the involved people all the questions that filled her mind now: why she didn't ask Mrs. Bledso about her boy who was killed in the war; why she'd never asked Aunt Clemma to tell her why she thought it was right to shout in church and have foot washings but not to talk in tongues or handle snakes; why she didn't ask her daddy what happened to Donny Stoddard; why she hadn't asked Miss Vickers what she meant when she said Nora Faye of all people should have sympathized with Trudy Morrow; what Dollie meant might be wrong with her when she said even if there was something wrong with Nora Faye that it didn't matter because she was not really kin to her; why she never felt like the preachers' sermons were meant for her, and why she hadn't felt more forsaken by her mother's abandonment.

Ted did not give answers, but to ask the questions made her feel she was participating in her own life in a way she hadn't before. He did tell her he thought maybe she'd been protecting herself. "You were just a kid, after all, when you were faced with more loss than some people have to deal with in a lifetime." He thought she'd worked out a way to sustain a sense of normalcy in spite of all her losses, that she knew her limits and knew what she had to do in order not to become a sum of her losses.

His experience with religion had been similar to hers. His mother had been a Catholic, attending mass sporadically over the years. His dad had not expected him to go to church after his mother died. When he'd gone with his mother, it felt like a play he was watching, not something he was expected to be part of. Nora Faye told him about Bootsie's traumatic conversion, and about the *Sullivans* movie and how Dollie had said Catholics don't go to heaven and how her grandmother had answered Aunt Stella.

He talked about his feelings of inadequacy as compared to his brother, wondering aloud if his appendicitis and the bout with the infection had been a physical manifestation of his fears about facing up to life with a lesser I. Q. than his brother's, or maybe an effort not to leave home until he felt sure his dad didn't value his brother more.

"Do you really think a person could make himself sick like that in a physical way?" she asked, and Ted said he wasn't sure, but that he was sure human beings knew only the tiniest bit about how the mind and body are connected.

It was Ted who brought about her meeting with Kenneth Mayhall. They were at a play, a student production of "Bell, Book, and Candle" at the Guignol Theater, when Ted pointed out a man a few rows in front of them. "I've talked to that fella in chem lab," he said. "I meant to tell you about him. I think I heard him say he was from Platchet County. I think his name is Linc something."

A tiny bell went off in Nora Faye's brain, but she forgot about it until the end of intermission. As the crowd started surging back across the lobby towards their doors, she and Ted bumped elbows with the man and the woman with him. They ended up stopping together in the back of the auditorium where the man introduced the woman as his wife Barb. Ted apologized for not remembering his name, and the man said, "I'm Linc Slaney."

As naturally as if it were fifteen years ago, Nora Faye asked, "Are you R. L.?"

He looked like he'd been shot. "You know me?"

"I knew your picture. And I knew your family if they lived on Dillard Creek back when you were in the Navy and I hadn't started school yet. My name's Nora Faye Houston. Your mother took care of me while my daddy went to work at the company store. I memorized your picture in your Navy hat. They all called you R. L. back then."

"You knew Conner?"

Nora Faye nodded.

R. L. looked like he was in a fog. The last stragglers were now moving intently toward their seats, and he got knocked this way and that before Barb took him by the arm. She turned to Ted and Nora Faye. "Would you be interested in skipping the last act and going around the corner for coffee or a beer? We know a place."

The next three hours sped by. As they talked, Linc remembered quite a bit about Nora Faye, considering that he'd possibly never seen her.

He remembered James and remembered that her family had moved to Dillard just before he left home. "Seems like maybe I saw you at the store with your dad one time when you were not much more than a baby. But maybe I just heard someone in my family tell about it. We still lived on the farm up the side hollow back then. I had just enlisted in the navy when my family moved to the camp house across the road from your dad's house, but my brothers and sisters wrote about you in their letters. I think you wrote me a letter once."

They talked about those letters and about his brothers and sisters. He told her Billy Ray had his tonsils removed shortly after the move from Dillard and that he never had another sick day in his life. He said he weighed more than two hundred pounds and was six feet tall. He was studying to be a Baptist minister and had been married since the summer he graduated from high school. He and his wife had their first child last year.

"Ruthie is a first grade teacher, wouldn't you know," he grinned. "She has all those little children to boss around now, plus one of her own."

Laura Jane and Lottie were both stay-at-home mothers.

"Did Lissie's husband ever come home?" she asked, and R. L. said Donald came home, but that he wasn't himself. They divorced. "Being in a prison camp like that makes it awful hard to adjust when they get back home." She didn't ask about his tongue. She assumed he still had it or R. L. would have said so.

His parents had passed away just recently, R. L. said. His mother hadn't been gone long.

And finally they talked about Conner.

He questioned her intensely. He wanted to know every detail Nora Faye could remember. She told him about the shop, the bee garden, the dead-board, the razor blade, and the letters he shook off the page like bugs while he re-read the *Tarzan* paragraph for her again and again. She told him about the books his teacher brought him and about him cutting glass under water, about the ice slide, and how Donny Stoddard ambushed any group Conner was in and how Conner kept him from tormenting the others by leaving the group to join him.

That was when Nora Faye commented about the rifle crack not waking his dad.

After that first run-in, Nora Faye and Ted met R. L. and Barb for beers or coffee every few weeks. (He'd been called Linc since his Navy days, but Nora Faye's tongue couldn't stop saying R. L..) He and Barb were both working on their masters. They had first met at the university after R. L. passed his GED test and started college on the G. I. Bill. They had no children but were closely involved with their nieces and nephews. They taught at a high school near Shippensburg, where his family lived, and they planned to return there when they got their degrees. He was pretty certain of getting the principal's job at the end of the year.

R. L. and Barb left town during spring break, and, during their first meeting after classes resumed, R. L. singled out Nora Faye and said, "Let me show you something. Let's see if you know what this is."

Nora Faye could tell it was something very important to him by the way he took out his wallet and opened it almost reverently to slide out a little folded slick white paper. It took her breath away. On first glance she recognized Conner's razor blade. It was only slightly rusty, and the paper was surprisingly clean. R. L. had driven up to Dillard and knocked on the door of the Slaney house. His eyes were dancing as he told her what he'd done.

"You can hardly recognize the place...or any of the houses," he said. "People have rebuilt them or fixed them up.

"I was afraid it was going to look like a boarded-up ghost town or a shantytown, but everything is spic and span." He said the store had burned down, and the post office and union hall and tipple were gone, but that all the houses on the lower level were still there. Most of the little houses high on the hills were gone, and the farmhouse where he had lived, but the remaining houses were painted and remodeled and shipshape. He was stunned to see Conner's shop still standing.

He said he knocked on the door and told the woman his family had lived there and asked if he could check for something in the shed. Remembering what Nora Faye had told him, he felt gingerly along the rafter tops until he encountered the little paper package he now held. His eyes went moist as he thanked Nora Faye for telling him about it.

"It might seem foolish," he said, "but having something he held in his hands makes me feel connected in a way I can't explain.

"My family handles their grief the way a lot of people do," he went on. "They don't talk about it. You've told me more about Conner than anybody in my family ever has. I felt his death like a double loss. In addition to missing out on all the years he would have lived, I missed out on those years away from him when I was in the Navy. My family's not been able to give me what you did."

All four sat silently with tear-filled eyes.

Later, when they were alone, Nora Faye told Ted about her mother's Cara Nome bath powder box and how she didn't know what had happened to it.

"Seems like I always considered it more of a nuisance than a treasure; I didn't have much drawer space, and it took up a lot of room. Somewhere along the way I took it out of my underwear drawer and put it where it wouldn't always be in the way. I remember making a place for it in an ice cream container I kept in the back of my half of the tiny closet I shared with Peggs after we moved to Johnston, and then I just let it get away from me."

She told him also about the hatbox with her mother's hair and the Kewpie Doll she'd let slip away as well.

"My mother's hair!" she wailed. "There must be something wrong with me not to take care of such a personal keepsake from my mother. Did you see how R. L. looked when he was touching Conner's razor blade? And I could have had my mother's hair!"

"Your mother's not dead," Ted said. "It might be different if she were dead like Linc's brother. Either way, it can get creepy when people dwell too much on things that belonged to people they've lost. Your way seems sensible to me."

It wasn't long until R. L. told them about running into Kenneth Mayhall at a ball game. R. L. had known Kenneth since their Navy days. They had shipped out together from San Diego, and they'd bumped into each other from time to time over the years: in California when they got back to the states, and then back in the east. Kenneth lived near Richmond now and worked as supervisor on a grounds crew at the Army Depot. When R. L. told him about Nora Faye he asked him to see if she wanted to meet with him.

Then, later, he helped to set up the meeting with Irene. R. L. had never met Irene himself, but he knew people—in addition to Kenneth—who knew her. She lived in Dayton. She came to Lexington just for the purpose of meeting Nora Faye.

CHAPTER 38
KENNETH AT GRANGERS

The Sandwich Shop on Grangers' Mezzanine proved to be the perfect place for Nora Faye to meet Kenneth. Summer term had not started yet, so she doubted that anyone she knew from school would be coming to the department store to intrude on a Saturday morning. She was already seated in one of the low-partition booths when she saw him come in through the store's second-floor entrance. He spotted her immediately, as though he had studied a map of where she'd be seated. He put his cigarette into the sand pot and came to her. She was glad he had not stood looking lost before he found her. He approached with strained severity at first, and it was only when she raised her hand in a little awkward wave that his face relaxed into a momentary twinkle.

R. L. had said only, "He doesn't look too bad." She didn't know what she expected, but this seemed not to be it; he seemed pitiful. For a moment she wished she could leave before he got any closer. She couldn't have said what made him seem pitiful. It wasn't the way he was dressed. His clothes were not new but they were not shabby. He seemed comfortable in a brown tweed sport coat with creased khakis and a soft white oxford-cloth shirt open at the collar. His shirt was slightly yellowed from time, with a collar a little longer than the present style, but he did not look out of date. His shoes were brown leather loafers, clean and polished, and his hair looked newly trimmed but without that raw-stubble look some dark haired men have on the neck just after a cut.

His narrow-brimmed khaki colored poplin hat seemed right for him.

It wasn't until he was closer that she realized it was his mouth that made her sad; his teeth didn't match his face. They were obviously false, and they must have been brand new, the way he seemed to be struggling not to put his hand over his mouth. All in all, he had the look of someone who had once looked much worse. His face was leathery and wrinkled past his years—like a coalminer's face without the grit—but he was clean-shaven, his cheeks highlighted with tiny broken veins, his lips twitching from time to time.

He stood for a moment just looking down into her face, and she almost panicked as she wondered if he expected her to get up and hug him. But then he dropped into the opposite seat, skimming his hat across the booth before him without looking to see how it came to a stop. She liked the way he did that. It was the mental picture she kept of him. She liked the grace and confidence of it, as though he'd made that move a thousand times before. He winked at her.

As soon as he was seated he took a Snap-Open Philip Morris package from his pocket and wordlessly offered her one, and then, when she refused, took one for himself, asking by raised eyebrows and a thumb paused on his Zippo if she minded if he lit up. "You're smart not to let yourself get hooked on these coffin nails," he said. "It's a nasty habit." He lit his cigarette and flipped his lighter closed.

Before she gave it any thought, Nora Faye said, "Oh, I don't want to give you the wrong impression; I do smoke sometimes..." He tilted the pack towards her again, and she waved it off again as she continued, "but not in front of my par...not with my family," she stammered. She felt flustered for a moment, but he simply pocketed the package.

As he inhaled deeply she glanced at his hands to see if that's where she got her tapered fingers. His nicotine stained nails made her even more aware that his teeth were new; his teeth were not yellow. The new cigarette brought an end to the twitches. He visibly relaxed with the first inhalation, but she couldn't stop thinking about his teeth. She wondered if he'd gotten new ones just because he was coming to see her. That possibility broke her heart.

She spoke before she had time to start feeling awkward. "How'd you know it was me?"

He grinned. "How did *you* know?"

"I don't know, but I didn't think it about anybody else."

"Me neither," he said.

After a moment's silence they started to speak at the same time. They laughed. Then he silently demurred to her.

"R. L.—Linc, I guess you call him—said he met you when you were both in the Navy."

"Yeah. I'd got to know Linc in San Diego before we shipped out, and then I ran into him a time or two overseas, and finally, at a joint here in Lexington not long after we got home." The timber of his voice, in spite of his smoker's rasp, was warm and melodic.

She was pleased at the way he made no issue of it when a waitress appeared and asked for their orders. He looked questioningly at Nora Faye. She said, "Just coffee," and Kenneth smiled up at the girl as he said, "Same here. Cream for mine, please." She was relieved he had not urged her to order a sandwich.

They took another moment to look at one another. Nora Faye was feeling more comfortable. She fished out the stinking, little, shallow, tin ashtray from under the jukebox selector and pushed it towards him.

He said, "I don't know if Linc told you I didn't know about you before your mother married James."

She barely shook her head.

"And then later, her last letters never got to me, the ones she wrote after she left Kentucky for California. She thought they did. I was on my way back to the states before she got to San Diego. I thought she'd dumped me; she thought I'd dumped her. Things got pretty crazy. It wasn't too long till she met somebody else, I guess. I'd heard she never went back to Plachet County."

Nora Faye said nothing.

"She never did tell me the truth about you. She told me she had a little girl, but I thought you were James's. She let me think that. She told me about you in the letters she wrote from Dillard. I didn't know you were mine till I got to talking to Linc here in Lexington."

"What'd he tell you?"

They fell silent while the waitress placed their coffees before them and set a little china cream pitcher and a spoon near Kenneth. The cream pitcher was shaped like Mrs. Bledso's chrome percolator. Kenneth quietly thanked her before he answered the question.

"He just said something about the rumors, and I sort of put two and two together when I got to thinking about the dates we'd…been together." He stopped himself, looking embarrassed.

Then abruptly, "I don't know how much you know about me…"

"I don't know anything."

He took his time stirring a dollop of cream into his coffee. "Well, even though I didn't know about you, I meant to marry your mother as soon as I could get things settled about my first wife. But things got crazy there, too. She'd agreed, before I went to Wolliver, that we'd get divorced, but then she tried to kill herself—took a bunch of pills, a real mess—and her family sent my uncle to come and get me. I didn't have time to explain anything to your mother…or anybody. When my wife's brothers said they were going to kill me, that's when I joined the Navy. It took me a long time to get in touch with your mother again. She'd been married to James a long time."

The sense of anti-climax was so great Nora Faye envisioned just getting up and walking away without

341

another word. Again, she didn't know what she had expected.

Kenneth raised his voice above the lilt of "Come On-a My House" that someone had selected on the jukebox. "I've got a wife now—a fine woman named Darlene—but no children on purpose. I don't figure I'd make much of a daddy. I lived a high old life for many a year before I met Darlene. Even if I'd known about you, I might have left you alone. I couldn't have been the kind of daddy I'm certain James Houston's been."

Feeling defensive in spite of no attack on James, Nora Faye said, "He's the only daddy I could ever want."

"I don't doubt it," Kenneth said.

Rosie Clooney chanted, "…a peach anna pear an I love-a you hair…"

"And if you just want to never give another thought to me," Kenneth went on, "I'll not do anything to keep that from happening. I don't want to cause you any kind of trouble. What little bit of money I've got, I'd be happy to share with you, but I'd never expect you to act like I'm your daddy."

In that instant, Nora Faye lurched several notches away from childhood. She had to strain to keep the pity from cracking her voice. "I won't forget that you offered, but I don't need money. I'm sorry you missed out on my mother and all, but you don't ever need to feel bad about how things turned out for me. Things just happened. I don't think there's any reason to want to make it different now."

"Yeah." The little smile he gave her was gentle and understanding, and she could imagine, for a moment, what her mother must have seen when he smiled at her like that when they were young.

He splashed a little coffee onto his wrist and instinctively started to reach into his back pocket for his handkerchief, but immediately pulled away and grabbed for a napkin. He had brought a handkerchief Irene had embroidered with his initials and mailed to him. It got to him just before he was shipped back to the states. It was the only memento he'd kept of Irene. As he had dressed for this meeting with Nora Faye, he'd thought it might be a good thing to show her. Now he wondered how he could have been so outrageously wrong and silly. He felt so embarrassed to have it with him that it seemed to burn warmly on his hip.

"Did anybody ever take you to the fire tower on top of Pine Mountain?" he asked suddenly, dabbing at his wrist with the paper napkin he wrested one-handed from the shiny chrome holder.

Nora Faye was surprised into silence by the sudden change of topic, and her mind went blank about the fire tower, confusing it with the one above Johnston. After a moment of bewildered silence she answered, "No. We always talked about hiking up to it after we moved to Johnston, but we never did."

Kenneth looked disappointed. A couple had seated themselves in the adjacent booth, so he leaned in toward Nora Faye as he visibly let go of thoughts of Pine Mountain and returned to family things. "Linc said your daddy got married again. I was glad to hear it."

"Yes. They suit each other."

And then Nora Faye said something that surprised herself. "I don't think my mother would have turned out to be that kind of wife even if she'd got to be with you."

They shared a quick, mischievous grin. She didn't know what she'd meant—didn't exactly know why they had grinned—but she knew what Kenneth meant when he immediately took on a look of solemn respect and said, "There's not a soul walks the face of this earth that's a better person than your mother."

CHAPTER 39
IRENE AT GRANGERS

The plans to meet her mother on Grangers' Mezzanine put Nora Faye in a state of nervousness even though she felt good about her meeting with Kenneth. She had a sense of having risen to the occasion with him. It was one of the few incidents in her life she could contemplate without some kind of regret; without thinking, "I shouldn't have," or "Why didn't I?" She felt like she'd probably left Kenneth feeling better about himself than he had before their meeting.

So, when she faced the truth about these plans to meet her mother she knew she was feeling challenged to make an even greater difference for her. It was exciting to think of walking away knowing she'd left her mother's heart at ease. She imagined Irene's appearance would be similar to Kenneth's, respectable but sort of ill-used. It would be sad if she looked worse than Kenneth—if she had rotten teeth or looked blousy and coarse—but she told herself to be realistic; women who've had it hard show it more than men. She still had a strong image of her mother with her sagebrush blond hair and her compact figure. She always pictured her in clothes that fit closely but not tightly. Her dresses—even the simple cotton-print housedresses she ordered from the Montgomery Ward catalog—seemed to move with her body, never riding up or twisting out of shape. Her slip never showed, and her blouse never pulled out of the waistband when she wore a skirt. Stella's slip straps always fell off her shoulders and down her arms below her short sleeves, but Nora Faye had never seen her mother's straps showing.

A few months had passed since the meeting with Kenneth, so Grangers' display windows and artfully placed mannequins reflected a new season. Festoons of fall leaves bedecked columns and stair rails, and the mannequins wore hues of rust and orange and brown. Instead of seating herself in a booth, Nora Faye decided to take a position where she could spot her mother unseen and watch her take a seat before she joined her. The Sandwich Shop had the perfect set-up for this kind of surveillance. There was the direct entrance Kenneth had taken into the shop from the store's second floor, then a half-story staircase that led down to the Sandwich Shop from a balcony hallway—the true mezzanine of the name—where elevator doors, restroom vestibules, and escalator access culminated in a steady come and go of traffic. There were potted trees on this level and mannequins in outfits of gold and burgundy and hunter green. Nora Faye decided to take up a position here that would make it possible for her to spot Irene no matter which access she chose. It suddenly seemed vitally important that she see Irene before Irene should see her. "What if I don't instinctively recognize her like I did Kenneth?" she worried.

She settled herself in an alcove at the end of the balcony, inconspicuous near some potted trees but close enough to the escalators that she would appear to have just stepped off in case someone wondered why she was there. She laughed at herself silently. Who was going to wonder why she was standing there…and why would it matter what anybody thought?

She heard the elevator doors open, and she knew her mother was going to appear. It was a large load, maybe seven or eight people. Irene was in the center of the group. She stood out as though a spotlight were on her. As the passengers dispersed in different directions it seemed the others deferred to Irene as she walked straight to the top of the stairs and stopped just for an instant to survey the restaurant below, giving Nora Faye a view of her profile.

She was the most perfect woman Nora Faye had ever seen. She radiated quiet composure. Of all the women in the entire store, she was the most beautiful. Of the entire town, even. It wasn't just that she was beautiful; she was well cared for. She had class. She looked exactly like she had the day she left Dillard, except everything about her was more deliberately tasteful.

As a little group of women left the restroom, Nora Faye stepped back where she could see around them. Irene's sagebrush hair curled softly around her face and around a shiny crown, just as Nora Faye remembered. She wore a straight-cut taupe-colored skirt with a long-sleeved cashmere sweater-set of the same hue. She laid a hand on the banister and let it trail lightly beside her as she descended the staircase while scanning the crowd. Her garments skimmed her body without being the least bit baggy or the least bit tight. She wore the cardigan unbuttoned with pushed-up sleeves. A small silk scarf at her neckline had pastel swirls of yellow, aqua, pink, and red. Her shoes were plain low-heeled pumps a shade or two darker than her outfit, but her purse was a little oblong leather clutch the same shade as the subtle swirls of aqua in her scarf. Her short, manicured nails were painted a transparent pink.

When her mother came to a stop midway down the stairs, Nora Faye turned away from her and stepped onto the down-escalator, holding her breath until she was on the first floor and headed toward the door onto the sidewalk. She actually ran away from Grangers, away from her mother.

When she saw Ted that night, she considered, for a moment, not telling him what she'd done, telling him instead that her mother hadn't showed up. Maybe because he had been uneasy about it from the beginning.

Before the date was set, when he had urged her to reconsider the meeting, she asked him what he was afraid of. "I just think maybe you've got more to lose than gain," he'd said. And then, when she asked what he thought she had to lose, he didn't say much more.

"It's not my place to say," he tried to conclude, but when he saw she thought he was keeping something back, he added, "I don't know what it is I think you've got to lose. If you want to see your mother, then that's what you should do."

After a pause he had asked if she was sure she didn't want to talk it over with Peggy.

"I know it seems like I would," she said. "But, think about it. Her mother's well-being is tied into my mother's well-being in a way that means I need to leave her out of this. I guess it's just about the first thing to come up that I can't talk about with her."

Ted didn't say anything to make her feel bad when she told him about running away. Just, "Maybe it's for the best."

They were sitting on the library steps where they'd stopped so Ted could finish his smoke. It was a crisply perfect evening, too pleasant to spend indoors. Nora Faye laid her books beside her and leaned against the Italian balustrade. The pungent smells of dry crushed leaves and wood smoke were hanging on the air. Girls wearing new jewel-toned suede jackets they'd been impatiently waiting to show off, and boys in chinos and pale oxford cloth shirts with button-down collars and empty suspender loops chattered and laughed as they came and went in pairs and groups, their footsteps still resonating with the kind of new-term enthusiasm that starts to fade by Thanksgiving time.

Nora Faye played with her long plastic beads, mindlessly tying them into a knot and then untying them. Ted took hold of her fidgeting hands. "You're out of date," he teased. 'I thought these were the beads flappers wore in the twenties." He was trying to take her mind off her mother.

She asked if he knew more about her mother than she did, if R. L. had told him things she didn't know. But he said he'd never talked to R. L. about her mother other than their brief conversation to set up the meeting, and he assured her he certainly didn't know anything she didn't know. "It just seemed like a set-up for disappointment, for anybody to see their mother after 15 years and after she left like she did…but, then, you feel disappointed about *not* talking to her, so who can say what's best?" he trailed off.

"I think I resented her looking so classy," she blurted.

"Well, you should resent it."

They laughed. He gave her a drag off his Camel, holding it tenderly to her lips, before he reached across her and through the banister to stub it out in the raised shrub bed.

Some people from his Trig class smiled and threw a wave as they passed on the far side of the broad steps. This was one of those moments when Nora Faye—as a rule—would have consciously savored the cozy enfoldment of the season and the reassuring comfort of Ted's presence. But this evening the subtle autumn odors, the friendly faces in the passing crowd, and Ted's warm, agreeable interest failed to block out the taint of her reaction to the vision of her mother.

"I've always thought I hoped she was happy, but I don't, do I? I want her to be miserable and look trashy."

"Trashy?"

"Well, the opposite of classy. Anybody else dressed as perfectly and looking as beautiful would have drawn attention. Most of the women in that store wore rundown loafers or some kind of flat shoes and carried one of those chunky, scuffed leather-and-burlap handbags with saddle-hardware trim and puffed pictures of thoroughbreds. But even though she looked so much better than the others, she was so classy that nobody gave her a second look. Even when the elevator doors opened like curtains opening on a stage, she was so contained that all those people making way for her did it without looking at her."

Ted was pulling Nora Faye to her feet.

As she clasped her books to her chest and fell in beside him to cross the veranda, she went on, "She inspired such respect that everybody acted like they weren't aware of her, like they knew she didn't want to draw attention to herself."

She mulled over what she'd just said, then added, "But like they would have looked at her if she had wanted them to."

"What?" Ted said. "I think you lost me."

"They would have looked at her. It was like she had an enormous hidden power, like people would have looked at her if that had been what she wanted, but didn't because that's what she decreed. Without words or even a turn of her head."

Ted opened the heavy door and held it with an arm extended over her head. He looked worried. "Maybe you'd *better* have a meeting with her, after all. To find out she's just human. Everybody is, Fayzie—just human. You could get Linc to see if she's willing to take another stab at it."

She made no response.

"I didn't check to see if she was wearing a wedding band—or if I could make out a corn pad on her little toe— or if her nylons were seamless." She had lowered her voice to a whisper. "I noticed her fingernail polish but I didn't look for a ring. I wish somebody could tell me what's wrong with me."

CHAPTER 40
TATTIE

After she buried Ben, Rose went back to Deep Fold where she took care of her folks for the next two years. They died within a month of one another. It was an existence requiring little of Rose except work so unrelentingly exhausting that, in spite of the anguish layered in her heart, she fell into blessedly dreamless sleep whenever she got a chance. There were no conveniences, so that she had to fetch every lump of coal and chop every stick of wood she burned, cook every bite they ate, draw every bucket of water from the well, and wash every piece of soiled bedclothes on the scrub board. Her folks were gentle, undemanding people who were too ill to be solicitous or inquisitive about her tribulations. The neighbors and relatives who dropped by were drawn so quickly into the hourly struggle to keep Mam and Pap Barton alive and tended to that they did not have time to impose their sympathy or curiosity on Rose. She existed for that time in a limbo that served to turn her out in one piece.

Taking one last walk through the little family plot to dress the graves with summer's last blossoms before she departed Deep Fold, she took a moment to look, as for the first time, at the six little stones marking the graves of her mother's six children who had either been stillborn or had died shortly after birth. She could not make out most of the worn names on the crudely carved slabs. There was a Chloe and a Rebecca. At one time she knew all their names as well as she knew her own. When she made her solitary childhood playhouses in the edge of the woods, she had made them each a bed of moss and a table-setting of flat-rock plates with twigs for silverware. But she had never really known more than their names. She wondered why she had not asked her mother to tell her about the lost babies. She wasn't sure if her reason for taking the losses for granted was because all six babies had come before she was born—coming between Jimmy and her—or if she had been made to feel it was a forbidden topic. She could not remember ever exchanging one word about the babies with Jimmy. She couldn't recall ever hearing him mention them. Tears stung her eyes for a moment, not because she was an orphan, but because she would have to look in the Bible to find the names of her mother's babies. She could not remember the names of her infant brothers and sisters whose only mortality now lay in her almost nonexistent memories of her mother's memories of them.

The anguish of death lies not just in the unbearable absence of the one who is gone and in the raw urgency to keep the essence alive, but also in the knowledge that it will be impossible to make others know what you know about the lost one. Part of the awful weight on the heart of the bereft is the burden he feels to bridge the gap between the seeming end and worldly continuance. The charge comes initially in undiluted surges of loss so deranging that when they are not contained they wipe out the possibility of laying groundwork for shared remembrance. To avoid alienating those who are there to share the sorrow, the survivor learns how to push down that early state of mourning bordering on mania, sometimes doing it so well it is eventually buried too deep to unearth in purest form, though it remains the compelling impulse of his existence.

And how much more urgently that impulse to keep the dead a part of earthly existence must weigh on the mother of an unborn infant who has had no actual interaction with anyone except that mother. Though her little Avanell was just a baby, Rose realized—when she finally regained her rational thinking—that the horror of her loss was made a little less excruciating by knowing the large Pennington family carried memories of Avanell's everyday existence along with their memories of her daddy. How much more unbearable it must have been for her mother to lose unborn babies....unknown even to their daddy.

Her mother's life would have been different if someone had urged her every day to talk about the babies. Rose realized now that the overriding frailty of her mother's existence sprang from the same kind of loss she herself had suffered. How could she not have seen this earlier? When Jimmy had so quickly backed off after Mam and Pap refused his invitation to come and live at his place, it had been because—she now saw—he was afraid to push too hard in any direction lest something should break, afraid his mother needed to walk among her babies' gravestones more than she needed to put the place of their loss behind her.

How strange, Rose thought, that she had not realized this when Avanell died, that she had not seen her own great loss as a repetition of her mother's. But, maybe she and her mother knew it would have been too much; knew it would have consumed and broken them both if they had commiserated openly with one another.

The thing people still wondered about Rose, of course, was if she was going to collapse again, the way she had the first time. But Rose had known, even as she stood with her hands in her loosened hair trying to take in the reality of Ben and the red-streaked bed sheets, that she was not going to fall into the abyss that had claimed her after her first great loss. She could not say why but, with all she felt giving away inside her, she simply did not feel her moorings giving away again. She felt herself withstanding.

Granted, the next few weeks were almost as much a blur as her weeks with the Penningtons after the loss of Garner and Avanell, but a part of her stayed connected to life-giving forces this time, the way an apple tree in

Jimmy's barn pasture had blown over in a windstorm but had not lost its tap root's grasp on the soil. Though barely grounded, it still produced apples, and she still produced the necessary human motions.

She took Ben back to Virginia to bury him. His relatives, the Calpers and the Lovells, were from Kendel Ridge beyond the Powell Valley in Virginia. Rose and Ben's sister, Mary Stenson, took the coffin on the first leg of the journey by wagon to Johnston, where they switched to horseback for the trip over the mountain on the treacherous trace that had been blasted and gouged out along the heights to bring train engine parts and large machinery from Virginia during construction of Johnston's railroads and first tipple. Ben's coffin was conveyed across the mountain on a mule drawn sled. In her state of suspended reaction, Rose felt no terror as her horse picked out its footing along sheer drop-offs where the crude road had crumbled away to leave such a narrow ledge that the men with the coffin sometimes had to dig into the hillside to make room enough for the sled to pass. Down the mountain a piece, on the Virginia side, they changed back to a wagon before they descended into the settlement called Stockard. There they caught a train that gradually took them up again through Wise to Norton— that Ben's people still called Eolia—and to Coeburn, before a final wagon trek out to Kendel Ridge.

Somewhere along the way they passed coke ovens glowing in the dark like the devil's furnaces. She thought a fellow traveler must have called them that. The image stayed with her all her life, but later she wasn't sure if they were real or part of some half-sleeping dream she'd had along part of the journey.

Kendel Ridge was a community truly following the undulations of an endless-seeming ridge surrounded by flowing mountains so different from the Kentucky mountains just over the state line that it seemed a different term was needed to name them. The mountains near Kendel Ridge brought to mind the ripples of a river making peaceful progress toward its destination, rather than the almost breaking waves of an agitated body of water like the hills on the Kentucky side of the Cumberlands.

Having those days of hard travel—the adversities of horseback and the uncertainties of the wagon journey and the train ride—had given her spirit time to make a transition. She and Ben's sister put out a hand to each other and held on, simply clung and held each other up...and got through it.

After her folks died, Tattie needed Rose's help with another difficult pregnancy and sickly baby. This made the fifth child for Tattie and Jimmy—and one baby, a little girl named Mary Ruth, lost the day it was born. Tattie's frail infants grew into sturdy children if they survived their perilous first year, but her body lost some of its resilience with each baby. However, when she offered Rose a home with them, she made it clear that she'd be welcome, not just because her help was needed, but because she was a sister in the truest way.

"Me and more than one of these babies might not be alive today if it wasn't for the tending to that you give us. I can't help but wonder if things might have been different for my little Mary Ruth if you'd a been here with me." They locked eyes solemnly for a moment. "But even if you never turn a hand to do another lick of work in your whole life, you can consider this place your home forever. That's what I want if you could want it," she'd said as she sat nursing the baby one morning while Rose did the churning.

Tattie expected no response, and Rose gave none. There was some measure of peace knowing she'd always have a home here if that were to be her fate, but a part of her knew she was not suited to a life as the widow-aunt.

Jimmy and Tattie's place felt as much like home as anywhere else. Ben's family and Garner's family also offered her a home, but she had discovered she'd rather not be besieged by the constant ache of loss she felt among their families. She continued to spend time with Ben's sister, Mary, now and then—living as they did on adjoining farms—and she visited a few days with the Pennington's after her folks died. Louisa and Drummond Pennington still ran their home with the efficiency of a well-oiled and warm institution. The losses they had suffered had drawn the rest of their family even closer. All those rooms were abuzz with life and industry. But, without Garner, Rose felt like a different breed there in spite of their warm urgings to make it her home again.

While she visited with the Pennington's she'd had an experience that both touched her and gave her a feeling of unease. Garner's sister Fern and his brother Tate's wife Mattie asked her to come up to the lady's loft with them. The lady's loft was one end of the attic partitioned off and fitted with conveniences to help a lady through her monthly time. In addition to lines strung where the women hung their rags to dry, there was a hand pump to fill their tubs and basins, and a drain pipe to empty them, both pipes going down into the ground inside a special closet next to a chimney so that there was no danger of them bursting in a winter freeze. There was a broad, table-high shelf built between two-by-four ceiling supports for each woman, and plenty of similar shelves and benches for their supplies and comforts, along with pegs to hang the washboards. The rough plank flooring was covered with a fresh piece of linoleum every few years, and bed sheets strung on wires made a private alcove for the times when total privacy was needed.

There was even a bathtub, a folding affair that looked like a camper's cot until it was opened and the frame locked into place to reveal—instead of a taut canvas bed—an envelope of thick, strong rubber suspended from the wood frame to hang down and rest on the floor. The filling and emptying were such daunting tasks the women seldom used the tub in the loft. Sometimes in summer months when one of them desired the rare luxury of stretching out in a tub with more length than the oblong galvanized tub, she used it in the summer kitchen where the bailing buckets could be emptied right out the door.

The lady's loft did not get the constant use one might expect on first thought of a house filled with women, for the women were most often pregnant or nursing a baby. But Mattie had been unable to get pregnant for the first several years of her marriage, and her more frequent use of the loft meant that she had fallen into the informal position of hostess. She had extended a welcome to the newlywed Rose those years ago by getting a shelf ready for her and decorating her tin pitcher and basin with hand-painted roses in honor of her name, and tacking a rose colored ruffle along the edge of her shelf.

When she and Fern took Rose to the loft during her visit, it was to show her that her shelf had been kept just as she left it. The basin and pitcher decorated with roses were turned upside down on the oilcloth-covered shelf with the rose colored ruffle along its edge. They said they'd kept things this way because this house would always be her home in their hearts, and she would always have this place waiting for her just as she saw it that day.

As deeply touched as she felt, Rose saw the pan and pitcher, in her mind's eye, sitting upside down for all eternity, and there was a definite unpleasantness about such an arrangement serving to represent her through the years, as though it were an altar to the halted state of her maternal function.

For the time being, she took more comfort from being homeless than from being attached to a place without the ones needed to make it her home. She was able to let the future hover out there beyond the reach of any plans she might make or expectations she might envision—like something beyond her control.

She thought maybe that was one difference between her reaction to Ben's death and to Garner's. Losing control of her life had felt like losing her very life when she was those few years younger. Now she knew that the outcome of a planned life is no more certain than the outcome of a life with no plans. Plans might help a person make the best of the journey, but they do not guarantee any predictable outcome, and they can lead to despair if a person puts too much stock in them. Life can continue, even though it turns out not to be what a person had thought of as life.

The rhythm she set up with the churn dasher drained her of strength momentarily, while at the same time it served to build up her long-term stamina and resilience. She could feel herself staying strong by pushing herself until she felt weak, the way she'd done with Mam and Pap.

Tattie was a true friend; she had loved Rose through thick and thin. But she did not love her like an equal. Rose had brought it to her attention not long back. "Why'd you leave me out when you called the married women?" she'd asked her after they'd had church dinner at their place one recent Sunday and Tattie had urged the crowd in groups to fill their plates. She'd dismissed Rose, who was taking a turn at the dishpan, by telling her that she and Florrie should fill them a plate as soon as the married women got finished. Florrie was Tattie's oldest daughter, young enough that she wasn't even courting yet. She was drying while Rose washed.

Tattie said, "Why, I never thought anything about it, and you know I'd a not wanted to hurt your feelings for anything in the world." Then after a little pause, "But you're not a married woman, Rose. You know you can fill your plate any time you want and eat it with anybody you choose, but you're not a married woman." Tattie was tender as she persisted.

"What am I then? What is a widow if she's not married? She's not a maiden, not a girl. I'm a married woman twice over," she'd said, having a need she didn't understand to establish something about her position in life.

More than she had realized, she resented not being included in any group of women: not the girls, not the wives, and not even the widows. Widows, it would seem, were women who'd lost the father of their several children after years of being married to him.

Tattie made that clear another time when a neighbor woman had been talking to them about Aci Capper's widow who was left with nine children after twenty-eight years of marriage. The neighbor woman had glanced sideways toward Rose as she referred to Romey Capper as a "real" widow, like there were qualifications for widowhood beyond losing a husband.

Again, Rose spoke to Tattie about it when they were alone, asking her why she had not spoken out for her.

Speaking gently as always, Tattie held her own. "Well, you know what she meant, Rose. There's no reason to let yourself be hurt by it. People don't say things like that to be mean. They think of a widow as a woman who was married long enough to tolerate a man after the shine wears off—who was married long enough to know all the reasons her man's not special, even if she does still feel like he is. You can't deny that you still thought of both your men as bigger than life. You hadn't been married long enough to see them as anything but perfect. Nothing had happened yet to make them seem like mortals to you."

"What's Jimmy done to make you see him as a mortal?" she'd asked.

"Lord a mercy, what's that man not done?" Tattie laughed. "The hay," she said. "Every year the hay."

"I know," Rose chimed in with a chuckle. "Every year you tell him not to cut the hay yet, that the rain's not done…"

"And, every year he goes on and cuts it, and it does rain, and then he has all the children out there helping him turn the hay right when I most need them to help me put in my kitchen garden. Every year," Tattie finished up. "And yet, when I see that man coming up from the field with the pitchfork on his shoulder I'm still mighty glad it's my hay he's been turning."

They laughed softly together.

"That's why you don't seem like a widow, Rose. They wasn't time for things like that to happen with your men."

"You're young," she went on. "You'll be getting another husband, and the Good Lord will surely let the next time be for your lifetime."

Rose did not say it out loud, but she knew she would not marry again, would never love that way again. Twice she had been blessed with the kind of oneness most people do not experience in a lifetime. That was over. The odds ruled out a repeat of such a union for a third time, while her experience of it ruled out her consideration of any other kind of union.

She thought maybe she could survive year by year if she did not look beyond the moment, if she could force her thoughts to remain in the present. She would stay with Jimmy and Tattie as long as it seemed right.

She swapped off the churn for the baby and watched as Tattie laid aside the dasher and took up the wooden paddle and began to work the butter, gathering together and scooping up the clots from the churn and patting them into a mound in a shallow dish. From time to time she drained the gathering milk back into the churn, holding the mound in the dish with the paddle. To watch was mesmerizing. The baby turned to nuzzle against Rose's breast before it fell asleep with a contented sigh, and she thought maybe as long as there were moments like this she could count it one more day worth living. If she could experience every moment like this to its fullest, then maybe she could let the moments collect like a set of silver spoons from famous cities or fancy hair combs from exotic places...or clots of butter.

But the situation seemed temporary. She could not envision an existence as the second woman on a place, not even Jimmy and Tattie's place. She's seen those women all her life, the aunts and grannies and spinster sisters who lived sometimes in the shadows and sometimes at the forefront and kept other people's families shored up over the years. She didn't reject the idea of that life; she just could not envision it.

If something different revealed itself to her someday, she would try to be open enough to pick up on it, but whatever was to come, she realized with some surprise, she did not need saving. Staying with her brother's family felt like diversion this time, not salvation. Her hands moved to mix the biscuits, chop the cabbage, swaddle the babies, shuck the corn, stir the gravy, boil the sheets, wrestle with the wash board and churn the butter, while her inner self stayed still and in one piece.

Steven, the oldest boy, dislocated his shoulder the next spring while he was helping Jimmy with the harrow. He got caught between the harrow and a large stone he had fetched to add weight, stumbling over a clod in such a way that his shoulder was pulled and twisted between the stone and the harrow's edge.

It was not something Jimmy could take care of without the doctor's help. Steven was in too much pain to ride the horse the few miles down to Bascom, so, once again, Jimmy borrowed the Stenson's wagon and Rose held Steven in the back, trying to cushion the jolts with her body.

Before they got to Doc Crenshaw's house they met a neighbor who told them they had passed the doctor. He was delivering Dicey Clay's baby up their way near the mouth of Lower Clive.

They retraced their steps and found the doctor caught in an oft-repeated dilemma. When a woman had a long, hard birthing and there was no woman with her who had the doctoring ways, there was nothing to do but stay with her until it was over one way or another. He had been sent for when Dicey's labor started before midnight, but things had come to a standstill during the early morning hours.

He laid Steven out on Dicey's kitchen table and gave him a whiff of the chloroform he pulled from his bag. With the help of Jimmy and Dicey's husband, Pete, he forced the bones back into place and—using strips of muslin he tore from the rags someone had readied for Dicey—he looped a piece around from back to front and on around to back again on each shoulder and tied it firmly, fastening the two pieces together between the shoulder blades before he tied the affected arm to Steven's side.

After the ease of his horrific pain, Steven fell into a deep sleep, and the doctor advised that they let him sleep for a while before they put him back in the wagon, While they waited, it became apparent that Dicey was in trouble, and when they eventually moved to carry Steven to the wagon, Dicey begged Rose to stay with her.

Rose promised she'd return, and when they got Steven home and the horse unhitched from the wagon, she saddled him and rode back down to be with Dicey. The baby was turned, and it took several arduous attempts for Doc to get it repositioned enough to make the delivery possible. Rose helped, and Doc said he wished he had her with him on every difficult delivery.

A neighbor woman tended to the baby while Dicey fell into a coma-like sleep. Rose cleaned up the bed and the room while Pete went out to bury the afterbirth in the garden and Doc sat in the rocker for a few minutes. Doc said, "I remember how that man of hers had to be nagged to take care of his duties after Dicey's past labors. I'm glad to see he got right on it this time." He rested his head against the back slats and closed his eyes, but he talked softly, and Rose and the neighbor woman learned the details of his varied schedule. In addition to his practice in Bascon, he worked for Staghorn Coal as the company doctor at three of their locations.

His first office had been in a little house in Wolliver where he and his wife set up housekeeping. He had moved his growing family to Bascon after his main practice took root there following Bascon's growth around the train yards. Then Staghorn had hired him. His Bascon office was open on Saturdays and Mondays. He spent one afternoon a week in his Wolliver office and one each at Dillard, Vargo, and Sledge, three coal camps between Wolliver and Bascon.

He said the offices at the coal camps were in the commissary buildings where somebody else dealt with maintenance jobs, but he bemoaned the beginning deterioration of the little house in Wolliver's upper bottom. Until recently he'd had arrangements with an aging couple to live there rent-free in exchange for general upkeep. But their health had deteriorated and they had gone to live with their children. "You know how a place starts to get rundown when nobody's living in it. There's nothing serious wrong with it yet, but it's going to go downhill fast now if I don't find somebody to take up residence."

Rose gave it no thought at the time, but, in a week or so, when Doc came by to check up on Steven, she asked him some questions: "Would the person living in your Wolliver office have to be somebody who could do carpenter work and roofing and such?"

"Wouldn't be necessary." He'd glanced up in bright-eyed surprise to see if Rose was asking for herself. "I can hire the maintenance jobs done if I don't find a resident who can take care of them; I mainly need somebody who can tell me what needs to be fixed before the problem gets out of hand."

By the time he'd finished with Steven's examination he'd made an agreement with Rose. She would live in his Wolliver house, doing the general housekeeping and overseeing any work he'd hire done. She'd not be open to office hours, of course, but she would make notes about the people who came in on the days when he was elsewhere and maybe dispense medicine he'd leave packaged for patients.

Once again, Rose felt herself coming to life after a time of dormancy. This was far from the life-force Ben had given her, but in its smaller way, it too was a milestone.

CHAPTER 41
MR. HOUSTON

Langdon Houston's father—James and Eldon's grandfather—came from Baltimore. He was one of the men who brought the railroads into Platchet County to haul out the coal early in the century. He was a geologist, an engineer, and a businessman who knew how to find the coal, how to blast it out of the mountains, and how to send it out to the ports and cities on the rails. Langdon was born in one of the first houses built in Johnston, one of the handful of pretty, two-story lakeside bungalows with more architectural detail than the row-houses springing up like mushrooms in all the dales and hollows surrounding the surprisingly beautiful coal town of Johnston.

He was still a child when he was sent out of the mountains. His mother died when he was twelve, and he was sent to live with relatives in Baltimore and have his schooling there. His interests leaned toward literature and history rather than engineering, and he had not returned to the mountains to make his living.

He did return to Kentucky to get his advanced degree at the growing state university in Lexington. He was teaching Latin and English Literature in a Lexington high school when he married a girl from Bourbon County and settled down with her on her family's farmlands near Paris. They had two daughters and a happy life together.

His wife died the year their youngest daughter married and moved away, and Langdon suddenly felt like a man without a home, like a man denied his heritage. He moved back home, if home is where a man was born. Not to Johnston, at that, but to Wolliver, the county seat. He bought a sturdy house in the Upper Bottom and taught Latin and History at Wolliver High School.

From the time his wife died, he had felt like everything was temporary, like he was on sabbatical from life itself or just filling in until his time was up. This detachment gave him an air of neutrality. People came to him when they wanted the opinion of a man who was truly disinterested, a man beyond the petty vagaries at the heart of most high-phrased decisions and pronouncements. He was warmly regarded at school and highly respected in the community.

During his first year in the mountains he was approached by every widow and spinster who had enough education or breeding to make her think he might consider taking her as his second wife. He had the ability to discourage them without diminishing them, and after the first year or so of kind but unwavering inaccessibility he was given more peace than most men in those circumstances can manage.

Though sought out to serve in more than one public office, he declined. The people of the mountains interested him, but not as much as the lay of the land. He began to explore the hills and hollows, following the streams and branches to their sources. He had made his way to Highcrest Rock up three different watersheds: up Crown Creek from the West and Perk Creek from the North, as well as up the Cumberland River and on up Brimstone Branch on the southeastern side of the mountain. As he covered the terrain, mental maps laid themselves over his substance, and he began to feel a oneness with the mountains that had pulled him back even when he had not known they had a hold on him. He and Rose lived near each other for some time before their paths crossed.

Rose was content in Dr. Crenshaw's little house. It was cozy but not cramped. Plenty of room for one person. There was a garden in the back yard and a couple of rock-ringed flowerbeds in the front. She lit right in to give everything the best cleaning it had seen in years, and she gave Doc a list of needed improvements the first day he came for office hours.

She joked with Tattie about how this way of getting the chores done was an improvement over having a husband who had to be nagged repeatedly before a job got any attention. She just gave Doc a list of needed repairs, she said, and a repairman appeared like magic, sometimes within a day's time.

This was a bittersweet joke to share with Tattie, for it was the kind of thing Tattie meant when she pointed out to Rose that she had not been married long enough to either of her husbands to have experienced the kind of exasperation—affectionate or otherwise—that entitles a woman to think of herself as a real widow after her husband dies.

When she got the house cleaned, she started right in on the yard. She was down on her knees cleaning several years' debris off a bed of cannies in the front yard when a man cradling a little red chicken in his arms came around from the back of her house, giving her a start.

She said, "Elt!" sitting back on her heels and trying to take in the man and the chicken. He said, "I'm sorry to startle you. I had to chase down my little hen. She likes your garden." He shifted his hen to his left hand and extended his right, saying, "My name's Langdon Houston. I live down the road here."

Then he jerked his hand back as she got to her feet extending her own hand. "I've been holding my chicken," he explained with a little laugh, tentatively dangling the hand between them.

"Well, I've been scratching in the dirt," she said as she wiped the sweat off her brow in the crook of her left elbow while she pursued his withdrawing hand with her right hand. "I don't reckon a hand that's been working in a flowerbed is any cleaner than a hand that's been carrying a chicken. I'm Rose Calper. I know who you are. I thought maybe you'd been out on one of your exploring trips."

"Oh, so you've heard about my meanderings?"

After he shook her hand, he unceremoniously tucked the little hen into his vest front where it made soft sounds of contentment while he talked.

Jimmy and Tattie had told her about Langdon Houston. He had eaten dinner with them one day when he was exploring over in their part of the county. He had crossed over Newcome hill from Millrun to come out on Lower Clive above their barn.

When she told him she was Jimmy's sister, he said, "Oh, yes, your brother and his wife told me you lived on my street. I'm greatly beholden to them for their hospitality and their interesting company. In fact, I mean to accidentally stumble onto their property again one day when the gooseberries get ripe. Your brother said his wife makes him a gooseberry cobbler worth tasting."

Rose laughed outright. That gooseberry cobbler was a subject of much discussion between Jimmy and anybody he could rope into a discussion of it. He looked forward all year long to the cloyingly sweet cobbler Tattie made him, but nobody else liked the pie made from the pale berries of the one bush he tenderly nurtured out by the smokehouse. Jimmy pretended to be glad to have the cobbler all to himself, while at the same time, he was always trying to find someone else who liked it, as if sharing it would make it taste even better.

"Well, you'd be the first to enjoy it like he does—if you should manage to stumble onto their property in gooseberry time and if you should happen to like the pie."

"Oh, I do mean to work it out so that I give that cobbler a try," he said, and, much to her surprise, Rose felt suddenly weak in the knees.

But several weeks passed before she saw Mr. Houston again. She knew which house he lived in—she had seen him from a distance—and had admired his confident, unhurried carriage.

The next time he appeared at her place she was working in the back yard, shaking out the featherbed she'd had airing on the clothesline all day. Again he held something in his arms, and she thought for a moment it was his little red hen again. But he said, "I didn't mean to show up with no notice again, but I've cut myself with a pruning knife. It's not such a bad cut, but I can't get the bleeding stopped because I can't get it wrapped tight enough. It's on my right hand and I can't do squat with my left."

When she realized that what he cradled in his arms was his right hand wrapped in a blood-soaked dishtowel, she crammed the featherbed under one arm and took hold of his arm with the other hand while she guided him over to sit down on the edge of her porch.

"Let's get you off your feet," she said. "You look a little peaked." She deposited the featherbed on the porch and began unwrapping the dishtowel while he explained that he had walked down to Dr. Betts' house but had not found anyone at home. "I knew Dr. Crenshaw wouldn't be here, but I thought maybe you'd be able to tend to me. I hear you've become a right good doctor yourself."

Rose gingerly examined the now uncovered hand.

"I was grafting an apple tree," he went on, "something I've done many a time without mishap, but I got careless this time. I don't think it goes to the bone, and I feel like a great big baby bothering somebody with it but, like I said, it's in a place that made me awkward with it."

Rose was relieved to find that the gash, though long, was not as deep as she first thought. "Looks like you jabbed yourself and then almost sliced off a piece of the fleshy part of your thumb. We'll need to wash this good and drench it with iodine," she said. "You just lie back here and I'll go get a pitcher of clean water and Doc's big bottle of iodine and some bandages."

He protested when she bunched up the featherbed and urged him to lie back on it. "You look like you might faint," she told him. "You probably haven't lost as much blood as that towel makes it look like, but Dr. Betts' house is a long way for you to have walked in this shape. You look like you're feeling swimmy-headed. I don't want to have to deal with a passed-out man." He gave in and lay back on the feather ticking before she went into the house for supplies.

The wound bled some more as she forced the clean water and then the iodine into the deep slit. "You need to show it to Dr. Betts tomorrow. He might want to put some phenol under the flap so it'll have a better chance of not festering, and he might want to put some stitches in it."

"Can't you do that?" he asked.

"Stitch it?" she asked, surprised. "Dr. Betts will do it in the morning. I think I could make stitches if I had to. I've watched Doc do it, and I believe I could if it was an emergency with no doctor available, but there's a doctor down the street that you can see tomorrow."

When she finished the wrapping, she had him swing his legs off the porch and sit up for a few minutes before he got to his feet. He didn't look quite so pale, but she urged him to come inside and sit at her kitchen table for a while before he walked back home. She gave him a glass of cold buttermilk and a dish of fried apples that he awkwardly spooned in with his left hand.

She sent him away with another warning about seeing the doctor tomorrow. "I might have wrapped it too tight," she said. "It's a thin line between wrapping it tight enough to stop the bleeding and getting it so tight that it can cut off the blood flow. Why don't you just lay down in your clothes to sleep tonight and then see the doctor early tomorrow?" From her front porch, she watched him head up the street.

He knocked on her door next morning to show her he'd been to the doctor. He told her Dr. Betts had put in a few stitches. "He said you did a fine job," he assured her. "You had it in such good shape that he started to just leave it alone, but then he said he'd better give it a stitch or two."

A week or two later he came to her door again to show her how well he had healed. He came just as she was making herself a late breakfast, and he ended up eating biscuits and sausage gravy with her. But, then, she did not see him again until the end of summer. She heard from neighbors that he had gone to North Caroline to stay with his youngest daughter, Ruby. Rose felt wounded that he had not let her know he would be away.

When he returned, he told her what had happened. His youngest daughter had come down with typhoid fever and had gone into early labor with her first child. He got a telegram from her husband and left for Ashville that same day. Things were touch and go for a while with the mother and the infant. He left Wolliver thinking he would be away only a few days, but had stayed to help out as long as he could, since he didn't have to be home until school started.

Once again he sat on the edge of Rose's back porch, this time giving her directions for cooking the Jerusalem artichokes he had brought her from his daughter's garden in Ashville. He told her to scrape them rather than peel them and then to cook them like turnips or parsnips or carrots. In fact, Ruby's husband, who had taken over the cooking while Ruby was bedridden, cooked all four together, he told her, and mashed them sort of lumpy. "He calls them sun chokes," he said, "but my folks always called them Jerusalem artichokes." Rose had never before heard of them with either name.

As it turned out, Mr. Houston came back next day with turnips and parsnips and carrots and stayed to help Rose cook and eat the mixture. As they sat in the tiny kitchen eating the pungent vegetables with the pone of cornbread Rose had baked, Mr. Houston said, "I don't know when a meal has tasted so good."

And then, "I don't know what I'm going to do now to get a chance to come in your yard and talk to you. I've already given you the artichokes, my little hen is long gone, and I don't reckon I ought to risk losing that much blood again."

After a faint smile, Rose stayed still and quiet.

"I don't know how to go about courting a woman, Rose. It's been too long since I've done that. Seems like it'd be sort of a silly endeavor for a man my age, anyway. But I've lived long enough to know when something seems right, and I hope you won't be offended if I just frankly tell you that I'm ready to ask you if you'd marry me whenever you'd feel ready to let me ask."

Rose said, "You don't offend me, but before you do any asking, I feel I need to make certain you've given thought to the fact that I don't have an education like you do, Mr. Houston."

He grinned and said, "Well, I don't have a doctor's certification like you, Rose Calper."

They smiled together for a moment. Then Rose said, "I don't mind if you speak frankly, and I need to be frank, too. I think it's right to tell you that I don't feel swept off my feet like I did with my two husbands. I missed you a right lot while you were away, and it's been a pure pleasure to sit here eating your artichokes, but I don't know if that's enough reason to marry a person."

Before spring, Rose found another tenant to live in Doc Crenshaw's house, and she married Mr. Houston and moved into his house. That's where James and Eldon were born and raised. That was home.

Once again she let a strong man's focused regard enfold her, so that she felt, not that she was giving up part of herself, but that she was blending the part that was herself into the part that was another, to make a whole. Her passion might not have been as intense at the beginning of her third marriage, but it was as riveting, having the advantage of time to ripen into something she had not known with her first two husbands.

She seldom called Langdon anything but Mr. Houston. The seeming formality was actually an intimate code between them, a secret key that reminded them, every time she said it, of the gratitude they shared for the deep happiness that had come to them in their unexpected union.

CHAPTER 42
MENINGITIS

Jamie died before James had a chance to call Peggy and Nora Faye, and it took him several hours to make contact after he started trying to reach them.

Phone calls in their dorm were a matter of hit and miss. The only phone was near the lobby office, and there was often no one working in the office to answer it. There was little chance you'd ever know about it when someone tried to reach you by phone. The casual effort to post messages on the bulletin board didn't amount to much, since the girls seldom thought to check the board unless they'd been dumped by a boyfriend they hoped would change his mind and call. An hour passed after James left his first message for them. He tried the dorm two more times before he called the dean's office. Betsy Owens, whose room was beside the phone booth, had taken the last call at the dorm, and she mentioned it to Nora Faye when they met on the steps.

"Oh, I'm glad I caught you, Nora Faye. Your dad's been trying to reach you and Peggy. It's something about your little brother being sick. You have some messages on the bulletin board."

The aide sent by the dean to track them down found Nora Faye just as she finished reading the messages. After she phoned her dad, she went, herself, to get Peggy from the Business Ed building.

Ted dropped everything to take them home.

Eldon and Stella and Rose were with James and Virginia when Ted got the girls to Johnston shortly before midnight. The suddenness made them all numb. The doctors had given Virginia pills to make her sleep.

James told the story over and over almost in a monotone. Jamie and Virginia had both developed runny noses two days back. Virginia had a little hacking cough that kept her awake that first night, but Jamie had been okay. He played outside all next day across the creek out back. He was so involved with the Kirby brothers, making roads around the hillside for their toy trucks, that he'd gone back outside after supper and played until dusk. He still had a runny nose, but he didn't seem sick as James gave his hair an extra rinse and helped him get out of his bath. He remembered scolding him laughingly about wiping his runny nose on the towel, and he remembered thinking he would ask Virginia if they had a thermometer, just in case. But everything was so normal for the rest of the evening that he didn't think of it again.

He'd told Virginia she should sleep in the girls' room by herself. That way, she'd not wake them if she had another night of coughing, and, if Jamie started coughing, it would not keep her from getting enough rest to make up for the sleep she'd lost the night before. She agreed after he said Jamie would sleep with him in their bed. She put the bottle of cough syrup by their bed, just in case. All three had gone to sleep with no trouble.

Though James was sound asleep, he knew exactly what was happening the minute his hip felt suddenly warm; Jamie was wetting the bed, something he'd not done for three years. He couldn't wake him. He got out of bed and lifted him out, but when he tried to set him on his feet, he collapsed like a rag doll.

He tore off the wet pajamas and wrapped him in a dry blanket before he woke Virginia. As he hurriedly dressed, he told her what had happened, and their only other words were about which would be faster, to carry Jamie to the hospital or to bring the car around and drive. Though the hospital was as close as the garage, they decided it would be best not to risk getting him chilled in the night air.

373

They put him into dry pajamas and rewrapped him in a blanket before James raced around the curve to get the car from the garage they rented. He was back by the time Virginia got herself dressed.

By rare coincidence, the doctor—a resident from Pittsburg—had a special background in spinal meningitis, quickly making a tentative diagnosis and giving them all—James and Virginia and the hospital personnel— several hours of hope. But in spite of the doctor's constant ministrations, Jamie never came out of his coma. He died in their arms just at daybreak.

As James talked, he removed his glasses and breathed on each lens before wiping them with his pocket-handkerchief the way he used to do. Until this moment Nora Faye had not realized her dad had given up his old habit. She couldn't pinpoint when it had stopped, but it must have been when he married Virginia. All those years ago she'd thought he cleaned his glasses so he could see better, but now she wondered if maybe he'd taken off his glasses so he would not have to look at reality for a few moments, so he would have respite from seeing clearly.

Virginia was inconsolable. She didn't wail; she hardly cried. But her words that would not stop were often indecipherable. She blamed herself. She should not have let him play outside and him with a cold. She should not have let him get dirty and sweaty. She should have noticed if he ate as much supper as usual. She should have taken his temperature. She should have checked on him in the night even though he was sleeping with his dad.

The doctor assured her that playing outside had not added to his illness and that he probably would not have registered a fever. But it made no difference. Virginia's self-condemnation increased by the moment. One of the doctors forced sleeping medicine on her by telling her it was for the little cough that tickled at her throat.

Nora Faye suffered her own personal agony. She was afraid she had given little thought to Jamie once she left for college. She remembered being aware that she considered him more Peggy's brother than hers...and telling herself it was natural that she should feel that way. She wasn't thinking about James not being her real dad; it just seemed to her that half-siblings with the same mother were somehow more kin than those with the same father.

It wasn't that she didn't love Jamie. Far from it. From the day he was born, she had thought he was the most wonderful child in the world. She was so proud of him she had rushed home from school to play with him when he was a baby and had showed him off by taking him with her to school functions when he was a toddler. (She'd taken him to a program to hear Peggy sing "Room Full of Roses," and for weeks after that he had babbled about hearing Peggy sing "Rueful Rosebies.") His face when he first started eating baby foods—the way it changed expressions when he took the first bite of a new food, like a chameleon changing colors—had fascinated her to the point that she vied for the chance to feed him. And the cute little things he said when he started talking—the way he said, "Me uh-ohed," when he did something he didn't mean to do, or the way he sobbed when he was a little older, "I not crying. I not crying," when he thought it was babyish to cry, touched her heart so deeply that she sometimes thought she would burst with love. The year when she was still at home after Peggy went away to college turned out to be a surprisingly happy time. She enjoyed being Jamie's only sister so much that it softened the pangs of being without Peggy.

She knew what a special place he held in James's heart. Not that James loved Jamie more than he loved her, but that he loved him in a different way. She had no doubts about her dad's love for her; every memory from babyhood to the present included his protective presence. She had always known he was forever there and that he would keep her safe no matter what threatened her world. But the look in his eyes was different when he looked at Jamie, his emotion intensified because of the way he knew

Virginia felt exactly the way he did, not just about this child they'd had together, but about everything.

And seeing this difference had not made Nora Faye unhappy. It made her feel free to start pulling away without fears that her leaving would seem like another loss for James.

But after she left home she didn't think a lot about Jamie. She was extremely happy to see him on school breaks, but she couldn't remember feeling remorse about not seeing him every day. She missed James more on a daily basis than she missed Jamie.

She couldn't shake the feeling that she was abandoning James when she left for college. If she had known what she wanted to do with her life, perhaps leaving home would have seemed a more natural step. But since her goals were vague, it worried her that James might feel she just wanted to get away. And, on one level, she did. She did not want to stay in Platchet County. That much she knew. And even though she did not know what she wanted to study, she knew she wanted a college education.

Peggy had known since her first high school typing class that she wanted to be a business education teacher. She knew exactly what courses her major required and the content of every future class syllabus. Her teachers could not keep from encouraging her to build a career around her voice. None of them doubted her ability to excel in business education, but even the typing and shorthand teacher, Mr. Heller, urged her to put her voice first. But, Peggy never wavered from her plans for a business major, and her departure for college was as natural as her graduation from high school.

Nora Faye figured everyone assumed she was just following in Peggy's footsteps rather than aiming at goals of her own. But people weren't aware of her burning determination for a college degree, a desire that was an ambition in itself, even if her pursuit of a teaching degree lacked the focused intensity of Peggy's calling.

Peggy and her college friends assured her it didn't matter. They said half the freshmen entering college didn't know what they wanted to be, and that many who thought they knew ended up switching majors, some more than once.

That gave her some consolation. And once she started college, especially after she started rooming with Peggy in her sophomore year—Peggy's junior year—her misgivings had faded. She realized the classes she was taking were classes she would want to take no matter if she didn't end up becoming a science teacher, and it did not bother her to let the future stay somewhat vague while she gave her attention to whatever she was studying at the moment. She enjoyed an elective literature class so much she submitted a poem titled "Undeclared" to an English department poetry contest and won an honorable mention.

But writing poetry was not a passion, and though neither science nor education were passions, her science classes were engrossing her more all the time. Maybe because of Ted. He loved rock faces the way Peggy loved office machines. Flora and fauna interested Nora Faye more than rocks and minerals, but she was beginning to enjoy all her science classes and considering how right it might be to teach science. Her last two years of college were beginning to take shape in her imagination.

After Virginia became more and more incapacitated by her grief, a horrid thought began to haunt Nora Faye. What would happen to her daddy if Virginia died and he was left alone again? Her own grief contorted her reasoning to the point that it began to seem to her that the purpose of her meeting with her mother might have been to form a bridge between her and James so he could reconnect with her if Virginia died. It so consumed her thinking that she found herself unloading on Granny Rose.

She had not told Rose about seeing Kenneth nor about running away from the meeting with her mother, so there was a lot of back-story with tears and self-recriminations before she got to the part about her daddy and Irene maybe being meant to reconnect.

"I should have talked to her," she sniffed. "I ran away like a baby, and I was meant to talk to her so they'd have some way to get back together in the future. Now, she's lost to him again, all because I was just a great big baby."

Rose said, "Elt." She looked up from the quilting frame where she was making tiny stitches on a lone-star quilt. It was a quilt top Virginia had pieced together—her first—and Rose hoped it might somehow prod her consciousness to show it to her as a completed quilt.

"You must be out of your mind, Nora Faye. There's no way your daddy and mother would ever be able to live together again. They don't have a thing to give one another. They didn't before, and they certainly don't now.

"You just said she looked like somebody from another world. Well, she is. She always was, and it sounds like she's even more that away now. James and your mother were lost to each other long before you came into this world."

Nora Faye took a bit of comfort from that assurance. She had a few almost peaceful days as she dwelled a little less on the possibility that she had let her daddy down by not following through on her meeting with Irene. But then, as Virginia appeared more irrational each time the girls made the trip home, Nora Faye's thinking became irrational in other ways as though in sympathy. She began to fear she had caused Jamie's death by not loving him enough, by letting him become vague in her heart after she moved away from home.

Most of all she remembered a time when her daddy and Virginia brought Jamie and came to an awards ceremony where she was presented with some kind of trivial certificate of excellence for her work in her education classes. Anybody with an average of B or above got one. She didn't even have an A average.

She was embarrassed, feeling they had come to her program to try to make up for the many times they had attended events where Peggy won true acclaim. She wished the school had not informed them of the occasion. They were staying with Virginia's cousin and were discussing, over lunch at Jerry's, whether they would stay another night or go on home this afternoon. She remembered with heart-wrenching regret how she had sat there forcing down a few bites of her fish sandwich, wishing they would go on home, how she was eager to get back to campus life with Ted and everything else.

The shame this made her feel in retrospect was so great she could not tell Rose about it. She just said she hadn't paid much attention to Jamie after they'd made the effort to bring him along and that she had let him start slipping away by not caring enough about him.

Again, Rose was blunt. "A person can't make things happen like that, Nora Faye." She straightened from the oven where she'd just slid in a pan of biscuits.

"Well, how come everybody says a person can make anything happen that they set their mind to?" Nora Faye persisted.

Rose returned her dough board—actually a large, shallow, wooden bowl—to the bottom shelf of the cabinet. Nora Faye felt like she'd watched her granny make biscuits thousands of times before. She kept the big bowl filled with flour, and when she got ready to make biscuits she'd make a well in the center where she would pull in some flour and dump in a little baking powder and salt before she mixed in a lump of lard with her hands. Then she would pour in some buttermilk, mixing in enough flour to get the right consistency before she balled up the mass and kneaded it a time or two. She let it sit a few minutes while she put away the buttermilk and lard can, and then she started pinching off biscuits. Nobody else could make them turn out right, no matter how determined. Stella had tried to gage the amount of each ingredient and write down a recipe, but her efforts resulted in the same disappointment as the dump-in method.

"You can make things happen to yourself, not to other people." Rose wiped her hands on her apron and pulled it off over her head before she took Nora Faye's two hands in hers. "If that was the case, they'd be a lot more good things happening...and a lot worse. You can't make something happen to another person just by what you think or feel."

She tilted Nora Faye's chin up with one hand as her voice went tender. "You know that, don't you?"

Almost in tears, Nora Faye let her head fall against her grandmother's shoulder. "If I'd just have paid more attention to him on school breaks—and had come home more often this year." She couldn't give it up yet.

"We can't keep people alive by loving them. We just can't." Her grandmother's voice was so wistful it made Nora Faye forget her own anguish for a moment.

CHAPTER 43
THE DIG

Ted's face broadcast something momentous. Long before he reached her where she waited on the library steps, Nora Faye could see he was going to tell her something that would determine how things would lie between the two of them from this moment on.

He took an envelope from his jacket pocket and waved it at her. She knew, then, as she had suspected, that it had to do with his application for the Wyoming dig.

"I got it." He was gasping, his breath visible on the cold air. This was one of the many ways she found him especially appealing, when he was so totally excited he looked like a little boy.

He clenched her two coat lapels in one hand and pulled her face to his while he made a gangster face. In a Jimmy Cagney voice he said, "You're looking at a happy man, doll. You're looking at a man who has everything, a man on top of the world." And when he kissed her it was different, still sweet but with no restraint.

"They accepted your application!" she gasped when she finally got her breath. "You're on the dig!"

She'd never seen his face like it was now, hiding something but ready to explode if she didn't ask the right question so he could reveal it. "Is it something more than you expected?" she ventured, seeing from his expression that she had not met the level of excitement he wanted.

"You!" he exploded. "You get to go with me!" He shushed her with a finger on her lips.

"You won't get paid, but we don't have to pay them for you. They'll cover your living expenses, your meals and a place to stay. You might have to do a bit of cooking and cleaning, but you'll get to do some scut work on the dig from the first day—and you'll get to do nothing but the dig eventually, if you take to it."

She almost laughed at the way he was making the hardships sound like privileges. Then, she bit her tongue to keep from saying the things that rushed her mind. "You're going to be late," she warned. "We've got to walk while we talk."

"Don't you want to celebrate?" She could see he was serious. "Isn't this worth skipping an afternoon of classes to celebrate?"

The sidewalks were thinning, with stragglers making that last lunge in an effort to beat the clock.

"I certainly do think so, but you'll end up getting kicked off before they take you on. Isn't this your afternoon for seminar, and haven't you told me Dr. Wheeler accepts no excuses for missing a seminar?"

He reluctantly fell in beside her as they headed toward the science building, making little celebratory kicks, like a kid, at the last brown leaves.

"We'll celebrate tonight," she promised as she kissed him bye before she turned off toward her classroom.

The reactions she'd held back had to do, first of all, with practical considerations. She couldn't afford to give up her job for the summer. She might even have to stay out of school and work fulltime for a year, because James could possibly end up without a job if Virginia did not start getting well immediately. The bottling plant, along with the ice plant and ice cream plant, had been phased out in early fall. James was given the store manager's position, working as an assistant manager until the present manager, Mr. Pomroy, would retire at the end of the year when James was scheduled to take over. The company had been very understanding about Virginia's situation and had agreed to give James a leave of absence until January. Mr. Pomroy had further assured James he would stay on for a few additional months if necessary. But unless Virginia made an enormous change for the better, James would be too tied down with her to assume the full responsibility even at winter's end.

Nora Faye and Peggy had already been promised places on Grangers' summer stockers' crew again, keeping the department store's racks and shelves replenished day after day. As boring as it was, and as modestly paid, it had amounted to a steady paycheck last summer. She and Peggy had saved enough money—by sharing the rent on a top-floor, run down Mill Street apartment with three other girls—that they'd never had to ask her dad for money after he paid for their tuition, dorm, and textbooks at the beginning of the year, Peggy's fees being less than Nora Faye's because of her academic scholarships. Peggy also had a student grant paying her to assist in teaching first-year business courses—shorthand and typing—to freshmen. With the war bonds her parents had bought for her when she was a baby, she would probably be able to finish school without James's help. Virginia and Charles had bought the bonds with the money Virginia earned when she worked part time in the Vargo store.

The thought of working full time to earn money for school didn't dismay Nora Faye. The thing that made her sad was that the prospect of sharing Ted's dream wasn't enough to make her give up her job plans without a thought. If she wasn't giddy enough to jump at the chance of turning her back on everything but him for one summer, then he surely must not be the one whose well-being she'd want to put before her own for a lifetime.

It came to her mind, on the other hand, that if she was hoping to spend her life with Ted, the practical argument would actually be one of passion. She could point out that a summer away from him—working to earn school money—would move them closer to the place where they could share their dreams forever, where they could get married. But she knew her conscience would not let her lay out plans for a future she could not clearly envision.

In the first second after he'd said she could go with him, her heart had leaped in anticipation of an entire summer immersed in his world. Her knees went weak when it flashed through her mind that surely they would sleep together at last.

They'd had opportunities. Charlie and Patsy's apartment provided the perfect place. They were the couple who let Ted keep his car in their garage. Ted fed their cat and watered their plants whenever they were out of town. Nora Faye went there with him the first time for that express purpose, going so far as to roll up a beach towel and squeeze it into her shoulder bag and to buy the paraphernalia, including condoms and a tube of contraceptive jelly with its clever applicator she'd got at a drugstore far from campus.

The condoms hurt Ted's feelings. "I figured you knew I'm always prepared to take care of you," he said.

"Oh, it's just me and my compulsion to be doubly sure," she explained.

He understood. "It's important to me, too," he said. "I've thought about it, and I'd never want to wonder if you'd married me for any reason except that you wanted to be with me forever."

"And for you, too," he went on." I would never want you to wonder if I'd married you just because I felt I had to. I'd want you to be assured, any time it might cross your mind, that it was my uncompromised choice to spend the rest of my life with you."

But, at the last minute, she became so tense that Ted stopped. He said it was okay, that he understood how she'd been raised, and that he'd never expect her to do something going against the way she felt.

She said it wasn't that she'd been raised a certain way, that she was just a natural-born idiot. She was overcome with sadness as he helped her refasten her bra and fold the beach towel. It was the first time she'd ever felt alone while she was with him.

Another time he asked if she thought it was because of her mother's situation, if it was something inside her that could not take the chance of *needing* to get married instead of *wanting* to. But, she could not talk about it, could not explore that possibility, even with Ted who was closer to her than her own psyche.

After that, they avoided getting into heavy clenches at the Banes' apartment or anywhere else fraught with too much opportunity. Ted kept assuring her he wanted to spend his life with her and that he didn't want to do anything to mess that up.

He asked her—with no teasing mixed in—if she would marry him right then. "We could take turns working for a semester and going to school for a semester until we graduate. It would prolong things, but it need not change our goals." But she did not want him to have further delays after his timetable had already been extended by the year he was sick and by his change of majors.

Then he stopped making so many allusions to marriage—in jest or seriously—when he saw how she could no longer abandon herself to the fantasy. But she knew he was trying to assume. And so was she. It wasn't that she'd lost her desire for him: it was that it seemed there must be some flaw somewhere if she could have all these opportunities without taking advantage of them.

The three weeks they'd gone their own ways last spring—after she told him she was afraid she didn't love him the right way to tie up his time and his life—she had missed him almost more than she could bear. When she would see him with Miggan Nestor, she felt like the ground was dropping away beneath her feet. She was so heartsick she couldn't study. She barely ate and sometimes threw up what she did manage to swallow. Her grades dropped. She was swamped with physical pain when she saw him one time on "their" bench with Miggan.

For, of all people, it was the little girl from the Wolliver fairytale stage who claimed Ted's attention after Nora Faye rejected him. Nora Faye would have been totally surprised if Shirley had not prepared her earlier with what she knew about Miggan. The moment Shirley first realized Ted was interested in Nora Faye, she whooped with joy. "I guess Miss Blessed and Perfect isn't as blessed as she thinks she is," she crowed. "She'll finally have to admit defeat. Probably for the first time in her life."

Shirley knew intimate details of Miggan's life. Not that they had ever been intimate friends, but she knew girls who were Miggan's friends. According to Shirley, Miggan fell for Ted the first time she saw him, and she'd managed to wheedle him into one date—a very casual date, Shirley always added—before he had the appendicitis attack. He'd visited friends on campus a time or two after he started getting well that spring, and whenever she learned he was in town, she'd track him down and throw herself at him. Shirley said Miggan invited Ted to her sorority fling that May. He came to town and went to the dance with her, but he left for home right after the dance and had answered her several letters with one breezy note, never giving her any reason to hope. The girls who passed this information on to Shirley took pleasure in Ted's rejection even though they were Miggan's friends. She was so poised and gifted and pretty and intelligent that even her friends were overcome with jealousy. And Shirley, who was not generally unkind and catty, belittled Miggan at every chance that came her way.

Being in a sorority, Miggan seldom crossed paths with Nora Faye at school, and with Peggy only when her date was in the same crowd as Peggy's date. Nora Faye had seen very little of her, in fact, after that second-grade reading class, and she certainly had no reason to dislike her. She'd always been in awe of her, and nothing had ever happened to make her think Miggan's many talents had given her a swelled head. It was impossible to tell if

Shirley had true reason to dislike her or if she just felt dwarfed by the girl who had so much going for her. There were some acquaintances who said she was as nice as she was talented. She was valedictorian of her class and was also voted the girl most boys would like to date and most girls would like to have as best friend. The spring they graduated, her picture was published beside Peggy's in the county newspaper's page of local high school valedictorians.

Nora Faye hadn't known, of course, that Miggan was one of Ted's "nothing serious" girlfriends when he first filled her in on his past. Not that he was hiding anything; he told her about Miggan as soon as he realized they came from the same county and that Nora Faye might know her. So it should not have surprised her when Miggan was the one he ended up with during their break-up. She knew the history by then, knew that—according to Shirley's sources—Miggan had never stopped hoping for a chance with Ted. Nora Faye told herself Miggan was a good match for him. Both were remarkable people, and Ted certainly deserved a girl who was as smart and interesting as he was.

But in her deepest heart she was jealous and resentful to the point of debilitation, and she wondered if knowing he might end up with Miggan might be part of what was making it hard for her to break up with him now.

Ted gave her security as warm as her dad had always given her. It was comforting beyond words to have someone to share everything, to have someone looking out for her, needing her, wanting to take care of her, respecting her opinions, making her feel smart and amusing, someone who made her laugh and who liked the same things she liked and felt the way she did about almost everything and opened her life to new possibilities when he did not. But what made their situation supremely satisfying was that the feelings were reciprocal. She simply cared more about his wellbeing than she cared about her own. He took her out of herself. There were no little snags of guilt making her feel he needed her more than she needed him nor jolts of fear that she might need him more.

Life fell into two kinds of happenings now: those that took effort and those involving Ted. A small routine like warming her hands in his overcoat pockets took on tender importance whenever they walked across campus on a frigid day, changing sides from time to time so he could warm first one of her hands, then the other in his pockets. And when they sat huddled in his coat on a knoll behind the darkened stadium one clear winter night watching stars that looked close enough to reach up and touch, she felt like she was inhabiting a dream. What could be more transcending than being with the person who could absolutely absorb you in twining eyebeams together toward the heavens? When she had been struggling with lab assignments until her brain felt gray one dark and heavy late afternoon and had looked up to see him threading his way to her among the lab tables, she thought her heart would explode.

Even though Peggy and Ted were comfortable together, Nora Faye and Ted seldom double dated with Peggy and her boyfriends because Peggy usually dated football and basketball players. Ted was a Wildcats fan—they went to most of the home games—but ballplayers do not have much in common with ball fans. Admiring Bear Bryant was not the same as playing for Bear Bryant, and the ball players lived in a world of their own. When it came down to entertainment, she and Ted had usually rather go to a play or movie, and Peggy went with them sometimes without a date.

The three of them saved enough money to take a bus to Louisville—that was before Ted got his car fixed—to see the stage presentation of *The King and I* at Memorial Auditorium. And after they saw the *South Pacific* movie, when Nora Faye was still struggling to master the Periodic Table—she had given it the least attention possible in high school chemistry, never thinking she might end up a science minor—Ted worked out a song of it for her to the tune of "You've Got to be Taught."

After he got his car fixed, they made it to Maysville to see Rosie Clooney at her homecoming appearance and to Cincinnati to see a stage production of *Mr. Roberts.* They could quote Henry Fonda's lines from *Mr. Roberts*, Humphrey Bogart's lines from *The Caine Mutiny*, and could sing all the songs from *South Pacific* and *Okalahoma.* It was Ted who took her to see Renoir's *The River*, and sat with her, unembarrassed, until she could stop crying after the lights went up. And it was Ted with her while she cried again in *Viva Zapata!* and who, like her, understood, for the first time, the to-do about Marlon Brando.

They took part in a '40s American Propaganda Film Festival, where they picked up a wealth of quotes recognized only by other students from the festival. They palled around with that gang for a while, enjoying it when the others were as quick as they were to spout lines from the melodramas they'd seen, especially the one they most liked to ridicule, the stilted *Keeper of the Flame* with Spencer Tracy and Katharine Hepburn. It was fun when a sudden quote of, "To worship anyone is the destroy him," would be met with a histrionic, "I had to destroy the man to save his image." Or someone would break a tense moment by suddenly intoning, "Clean death in the rain was the best thing that could happen to Robert Forrest." One day when they were hiking with some of those friends and came to a place with no bridge where the trail crossed a little creek, Nora Faye was trying to get up the courage to jump it when Ted dropped to a knee before her, saying, "I can believe in you so much that you can't help yourself. You must be what you are." She jumped the creek, then, while the others clapped and whistled.

But frequent company, even when it was good company, was not what they wanted. They wanted to be alone together. They were enough for one another. Her dorm, the stately Arden Hall, had a side room off the lobby with a phonograph where they could play their records, usually without interruptions. They played Gordon Jenkins' *Seven Dreams* until its grooves wore thin. "Living on a Houseboat" became the code for what they had between them, whatever it was.

They read Hemingway and Steinbeck and Faulkner, starting with the obscure *Across the River and into the Trees* and *To a God Unknown* because the English majors had checked out the more familiar titles. They plowed through *Invisible Man*, frolicked through *Why I Live at the P.O.*, and devoured Fitzgerald. They read and reread *Jude the Obscure* and every Hardy novel they could find in the library.

But being with Ted never got old. An accidental brush of his hand as he gestured could make her lose her breath, and the sight of him across a room full of people—gesturing with those beloved hands—could make her feel she was the luckiest person in the world that he would rather be with her than with any of those people between the two of them.

But because she could not abandon herself to the ardor she felt for him, she gradually became unable to abandon herself to the idea of a future with Ted. As preposterous as it would be, what if there was some kind of euphoria missing, a kind that would have made it impossible to be with him without sleeping with him? She feared she might be unable to resist going for the euphoria if it should appear in another person.

If she had known about Miggan before she started going with Ted, she would have wondered if she was trying to outshine the little girl who danced in the spotlight by taking her prince away from her. But she had never really thought of Miggan as a real person, and had not had much reason to think of her at all since second grade. It was astounding that, of all people, the girl who danced with the brownies turned out to want Ted just as much as she did. Maybe more.

And when he'd turned his back on Miggan to make one more attempt to win back Nora Faye, she, of course, could not resist. The way she'd missed him was a suffering as intense as the dream-muddled onslaught that wracked her being the time Stella nursed her through that fever-fraught interlude. And returning to him was like gulping down the jars of cool water she stashed in the refrigerator following that assault.

Though still confused that she should feel such passion and yet fall short of total surrender, she knew only that she had to be with him, had to feel her heartbeats echoing off his chest in order not to lapse into emotional arrhythmia. Her joy, made up of bliss tinged with self-reproach, was something she could live with... until the summer dig became reality. The dig threw her into a moral dilemma. She knew he'd be wounded if she refused to go with him, but on the other hand, she feared it would be wrong to go, feeling, as she did, that something she required might be missing. She was humbled by the confident way he had assumed she would be part of the experience that was so important to him, had assumed they were a unit, not two separate entities. The purity of his assumption frightened her so much that even while she felt she had to be with him, she knew she had to break up with him now, knew how cruel it would be to wait until the last minute, until it was too late for him to ask Miggan—or whoever—to take her place on the dig.

But, what if she was wrong? What if this was as good as things got between a man and a woman? What if she would be giving up the most intense emotion she would ever be able to feel?

CHAPTER 44
PEGGY

Peggy didn't take it seriously when Nora Faye told her she was going to break up with Ted because she wasn't sure she loved him enough. "What is it you're looking for?" Peggy teased. "Doesn't the ground move?"

"Earth," Nora Faye said. "Earth move." Then, "It's not that. We don't make out. Did you think we make out?"

Peggy looked a little scared to realize Nora Faye was responding to her teasing by talking seriously about intimate things. She began rummaging through her notebooks to keep from looking at Nora Faye who was sitting cross-legged on the floor sorting records. "I guess I did," she squeaked thinly. "I thought everybody on campus except me was making out."

They avoided eye contact. Sharing a room again had made them feel as cozy as they felt when they were six and seven and had first shared a room and a bed in Johnston, putting themselves to sleep at night by pretending they were baby animals in the forest unperturbed by the absence of a parent since they had each other for company as they pressed up close against their pillow-logs.

They'd considered keeping the Mill Street apartment, but had given up the lease when they weren't able to find replacements for the girls who left at summer's end. Nora Faye was glad they were in a dorm room. It was good to have Peggy to herself again.

However, as close as they felt and as much as they confided in one another, they did not usually talk about what they did privately with their boyfriends.

"You mean you and Wayne haven't done it?" Nora Faye was truly surprised.

Peggy stayed quiet, just shaking her head. Nora Faye probed, "Why not?"

Peggy shrugged. "He doesn't appeal to me that way," she finally answered.

"Then, why in the world are you going with him, Peggs?" Nora Faye screeched in a whisper. "You know you could have your pick of the sexiest guys on campus."

After the thick walls and heavy doors of Arden Hall, the historical freshman dorm, this much newer building felt like a house of cards. The flimsy walls of the room they now shared may as well have been Japanese paper screens compared to the fortress-grade construction of Arden Hall. This building gave the impression of a stage setting, temporary and built to knock apart easily.

"I thought it wasn't about having sex," Peggy admonished. She was conducting a mock search through a desk drawer now, to give her eyes a place to go.

"I guess I wasn't being honest," Nora Faye admitted.

She slapped at Peggy's hands when she reached to take a record she had just sorted out of the crate. "Don't mess up my stacks," she pleaded. "It's hard enough already. There's no way to know which are mine and which are his; they're ours. I can't break up with him; I can't sort the LPs. The 78s are his, and most of the 45s are mine, but, the LPs, we bought together."

Peggy ignored her and picked up the record anyway. "Oh, you can't give him 'Rhapsody in Blue'," she gushed. "I love 'Rhapsody in Blue'." She clutched it to her chest before she put it back on the stack.

"What's wrong with us?" Nora Faye moaned dramatically. "Why do we find it so hard to talk about this stuff—and do it?" She was turned away from Peggy, bent over the record crate, or she would have been unable to ask something so intimate even in a mock-serious way. "Why are we such prudes? I don't remember anybody giving us any special lectures about keeping our reputations unsullied. Why can't we just do it like everybody else?"

"Oh, well, for one thing—for myself, that is—I know I'd get pregnant. Just one time doing it, I know I'd hit the jackpot, no matter how many precautions."

"Me too!" Nora Faye agreed in a conspiratorial whisper. "Contraception sounds like a fairy tale that doesn't apply to me. All that foam and jelly and douches and diaphragms and condoms and thermometers and calendars; just magical props for people who believe in voodoo."

They giggled quietly, then Peggy abruptly confided, "It's no temptation when I'm with Wayne, but I almost went all the way with Burt." She looked very serious now, staring into a corner as she continued. "The day of his graduation, before he left campus, I almost risked everything and did it with him."

"But I thought the girl he was engaged to was here with his parents!" Peggy gasped.

"She was. That's part of why it was so exciting. Knowing he wanted me more than he wanted her. Knowing he was feeling something stronger than all his well-laid med-school plans. It's a wild feeling. I didn't care about my well-laid plans either. I didn't care if I got pregnant."

"What stopped you?"

"Mother," Peggy said. And before Nora Faye had time to get confused, "I feel like Mother knows everything I do, even when I don't tell her. I feel like it's written on my face for her to read." Her voice faltered. "Or, that's how it used to be when she was still herself."

They were quiet for a few moments with the sounds of the dorm thrumming around them: footsteps, voices, running water, sudden peals of laughter, Doris Day singing "Que Sera, Sera" from one end of the hallway and Eddie Fisher singing "Oh, My Papa" from the other.

Then Peggy resumed, "I think it has to be something irrational—like Mother's face—to make a person resist, because there's nothing rational about the feeling."

"That's the key, that thing about it being hard to resist," Nora Faye said. "I've always figured that's how I'll know when it's the right one—when I can't resist."

"Yeah, the thought of doing it with the wrong person turns my stomach, too. Like Wayne. Everybody thinks I'm so satisfied being with the big football star." She hurried to make herself clear, "I'm not putting Wayne down; we do have a good time with the crowd, and I'm proud to be with him. I do actually like him. But I think I'll throw up when it's just the two of us and I make the mistake of letting him kiss me and he starts trying to do more than kiss. I know just what you mean."

"No, no! You don't know what I mean." Nora Faye strained her throat trying not to scream the words. "That's not how it is at all! I love kissing Ted! He's not the wrong person!" She jumped up and put out a hand to keep Peggy from interrupting. "I love kissing and snuggling and lying together, and I love the thoughts of going all the way with him. But, evidently I'm not compelled. It seems like it would be wrong to take that final step if I can resist. And I can resist. Every time, I can resist. If he was meant for me, I wouldn't be able to resist, would I? I'd feel every bit as compelled as he does."

"Oh, Fayzie, don't you think what you feel is enough, then?" Peggy's voice was deep with compassion. "What more can you want? If you love everything about him, even the physical part, what is it that's not enough?"

They were whispering, as though the walls were truly made of paper screens. Nora Faye was barely audible as she answered. "It's that I think there might be somebody out there somewhere who will make me feel like I will truly die if I can't go to bed with him, and it would be horrible to be married to Ted if that person should cross my path. It would be unbearable to betray Ted or even to want to betray him. I couldn't live with myself if I had that longing for someone else."

"You mean you love him too much not to break up with him?" They got the giggles then. Both were a little teary-eyed by that time, and they snuffled and blew their noses and giggled like they had when they were little girls in bed after their light was out and they were supposed to be asleep.

The time when she broke up with Ted for a few weeks, Nora Faye had tried to tell him how she felt without hurting him. She told him she was afraid she'd be doing wrong by him if she married him without having anything to compare to how she felt about him. He said, "Silly. I don't have anything to compare you to, either."

When she started to protest that he had slept with other girls, he said, "I don't mean that. I mean I've never felt this way about anybody else." Then, his face clouded with an unconsidered possibility. "Have you found somebody you love more than me?"

When she assured him she had not, he told her to think of how terrifying the train had seemed when she was a little girl and had first moved to Dillard. "You told me how you had to trust your dad when he said it would not run into the platform, how you just gritted your teeth and clenched his hand and trusted him. You can trust me, Fayzie, when I tell you there's nothing to be afraid of."

Another time he went to their past and brought up *The Razor's Edge*. "Remember how you belittled Maugham's Larry for dropping out of life to learn about it? You said the only way to get answers about life is to plunge right in and live it." He shushed her as she tried to comment. "The only way you'll know if I'm the one is to live as if I am. If it turns out I'm not, it won't be any harder on me to learn about it that way than it would be to have you out there trying to figure it out without me." That's when they got back together.

"I guess I can be grateful my reasons for never taking the plunge are not complicated," Peggy said, looking very serious again. "I don't mean with Wayne; I mean the boys that turn me on. Burt wasn't the only one."

"Was Parilli one that turned you on?"

"*Babe* Parilli?" Peggy laughed.

"How many Parillis do you know of?"

Peggy laughed again.

"No, seriously, I heard…"

Peggy interrupted. "Parilli was gone before I got here."

"I know that," Nora Faye said, "but I heard he put the moves on you when he came back for some sort of ceremony for Coach Bryant."

"Why, I think he was married."

"I heard he wasn't married then, and, anyway, when did that ever stop somebody from flirting?"

"Well, I wouldn't know about that. In fact, you seem to know a lot more about Babe Parilli than I do. I didn't speak more than two words to him that time I met him."

"You're blushing," Nora Faye taunted.

"I am not." Peggy laughed again, then suddenly became very solemn. "You make me feel like you think I'm a freak when you act like you'd really expect any guy that looked at me to be interested in me."

"Not a freak; just a different species. I admit that when it comes to boys, you do seem like a different species. I cannot imagine what life would be like to have boys falling all over me the way they do you."

"And yet you're the one who has the total adoration of the boy you totally love, the only boy you've ever really cared about."

She shushed Nora Faye and went on. "It's not so much that boys haven't fallen for you; it's always been that you didn't care much for the ones that liked you, and you only liked the ones that weren't interested."

She went on when Nora Faye tried to speak again. "A highly effective and not uncommon form of population control, by the way. Think how densely populated the world would be if every girl had the hots for every boy who first had the hots for her and vice versa.

"And, let me tell you, Fayzie, it seems like more than a miracle to me the way you and Ted found each other almost your first day on campus and how each of you loves the other with matching intensity. I do feel I'm of a different species when it comes to that."

Nora Faye said nothing.

"Anyway, I was talking about Johnny. That's why I quit Johnny last year. I knew I'd end up pregnant if I kept going with him.

"And back when we were kids, I had such a thing for Gary Alton. Did you know that? You did know that. I wanted to make out with him so bad."

"Behind the smokehouse at Aunt Clemma's," Nora Faye chimed in, "where the grape arbor was dense as a wall. I knew all about it." And then when Peggy looked horrified, "Nobody else did though. Everybody else thought of him like he was our cousin. But he wasn't. He really wasn't kin to us at all. And of course, he wouldn't have been kin to you even if he was kin to me." She laughed. "Actually, he wouldn't have been kin to *me* even if he was kin to me." Nora Faye was putting the LPs back into the crate. "Why didn't you, then? With Gary?"

"That Mother thing."

"You mean all those boys that stood in line to fight for your attention back home...you never...with any of them?"

Peggy just shook her head.

"I still don't get it about Wayne." They had pushed the record crate back under the bookshelf made of planks and cinderblocks and were straightening their clothes and putting on lipstick in the one shared mirror as they got ready to go get something to eat. "Why are you going with him if you don't like him?"

"Like I said, I like him well enough," Peggy answered. "I just don't want to go to bed with him. I figured if I wasn't going to allow myself to shack up with boys that turned me on—like Johnny—that I might as well choose somebody to go steady with that comes without that temptation but is still an asset in other ways." She froze, looking into her own eyes in the mirror built in above their built-in dresser drawers.

"I've never said that out loud before. It sounds so cold and scheming. But that's how it is. Going with a football star solves so many problems. I never have…"

"You never have to wonder if you'll have a date for a dance, you never have to worry that you might be excluded from something you want to be part of, you never have to decide where you'll go or what you'll do. I don't think it's scheming; it's just practical…and easy."

"That's the sad truth," Peggy said, "I go out with Wayne because it's easy. I'm sorry there's nothing easy for you about loving Ted."

"Oh, everything's easy about loving Ted; it's my warped psyche that's difficult," Nora Faye murmured. Then, "How come Wayne puts up with it? Doesn't he make things miserable trying to talk you into it?"

"He did at first. Then, when he realized things weren't going to change, I think he made his own little deal with the devil. I think he decided it would be ideal to have me as his campus girlfriend. I don't give him any of the problems a girl would if she wanted to sleep with him or marry him. We don't talk about it, but I assume he has other girls he makes out with. Back home or somewhere." She glanced over at Nora Faye. "This must sound absolutely sordid to you. But we would never do anything to embarrass each other. Come to think of it, we sort of pretend to the others that we go all the way. It's really no longer an issue."

"Do you realize how funny that sounds, that *not* shacking up with a boy could sound sordid?"

"It's not that part that's sordid," Peggy said. "It's that I spend so much time with a person knowing I don't want to be really close to him."

"I'm sorry anyway. I should have realized how it is with you and him."

"Yeah," Peggy gave herself a final look in the mirror as she gave her hair one last pat, "I certainly don't appear to be a woman who is experiencing ecstasy on a regular basis, do I?"

"Neither do most of these girls who say they're doing it," Nora Faye murmured. "I thought maybe a letdown demeanor was part of the experience."

CHAPTER 45
THE STORM

At Thanksgiving time, Virginia didn't recognize Peggy, and by December, she didn't know James. She paced the floors night and day, twisting at her hair and fidgeting with her clothing. If James tried to soothe her, she became hostile, knocking him away and making unearthly sounds. The only time she slept was when she literally dropped from exhaustion—often on the bottom few stairs—and then her naps lasted only a couple of minutes before she woke flailing at the air.

James brought her to Eastern State Hospital in December. The dorm would be closed over Christmas vacation, but Nora Faye and Peggy were planning to stay with James in Virginia's cousin's house near the hospital. They had withdrawn their applications to work at Grangers.

It had been agony for Peggy to watch her mother's inconsolable agitation and for Nora Faye to watch her dad as he tried to ease Virginia's misery at home; it was a relief to both girls when he decided to bring her to the asylum in Lexington.

But the situation brought its own stresses. James very reluctantly agreed to electroshock treatments, but he felt hopeless when they were discontinued after the first one made her worse rather than better. When the doctors first mentioned a lobotomy, the girls went to the libraries—the university library and the public library—to read up on it. They found very little, and they were horrified with the little bit they found. A friend of Peggy's who was an intern at St. Joseph's dug up a bit more information for them, and it only added to their apprehension.

If they'd paid attention to weather predictions they might have avoided the complications that started when Peggy caught a ride to Wolliver with Platchet County acquaintances on the first day of Christmas vacation so she could gather some of Virginia's things they were told might help to settle her down: a few of Jamie's toys, some family pictures, and some of Virginia's favorite knickknacks and belongings. Hospital personnel told them dramatic tales of how such items had brought about a change for the better. When they pointed out that none of those things helped at home, they were told that it might be the contrast of seeing familiar things again after time spent in unfamiliar surroundings. So Peggy headed to Platchet County as soon as possible with plans to have the items packed and ready to go when Nora Faye and Ted came to fetch her. That way, both girls would be back in Lexington with James for most of the Christmas vacation. When Peggy got to Wolliver she caught the bus to Johnston—Rose went with her—to collect Virginia's things, and then she got the items all sorted and packed at Rose's house, along with the quilt Rose had finished, so she'd be ready to leave as soon as Nora Faye and Ted showed up.

Ted was at Mammoth Cave on a class field trip until Christmas Eve. The plan had been that he and Nora Faye would leave for Platchet County as soon as he got back to campus. That was before the doctors suddenly wanted to schedule a lobotomy between Christmas and New Year's Day, saying a surgeon would be available at that time. A well-known psychosurgeon who was traveling from city to city to perform lobotomies would be at Louisville's Central Kentucky Asylum during the last week or so of December. He might come to Lexington, or he might have Virginia delivered to Louisville. James had been told it was a very simple operation with no special set-up required. Sometimes it was performed in doctors' clinics with the patient walking out unassisted within a few hours.

Nora Faye was as stunned as James at the suddenness of the proposal. She called Rose and Peggy to bring them up to date. "It's what Peggy's been telling you about, Gran, the lobotomy. They make a cut that breaks the connection to the part of the brain that's been causing the trouble, but it doesn't do any damage to the other parts."

"I know about lobotomies, Nora Faye," Rose grunted.

Nora Faye went on. "We knew they were considering it; we just didn't know they'd want to do it so soon." Nora Faye gave her the details about the sudden availability of the psychosurgeon within the short time frame.

Rose said, "I know the doctors have been nattering about it, but I didn't know your daddy was taking it to heart. You can't let it happen, Nora Faye. I'm not sure I can make your daddy understand over the phone. I need to come down there right now so I can talk to him face to face."

"Maybe it's not as terrible as it sounds, Gran. Maybe it's for the best. It's been a few weeks since you saw Ginny. She's a whole lot worse."

"I'm trying to tell you that it won't be for the best. I've been telling Peggy it's not like they make it sound, Nora Faye. It's not just one part of a brain that gets sick. A person's whole brain goes haywire." Rose was getting a knot in her shoulder from stretching up to reach the mouthpiece of the wall-mounted phone on her stair landing while she kept the earpiece at her ear. The girls had urged her a million times to have a tabletop set installed in her front room, but before tonight, she'd never really used the phone enough to feel the need to sit down while she talked.

"Slicing through a certain part of her brain can't make her well," she continued. "A lobotomy is what they did to Maureen Porter. Do you remember Maureen?"

"Frankie's mother? That lived down the street when we first moved to Johnston?"

Rose said yes.

"I remember her, but a lobotomy surely can't be what they did to her. Maureen Porter didn't know much of anything after her surgery. With a lobotomy, you're normal; you just don't remember the things that were driving you crazy." Nora Faye was trying to sound more optimistic than she felt.

Rose was becoming desperate, "Lord a mercy, Nora Faye. That's what they told them it would be like for Maureen. Let me talk to your daddy."

James was so exhausted he could barely make sense of anything his mother was saying. She went on and on about things he could not remember her ever talking about before, about her first husband and how she became just a living shell after he and their little girl died of the flu, how she had no memory of her life for months on end after that, and only knew what others had told her about it. He listened a long time before he asked, "Why didn't you ever tell me all this?"

Rose said, "Elt." She knew she could not make him believe that she had never tried to hide any of her past from him. She ignored the question and stressed what she and Virginia had in common, the breakdown after the unbearable loss.

After he listened for a while James sighed. "Well, you couldn't have been like Ginny is, Ma. She's almost worse than dead. And she will die from what she's doing to herself."

Rose agreed that she hadn't behaved like Virginia. "But the reasons are the same. The reason I was the way I was is the same reason Virginia is the way she is; we went crazy to keep from remembering what we'd lost. They thought I was never going to be the same, James, that I was never going to snap out of it. But I did. Virginia will, too. It will happen if you can just wait it out and try to keep feeling good feelings about her while you take care of her. One day something will happen that starts to turn her brain around, and she will be herself again. But you have to let time take its course. You can't make it happen by cutting her brain. That makes something awful happen." James wearily shifted position, trying to get comfortable on the cousin's rickety little phone bench that gave no more perch than a fence rail. "You saw how she was, Ma. Well, she gets worse every day. She'll die from the way she's treating herself. Anything that gives her some peace will be better for her."

"That's what I'm saying. It won't be real peace. It will just make her sick in a worse way. People looked at Maureen Porter after the surgery and said anything would be better than how she'd turned out."

James said he could not talk any more. Rose begged him please not to let them do the surgery before she got there.

"Get where?" he asked in a daze. "Here? How could you get here?"

She told him to give her back to Nora Faye. This had already been the longest time Rose had ever talked on the telephone at one stretch, but she felt she had to make James and Peggy see that a lobotomy was to be avoided at all costs.

By the time she finished talking to Nora Faye and then gave the phone to Peggy, the three of them had come to an agreement about the necessity of getting her to Lexington in time for her to talk face to face with James before the doctors pressed him for a decision. They had the beginning of a plan.

Nora Faye would drive Ted's car to Wolliver today and take Rose and Peggy back to Lexington tomorrow.

"I didn't know Nora Faye could drive," Rose said when Peggy told her the plan.

"She doesn't have her license, but Ted's been teaching her. You know that's how I was going to get back to Lexington, anyway— with them."

"But that was going to be after her friend got back to do the driving, wasn't it?"

Peggy said that had been the original plan but that they wouldn't wait for him now. "I think you're right, Gran. I think we've got to make James see that a lobotomy might turn Mother's life into a worse nightmare than it is already. I'll make it clear to him that I'll stay out of school next term to help him take care of her. I'll take care of her by myself if he can't do it. I'll stay out of school as long as I need to and take care of her night and day if I have to. I'd rather see her dead than see her turn into a zombie like Maureen Porter."

Rose felt a moment of relief. She gave Peggy's arm a squeeze. She had seldom been more desperate for people to understand what she was saying. It wasn't just for Virginia; it was for Nora Faye and James and Peggy, too. If Virginia had her personhood taken from her and was left to walk around like an empty shell, it would be worse for her family than if she were dead. She racked her brain for some way to make James understand.

How strange, she mused, that James could not remember ever hearing about what happened to her after she lost Garner and Avanell. He did not even seem to remember that she'd been married to Garner, much less Ben.

It shouldn't have surprised her, though. She shouldn't have expected James to be different from most people. Most people had forgotten about her early losses. It seemed to her that it was human nature for people not to be interested in hearing about a person's past if nobody was trying to keep it a secret, but on the other hand, that they always wanted to know more about things that people didn't want known.

Like the difference in the way people treated her past life and Nora Faye's. Rose wanted her family—and everybody else—to know about her past. She wanted her sons to know all about their half-sister and the two husbands she had lost before she even knew their dad. She had never tried to hide her past from them, had never tried to hide it from anybody. She would like it if people would ask her to talk about Avanell and Garner and Ben—and Langdon. But Langdon was the last person ever to let her talk about her losses without getting uncomfortable—and now he'd joined the ranks of the gone. She and Langdon had never stopped telling one another about their past loves, but if she mentioned her dead ones to most people now, they generally acted like she had said something embarrassing, like they thought there was something in particular that they were supposed to say and that they felt put on the spot because they didn't know what it was.

On the contrary, people with no good reason to be curious about Nora Faye wanted to know all about her history. Relatives who should know better asked questions right in front of her, and acquaintances with no business even wondering about it did not hesitate to make flat-out personal queries.

And then Rose was struck with mournful regret along with her bewilderment when she thought about how she had not given her mother a chance to talk about her dead babies, how she had felt uncomfortable when she thought the subject might come up. How strange, she thought, that well-meaning human beings cannot figure out what's right even when they are hit in the face with it.

The snow started shortly before Nora Faye crossed the line into Pike County around midnight. In spite of the horror of realizing that she was not capable of making this drive, the trip had been blessedly uneventful for the first many miles, giving her a chance to get a feel for the basic operations of the car before she had to deal with night-driving. She hadn't lost a minute getting on the road after she hung up with Peggy. James had dropped into fitful sleep on the couch. She crept around so as not to wake him as she got ready. The house was all theirs. Virginia's cousin and her husband would be in Florida until March.

Just before she left, she tiptoed to the sofa and carefully slipped off James's Florsheims and spread an afghan over him. He opened his eyes and started to sit up. She gently pushed him back down.

He complied like a trusting child and lay back on the rough throw-pillow, closing his eyes and then opening them to stare into space for a moment. "Oh, Fayzie, your daddy's feeling like a lost soul these days," he sighed. "It's like I'm in the dark and don't know where my next step will take me."

"It's okay," she whispered. She had a flashing memory of Callie Bennet's horse and the road up Dillard where it came to an abrupt end beyond the schoolhouse. She felt there was something about Seelom she could say to comfort her daddy, but the thought would not stay with her. It didn't matter; he wouldn't have heard her. He was already asleep, breathing regularly at last.

She took a bus several blocks to Charlie and Patsy's apartment where Ted parked the 1950 Ford Crestliner he had worked long and hard to put back in operation after an uncle wrecked it and gave it to him. He could not afford the gas to drive it for everyday use, walking instead to get around on campus, but he'd been taking Nora Faye out for driving lessons every chance they got.

He had praised her for picking up on things quickly, but she hadn't had enough experience to cause her to realize how far she was from being a driver. As it turned out, she learned the most difficult things she'd ever need to know about driving on this, her first trip on her own. She learned how to drive in the dark on the trip east from Lexington to Wolliver and how to drive in a blizzard on the way out of the mountains back to Lexington. Ted had warned her how different it would be to drive in the mountains, but she had been eager to give it a try as they made their plans to go for Peggy. She had no idea how very different it was going to be without him.

When she got to the Banes' apartment she learned about a freshman girl from Bascon, Ramona Clumner, who had not found a way home yet. She was a friend of the Banes and had asked them to find out if she could catch a ride with Nora Faye. Nora Faye called her and told her the situation, that she did not have a license, had driven very little, and had never driven by herself. The girl accepted the offer with no hesitation. She was desperate to get home. She'd heard that her boyfriend back home was spending all his time with her best friend. Nora Faye had hoped Ramona would be able to help with the driving if needed, but Ramona said she'd never been behind the wheel of a car.

Charlie and Patsy asked Nora Faye why she couldn't wait the couple of days until Ted got back to do the driving, and she knew her answer had left them feeling like she had made a childish, irrational decision. There was no way she could make someone understand how much hinged on a few hours delay. James was so weary, and the doctors could be so persuasive just by not saying much, that even if she got back with Granny Rose tomorrow, she knew there was the possibility that the surgery would have been done while she was gone. She wondered if she should try to prepare Peggy for that possibility or just let well enough alone.

She had left James a note telling him what time she left and when she expected to return. She was glad he'd fallen asleep; she knew he would have tried to stop her. The cousin's house was a sparsely furnished bungalow with cold, bare hardwood floors and a boxy sofa with maple arms and removable leather cushions. It chilled her to think of James sleeping alone on those cold leather cushions, but how she hoped he would sleep all day and not get back to the hospital where the doctors might push him for a decision. She wished she'd known about Ramona when she wrote his note. It would have given him some peace of mind to know she was not alone. It gave *her* some peace of mind. She laughed to herself. How ridiculous to take comfort from the company of a total stranger, a ninny who did not have sense enough not to put her life into the hands of someone who readily told her she did not know how to drive.

All along the way she realized what a difference it was making for her to have Ramona with her. She would have abandoned the effort before she got to Winchester if Ramona had not been sitting there beside her with no indication that she had been told she was riding with an incompetent fool. How strange that, as much as a person needed to be alone at times, there were other times when any kind of company was better than none.

And how curious it was that people—like Ramona—could just completely overlook the reality of actual physical dangers when they were preoccupied with thoughts of other kinds of danger. Ramona never one time gasped nor groaned nor held her breath while Nora Faye ground the gears or came to jerky, jolting stops or took curves in cautious stutters.

The enormity of her misjudgment was obvious to Nora Faye from the first block of the drive. Panic set in as she maneuvered her way along Broadway and out of town. She hadn't thought about how overwhelming it would be without Ted's help to deal with traffic and traffic lights at the same time she was learning how to operate the car and slow down and then resume speed without stalling out.

Before she left the Lexington city limits she was aware of the magnitude of her folly. There would be no shame in backing out. In fact, the truth lay in the other direction; it would be foolhardy to continue. But then she'd think of her dad lying drained and spent on that cold, hard couch, and she would think what a difference it would make for him if Peggy and Granny Rose were with them when he was forced to make the horrendous decision—or to face the aftermath of the decision.

Ramona's constant chatter helped to keep Nora Faye from slipping into hysterical paralysis. She learned all about the boyfriend, Chad, and the best friend, Yvonne, who were still in high school. Ramona had told Yvonne to keep an eye on Chad for her when she went away, only to learn from her sister that Yvonne and Chad were being seen together all over town every day.

Ramona's chatter required no response, so Nora Faye could give her full attention to her driving. The flatland curves, before she got to the mountains, gave her practice in taking curves at the right speed and then giving a little more gas at the precise moment. She practiced with the dimmer switch before the headlights became a necessity, getting the rhythm with her left foot, clicking the button on and off without letting that function interfere with the use of the clutch pedal, and she thought to locate the wiper switch and fool around with it before she needed it. She could not recall what Ted had told her about the choke, so she decided to ignore it. The thing she thought would be the greatest challenge, learning how to keep from being blinded by oncoming lights without taking her eyes off the road ahead, proved not to be as difficult as she had imagined.

The great realization about driving was that it depended on a perfect combination of putting learned information into practice, while at the same time making many decisions according to how things felt at the moment. Later, on the slick roads, she found it exhilarating to sense the back end of the car start to stray and to force herself to give in to the motion so she could get the feel of it before she turned the front end into the slide like Ted had instructed. It worked. The secret of not losing control was a matter of going with the frightening feeling as long as you could, and then making your move at exactly the right moment, like crossing one foot over the other to round the curves at the roller rink, or letting go at just the right moment to ride a bicycle with no hands.

She had thought to tell her dad in the note that she would go through Pikeville, not Jackson. She knew how much more he would have worried about her if he thought she was navigating the snaky terrain of the Jackson route.

Her only regret at having Ramona with her was that she would have to go out of her way to take her up to Bascon before she went on to Wolliver. Then, once the snow started, she decided to take Ramona to Wolliver with her for the night and have someone come to get her in the morning. When they stopped for gas and a bathroom at a lone service station they found still open in the Pikeville outskirts, Ramona called her dad collect and asked him to come and get her at Rose's house next morning.

They were already up and packing the car when he came for her well before daylight. He was concerned when he learned they planned to head right back to Lexington. "The roads aren't bad yet, but they're predicting a blizzard for later in the day. I wouldn't let anybody I know start out to Lexington this morning, even if it meant they'd miss out on Christmas." He had the idea that their rush was due to Christmas plans.

It was Rose who stepped in to keep him from trying to get hold of James or Eldon. Come to find out, he knew the family, remembered Langdon, had been acquainted with both her sons since school days and had done business with both of them. "I'll tell you what," he said, " you let me call one of your boys and see what we can work out. Surely one of them can take you."

When Rose told him it was James they were returning to in Lexington and that Eldon was on the road himself, fetching his girls from Lincoln Memorial College in Tennessee, he said, well, he wished he was in a position to drive them himself, but that he couldn't let down the people that would be depending on him today. "I've let my help off a few days early for Christmas, so it's just me till the 26th; there's no way I can close up my store. You know how people's electric ovens always stop working just when they start to cook a big Christmas turkey," he finished with a little laugh. He owned an appliance sales and repair shop in Bascon. Rose thanked him for his good intentions.

Nora Faye's biggest decision the night before had been whether or not to call her dad before she went to bed. As much as she wanted him to sleep, she was afraid he'd freeze to death if the furnace should go off before he woke. She was also afraid he would forbid her to make the return trip if he'd heard a weather prediction. Finally, she thought to call the nurses' station to ask about him. They said he came to the hospital during evening visiting hours and that he did not talk to any of the doctors while he was there, so Nora Faye didn't call him. She left a message for him with the nurses, just telling him she got to Wolliver safely.

Mr. Stillwell at the Standard Station in Johnston also tried to talk them into postponing their start. He and James were friends, and he knew about Virginia. He said, "You all can just go up to your house and get some sleep today. My boy will be in from school today or tomorrow, and I'll have him drive you to Lexington as soon as he gets here. He won't mind if we have to go on and have Christmas without him. We'll make it up to him later." Like Ramona's dad, he seemed to have it in his mind that their haste had to do with an effort to get to Lexington for Christmas day.

When they thanked him from their hearts and told him—without going into any detail—that they could not lose a minute, he said he'd close the station early in the evening and take them himself. Nora Faye was almost in tears before she got him to see that they were not going to be detained. He said they did have snow tires. Nora Faye hadn't been sure—she couldn't tell by looking and she didn't remember Ted ever mentioning it—and when he saw that they would not consider enough delay to let him put on chains, he insisted on putting a set in the trunk. He said James could bring them back to him. He could not refrain from making one last attempt to persuade them to wait, kindly reminding them that even snow chains couldn't improve visibility in a blizzard.

It was not yet daylight when they got on the road with a topped-off tank. They would have plenty of gas money; Nora Faye had taken some bills from her dad's wallet, and

Rose had gone to her bank and made a withdrawal after yesterday's phone call.

Mr. Stillwell had insisted on marking a map for them and had advised that they go by way of Hazel Green instead of Morehead. Nora Faye took his map, but she knew she was going to stick to the route she knew. She didn't dare add the difficulty of following a route with no familiar landmarks. She just hoped the landmarks she knew would not be obliterated by snow.

The first few hours went amazingly well. Nora Faye could feel her driving skills improving by the minute, but she also felt the dangers increasing by the minute as the winter storm began to take on the characteristics of an assault. When they left West Liberty behind them around noon, the snow was blowing in blinding sheets atop the long, narrow ridges that dropped precipitously on both sides. She began to think maybe she'd made a mistake in taking James's route. She couldn't remember why he came this way, but she could remember times when he was driving in this very same area under similar conditions and how it had seemed cozy and adventurous to her when her daddy was in charge.

From the time they got away from Prestonsburg she had been on the edge of panic, but she struggled not to let it show. An unreal quality enclosed them as she watched other cars spin out and bog down. More than once she watched as cars lost traction in curves on upgrades and slid backwards and sideways and off the shoulders, and yet she kept moving, somehow continuing to pull the grade and not get entangled in the other cars' mishaps. Her greatest fear was that she'd have to stop for another car and would slide into a snow bank. The more she willed herself into a pose of peaceful competency, the more she felt like she had some real control.

On the ridges she had to deal with the nauseating visual onslaught. The effect of the snow coming straight at her face was the same as watching waves from a boat. Just when she'd think she was going to be sick, she would be saved by a sudden change in wind direction or a halt in the snowfall.

Somewhere along the way—without realizing when it happened—she gained an understanding of how the gears could help her. Ted had commended her on her use of the clutch, but she had not really known what she was doing with it. Now, as the roads became slicker and more rutted, she instinctively knew that she must keep the wheels rolling as steadily as possible. She stayed in the ruts and kept accelerating, sometimes pressing the clutch in and sliding smoothly into a lower gear if she began to lose traction.

At the bus station in Morehead they got cold cheese sandwiches to eat in the car, afraid to lose time enough to wait for a grilled sandwich or a sit-down meal. Rose had thought to throw some crackers and apples into a paper sack just before they left the house, so they'd not starve.

For several miles they sang the Christmas carols they'd heard on the jukebox at the bus station. The car radio didn't work. The heater worked, but it seemed to either blast them with hot air on high or let things get too cold on a lower setting. They had to scrape the insides of the windows when the condensation froze.

And then, around Owingsville, the snow began to let up. The wind continued to blow drifts across the road, sometimes in gusts so strong there were momentary whiteouts, but there would be a lull before another assault.

Finally, with the Owingsville curves behind them, Peggy got a chance to bring up yesterday's phone conversation. Listening to Rose talking to James, Peggy had learned things she didn't remember ever hearing before. They were all three in the front seat, with Rose wedged in between them where they thought the heater would best hit her feet. During a lull, when the wind had died down and the snow had let up, Peggy leaned her head on Rose's shoulder and stroked her coat sleeve. "I'm so sorry about your little girl, Gran. And your husbands. I didn't know you'd had such bad times. Does Nora Faye know?" She sat up and peered around to see Nora Faye's face. "Did you know about Gran's little girl, Fayzie, and about the husbands she had before your grandpa?"

"I know a lot. Remember when I used to go to the Sanghill cemetery with Gran—and at least one time to Virginia—before we went to Grandpa Houston's grave, and you couldn't get straight whose graves we were going to at which place?"

Then to Rose, "I know about it all in bits and pieces. I know about your little girl. Remember? You used to take me with you to the Pennington cemetery to put flowers on Avanell's grave—and on her daddy's—on Decoration Day. And you and Aunt Mary talked about your husband Ben…that was Aunt Mary's brother?" Rose nodded. "But I've never heard about your life all at one time. Tell us, Gran."

And over the last leg of their journey, as Nora Faye adroitly avoided snowdrifts and fish-tail slides, Rose recounted her life for her granddaughters who could not have felt closer to her heart if they had been of her blood.

Nora Faye kept asking, "Why didn't you tell me?" or "Why didn't you want me to know?"

"Oh, I wanted you to know. I never tried to keep anything from you." Rose groped for words. "Everybody that knew me while I was living through it knew all about everything." She thought quietly for a while. "But by the time you were born, all that was part of the past…and not important to many people but me."

Peggy said softly "I can see how it happens, how people end up not really knowing what went on with their mothers and daddies and grandparents. It's come to my mind that my children will never know Jamie except for what I can pass on to them. And how can I do that? How can I tell them enough to make them really know him?" Her voice broke. "I can't, even if I would talk about him day and night without a stop."

"I know," Nora Faye joined in. "I think about that too; that my children will have no actual knowledge of the little person that was once the center of my life."

"How does a person tell their children about things that happened before they were born? " Peggy was sitting up straight now. "Do they set them down on each birthday and say, 'Now, listen while I tell you what I think you're old enough to hear this year?'"

"That's what I mean," Rose said. "If things don't just come up in everyday talk, how's a person supposed to pass it on without dwelling too much on the past...and on the dead?"

After a silence, Rose went on. "I talked to you about my little girl, Nora Faye. I even named one of your dolls Avanell. A little rubber doll. You asked me to name her, and I told you we could give her my little girl's name."

"What happened to her? I don't remember having an Avanell."

"No, you wouldn't. I put her away. I'd thought it would make me feel good to see you playing with a doll named Avanell, but it turned out different. It made me sad when I'd find her laying in the floor without any clothes on.

"You always took off your dolls' pretty little dresses. Sometimes you switched things around from doll to doll— with a tiny hat on a great big doll or a great big frock on a little one—but most of the time, you just left them all bare naked while their pretty little outfits got crumpled and mixed in with your other play-pretties."

They couldn't have said why it was amusing, but all three had a soft, contented laugh together.

Rose promised to look for the doll next time they were at her house. It made her feel good to talk about Avanell and even about the deaths and the terrible times that followed.

"How did you bear it, Gran?" Nora Faye asked. "How did you make yourself start living again when you came to your senses and realized your little girl was dead and your husband too?"

"Well, I reckon I didn't bear it for a while. I reckon that's why I was out of my mind. I don't know how it was that I had come to a point where Ben Calper could get through to me when he first crossed my path." They said nothing for a few moments as the wind drove the snow directly into the windshield. "It's not something I understand."

Even with this opportunity for total frankness with her dear girls who wanted her to share with them, Rose was not able to speak the words that framed her survival. To say that Ben brought her out of the paralyzing grip of sorrow seemed to trivialize her life with Garner, just as Ben in turn seemed trivialized if she said her compounded loss was eased when Langdon Houston came into her life. She did not have the words to tell them.

Peggy's sudden next comments sent them all three into choked-back tears. "I thought I was never going to be able to draw another normal breath after Jamie died. That's why I can understand how Mother got to be the way she is.

"Gran, how come an absolute angel-child like Jamie can be killed off when he's an innocent baby, while evil people like Tojo and Mussolini and Hitler are allowed to live long enough to do all that horrendous evil?"

She went on, not waiting for an answer. "When I think about Jamie I can still smell his warm neck and hear that little chuckle he had—the way he laughed whenever somebody ran that little tank over his head." When the other two made no sign they remembered, she reminded them, "You know, the little tin, wind-up toy tank that James used like a pair of clippers to get him used to going to the barber? If you'd wind up that little tank and run it over his head, he'd sit like he was hypnotized till it ran down. Then he'd do that little chuckle and say, 'One bore tibe'."

It was good for them to be able to cry without the worry of making things worse for Virginia or James but, even with that freedom, they all held back for unfathomable reasons, maybe having to do with the concern each had for the other two and maybe with the fear of not being able to stop if they got started. It's seldom that even the fortunate mourners who are offered true comfort can completely take it. Rose knew that was part of the key to her healing, that she had ultimately and repeatedly been able to accept the offer when she'd been given the chance to share her grief. She wished she could pass that understanding on to the girls.

Nora Faye said, "We were discussing Mark Twain in American Lit., and all I could think about was Daddy calling Jamie his Huckleboy. I can just see him tiptoeing downstairs after Ginny put him in his pajamas. He would crawl in behind Daddy's chair, and Daddy would say, 'I smell a Huckleboy! Where's my Huckleboy?' They went through their hugging and tickling every night before Daddy carried him up to bed."

"And remember the time at Aunt Tattie's house when Preacher Alston asked him his name and he said it was Huckleboy Houston?" Peggy chimed in. The three of them reminisced and laughed and cried, and Rose felt more peace than she thought she'd ever feel again when she had been their age.

"I thought that was nice of Preacher Alston to come to his funeral from way up on Upper Clive. In fact, it was amazing how many people, period, came to his funeral, and him just a little boy. Part was for Mother and James—and you, of course, Gran, and the rest of us—but a lot of them were people who just remembered him as being a special little boy," Peggy said.

They were in the home stretch—leaving Winchester and seeing a definite let-up in the snow—when Peggy said, "I don't think I could go on believing in God if I woke up like you and Mother and found that my little child was dead or dying. I've heard Mother talking about it in her prayers. Before she got so sick she didn't make sense, I heard her asking God why Jamie, when he had never been anything but good. She asked God what she was supposed to do that she hadn't done right."

After a few moments with only the drone of the heater filling the pause, Peggy went on. "You don't talk about God, Gran, the way other grannies do. You don't blame Him or give Him credit for things, and you don't ask why He lets things happen. At least, you don't ask out loud. Did you stop believing in God when your little girl died?"

Rose sat quietly for a while before she answered. "That happened before I'd ever given much thought to that kind of thing. Looking back on it, sometimes it seems to me like I might have found it easier to bear if I'd had a strong belief in The Lord, but sometimes it seems like that's what saved me, that I hadn't thought a lot about things like that and that I didn't feel like I had to try to figure out why He let it happen."

She fingered the seams on the back of her gloves. She thought maybe she'd never consciously formed the thoughts she was now voicing. It seemed important that she say what she meant to say.

"My folks never were wrapped up in church things like some people around us. If I'd been raised to think the Lord has reasons for everything that happens and that we're supposed to be able to figure out the reasons, I might never have stopped being crazy."

"But they taught you about Jesus in Sunday School, didn't they? Peggy asked. "Did you ever take the story of Jesus too much to heart, like Bootsie did?"

"There wasn't any Sunday School, and church wasn't for children. I think maybe the old-time people knew that it was too much for little children to handle, knew that they might do what Bootsie did and try to understand things past understanding.

"I don't remember much talk about Jesus when I was a girl. My mam went to church when it was near enough that she could get there, and we had the whole church crowd to dinner sometimes, like Tattie and Jimmy still do. But not as often as they do, thank goodness, because, for me, those church dinners meant I had a whole morning in the kitchen cooking to get ready and then the rest of the day washing dishes."

Rose sat silent for a bit, comfortably aware of Nora Faye's alert grasp on the wheel and Peggy's renewed efforts to snuggle down and get comfortable.

"Pap would say grace at the Sunday table when we had company, and a Bible was always laying on the mantle—that's the Bible I have now—but I don't remember Mam and Pap reading it. It was for putting down births and deaths.

"My folks—and all the neighbors round—said things like 'Thank God' and 'The Lord willing' and all that, but Mam and Pap didn't do any talking about what they believed. I hadn't thought much about church things. When Garner and Avanell died I was still a girl myself, just about the age you are now."

After doing some calculations about their ages compared to Rose's, the girls fell silent. The heater hummed, the windshield wipers scraped back and forth, the snow tires thumped. Peggy nodded off to sleep.

After a bit, Rose said, "You and your friend sang a song one time when he brought you all home. He said his grandmother used to sing it. Do you remember which one I mean?"

Without a word Nora Faye began to sing softly. The song sounded like a hymn, but Ted said he didn't know if it was or not.

Though Rose had heard it only once before, it flowed so naturally she joined in now and then as Nora Faye sang:

Someday the veil of life will surely rise
Revealing scenes immortal to our eyes...

She hummed parts of the next lines when she couldn't recall the words.

And then the da da da we'll realize.
Oh, then we'll understand.
Someday where healing waters ever flow,
Someday where fadeless flowers ever grow,
The mysteries of life we'll surely know.
Oh then we'll understand.

After a bit Nora Faye asked, "Do you think that's heaven it's talking about?"

"Like as not," Rose answered. " Somebody's heaven."

They sang through it a time or two, trying different words where Nora Faye couldn't remember, and coming out confidently on the chorus.

Then, so suddenly it took Rose several moments to follow her line of thought, Nora Faye said, "I can tell that you think I shouldn't marry Ted, Gran. I think that's why you won't say his name, why you call him my friend. Is it because you think I would have married him already if I loved him the right way?"

Rose stammered internally for a moment, not sure what she was being asked. Before she got her thoughts together, Nora Faye went on.

"It must seem to you like what I'm feeling can't be the right thing, the way you knew immediately about all three of your husbands and the way you didn't hesitate for a moment.

"And then there's the way my mother got married knowing she didn't love the man she was marrying. It seems like that would be as hard as not getting to marry the man you want to marry. But that doesn't really have anything to do with me, I know—even though it was all about me."

As loopy as she might have sounded to an outsider, she was making sense to Rose. It seemed she was saying things Rose had been waiting to hear her talk about since the day Irene left her.

"The really sad thing," Nora Faye continued," is that she knew when she married him that she wasn't going to stay with him. She married him for a reason having nothing to do with her feelings for him one way or another. It was all about his feelings for her, and he loved her enough to marry her knowing what he knew. It would have been a miracle if she'd started loving him.

"And Daddy, being so kind and so easy to love, just shows you how it's not something a person can make happen and not something a person can earn by loving a person the way he wants that person to love him. You would have thought she couldn't help but start loving him after living with him all that time while he treated her so good, but actually it must have been as terrible for her to be married to him as it would have been for her to be married to an ogre like in the fairy tales."

Rose didn't move.

"Maybe I'll never be in that kind of desperate situation no matter who I love or don't love. Maybe I'll be able to make the decision based on what I want to do and nothing else."

She barely took a breath before she went on. "But, the problem now is that I'm not clear about what I want to do. I thought I'd know who I wanted to marry the minute I met him. I thought it was going to be as clear for me as it was for you all three times, and it was at first, but..." She fell silent at last.

"Have you decided not to marry him, then?" Rose ventured to ask.

"I don't know." Her voice was small and forlorn. "Before I started talking about it just now, I thought I'd decided to end it. But once I started talking, I felt like I'd die if I knew I had to live my life without him." She reached to adjust the heater fan, turning it down a notch.

"The way you loved all three of your husbands in a way that left no room for doubt, that's the way I loved Ted at first. But when I didn't do something about it, then my feelings got all tangled and complicated.

"I must seem so silly to you, the way you knew what you wanted to do and just did it. But you're absolutely right when you call him my friend. He's the best friend a person could have."

She gave her attention to the road for a few seconds as the wind gave one last gust in all directions like a dog shaking water from its coat. Her mind was yet enough in the present moment to give herself a silent warning about staying especially alert now that the worst roads were behind them. It would be easy to become falsely complacent now that the highway was flanked by softly rolling muffled pastures instead of looming cliffs and sheer drop-offs.

"He's so much more than a friend, but at the center of it all, that's what he is to me, the best friend I could ever dream of having. It's because of him I feel happy most of the time, that I feel at peace with myself and the world. But then, I don't see how it could be that I love him the way I need to love the man I'll marry. If I did, I'd have married him already…or something."

She gave her grandmother a glance of solemn portent. "When we get back, I think I have to tell him I can't go with him on the dig." Her voice fractured for a second and she ended in a whisper. "I have to break up with him, but I don't know how I can live without him."

There was no traffic except for a snowplow that buffeted them in its wake as it went by in the other direction. Darkness was already falling, but wind gusts had subsided. Banners of snow no longer ripped across the road at gale force. Ruts were easier to follow. A few colored Christmas lights glowed faintly at a big farmhouse set far back from the road, its long lane a slight depression in the pristine snow blanket. It was like they were alone in a world composed of snow. Peggy, sleeping soundly now, breathed rhythmically. Rose stayed still.

Nora Faye picked up on what she'd been saying. "I think some women can have a good marriage with just about any man they might marry, as long as he's a decent person, but I think other women have to love the man they marry so much it blots out…everything else. Not like letting yourself get lost in the other person, but like finding yourself there. Or finding something that lets you be yourself"

She glanced sideways at Rose again. "I think you loved your men that way, the way my mother must have loved Kenneth. And I think I'll have to love that way. With a sort of quietly wild devotion."

Rose managed to hold her reaction down to a slight blink, though it seemed to her the best description she could imagine of how she felt about her husbands.

"And even though that's the way I feel about Ted, I've let things get all foggy. We no longer talk much about the future beyond the dig, and my chance of having a future with him will end if I can force myself to do what I think it's right to do about the dig." She reached a hand to the windshield and swiped at the condensation with the back of her glove before she cracked the wind-wing a bit. There was a loud swoosh until she worked with the panel, getting it where it was open a mere hair's width. Peggy stirred and then fell back into regular breathing.

"And, who knows," Nora Faye went on, "maybe whatever happens in these next few hours will make it easier for me to face up to what I have to do." The sideways smile she gave her grandmother was more sorrowful than reassuring. Then out of the blue she asked, "Was this the shortest day of the year? I've lost track of time."

Rose ignored that question. She recalled Tattie saying just recently that she'd never heard Nora Faye say more than two words at the same time. "All these other young'uns, you can't hardly stop their nattering, but you have to drag ever' word out of Nora Faye one at a time." Rose smiled to herself.

In spite of all Nora Faye had said since she asked her first question, Rose had not forgotten it, and she felt compelled to answer it. "You're wrong about me thinking you shouldn't marry Ted," she said. "I think I've been taking for granted that you would. Everything lately's been overshadowed by what Virginia's been going through, but from the little bit I've seen of the two of you together, it seems like you're different with him than you've been with other boys. It seems like you feel at home with him."

She looked right at her before she went on, waiting until Nora Faye could return her look for a moment.

"In my day they wasn't all that effort to figure out how things might turn out to be in years ahead. A girl couldn't give much thought to how she might be feeling in the future because she might not have more than one chance for making a future with a man. She might never get another chance to see him or to hear from him. She had to make a decision more on what she knew about herself than what she knew about him."

Nora Faye tried to say something, but Rose talked over her.

"Thing's are awful complicated now, what with cars and trains and telephones. It's a different world. But one thing that's not changed is the way the future doesn't always turn out to be what you think it will be."

She paused while Nora Faye cautiously made her way through a spot where great chunks of ice were strewn across the road, probably fallen from the snow plow.

"Could be that you're making your life complicated now because of all the times you've had to go on with things after you've lost somebody. Could be that you've got better at losing people than keeping them."

Nora Faye jumped in. "But that's just it. You'd lost two husbands and your little girl, and yet it doesn't sound like things were complicated when you met Grandpa Houston."

"That's what I mean about things being harder for a girl to figure out these days. I just didn't have any reason to question what I was feeling for all three of my husbands. It's like you said; sometimes the longer you hold off on doing something, the more mixed up you get about how much you want to do it.

"Maybe the only way you can know if you have the right kind of feelings is to tell yourself you do, and then to make it happen. No matter how right it starts out, part of what keeps it being the right thing is making up your mind over and over again that it is."

Nora Faye stayed quiet. They fell into a comfortable silence. The lights of Lexington had become a fully discernable glow.

Rose tried to remember if she had ever looked to the future when she was as young as Nora Faye. It seemed that things just happened, that she had not planned anything.

Even later in her life, she had not tried to plan the future. After Langdon's death, making plans was not the issue. Existence became a matter of making herself as hard or as soft at any given moment as Eldon and James needed her to be while they were learning how to be alive without their dad's constant example. They were still in high school. Though not suffused with as much horror, Langdon's death was as sudden and devastating as those of Ben and Garner. He suffered a fatal stroke while sitting at the kitchen table slicing the green tomatoes she was frying for their supper one late-summer evening. But she was spared the anguish of deciding what to do next: she had Eldon and James to see to day by day.

She thought about what a little bit of control human beings have over their lives and how the control that's called for often does not turn out to be what a person expects, how life's dangers do not necessarily lie where it seems they will lie, and how comfort can come from unexpected sources.

She felt humbled by the unknowable quality of human nature that can sometimes bear up to loss and that sometimes sinks into a mire akin to death. Having experienced both reactions, she felt more baffled than enlightened. And, rather than attributing her survival either to her own willpower or to an otherworldly power, she was mightily aware of forces that just are—forces neither all good nor all evil, like fire and water and honeysuckle vine, forces that, under varying circumstances, can be either good or evil to the utmost extreme. Having found herself repeatedly at the mercy of this incomprehensible influence, she wondered at the ease with which many good-intentioned people so readily offer ungrounded advice about how to deal with death and loss and sorrow. She marveled at the astounding ways comfort can elude a person on the one hand or, on the other hand, can sift down with no more fanfare than the sticky little "bamma gilly" flowerets…with a difference she suspected would remain a mystery for all eternity.

She broke the silence. "Seems like it might be a mistake to end things before you know what you're ending. Whatever it is you think you're not feeling, seems like spending the summer with him might be the way to find out.

"One thing different these days is that a girl is expected to find out as much as she can about what she's getting into before she marries. A girl today might be thought foolish to do things the way that was right for me in my time…just like taking the kind of risk that could ruin a reputation in my day—could ruin a life—is what a sensible girl might be expected to do nowadays."

"Elt." Nora Faye's eyes blinked a couple of times then stretched wide. "Granny *Rose*!" she laughed, the first time she'd laughed since she'd been away from Ted. "What did you just say?" Rose smiled faintly, her gaze fixed on the dashboard.

Peggy stirred. "Wake up," Nora Faye giggled. "We're almost there, and you won't believe what Gran just advised me to do."

Tension drained from her body like melting snow. Her hands, clenched on the steering wheel, relaxed as they had not for two days. Entering the Lexington city limits, she maneuvered the snow-choked streets like someone who'd been driving for decades.

13749559R00230

Made in the USA
Charleston, SC
29 July 2012